The Black Horns

Joshua Yoder

ISBN: **1-7329138-0-3**
ISBN 13: **978-1-7329138-0-6**
Library of Congress Control Number:
LCCN Imprint Name: **City and State (If applicable)**

Cover art by Joanna Hill

Very special thanks to my sister, Joanna Hill, for creating such a fantastic image to use as my book cover!

Also by Joshua Yoder:

Mark of the Tiger's Stripe

For in the realms of the Heavens and Mortals

One truth does ever persist

That in truth there are no angels

Only the demons a man makes for himself

And as the sun sets on this life

So the dues of the demon come to pass

- Kailepias, Meccinai philosopher, AC 2

1 – Strong Hand

The fortified city of Det was one of the few green places in the arid nation of Pytan. It nestled in the arms of a nameless river that twisted its way south from the Nefrit Ishem Mountains and joined with the wide winding ribbon of the Tuunesh-Et River, the watery border between the continents of Estan and Mwungo.

Det was not large, but it saw its fair share of trade from ships passing between the port cities of Ghadir and Tanahwi, which sat at opposite ends of the Tuunesh-Et. Or at least it did for now. Events were unfolding in the northern capital of Kairran that might have a significant impact on ships travelling from the Medean Basin into the Strait of Adrakar.

None of those things mattered in the least to the small boy, about four years of age, who sat on the tasselled carpet as he traced the intricate floral patterns of the Pytian designs with his tin-plated toy cars.

Of course, boy wasn't really the right term. He was a kidd or young goat; specifically, a subspecies of the subfamily *Caprinae* known as *Ovis orientalis*, or mouflon. This was in no way strange to him as there were many sentient inhabitants on Amarthia just like him and many more of entirely different species; some with fur, some with scales, some with feathers, and even a rare few with insectoid chitin.

Academically the people of Amarthia were members of the kingdom *Animalis*, phylum *Chordate*, subphylum and supergenus *Homo sapiens animalis*, or "wise man-animal" in the long dead language of Ariculm. This was often shortened to the sobriquet "hom-an", but appealing to ones "hom-anity" never sounded quite right, so the masses simply bastardised into "human". Of course, that is when they used the word at all, which was rare; and not one sentient creature on Amarthia was even aware that the term might already be in use elsewhere in the grandness of the universe.

Again, all this had little bearing on the child playing with his cars. He was far too busy running the tin vehicles up to the edge of the carpet and fiddling with the tassels, make believing they were the grasping tentacles of Moana Kaitiaki, the dreaded Sea Guardian, threatening to drag his imaginary heroes down into the depths of the sea.

But Moana Kaitiaki was not an imaginary beast. In fact, much of the recent news had centred around the creature, usually connected with reports of missing trade fleets or the discovery of a torn and twisted vessel washed up on a distant shore. The leviathan had proven resistant to all types of conventional weaponry, and the ecconomic devastation had finally reached a point where several of the worlds top scientific minds were brought together to create a weapon powerful enough to destroy the creature; they called it an atomic bomb.

As if to highlight the arrogance of hom-ans, it remained uncertain if the device succeeded. Moana Kaitiaki retreated into the depths of the sea and hadn't been seen since, leading many to believe it died of wounds sustained in the blast, but leaving no concrete proof. This was quickly forgotten as the eyes of the world turned to a new threat: the nature of the atomic bomb device itself.

The young mouflon didn't care about this news, even though it would forever shape the world he would grow up in. He pondered the loose cloth strings in his hand, his child's mind briefly seeing them for what they were instead of what he wished them to be. He sat up and ran a hand over the tuft of dark long-fur growing atop his head. His horns hadn't grown in proper yet, but perhaps when he was older, he might start wearing tassels on the tips as he had seen adults do.

The adventure of his toy cars momentarily forgotten, he took in the room around him, scratching the white patch at the end of his muzzle that stood out against the woolly brown and black fur the covered the rest of him.

His father's home wasn't lavish, but it was comfortable, with two stories and the bedrooms on the lower floor where the air was cooler. Afternoon sunlight filtered in through white cotton curtains and bathed the second-floor living room in soft light. The boy didn't know it, but his country was currently revelling in the midst of a cultural revolution, and the so-called Mid-Century Modern styles from Locke and the West United Kingdoms were quite popular with the citizens of Pytan. The furniture was all squares and sharp angles, and the paintings on the walls displayed dashes of colour with no real discernable shape or pattern. Pastels were everywhere from floor to ceiling, mostly blues and yellows.

A voice from the next room made him turn. The old cow who was his nanny—this wasn't an insult, she really was an aged woman of the bovine species—slept fitfully in a chair by the door, her head wrapped in a floral-pattern hijab. The kidd was unaware that her choice of pattern was actually considered daring at the present time, since Nuadinite tradition typically demanded something much plainer.

But the nanny's choice to subvert some of Pytan's more radical religious elements was not the reason the kidd didn't like her much, or his previous nursemaids for that matter. His guardians tended to yell at him for the smallest offence and continuously fussed at him should he do anything but sit quietly with his toys, and his father had done nothing to correct them.

The rough voice sounded from the next room again, and the kidd crept towards the crack in the door. The man who was his father sat at a large oak desk on the far wall. The trimmings of Saifullah El-Hashem's office where older than the rest of the house; the boy guessed this had something to do with his father selling "anty keys"—it would be a few years before he learned the word was "antiquities".

The adult mouflon had positioned himself turned partially away from the door, watching a black-and-white television along the far wall. His paisley vest and matching tie bore the wrinkles of a man who had slept at his desk through the night, again. The white linen shirt underneath was tucked haphazardly into a pair of tweed slacks, and a matching dinner jacket hung from a corner of his leather-cushioned chair. It was bolvin leather, of course; there might be distant relations between the domestic beasts and the boy's nursemaid, but the very thought of tanning a sentient animal was barbarism of the highest order, no matter one's religious affiliation or lack thereof.

A glass of amber-coloured liquid sloshed in Saifullah's hand and even from the doorway his son could smell the alcohol.

"Fucking imbeciles, all of them," Saifullah said, glowering at the TV. "That canal is going to play hell with this region."

The canal in question was an expansion of the Hutseph River, creating a swift, direct route from Kairran to Meshim. It would also create an artificial border with Kirque, Pytan's northern neighbour.

Saifullah downed the rest of the amber liquid from his glass. "How the hell am I supposed to support that bastard child if all the trade traffic is flowing through the northern route?"

The elder mouflon began muttering again, and the younger leaned forward, curious. In doing so, he nudged the heavy wooden door to the office, and it moved inward with a terrific *creak*.

Saifullah turned, the brown bloodshot eyes with their odd bar-shaped pupils coming to rest on the child. "Ah, speak of the demon and it shall appear. Where is your nanny, boy?"

"S-she's asleep," the kidd stammered, "I didn't mean—"

"No, I suppose you didn't," the elder cut him off, his thin lips spreading in a disgusted sneer. "You didn't mean to do a lot of things. Didn't mean to make a noise; didn't mean to disturb your drunk of a father; didn't mean to tear the heart out of your whore mother." He sat back and hiccupped loudly. "Gods be damned, you even stole her eyes."

The boy's pale-yellow orbs began to glisten with tears.

The bovine nanny awoke with a start and rose from her chair. "Jirair!" she cried, "Come away from their, child!"

"Jirair," Saifullah's voice dripped with disdain as he pondered the name, "Yes, how fitting. My little Strong Hand. Perhaps one day you will choke the life from me as well."

The kidd clasped his hands in front of him, pleading. "Please, father. I—"

The nanny poked her head in and roughly grabbed Jirair by the arm. "I'm sorry, sir. It won't happen—"

"Get out," The elder mouflon growled. "Both of you get *out*!"

Saifullah reared back and hurled the empty glass toward the door. It shattered against the heavy wood frame, and a shard of glass cut across Jirair's cheek under his left eye. The nanny shrieked in terror and ran down the stairs and out of the house.

Jirair never saw her again, but there would be others.

The boy stood resolute in the doorway, and his father rose to his cloven-hoofed feet angrily, although the younger mouflon couldn't tell if the elder's shaking was from rage or the booze.

Saifullah grabbed the bottle of bourbon from his desk and raised it high about his head. "Do not test me, boy!" He shouted, "I said get *out*!"

He took a heavy step forward.

That was when Jirair fled, not knowing that the crash of glass and heavy *thump* he heard was his father falling to the floor and passing out in a drunken stupor.

2 – Fallout

Jirair al-Seif started awake behind the thick black marble slab that served as his desk. He rubbed the long fingers of his hands across his face, digging the caps of his fingernails into his pale-yellow eyes to get the sleep out.

It had been a most peculiar dream, thoughts about his younger years hadn't plagued him in a long time. After the events of last night, he wondered if this was what people meant when they said they saw their lives flash before them. Yet all he had seen was his childhood self, playing with his tin-plated cars, and his drunken father tossing the glass. The scar under his left eye was so faint it was barely noticeable now.

That cut was the first injury his father had given him, but the others hadn't been physical.

He wondered ever so briefly if his father was even still alive; he hadn't spoken to him in almost thirty years.

Al-Seif ran a paw through his dishevelled shock of slate-grey long-fur, now streaked with white at the temples. The white patches on his muzzle and hands had also grown larger as he aged. His alabaster horns were no longer childhood stubs and made almost a full turn back onto themselves, the tips levelling off at his cheeks. He capped them with gold and purple tassels, one of which had fallen off, and lay on the floor unnoticed. The long greying goatee on his chin was desperately in need of brushing, and the finely-cut white linen suit he wore was rumpled and unkempt.

His disorganised appearance was very out of place in the confines of his private office. It was the only hexagonal-shaped room in the multi-tiered structure of his ultramodern villa and occupied a corner of the house overlooking both the expansive gardens and his own modest stretch of private beach.

White was the predominant colour of the room. Behind al-Seif were the built-in bookshelves of his personal library, containing the complete works from ancient Pytian and Kirque poets—some of which were originals he had paid handsomely for. Clockwise from the shelf was the entryway, a pair of double doors flanked by Benese watercolours with mercantile themes. Next was his entertainment centre, a large projection TV paired with a hi-fidelity stereo. The remaining three walls were solid glass, broken only by a pair of glass doors set in the pane directly opposite the desk.

The morning sunlight caught in the square-cut crystal chandelier that hung from the high ceiling, casting bright shards of white across the walls along with the odd prismatic rainbow.

The cypress trees in al-Seif's gardens were beginning to blossom, even though it was only the twenty-seventh day of Ferrus, the second month of the year. Winter was releasing its grip early in Medocci, and soon the hills of the western province of Pianure Rosso would be a blaze of spring colours.

The mouflon couldn't have cared less at the moment. Al-Seif picked up a purple feather from the desk and toyed with it, idly rolling it between his fingers while the thick nails that capped each digit clicked together.

The plumage came from a cauracua; a feathered, reptile-like avian creature that had been a significant influence on his life. He was inspired by the way they used the small horns on their head to deliver quick blows and stun their prey. That was how he had become Assad Alabwaq, the Black Horns; striking swift and building his empire from the corpses of his enemies.

And now that empire was in danger.

Al-Seif's pale eyes, red-rimmed from lack of sleep, transfixed upon the smouldering remains of Vigo De Palma's villa only a few kilometres away on the next hill.

He flicked on the stereo via remote and tuned the radio to the local news station. His grasp of Mecci wasn't perfect, even after living so many years in the country, but he understood enough to put the story together. The official report proclaimed there had been a series of Medoccian bandit attacks during the night, several compounds suffered damage during the raids including the utter decimation of the De Palma estate. The entire family of Vigo De Palma and several of his chief business associates were rumoured to be among the dead.

Well, not the entire family, al-Seif thought darkly.

It was quite a story, especially considering al-Seif hadn't seen a single journalist's vehicle visit the scene since the attack occurred. Curiously, none of the other nearby villas appeared to be on fire. Even a casual observer could see that the De Palma's compound was the only one these so-called bandits had managed to overcome.

Yet as sensational as the news was, it did have a basis in fact. Bandits often overran inexperience millionaires who moved to the countryside without proper planning. That's why raids were still a problem.

However, the De Palmas were anything but "new blood". In fact, they were one of the most powerful mafia families in the region and long-time residents of the hills. For them to succumb to a mere band of roving thieves was unthinkable.

Jirair al-Seif didn't need to check his sources to know the underworld rumour mill was in full swing. The rival mafia families would be near the top of the suspect list, but it was only a matter of time before the fingers started pointing to him.

Al-Seif knew the truth, he had been there, and he had a pretty good idea who the real villain was. Why else would Freggs have called him only moments before?

"The meeting is over," the mechanical voice had said. "You have two minutes."

Al-Seif understood the unspoken suggestion and had taken his leave soon after. What he witnessed as he stood on the De Palma's driveway would haunt him the rest of his days. The drone of the helicopter gunships and the mechanical whine of their machineguns still echoed in his ears.

None of this had been the mouflon's plan. Al-Seif's ten-year business partnership with Vigo De Palma had started with an arranged marriage to his daughter Yursa—an old custom according to Vigo. From there al-Seif had gained the old deerhound's respect, if not his admiration.

After all these years, the mouflon had finally been ready to deliver the masterstroke that would cast aside his legitimate façade and place *himself* as the head of the De Palma's mafia empire. Al-Seif owned the controlling shares of De Palma Shipping, and with the aid of his criminal alter ego, Assad Alabwaq, the mouflon had expertly manoeuvered several of his defunct criminal enterprises into the possession of Vigo De Palma.

One word from al-Seif and the De Palma family would end up in a legal quagmire that spanned two countries with their financial assets tangled for months if not years.

It was brilliant if the mouflon did say so himself.

And then he had it all stripped away from him.

After last night's attack, Yursa was the only survivor, and without Vigo's signature on al-Seif's agreement, everything on the illegal side of the family business passed to her. Al-Seif might still be able to use the blackmail, but if he tried to exercise his rights as the major shareholder, it would draw unwanted suspicion to him and his possible involvement in the attack. And that might lead to uncomfortable questions about al-Seif's mysterious benefactor, a mechanical voice he knew only as "Freggs". If there was one thing the mouflon knew, it was that the mechanical voice wouldn't want that kind of attention and might even decide that al-Seif was a liability to his operations.

Al-Seif could deal with threats from two fronts, but only if he saw them coming. And Freggs had proven he could keep to the shadows much better than al-Seif could.

As for Yursa, the De Palma's reign at the top of the organised crime pyramid had been a long one, and she would have a tough fight to maintain that power. No doubt the predators were already circling around, seeking to fill the presumed power vacuum. But fight she would, and more tenaciously than anyone al-Seif had ever known; and *he* would be her first target.

All he could do was try to compose himself as he waited for the inevitable arrival of the *Polizia*. With his relationship to Yursa De Palma—and her influence within the *Polizia*'s more corrupt elements—it was only natural for him to be a suspect. Perhaps it was fortunate his plans had fallen through; despite a few small operations, his partnership with Vigo De Palma was strictly legitimate, and his reputation in Medocci was not as strong as it had been in his homeland of Pytan.

Of course, maybe Yursa wouldn't use the police against him at all. This was personal now, and her revenge would involve more than just toppling her soon-to-be-former husband's criminal empire. She would want blood.

The phone on the desk chirped, starting him out of his brooding.

"Good morning, Jirair," the electronically filtered voice greeted him when he answered. Despite the mechanical sound, al-Seif could always detect a faint Locke accent and the tell-tale glottal clicks that marked amphibian speech.

The mouflon's mood darkened even further.

When Jirair al-Seif spoke, his voice had a higher pitch than one might expect from a man in his position, but that didn't detract from the aura of command in his tone. "I don't know what kind of game you're playing, Freggs," he said, "but I won't be your pawn."

"It's too late for that," Freggs replied, "But don't trouble yourself. You are a valuable asset, Jirair. Rest assured you will not be sacrificed as easily as Vigo was."

"Yes, exactly what am I supposed to tell the authorities after that little stunt?" al-Seif growled.

"Whatever you wish," Freggs responded, and gave a mechanical chuckle that made al-Seif's fur stand on end. "Tell them the truth, for all I care. I would be more concerned with what you tell your *wife*."

The line went dead.

Moments later the soft voice of Abar Kami called him on the intercom. "Yursa De Palma is here to see you, sir."

Gods damn it all, al-Seif thought. He pressed the speaker button and said, "Send her in." Another button remotely unlocked the door.

The tall wolfhound who entered was somewhere on the upper end of thirty; not that you could tell from her wiry body-fur, which had been naturally grey since puppyhood. She appeared surprisingly composed after the events of last night. Al-Seif recalled she had looked almost pretty with her rust-coloured long-fur cascading down around her shoulders, now it was back into the tight, stylish bun she preferred.

Her posture was erect and confident, ready to pick up the mantle her father had left her. Al-Seif had to admit she was well-built, for a canine, and even while in mourning her fashionable black dress hugged all the right curves.

He didn't offer her a seat, and she didn't take one. She stared at him in silence, ears back, and the deep grey eyes behind her black veil burning with hate.

The mouflon's own drooping ears began to twitch, and eventually, he gave in to his anger. "What do you want, *la cagna*?" he said, addressing Yursa in Mecci to emphasise his words and ignoring the irony of his insult.

"I was just studying the face of the man I'm going to murder," she said coolly. "If you're waiting for the police, don't bother. I understand the chief inspector is still indebted to me. I informed them we witnessed the same chain of events."

The mouflon's eyes narrowed sharply. "Which where?" he asked.

"We invited you to dinner to welcome you back to Medocci after a long absence. You received an urgent call from your villa guards that a bandit gang was approaching. I saw you out to the car, and the gates blew open, followed by a bandit buggy with a mounted machinegun. Both of us were equally startled and barely escaped through the gardens." She smiled coldly. "It's close enough to the truth."

"An investigation would not corroborate that account."

Yursa shrugged. "As I said, the chief inspector owes a great deal to the De Palma family."

Al-Seif leaned back wearily. "I did not order your father murdered."

"I know. It doesn't matter. I was there when the spotlight trained on us, yet we're still alive. Whoever it was, you are obviously still of value to them. I intend to prove them wrong."

Al-Seif rubbed at his temples and wondered when everything had gone so wrong. Last night he thought he had planned for every contingency. He thought about the blackmail again, but after Vigo's assassination, al-Seif was almost certain that would mean little to his enraged wife.

He tried anyway.

"My contracts still stand," he said slowly, "If you so much as blink I'll release the documents and have you under investigation for bioweapons manufacture and extortion."

"I've already lost everything," the wolfhound growled defiantly, glaring down at him. "I'm going to hurt you just as you've hurt me. I'm going to make you wish you had never heard the De Palma name."

"I must warn you," the mouflon said coolly, "that the people who executed your father can make it so that no one remembers the De Palmas even existed."

"Let them come. You'll find I'm much more aggressive than my father. After I'm through with you, I'm coming for them as well." Yursa leaned forward and placed her hands on the desk, baring her teeth in a grim smile. "Let me put it in simple words so you'll understand: *vaffanculo*, Jirair."

Al-seif didn't need a translator to understand her final comment.

The wolfhound pushed away sharply and made her way to the door, pausing just for a moment in the entryway. "You'll have until Faerday," she said over her shoulder, "Papa would want you at his funeral. After that, will be yours."

Then Yursa brusquely left the office.

Al-Seif stared out the open door for a long moment then turned his gaze back out the window. The fires at the De Palma villa had started anew.

* * *

On a hill outside al-Seif's compound, a canine figure lounged comfortably in the shade of a grove of palm trees. The fauna wasn't native to Medocci, but many unusual plants had found their way onto the fertile volcanic soil over the millennia, especially when the great Meccinai Empire ruled much of the Medean Basin. Of course, this mattered little to the greyhound; all he cared about was that from his shady vantage point he had an excellent view of the villa, the private beach, and the front drive of Jirair al-Seif's fortified compound. A battered brown leather case sat on the ground by his feet.

He adjusted the sling over his right arm and watched as Yursa De Palma left the house by the front door and climbed into the back of a waiting armoured limousine. The vehicle rolled through the compound's gate and glided down the hill towards Pacé Acqua and the wolfhound's apartments.

A mechanical chirp sounded from the pocket of his long brown trench coat. He removed the bulky handset of a satellite phone and placed it next to a pointed ear.

"*Oui?*" his low voice answered in the musical strains of Marisian.

"We want her," the mechanical voice of Freggs replied in Locken. "I hope you have clothes for a funeral."

"But of course," the figure replied, switching to the same language.

"Good. First, we need you back at Jar-Geshim. The snake may still be of some use to us."

"Understood," the greyhound said and disconnected the call.

He dropped the handset back in his pocket and reached up to pluck the receiving dish for the satellite phone from the branch above his head; stowing it carefully in the case at his feet next to the dismantled frame of a rifle.

His kit packed, the greyhound silently melted back into the shade of the trees and vanished from sight.

3 – Carmen

From a shadowed alcove near the kitchens, a pair of stunning pale blue eyes gazed coolly at Yursa De Palma as she left the villa. The slight, voluptuous female ibex was in her early forties now, but still as vivacious as the retreating De Palma matriarch. Her polished ribbed horns gleamed with a bright ebony sheen that matched the shining ringlets of her black long-fur, which fell to her shoulders and was just a shade darker than her woolly body-fur. The melanism was unusual for an ibex and gave her an exotic appearance that she bore with pride.

After several long minutes, the ibex moved toward al-Seif's office as delicately as she could, her polished hooves making only the slightest *tic tic* against the marble floor of the foyer. She raised her hand to knock on the frame, then decided against it and stepped into the office unannounced. Pausing next to the desk she gazed down at the mouflon seated behind it with a mixture of affection and concern.

Al-Seif didn't acknowledge her presence, even when she leaned forward into his view. Her floral-patterned silk dress left very little to the imagination, but her veiled curves could not seem to draw the mouflon's eye. Finally, she reached out and gently took one of his hands; the one fiddling with the purple feather.

Al-Seif looked at her, and for a brief moment, the worry melted away from his face. "Carmen, my love," he said.

Carmen Abbatelli smiled and sat on the edge of the desk, still clutching his hand. "Jirair, *mi amore*, you must sleep. I am worried sick for you."

He listened to the silky streams of her voice, and she could tell from the look in his eyes that he wanted to smile, but the weight of his predicament was heavy on him.

"I cannot," he said, "With Vigo dead, it is only a matter of time before the other families begin vying for their assets. Yursa will fight, and hard, but I think she has forces working against her that she cannot comprehend."

Carmen had always tried to distance herself from the illegal practices of her paramour; even so, she was wickedly intelligent and always spoke her mind when she identified a flaw. She saw one now.

"Freggs is playing you both," she said, "This game of his seems to cover the whole world. He must have many pieces on the board."

Al-Seif did smile now, a mirthless twitch of his lips that made Carmen shuddered involuntarily. "It does appear that Freggs has other ideas," he said, "I fear that things are swiftly moving out of my control." He reached up with his free hand and stroked a delicate cheek. "I fear he may eventually try to take that which is most dear to me."

The ibex frowned and seemed on the brink of tears. "If it is not safe, we should move. Get far away. Surely there must be someplace where we can go. You know these material things mean very little to me." She waved around the room vaguely.

Al-Seif nodded and gently but firmly removed his hand from her grasp. "First I must make sure I am still useful. Since leaving Pytan, my position has grown untenable. The assassination Ambassador bin-Aden's daughter has stoked the fires of war between Pytan and Barju, and I have no doubt Freggs is pulling the strings from behind the curtain. His associates want the region destabilised, and I intend to find out why."

"Be cautious, *mi amore*," Carmen said, "You cannot return to Pytan yourself, Freggs will be watching you too closely. He ordered you to let your Pytan businesses go, and it may be wise to do just that."

Al-Seif shook his head negatively. "You know that is the one thing I cannot do," he said firmly, "But you have given me an idea. If that cursed amphibian is focused on us, Delshad may be able to get back in unnoticed. He has grown as cunning as his father, and if I grant him authority to stabilize my holdings in Pytan, my men will obey him. That should net us the capital we need to start again elsewhere."

He paused and glanced at the growing look of concern on his lover's face. "Forgive me, my dear," he said gently, "I know sending our son out will be dangerous, but there should be no reason for us to lose everything and subsist in squalor."

Carmen nodded and pushed off the desk. "That is so. But please advise him to be careful and assign your best men to protect him."

Al-Seif nodded. "Abar must stay here with you, but Rashid has proven to be nearly as competent. He is not a fighter himself, but he will hire those who are. And my gladiators are still in Pytan, no one would dare challenge them."

Carmen noticed the fallen horn tassel on the floor and bent to pick it up. Rising, she embraced the mouflon, laying his head against her chest, and carefully replaced the ornament. Then she moved her hand to stroke the curve of his horns.

"Thanks to your bond with the De Palma family the mafia will be looking for weakness even in you," she said huskily, "We must continue to appear strong to them, and you should start by keeping yourself groomed. It might also be wise to meet with the other shareholders now that the business has changed hands."

Al-Seif tilted his head to look up at her, and his lips curled in a genuine smile now. "Ever you continue to amaze me at your grasp of this dirty business. But no, not until after Vigo's funeral. I may have taken the name Assad Alabwaq to reflect my swift action, but I respected Vigo too much to act so hastily. Besides, there will be other distractions between then and now."

The ibex's smile was warm as she moved her hands to his shoulders, then down the front of his jacket. "Distractions like me?" she whispered in his ear.

Al-Seif nuzzled against her. "Always, my angel."

"There are no angels in this world," she said, "Only the demons we create for ourselves."

4 – Mody Nahas

Kairran, capital of the nation of Pytan. An arid city commanding an arid country.

Just over one week had passed since the war had officially started with the country of Barju to the northeast, but to be perfectly honest, Mody Nahas didn't see much of a difference.

The obscenely obese orangutan leaned his bulk against the wide window sill and gazed out at the bustle of the market streets in the Dahley District. Vendors still barked their trade, and veiled prostitutes continued to entice the weak-willed to sample the luxuries of their patron opium dens. Beyond, on the distant edges of the city, the formidable outer wall still protected them from blasting sandstorms and bandit invaders. Soon it may have to withstand mortar fire as well, but on this wonderfully warm late winter morning, the conflict felt as many hundreds of kilometres away as it really was.

True, the military presence was heavier than usual, but it didn't appear to be affecting trade. Not yet.

Nahas knew it was only a matter of time. The government had sealed the borders and the ports; that meant there were many goods, even in legitimate markets, that would soon become scarce. Demand was going to skyrocket. This was an excellent time for smugglers such as himself.

Knowing this made the heavy brow over Nahas' beady, pale-blue eyes furrow and his purple lips turned down in a droopy frown. Why had Assad Alabwaq, one of his fiercest competitors, decided to cut and run after the events that had brought this most fortuitous circumstance?

True, it couldn't have been easy to discover that one of your slave girls was actually the daughter of the Barjan ambassador, and then witness an assassin spatter her brains all over the stage. Nahas would be shaken to the toes of his large feet, but he had known the mouflon for a very long time, and Alabwaq didn't scare so easy.

Nahas had been there from the beginning, running textiles with Alabwaq for the leopard Ricky Tan. The mouflon had always proved to be quick-witted and resourceful. On every job there was a gleam in Alabwaq's eyes unlike anything Mody Nahas had ever see. It was not the look of a coward. For the mouflon to flee the country entirely, abandoning all his local business interests, felt like economic suicide.

Or at least it did to Nahas.

The orangutan ran a large hand over his swept-back long-fur. Strands of grey had started appearing on his head, but most of it was still a shade darker than the orange body-fur that covered his immense frame. He turned away from the window and shifted ponderously toward the low stone chair along the back wall.

The room that served as Nahas' meeting hall would rival the sultan's own palace. Silk draperies in a rainbow of colours cascaded from the high ceiling. Hooka tables, surrounded by piles of pillows and plush divan couches, lay scattered around the outer edges. His highest-ranking lieutenants lounged at their leisure, enjoying the company of the beautiful veil-clothed women who served as part of the ape's personal entourage. Mody Nahas played no favourites with his women. Carnivore, omnivore, herbivore, furred, feathered, or scaled; all had their own particular fancies with him. Although he did have a disproportionate number of primates.

The orangutan eased his bulk onto the stone chair and waved one such beauty over. The serving girl—a petite rhesus monkey with ample bosom—bowed respectfully as she held out a tray laden with fresh grapes. He grabbed a cluster and began nibbling it thoughtfully, his large lips smacking and sucking on the juicy fruit.

Nahas hadn't been idle during Assad Alabwaq's absence. Already some of his competitor's assets had fallen under his control. Alabwaq's slave and drug trades were still too highly protected; but his weapons, textiles, electronics, and small goods operations had all been vulnerable—especially now that Vigo De Palma was out of the picture. All it had taken on Nahas' end was a careful reassignment of personnel.

What troubled the orangutan most was that he shouldn't have able to move in so quickly.

Of course, holding back would have been equally stupid. Someone else could snatch up the resources first; like maybe that Dollan fox-shepherd, Weis. But Nahas was still cautious.

Pytan's new Regent and his Governor General were loyal Alabwaq customers, and if this was a trap, Nahas was going to be ready for it.

A comfortable sensation grew in the ape's gut, and he let his blue eyes wander over the serving girl. The rhesus was a new hire, young, barely into her twenties. Beneath the veils, Nahas could make out intricate floral tattoos on her arms that he found dizzying to look at. She had many other designs as well, one in particular that had drawn his interest when he hired her.

Tattooing was rare for Amarthians, no matter the culture. Reptiles could permanently dye their scales without much loss of function; but in mammals, once inked the fur would not grow back and deprived the individual of its natural weather protection. One could always permanently dye their fur, but it could be costly, and quality designs were rare. "Mom" spelt in fur often looked particularly garish, but tiger stripes or leopard spots on species that such patterns weren't natural could be quite becoming.

The rhesus servant was a local girl and had reasoned that since cold days in Pytan were rare, losing her fur by turning her body into canvas was an acceptable risk.

The look in Nahas' eyes turned lustful, and he was just about to ask her to show him the "special" tattoo again when he heard the old fashion bells of the phone next to his chair.

The serving girl backed away respectfully as Nahas answered it. "Yes?"

"Mody Nahas?" The feminine voice on the other end was rich, cultured, and spoke Locken with a faint trace of Medoccian heritage and the roughness of a canine.

"Speaking," Nahas answered, his own deep voice had a slowness to it that drew out his *es*.

"I have an...unusual proposition for you," the woman said pausing. "I believe we have a mutual enemy, Jirair al-Seif."

Nahas' eyes narrowed. He was one of the few that knew al-Seif was the real name of his competitor, Assad Alabwaq, but he said nothing.

"No doubt you have already begun to pick apart his interests in Pytan since he left," the woman continued. "How would you like to solidify those holdings and perhaps even move into Medocci?"

Nahas leaned back, the stone chair grinding slightly. "And how would I do that? Does the matriarch of the De Palma family still have the power to grant such a boon?"

There was a low growl on the other end, but Yursa De Palm brought herself under control. "I can, and with your help, I can do much more."

"What you ask is a tall order. And I am currently quite busy here in Pytan."

A pause.

"Understandable," Yursa replied, "What would it take to lighten your load? Perhaps there are some local matters you need assistance with."

The orangutan grinned widely. He had heard of Yursa De Palma's shrewdness, it was a pitty al-Seif did not appreciate her.

"You are a fine bitch!" Nahas laughed raucously, bits of grape flying from his mouth. "There are a few matters which may help both of us. For instance, this war has significantly decreased the desire for gladiator games and slaves, but significantly raised the demand for arms. Ah, how conflict conspires to release the ancient bloodlust in us all." He sighed. "I have already struck deals with a few of Alabwaq's— or al-Seif as you call him—suppliers, but there are more still who seem intent to shell up entirely and wait out the storm. I believe many of them might actually be some of your father's old clients."

"And if someone could convince them their need was greater than loyalty," Yursa said, "You might be willing to offer goods at more than reasonable discounts."

"Precisely! I have tried to crack these supply lines before, but perhaps someone with a more...intimate knowledge of their workings could provide the leverage I need?"

"My father's old clients will listen," she said, "Jirair's more loyal customers might be a problem. That bastard is as stubborn up here as he was in Pytan. However, it appears my recent misfortune was not a part of his machinations either. I have no doubt he planned to annul our marriage after taking over papa's business, but he might be thinking twice now. That reminds me, there is a favour you could do for me in return."

"I am listening."

"Carmen Abbatelli," Yursa growled, the disdain dripping from her voice. "Al-seif's whore mistress. I want her dead."

Mody Nahas ran his long fingers through his rust-coloured long-fur. "That is a tall order. I do not have many resources outside of Pytan, let alone in Medocci."

"I can get your men in, but it will take some time," she answered, "While you wait, I have something else that may appease you. You have already mentioned seizing some of al-Seif's assets, if he wishes to maintain his hold in Pytan, he will need to send someone to either liquidate or reacquire them. I believe that someone will be his son, Delshad. His presence may provide an...opportunity."

Nahas chuckled dryly. "Indeed. We shall see. You have given me much to think about, Ms De Palma. May fortune favour us both."

"Indeed." De Palma disconnected the call.

Mody Nahas hung up the ivory handset and rubbed his chin thoughtfully with long fingers. A familiar rumbling in his stomach disturbed him. He waved to the rhesus serving girl.

"Come, my dear! Thinking requires food. And perhaps you can give us a dance later. I find myself wanting to see your tattoo again. That one that looks like a tiger's face."

5 – Formative Years

Jirair wrapped his morning robe around his scrawny frame and brushed his long-fur until it no longer fell in front of his eyes. He studied his appearance in the bathroom mirror, satisfied that he was presentable but still disappointed that his horns had not grown much further than his narrow jawline. He had a couple years left before he reached maturity and with luck, the horns would start to curl around until the tips lined up with his cheekbones. At least they were even, his father constantly complained that a *Caprinae* with uneven horns was little better than a thug or a beggar.

Jirair checked his wristwatch. It was a cheap model, but one of the few gifts his father had given him; even if it was for the sole purpose of making sure he was never late for anything important. As usual, he had just enough time to dress and climb the stairs to the kitchen for a light breakfast before his tutor arrived.

There were plenty of religious schools around, eager to teach the values of Nuadinism or Aabanism or even the numerous scriptures of the Antheon alongside reading, writing, and arithmetic skills. However, Jirair's father had made it quite clear that his reluctant offspring wouldn't be participating in any foolhardy religious fanaticism; although Saifullah did keep a small shrine to the various goat gods in his office, for luck.

At the impressionable age of twelve, Jirair wasn't quite sure what to believe. Currently, he was under the impression that the universe was too complex to be a cosmic accident; but if a deity, or deities, did exist, they didn't seem to have as much influence on the modern world like they did in the "old days"—whenever those were.

He wiped a bit of fruit from his mouth and rechecked his watch, then matched it to the kitchen clock. It was almost a quarter until nine in the morning. His tutor should have been there by now.

Jirair frowned. This was not the first time he would be studying on his own. In fact, he had a pretty good idea where his tutor was.

She was a mink this time; young, supple, and attractive. They were always young, supple, and attractive. Jirair was entirely convinced at this point that his "tutors" were as much to fulfil Saifullah's appetites as to actually teach his offspring. For all Jirair knew, tutoring was merely an excuse for them to visit the home of the moderately successful antiquities dealer. After all, "whore" was still a blaspheme in most parts of the world, even in Pytan where prostitution was legal.

Jirair sighed and cleaned up his breakfast dishes. His father had yet to hire another housekeeper after he fired the last one; why should he when his son could do most of the work for free?

The young mouflon strolled through the living room heading for his bedroom and his books, sparing a sideways glance at the closed door of his father's office. A faint noise caused him to pause, his foot halfway toward the first step.

Jirair cocked his head to the side, listening.

The noise came again, a breathy, high-pitched, and very feminine giggle.

Jirair didn't quite understand what came over him at that moment, but he suddenly thought of his mother. Saifullah never talked about her, and it was only through careful guesswork that Jirair had been able to deduce that she was deceased. The young mouflon had only seen one picture of her, and when his father caught him staring at the folio, he had come very close to beating his son. Jirair still didn't understand why he hadn't, or what had made his father so furious.

The giggle came again, punctuated by a laughing shriek.

Jirair's fists balled with sudden rage. It wasn't right. For too long his father had been keeping him from knowing who his mother was. Was she just another of Saifullah's whores? A summer fling that had produced him, and then tore his father's life apart?

He stepped over to the heavy wooden door. An itch under his left eye made him rub at the scar there. He raised his hand to knock, then decided to throw decorum to the wind, grabbed the handle, and threw the door open.

Jirair's tutor was there, all right, her shirt half open as she lay sprawled across the large antique desk. His father loomed over her, the fingers of one hand playing with the tuft of soft white fur on her chest.

Saifullah stood up with a start—Jirair was honestly surprised his pants were still on. The tutor shrieked and gathered the folds of her shirt around her.

"You wicked little boy!" she cried.

But Jirair ignored her, he just stared straight into the eyes of his father.

"Well?" the elder mouflon asked, returning his son's gaze. "What is it, boy? Come to wonder what happened to your teacher? Seems to me you're doing well enough on your own."

"Is she here to teach me or to please you, *father*?" Jirair spat the word as if it left a bad taste in his mouth.

"You watch your tongue, whelp," Saifullah said, pointing an accusing finger at his son. "While you live under my roof, you will obey my rules, and the rule of the day is to keep your nose in your books and out of my office!"

The mink tutor rolled off the desk and started gathering up what clothing she had already discarded.

"I'm not finished with you," Saifullah told her bluntly, and she promptly folded herself into a chair against the wall.

"Did you order my mother around like that?" Jirair asked.

Jirair could almost swear he saw a vein on his father's forehead pulsing with anger beneath the woolly fur of his brow. The younger mouflon had only seen his father so furious once: when he had stolen a peek at the folio with his mother's picture.

"Get out, gods damn you!" Saifullah roared, slamming a balled fist onto the desk. The mink whimpered slightly from her chair.

Jirair stared at him a moment longer. He had struck a nerve mentioning his mother, he must remember that. He was not going to win any argument he started now, best to let his patron have his way. He turned on his hoof and left, slamming the heavy door behind him.

* * *

Jirair al-Seif started awake in his bed. Fosday morning dawned bright and clear on the hills outside Pacé Acqua. He rubbed at the sleep in his eye and felt the tingle of the scar under it.

He had dreamt of his past again. Why? He had already learned the lessons he needed, they were what made him the man he was. They were what had created Assad Alabwaq.

The mouflon looked at the slender form of Carmen lying next to him, still asleep.

Unlike his father, al-Seif had remained faithful to her alone through the years. Every moment they were apart was unbearable to him. He couldn't avoid that, of course. His double life as Assad Alabwaq required him to spend weeks or even months in Pytan; but rarely did he go more than a few days without calling her.

Carmen was the most unique woman al-Seif had ever met, and even though he didn't consider himself a religious man, he thanked the goat gods for her all the same.

Yursa hated her almost as much as she hated Jirair, and it wasn't just because the ibex "whore" was an affront to their sham of a marriage. No, al-Seif well and truly loved

Carmen, and that was one thing Yursa knew she could never gain control of.

Al-Seif pondered what the wolfhound might be doing that morning. Fosday was a holy day for Aabanite Catholics, and the mouflon assumed Yursa would be attending morning services, feigning piety and asking absolution for the sins incurred doing the dirty business she was now in charge of.

Hypocrites.

Al-Seif didn't care what sort of rationalisation the De Palmas used to make them feel they had the moral high ground. Al-Seif had determined long ago that the goat gods didn't care much what happened to their subjects, and it was unlikely any other deities did either. When he offered a half-hearted prayer to the goat gods, his only thought was that maybe in the end his own little corner of hell wouldn't be quite so bad.

Gently he woke Carmen and spent Fosday morning as he always did, making love to his "whore" mistress and caring not a wit that his wife must be begging all the Saints to call down curses upon him.

Afterwards, al-Seif showered and dressed in one of the white suits he had grown so accustomed to wearing.

As he sat down to a breakfast of fruit and oats, the mouflon began to wonder if his misfortunes over the past week might have been an answer to Yursa's prayers.

Al-Seif discarded the thought almost immediately and tried recalling his dream, wondering if there was some small piece that connected it to his current state.

At first, the young mouflon had thought the "tutors" were just a way for his father to appease his appetites. But as he grew older, al-Seif began to see it was more than that. In his own way Saifullah El-Hashem was trying to crush his son's spirit; to give the boy all the tools he needed to succeed, then show him that it was a pointless endeavour because he meant nothing, not even to his teachers. Saifullah was the master of the house, and he let his hated son know it in every way he could think of.

Naturally, it had backfired, and al-Seif only strived harder to prove his father wrong.

No, that wasn't right. Al-Seif didn't need to prove anything, and that became his goal. At twelve years old al-Seif had realised that he was alone, and if he were to stay that way, he would be alone from a place where he could look down on everyone.

Then he had met Carmen and not long after became a father himself. His dreams of power and station didn't change, but he suddenly realised he didn't have to be alone at the top.

Thinking of this brought al-Seif's thoughts to the present. By now Delshad should already be on his way to Challan from Libris, and from there he would circle southwards to Pytan; he should arrive in Kairran sometime mid-Miriday morning. As much as al-Seif would like to just enjoy the pleasant late-winter day, several items required his attention to assist his son's mission. And most of them centred on trying to distract Freggs.

He left the dining hall and made his way to his office, seating himself once again behind the black-marble desk.

The more al-Seif thought about the events of the past week, the more he realised just how much of a pawn he had been to the mechanical toad—that was how he pictured Freggs behind the voice filter.

First Freggs had set up the auction and subsequent assassination of Rijay din-Aden, a disturbing stunt in itself. On the same day, al-Seif's brand new and not even completed gladiator arena went up in flames; taking a healthy chunk of the warehouse he used for legitimate trading with it.

Had Freggs rigged that as well? The arena had been the toad's idea and his design; al-Seif wouldn't have placed such a destructive security device himself, the venue was too costly to replace. And Freggs certainly didn't seem at all surprised to learn someone had been snooping around the arena. In fact, he seemed more interested in the intruders than the loss of al-Seif's business revenue.

Had they been the mechanical toad's actual targets? Was it for the benefit of this third party that Freggs was putting on a show?

It had to be. It couldn't have been just coincidence that those same "agents" had reappeared in Jar-Geshim. And after they managed to bring down Freggs' pet mad-science project, the toad had all but force al-Seif to call in a marker with Agabe Hassan, now the self-appointed Regent of Pytan.

Hassan had sent his best assassins, the *Alqarmizi Alhulm*—the Scarlet Dream—to remove the threat.

In the end, they had failed too.

The Marshal of Jar-Geshim hadn't contacted al-Seif since the incident, which was just as well. Cobra or not, if al-Seif ever saw the snake again, he would milk the venom from his fangs and make him drink it. Then he might skin him and hang him on the wall in his office, or perhaps in the living room above the fireplace.

Al-Seif plucked the cauracua feather from the lapel of his suit and started playing with it again. He wondered what had happened to the hunters after they vanished into the Warren. The labyrinth of ancient Jar-Geshim held enough dangers to keep an army at bay.

Perhaps they had met their end within the Warren's walls?

Jirair al-Seif's eyes narrowed and he frowned contemptuously at the thought. No, after everything he had done to try and stop them, he didn't feel he was that lucky.

6 – A Minor Inconvenience

Detective chief inspector Codwithe glared through the single-sided mirror at the figure seated in the room beyond, his large eyes squinting almost comically as he folded his arms across his narrow chest.

Despite being a red squirrel, the inspector loved dealing with predators. Maybe it had something to do with overcoming the ancient myths where primitive versions of his species served as prey to creatures with bigger teeth and sharper claws. Now Codwithe could play the tough guy because, in the modern "enlightened" world, only a deranged maniac would ever dream of eating another sentient creature.

But then again, only a deranged maniac would dress like the occupant of the other room.

The tight, ratty jeans; the heavy-metal band T-shirt; the studded leather bangle on the left wrist; all of them were trademarks of the radical "punk" style the young hooligans were wearing today.

And then there was that weird mark on her arm. It wasn't a tattoo, but Codwithe had never seen a birthmark that took on such a distinct shape before. It kind of looked like half a tiger's face. He found it really creepy.

Well, time to get this freakshow on the road, the squirrel thought.

Codwithe grabbed his file folder, took a swig of cold coffee, and set the cup down on the soundboard. Heath, the engineer, promptly swore at him and moved the cup to a table.

"Oi, this shit is delicate, you knob!" the orange tabby whined.

Codwithe just smirked as he left. How mighty were the predators now?

The white tigress in the interrogation room didn't even look over as the squirrel entered. She just sat there, arms folded across her chest, unshod feet propped on the metal table with her chair balanced on the back two legs, and staring at an undefinable point somewhere above and to the left of the observation mirror.

Her fur had the faintest touch of pink to it; Codwithe guessed it was part of her "punk" getup. The squirrel was mildly surprised the tigress hadn't dyed the black long-fur on her head to match. The hair was too long for a pixie cut, but stopped short of her shoulces. It was still shorter than what Codwithe deemed attractive for women, and there was a thick strand in front that kept falling across her left eye.

The inspector reached backed and pulled a large handgun from his belt; the magazine had been removed, and the slide was locked open. He rested it on the table, tilting the white-gold barrel at the tigress. Her gaze did shift now, first to the gun, and then to him.

What was that look? Not defiance. It seemed more like disapproval. It reminded Codwithe uncomfortably of the look his safety instructor gave him during the firearms portion of his academy days.

That was absurd, of course. Imagine, a street punk like this tigress actually concerned about gun safety. Especially when she carried something so large and ostentatious; she'd even scribbled some kind of engraving along the sides. Typical wannabe crime-boss mentality.

"You are aware of Locke's gun laws, aren't you, miss—" He checked the file. "Miss Katral?"

The tigress remained silent.

"You didn't really think you and your cohorts could get that whole plane-load past customs, did you? Even if you did, you must have gotten someone's knickers twisted, because we got a nice juicy tip that you lot were coming through." Codwithe leaned back and crossed his arms smugly. "What happened? You cheat a mate out of his cut?"

The tigress continued not to answer, but a subtle flicker in her eye told the inspector that something had hit a nerve. He had to admit she was good, but she would break, they always broke eventually.

There was a knock on the door, and Superintendent James stuck his big bison head into the room. "A word, Codwithe?" he said and gestured outside.

Codwithe picked up the pistol and followed. James led him into the observation area and told Heath to leave.

"We get something else, Captain?" the inspector asked.

The super frowned and handed him an official looking piece of paper. Codwithe took it and read it. Then he reread it.

"They can't be bloody serious?" the squirrel said, barely able to keep the rage out of his voice, "The whole lot?"

The bison nodded his woolly head. "That note comes from the Minister of Intelligence himself. They're to be released, their weapons returned, and the plane released."

Codwithe partially crumpled the note, his hands shaking with anger. "Bloody hell!" he blurted out, "When's the bloody Ministry ever going to tell us they've agents coming through? What about the tip?"

"Probably someone trying to blow their cover," James said, "Look, it's not like we've never dealt with this before, you know these cloak and dagger types. Go on, go let off some steam. I'll see to it they get a swift boot out the door."

The squirrel turned to leave.

"Ah, Inspector," James stopped him and held out his hand.

Codwithe shoved the heavy pistol into the super's paw and stormed out the door.

The bison went to the entry and made sure the squirrel had turned the corner, then he returned to the control board. He turned off the camera and the recording equipment then went into the interrogation room himself.

James placed the pistol on the table again, pointing the barrel towards the wall this time, and produced a loaded magazine, which he set next to the weapon. He pushed both towards the tigress.

"You're free to go, agent Katral," the superintendent said, "The rest of your team will be waiting outside."

Kitty Katral picked up the gun, inspected it, and inserted the magazine. Then she stood and shoved it into the back of her jeans next to her tail, covering the weapon with the hem of her shirt. She seemed uncomfortable with the arrangement, but there were no other options without the weapon's holster.

"I understand you're a hunter team," the bison said, a note of agitation in his voice.

The tigress said nothing.

"I hope you aren't here for a reason," James continued.

Kitty shook her head negatively. "No worries, mate," she said.

As she made for the door, James called to her. "Agent Katral?" the tigress turned to him, and the bison tapped his right shoulder. "Strength and honour."

Kitty pointed to her marked left arm. "Wisdom and justice."

Then she was gone.

* * *

Within the hour the tigress had rejoined her comrades aboard a train heading from the Locke capital of Hempsford to the northern city of Grettasburg.

None of them spoke about the incident at the police station; they didn't need to. Ever since the assassination of Rijay din-Aden, the agents of the *Laohu Tiaowen*—the Tiger's

Stripe—had been hounded by a mysterious adversary that seemed intent on making their lives very uncomfortable.

By rights, they shouldn't even be in Locke. Their team was assigned to the continent of Estan, where they had been tracking the crimelord Assad Alabwaq, A.K.A. Jirair al-Seif. However, despite the mouflon's numerous offences, bringing the mouflon down hadn't been their goal.

Hunter TS Three—or Mohan's Scrappers as they called themselves—were monster hunters. Their prey were the nightmarish beasts called fiends, whose destructive power was unmatched by even the deadliest of Amarthia's native predators. The creatures also happened to carry Daeminox syndrome, one of the deadliest sleeping plagues in the world.

The Elder Council, Tiger's Stripe's ruling body, believed Assad Alabwaq wished to harness the power of the fiends, and it was the hunters' job to make sure that didn't happen.

But there had been an unexpected wrench in the works. He sat across from Kitty as she lounged on the bench seat reading a computer magazine. Out of the corner of her eye, the tigress watched Sedric Barnes yawn widely, baring long feline fangs and blinking away the sleep from his emerald green eyes.

Kitty fought the urge to follow the lynx's yawn with one of her own. All the agents felt the lingering tendrils of weariness that seemed to plague travellers. They had been in transit nearly sixteen hours and had crossed three time-zones on their journey westward.

But hopefully, this was the last leg. Once Ric had his affairs in order, they could get back to al-Seif and give him the justice he so richly deserved.

Bastard deserves a bullet for the slaves alone, Kitty thought.

Much to the tigress' chagrin, Tiger's Stripe didn't operate that way; after all, they were the good guys. Their code of honour demanded they make things all nice and legal; get al-Seif on trial and let the proper authorities lock him away for good.

Thinking about it only made Kitty angrier. She lost her place in the article she was reading and fought against the urge to toss the circular across the cabin. Exasperated, the tigress tried distracting herself by stealing a glance around the compartment.

Her father, Mohan, sat slumped against the seat near the door, his broad-brimmed slouch hat—left side pinned up—pulled over his eyes and his powerful arms folded over his barrel chest. The massive tiger's two-point-two-metres frame seemed to fill the cabin, even though they had booked larger accommodations for the trip. Despite his casual clothing, two items stood out: a trophy necklace made of long teeth and claws and a pocketed vest of greenish-scaled hide.

Both items were fashioned from fiend monsters that Mohan had slain with his bare hands. The proof of these deeds was hidden beneath his shirt: three large jagged scars across his chest and two more on his left bicep.

Kitty's eyes moved to Ric again. The lynx was staring out the window, but there was little to see along the rolling green and grey hills apart from forests and the odd castle ruin. Kitty guessed he was probably thinking about everything that had happened over the last week. It was ironic, but Ric had doubtless been shot at more often as a journalist than he probably would have had he followed his late father's career and join the Royal Grettasburg Police.

And all because of that birthmark, Kitty thought.

The mark in question was on Ric's right forearm, just behind the wrist. The peculiar arrangement of stripes twisted into the distinct form of a tiger's face with a broad *S*-shaped stripe between the eyes. It was just like the one Kitty and her father had, except Mohan's was spread across his back and shoulders and hers was split between her left breast and arm.

Ric had seen her mark in full, but the events that made Kitty expose herself were not something she wished to focus on. Codwithe had been wrong about her fur, the pink colouring wasn't dye, it was blood. Blood from dozens of bandits the tigress had slaughtered in a blind feral rage.

By the end of the weekend, Kitty's fur would return to its normal cream colour; the faces in her dreams would never go away.

And there'll be more, Kitty whispered to herself, *More unless I embrace my deepest fears and accept—*

She flipped a page angrily. No, she needed that pain, it kept her senses sharp.

Out of the corner of her eye, the tigress noticed Ric staring at her.

"Enjoying the view, mate?" Kitty asked. Her dialect was lazier than what was generally heard in Locke, a clear indication she was from the colony that eventually became the United Plains.

Ric realised his gaze had unconsciously shifted to the tigress' long, jean-clad legs and he snapped them back to her eyes. Two pools of sapphire ice gazed back at him.

"Sorry," the lynx replied.

Kitty went back to her magazine.

Ric ran a hand through his shaggy dirty-blond long-fur then over the scruff on his chin and muzzle; he hadn't had the opportunity to trim it in days. Mammal beards grew the same colour as their facial markings unless dyed, and without proper care they often gave the bearer a wild and most uncivilised appearance.

A flash of chrome and car-paint caught the lynx's eye, and he turned to watch a motorist zoom by.

"Safer to use the train," the journalist said idly, "Although these white-lines don't stop at some of the smaller hamlets along the route."

Kitty said nothing, Mohan remained asleep.

Ric continued trying to make conversation. "To think, our ancestors once huddled in thatched-roof stone houses, listening to the rumble of vicious beasts prowling outside. And now we're the masters of our environment."

"Or at least we like to think so," Kitty said.

Ric glanced at her, but the tigress' nose was still in the circular.

"True," the lynx said, "I wouldn't want to get jumped by a hargaer out here."

Locke's wilderness was still full of all manner of wild beasts. Not the least of which was the hargaer, a feather-covered bear-like creature sometimes called an "owl-bear".

Naturally, the term was quite offensive to both owls and bears.

The armour-plated diesel-electric train wasn't in any real danger. Armed guards were on hand should any beast be bold enough to attack the train, but Ric had to admit such assaults had grown few in Locke. In fact, the citizens of the great walled cities were so comfortable in their modern ways that they had started expanding beyond the concrete bulwarks.

"But nature's always ready to swat you one should we get too presumptuous," Ric said as the first outlying buildings of Grettasburg approached.

Kitty said nothing, apparently trying to ignore any further conversation.

Ric sighed. "Only we sentient hom-ans could be arrogant enough to try to tame the native beasts of Amarthia," he said, more to keep himself awake than anything. "I wonder how the city would fair if attacked by one of those fiend creatures?"

"Don't even joke about that," Kitty said, lowering her magazine and staring at the lynx intently.

A knock on the door interrupted the journalist's reply.

Mohan was instantly awake and alert. A stocky badger opened the door and the tiger relaxed when he recognized it was Ezekiel, the team's tracker.

The badger was much shorter than Mohan—everyone was—but his broad shoulders still barely fit in the door. Ezekiel had swapped his customary thawb robes for a less conspicuous button-down shirt and casual slacks, but the badger still wore a sky blue keffiyeh around his head. The colour and style of the turban identified him as a Soketh from the Tribe of the Brown Paw, one of the mysterious nomadic tribes who thrived in the desolate wastelands of Amarthia's wilderness.

Ezekiel was also the only member of their party who was not born with the Tiger's Mark. He earned his place among them through an intense and extensive initiation process and had the mark tattooed on the back of his right ear to prove it.

"We will be arriving shortly," the badger said in his rumbling, formal, and unaccented voice.

"Thanks, Zed," Mohan replied, instantly resorting to the badger's nickname. The tiger's voice was as sonorous as Ezekiel's, but with Kitty's lazy Plainsman accent.

The huge tiger rose and stretched sore muscles, reaching back to straighten the short pony-tail of greying long-fur that had gotten tangled during his nap. Then he bent almost double to glance out the window.

The outlying homes and businesses of Grettasburg expanded nearly ten kilometres beyond the primary fortifications, which already encompassed seven hundred square kilometres around a tall hillock with a remarkably well-preserved castle at the centre.

As the train began to slow, Mohan and Ric watched as a group of uniformed police officers interrogated a cluster of youths standing near a crossway. The teens represented a variety of the so-called "woodland" species, both carnivore and herbivore, but the train passengers made note that their clothes bore matching colours. An array of spraypaint cans were scattered at their feet.

"Are gangs a major problem in Grettasburg?" Mohan asked.

"No more than usual," Ric answered, "Locke bandits are a different breed from what we encountered in Pytan. Exile is rarely used as a punishment here; a valiant attempt to keep the bandit population low. Most of the brigands in the wilds are just thieves and convicts living in caves to escape judgement. The local authorities are more worried about adolescents venturing beyond the city limits, where they're easy targets for kidnappings, or worse, recruitment."

The lynx turned his gaze to the approaching wall. "And while the police spread themselves thin worrying about bandits in the outer city, the inner city is vulnerable to the syndicates. Organized crime may not use the chaotic violence of the wild bandit clans, but their detriment to society is equally severe."

"Bandits within, bandits without," Mohan said with a chuff, "Amazing how it all somehow manages to remain more civilised than Jar-Geshim."

"That's Locke pragmatism for you," Ric replied, "Even the thieves have a code."

"Oh, good," Kitty scoffed, "Shall we invite them for tea?"

The train crossed the threshold of the main wall, and Mohan noted the guards stationed at the open gates looked almost bored; a sharp contrast to their counterparts in Kairran, where sandstorms or bandit attacks were constant. The ramparts themselves were cement walls fifteen metres high and at least eight metres thick, with fortified battlements dotting the top. Murals of landscapes or depictions of everyday life adorned the broad wall sections.

Mohan observed these with a raised eyebrow.

"Parliament thinks they help present a more positive image of life within the city," Ric said, noting the look on the tiger's face. "Doesn't always work of course. There's no measurable difference between inside or out on economic, social, or even political scales. But you can still find an element of classism between those who live inside and those without."

"Is that the voice of experience talking?" the tiger asked.

Ric's ears folded back slightly. "I grew up on the inside," he said with some hesitation.

Mohan chuckled. "Don't be hard on yourself, mate. My family's lived on a compound well beyond the walls of East Plains for at least a generation. It's a good fifty clicks along dirt road just to make a run to the market. Most people inside think we're crazy to live out there, but there's nothing like the freedom of the living in the bush."

It appeared that Ric wanted to ask more about the tiger's life outside his monster hunting, but the slow squeal of the train's breaks interrupted him.

"Weatherford Station," came the announcement over the train's public-address system.

Mohan straightened and turned to the journalist. "Welcome home, Ric."

7 - Grettasburg

As the passengers stepped onto the platform, Ric took in a deep breath. The air was thick with the rich sent of iron and damp pavement. Out beyond the covered portion of the station platform, a steady late-winter drizzle was falling. But the dreary weather couldn't mute the brightly painted storefronts that made up the city centre, nor stop its citizens from getting where they needed to go along the cobbled sidewalks.

Kitty watched Ric as he took all the familiar sensations in. The nostalgic contentment of being home was evident on the journalist's face. It was an emotion that Kitty had not felt in several years.

Four other passengers soon joined the party and allowed the tigress to force her attention to something other than her own regrets.

The first to join them was a tall tawny-furred hare, whose long ears protruded through the crown of a weathered white fedora. Vincenzo Nieves carried himself with an air of effortless charm, shifting his weight from one long rabbit foot to the next with measured hop-steps, and showing the world a dazzling buck-toothed grin. His Hamilton slacks and polo shirt were much pricier than the threads worn by his companions, but he wore them as casually as a suit from a chain department store. Ric's impression was that if someone spilt coffee on Vince's shirt, the hare would merely shrug it off and buy another without any complaint, and he might even buy a set for the offending party.

Behind Vince came a female basilisk with a short blue plume atop her head. Emperatriz "Rizzo" Vega was roughly the same height as the lively *Lagomorph*—minus his ears— and carried herself with a similarly relaxed gait, her long whip-like tail swishing behind her with each swing of her hips. She wore conservative slacks and a tube-necked shirt in earth tones that complimented her bright green scales. The claws on her hands and feet were noticeably longer than those of her mammal companions, with the possible exception of Zed's badger claws.

Next to Rizzo hopped a short, narrow-framed female bullfrog. Victoria Littlepond was a constant ray of sunlight wherever she went. Naturally, the damp Locke weather was more to her liking, but even in the arid deserts of Pytan, she had kept up a perpetually cheery disposition. She wore her pink dress in amphibian style, a billowing cut that kept most of the loose fabric from sticking to her moist skin except where it was unavoidable. The garment remained secured around her narrow waist with a broad belt of red plastic clasped with a large white circular buckle.

The last to join the group was a female golden eagle.

It was easy to determine the femininity of Rizzo and Vicki by the curve of their hips and the subtle swell of the false-breasts that characterised all non-mammal females on

Amarthia. However, Basira Tyrsus had adopted the uncommon practice of surgically augmenting her chest with more mammalian-type implants. While unusual, there were many males on Amarthia who found the appearance of feathered cleavage attractive, a fact the eagle was clearly well aware of.

Birds, reptiles, and amphibians aged gracefully on Amarthia, and it was nearly impossible to tell that Tyrsus was in her mid sixties. She flaunted it by wearing a figure-flattering turtleneck sweater, which was sleeveless to let her feathered arms free. The wings attached to her shoulder blades protruded through a hole in the sweater's back. Tyrsus completed the outfit with a pleated skirt that came to her knees, showing off her scaly lower legs and taloned feet.

Once the group was assembled, they milled about the platform for several minutes until most of the other passengers had gone on their way and the train left for its next stop.

"Well, where do we go from here?" Vince asked in a melodious baritone with a Banton drawl. He stroked the goatee on his chin, which he had dyed the same golden colour as the wavy long-fur partially hidden beneath his hat.

"Search me, Vince," Mohan said, "After that ripper of a welcome in Hempsford you'd think His Majesty wanted the war back on. Sorry, mate."

This last was directed at Ric, but the lynx just waved it off. The United Plains' struggle for independence from Locke rule hadn't been a pleasant experience, but it happened well over a hundred and seventy-five years ago.

The tiger turned to the golden eagle. In addition to being the eldest, Basira Tyrsus was also a member of the *Laohu Tiaowen's* Elder Council and was thus the ranking agent. She assumed command effortlessly.

"Originally," Tyrsus said, "Our objective was to let Mr Barnes prepare for his journey to Sanctuary. But since we lost Blue Wing, we must reconnect with our intelligence service and get a status update."

After landing in Hempsford, the agents had placed a call to announce their safe arrival in Locke. However, instead of reaching Blue Wing International Incorporated, they had received a recorded message that the number was no longer in service.

The purpose of Blue Wing was to guide agents who had temporarily lost direct contact with the Watch Command at their hidden headquarters, the Sanctuary. With the relay disabled, the agents were adrift until they could make contact with a backup.

Before they could make the call, the police had arrived to seize their plane. Tyrsus didn't say so allowed, but she had a suspicion that the old number had been tampered with to track anyone who attempted to call it.

Mohan yawned widely and stretched his arms above his head. "You see him, Basira?" he said quietly.

The eagle nodded slowly. "Same sport jacket and hood as in Hempsford."

The figure in question was seated two platforms away as if waiting for the connecting train, but the more experienced agents had recognised a tail when they saw one. His first appearance had been at the terminal in Hempsford, and again after they had been released from police custody. All they knew for sure about him was that he was canine and had taken more than a casual interest in the agents of Tiger's Stripe.

"Police?" Ric asked casually, keeping his back to the figure.

Mohan looked up at the departures board as if checking the information displayed. "No, he isn't sloppy enough. When we got off the train, I had actually thought we lost him until a few minutes ago. Whoever he is, he's good."

Elder Tyrsus turned to Ric. "Can you recommend a good hotel, Mr Barnes?" she asked.

The journalist blinked, stunned by the sudden change of topic. "You don't have a safehouse here?" he said. His surprise caused him to voice the question aloud.

"Oh, real smooth, nutter," Kitty whispered fiercely, "Just let the whole station know we're spies."

"Knock it off, Kitty," Mohan growled and turned to Ric. "We're a bit short on resources now. First rule is to make use of local hospitality."

"That said," Vicki Littlepond interrupted in her brusque but cheery New Port fashion, "I agree with Ric. Shouldn't KLAWS have a lot more resources available at the moment?"

"That is assuming our leak isn't from within," Rizzo added. The basilisk had a musical, if slightly pretentious, Marisian accent that made her first words sound like *zat ees ah-soo-meeng*.

The agents let the awful thought hang like a cloud for several moments. The *Laohu Tioawen* operated in deep shadow; their more public face was KLAWS, a secret organisation designed to be seen by other such organisations. If KLAWS had been compromised, it could spell disaster for its parent company.

"We always run that risk," Tysus said patiently, "Right now, we need to look as normal as possible." She turned to Ric again. "Until we can re-establish a link to the Sanctuary its best if we rely on our own resources."

Ric only hesitated for a moment, then nodded. "I think I know a place," he said.

They left the platform and headed straight for the rental office to acquire a vehicle large enough for all of them. To Mohan's disappointment, they didn't have any Tracksman Hikers like the Scrappers had used in Pytan; but the squat Rutherford Motor's Camp Wagon served its purpose well enough. Mohan and Zed took the front seats while the others squeezed onto the bench seats in the back.

Grettasburg was an older Locke city built around the tallest hill in the region. The ancient stonework walls were long gone, but the ruins of the old castle on the hill crest still served as a tourist attraction—the actual seat of the city government rested in the much less draughty brick buildings nearby.

Vince noted the look on Ric's face as they drove. "Good to be back?" he asked.

The lynx nodded. "I admit I feel a bit guilty about having been away so long, even if it's only been two months. It's hard to think that I'll just be going away again, perhaps for much longer."

"Once you're fully trained you can manage your time however you like," Mohan said, "I've been away from home too long as it is and can't wait to get back."

Did you feel that way when I was growing up? Kitty thought from the back seat, *You never seemed to be there for Nini and me.*

That's not fair, another voice argued with her, this one sounded like her younger sister, *Dad was there as much as he could, you know that. And when he was home, he spent every minute with us.*

Shut it! Kitty thought, squeezing her eyes shut, *I'm losing my bloody mind! Arguing with my own internal monologue.*

When she opened her eyes, Kitty caught a flash of movement as a motorcycle manoeuvred behind a lorry a few car-lengths behind them. Their tail hadn't gone away.

Ric directed his companions to an inn roughly halfway between his family home on the north end of Grettasburg and the offices of *LBC World Press* located in the city centre.

"Never spent the night here, per se," Ric explained, "But I pass it every day on the way to and from work. Plus, my best mate, Ed, has a flat nearby, so we often pop in for a pint."

"Thinking of visiting?" Tyrsus asked.

Ric hesitated a moment. "No," he said, "No, I'll see him when I head to the office Miriday."

While the journalist assisted Mohan with the check-in, Elder Tyrsus used the phone booth on the corner outside to connect with their new forwarding station—the packaging department at Jacobson Industries Limited. Kitty noted the troubled look in her eyes when she returned, but the eagle only recommended that the agents lay low until Miriday morning.

"Suits me," Ric said, "I'm knackered. Plus, the extra day will give me time to jot down a quick list of notes. Naturally, you'll have to look through them first, but I have to produce something. Getting trapped in a war zone is no excuse for Wilson Kneedy."

Tyrsus nodded. "By all means," she said and glanced meaningfully at Mohan, "We have some things to take care of tomorrow as well."

* * *

When Kitty woke the next morning, it was to find Mohan and Elder Tyrsus waiting for her in the lobby.

"We need to find somewhere to set up the radio," the eagle said, "Zed thinks he's found a spot."

"And Ric?" Kitty asked.

Tyrsus hesitated for a moment. "I know it's breaking with tradition," she said quietly, "but Rizzo, Vince, and Vicki can watch him. I want you on this one, agent Katral."

Kitty nodded.

Within a half hour, the tigress was sitting in the back of the Camp Wagon. Zed occupied the centre bench seat and Elder Tyrsus road shotgun with Mohan driving. All of them were armed.

The "spot" Tyrsus had mentioned was the old castle in the centre of the city. It was closed to the public on Fosdays, which made it the perfect location to set up a radio transmitter. Or an ambush.

The gardens surrounding the old citadel were still open, so it wouldn't be too odd for their truck to park in the lot, even if most of the citizens were either in bed or at church that early in the morning.

After parking, the four agents strolled casually through the grounds until they reached one of the service gates for the castle itself.

Kitty looked up at the closed-circuit cameras pointed at the entrance. "I don't know why you wanted me along," she said, "Vince should be here to handle security."

"Oh, but he is," Mohan said flatly.

Kitty raised an eyebrow.

"The guard on duty today just happens to be a lovely fox vixen," Elder Tyrsus explained, "We, uh, introduced her to Vince last night."

Kitty groaned and rolled her eyes. That was one vision she didn't want in her head at the moment.

"And besides that," Mohan said, moving to the gate, "Vince isn't the only one who can take care of a lock."

The gigantic tiger produced a ring of plastic keys. Undoubtedly, they were a gift from Vince, made using moulds of the real keys that were probably resting on the hare's nightstand at the moment. It was necessary to use plastic because it set faster than metal, and the keys needed to be back in place before Vince's guest knew they were gone. The down-side was they were brittle and rough on the edges, Mohan would have to be careful not to force any of them.

Which he did when he tried the key for the garden gate.

"Bollox!" Mohan said, tossing aside the broken key.

"Oh, ripper, Mohan," Kitty said frowning.

"Right, plan B," the tiger said.

Plan B involved Mohan grasping the chain with both massive paws and giving a sharp pull. It held for a few seconds, but eventually, the metal links buckled and snapped under the tiger's strength.

Once through the gate, Mohan handed the keys off to Zed and let him open the door to the security office. The badger had a much lighter touch and gave the tiger a placating smile as the locked clicked open. Mohan made a face, but returned the smile and waved the Zed on. First, the badger went to a bank of cassette decks and began erasing the tapes for the cameras, then he moved over the control board and switched off whatever electronic locks were in place.

"There are still several manual locks throughout the castle," Zed said, handing the keys to Kitty, "I shall disable the recording functions and monitor the camera feeds from here."

"Bonza," Mohan said, "Kitty, you and I are the darzl-catchers." He turned to Elder Tyrsus. "Hope you don't mind being the bait, Basira."

"Let us just hope there aren't any real darzl up in the tower," the eagle said.

"For their sake or yours?" Kitty said.

The elder just ruffled her wings and left. Darzl were small scaly vermin with an unfortunate resemblance to rats crossed with frogs. Though mostly considered pests, there were those among the raptor bird species who thought they made great snacks. From her tone, that wasn't how Basira Tyrsus viewed them.

"Right," Mohan said, "Kitty, you take the furnace, and I'll watch the gallery. Then we wait and see what our trap catches."

* * *

And wait they did, until the sun was well past noon. Not that Kitty could see it, being stuck in the grimy furnace room that used to supply the draughty building above with heat. The boilers were cold now, and from the refuse piled in the corners, it was evident that this section of the fortress was not on any tour.

As the team's sniper, Kitty prided herself on her patience, but this was getting to the point of ridiculous. However, it was her father that broke radio silence.

"I'm surprised the guard hasn't come back," Mohan said in a burst of static, "Guess you gotta praise Vince for his stamina."

"No!" Kitty said, "No you don't. Oh, that's gross."

"Indeed," Zed said, "Not the image I wished to conjure up."

"Not that," Kitty said, "Well, that too, but I meant the huge darzl nest I just saw in one of the boilers."

"Darzl?" Elder Tyrsus' voice came on the line.

"I am *not* catching one for you," Kitty said.

"No!" the eagle said, "Keep them away from up here, they're disgusting creatures!"

"South gate," Zed interrupted them, "Our target is approaching the undercroft entrance."

"Damn," Mohan said, "Slipped right past you, Zed?"

"It is possible to avoid the cameras overlooking that side if you know where to step," Zed answered, but there was no hint of defensiveness in his voice.

"Kitty," Mohan said, "Move up here. I think the undercroft has a hidden entrance into the gallery; I found the trigger earlier but left it alone."

"He is in the undercroft now," Zed reported, "It appears he is—by Mbektar! That is the security guard! He has her over his shoulder. It appears he plans to use her as a hostage." The badger paused. "No, wait. Mohan! He is going to—"

The badger was interrupted by the loud crack of a pistol shot.

"Kitty, move!" Mohan shouted, "Cut him off if you can!"

Down in the furnace room the tigress darted off between the old boilers.

Up in the gallery, surrounded by medieval tapestries and mounted suits of armour, Mohan took two long strides over to the ornate fireplace on the south wall. He extended the claw of one finger and shoved it indelicately into a slot carved into one of the stone feline figures bookending the hearth. There was a clank of metal, and a creak of wood as a panel next to the fireplace popped out.

Mohan dug his claws into the newly opened slot and tore the passage open; there was no time to be delicate now. The opening was almost too narrow for his massive frame, but he let his adrenaline push aside the claustrophobia that threatened to overcome him.

After traversing no less than three narrow staircases, the tiger reached the end of the passage and gave a mighty kick at the solid wood wall. Architects who studied medieval engineering always marvelled at the strength of the lumber used long ago, but under the weight of an adrenaline-fueled two-plus-metres tiger, the panel splintered like kindling.

Mohan moved out of the passage cautiously, his massive revolver drawn and at the ready.

The undercroft was cleaner than one would expect from a dungeon. When the castle was in its prime, these passages served as the crypt for the family members of whatever lord or duke ruled at the time. Later, when the chapel above became the more prominent structure, other influential members of the aristocracy were interred below.

This part of the castle was included in the tour, but since the premises were closed the lighting was dimmed. With his feline night-vision, Mohan could see the body of the security guard, bound and gagged, sprawled on the floor in the middle of the chamber. She was still alive and whimpering.

"Come to play, Mountain Cat?" a voice echoed from the darkness. It had an accent Mohan couldn't identify.

"Mohan," Kitty's voice whispered over his radio, "I'm at the exterior entrance. He can't get out."

Mohan wasn't so sure about that, who knew how many other hidden passages lay within the old ruin.

There was a clatter of stone off to his right, but Mohan's sharp ears could identify a tossed stone when he heard one. He kept his attention focused ahead.

"Ah, he's clever!" the voice said.

"And my claws are very sharp," Mohan replied, thumbing back the hammer on the revolver.

The tiger felt an itch on his back between his shoulder blades, his mark was tingling, signalling that some unseen danger was close. Mohan sensed rather than saw that the air was moving ahead of him and ducked just in time for the thin blade of a knife the whistle past his cheek and embed itself in a beam.

"Clever and quick!" the voice said, "Well, now that I have your attention..."

His words trailed off as Mohan heard the hammer of a pistol cock. The tiger realised too late what their assailant intended to do, and a pistol shot rang through the undercroft. Mohan saw the body of the guard jerk and go still.

"You bastard!" a new voice roared, and Mohan heard the thunder of a pistol shot. It was a heavier calibre than the assassin's gun, and the tiger knew it well.

"Kitty!" Mohan shouted, "Dammit, I told you to wait out there!"

"No, you didn't," Kitty's voice came back.

It only took a moment for Mohan to realised she was right. Ahead of him, the mystery voice gave a cry of pain, and something heavy collapsed to the ground. Maybe Kitty hadn't killed him.

There was a series of metallic *thunks*, and the lights of the undercroft came on. Less than three metres from Mohan sat a wolf who couldn't be older than twenty. He had collapsed to the floor clutching at a bloody knee and howling in pain.

Kitty was at the far end of the undercroft and already moving forward with murderous intent.

"Kitty! Stand down!" Mohan roared.

The larger tiger was on the wolf in three strides. He grabbed the assassin by the neck and shoved him against the wall. The wolf's eyes had a peculiar slant at the corners that Mohan recognised as characteristic of Amarthians who had a Benese heritage. That also explained the wolf's strange accent.

Kitty came around the corner, her pistol grasped firmly with both hands and trained on the wolf's head.

Mohan glanced over at her. "You're lucky you only wounded him."

"I missed," Kitty said, "Out of the way, it won't happen again."

"Back off, Kitty," Mohan said, "I won't warn you again." He turned his attention back to the wolf. "Now," he growled, bearing his teeth, "Let's see what it takes to make you wag your gob."

The wolf stared at him with a defiant grin. "Wouldn't you like to know," he managed to choke out.

He twisted his head and made a motion like he was biting down on something.

"Cyanide tooth?" Mohan said, his eyes widening.

"No, wait!" Kitty said, but her warning came too late.

Mohan shifted his grip on the wolf's neck in an attempt to fish the phoney cyanide capsule from his mouth. Kitty saw what her father hadn't: a hidden blade popping from the wolf's sleeve and into his hand.

Mohan grunted in pain as the assassin drove the knife into the tiger's arm, causing him to release his grip on the wolf entirely. The assassin shoved the tiger away and made a leap at Kitty.

The tigress was already fuelled by the murder she had just witnessed, but something else came over her at that moment. Kitty looked into the eyes of the wolf and her mind flooded with images. The corpse of the vixen security guard was among them, but there were others, countless others. How could she know that?

He must pay for his crimes!

The voice the tigress heard was her own, but it was cold, cruel, and filled with the thirst for vengeance.

"Wait!" Mohan shouted at the same time Kitty pulled the trigger.

The wolf's head jerked up as the back of his skull exploded.

Mohan yanked the knife out of his arm and put his hand over the wound. "Goddammit, Kitty!" he grunted, "We wanted him alive!"

Kitty didn't seem to hear her father. She had lied when she told Mohan she had missed. The tigress wanted to get the assassin in the knee, wanted him to suffer before she finished the job. She stared past the smoking barrel of her gun at the corpse of the wolf, a red mist creeping in at the edges of her vision. She didn't have to do that. The wolf was fast, but Kitty knew she was faster, she could have taken his other knee. Why hadn't she?

Moments later Zed and Elder Tyrsus rejoined them. Mohan filled them in on the details while Zed searched the body of the assassin.

"Most interesting," the badger said holding up a ruby pin.

The brooch depicted a sentient eagle in flight, wings out, arms and legs stretched out behind it as if the figure had been fired from a cannon.

"The emblem of the Red Eagle," Tyrsus said.

"What the bloody hell are they doing way out here?" Kitty said returning her pistol to its holster at her hip.

"Well we won't find out from him, will we?" Mohan growled.

Kitty folded her arms across her chest and said nothing.

Zed turned the pin over carefully. "Perhaps we are only meant to think that was his allegiance?"

The agents shared a quartet of speculative glances.

"Can the PR in Hempsford help us?" Mohan asked.

"They will," Elder Tyrsus said, "But we will have to wait here for their arrival and make sure nobody else wanders into the area."

Zed nodded. "I will head up to the radio and make the call."

* * *

The quartet didn't return to the inn until much later that evening.

Ric noted the haunted look in Kitty's eyes. Or was it a hunted look? He also noticed that Mohan's shirt sleeve was bloody, and beneath it, Ric could see a fresh bandage.

"Everything all right?" Ric asked.

Mohan gave him a look that the journalist found a bit unsettling.

"You have other things to worry about tomorrow," the tiger said, "As per my arm, let's just say being followed isn't something we have to worry about anymore."

Ric didn't like getting cryptic explanations, but he had learned to accept them at this point. All the same, he stayed awake for a long while that night wondering precisely what had happened—and why Kitty had the same look in her eyes that she did after her bloody rampage in Jar-Geshim.

8 – LBC World Press

The glass and steel headquarters of Lund, Brandon, and Chelsey World Press stood out sharply against the tan brick of the traditional buildings in Grettasburg's city centre, all the more so with the ancient stone castle perched on the hill only a few blocks behind it. All five stories of the narrow LBC World Press building gleamed in the morning light, the glare partially obscuring the reflection of Druna, the pale orange day-moon.

Only Mohan and Kitty accompanied Ric Barnes on this leg of his journey, and Kitty was obligated to do so as per protocol—she was the one who found him in the black markets of Kairran.

Kitty was glad she wouldn't have to follow him inside. She was growing increasingly annoyed with how readily the journalist accepted all the strange things happening to him and couldn't help but reflect on her own experience a handful of years previous. She could still see the expression on Nilani's face, watching as her older sister was pulled into a life she didn't ask for.

Kitty shook the thought away. She had every right to be upset. Her father had kept her birthright a secret for many years. Then, on her eighteenth birthday, when she had finally made up her mind to go to university for a computer science major, Mohan decided to ruin everything by telling her she was "destined" to be a secret agent.

To make things worse, two days later—

Stop it! she shouted at herself, You can't fix that now.

Kitty waited in the truck while Mohan and Ric got out. Mohan handed the journalist a yellow envelope.

"What's this?" Ric asked, opening it uncertainly.

"A little gift to help ease your departure," Mohan grinned.

Ric pulled out a handful of glossy photographs. It was the film the agents had taken from Ed Sanders, his photographer when they had stumbled into each other in Kairran.

"Oh, and the camera," the tiger added, handing him an expensive 45 millimetre. "Not a scratch, I swear."

Ric flipped through the stack of images. "I notice there are quite a few missing; particularly from the market auction. And no negatives."

The tiger just gave him a knowing wink.

Ric smirked and tucked the folder under one arm before heading for the lobby door. Mohan leaned against the side of the truck and crossed his arms, watching intently as the journalist vanished inside.

The silence drew out for several minutes before Mohan broke it. "I'm sorry," the tiger said to his daughter through the open window.

Kitty said nothing.

"You were defending yourself, and I had no right to be angry with you," Mohan continued, "Will you be OK?"

"Why wouldn't I be?" Kitty answered sullenly.

"Fair enough," Mohan said, "Just we haven't had much chance to talk in a while."

Kitty responded by grabbing the doorknob and cranking the window shut.

Mohan sighed. "Right then."

Kitty chuffed in annoyance. She had her own concerns about the events in the castle undercroft, not the least of which was how she had intuited the past crimes of the wolf henchman.

The mark on her arm had burned fiercely during the encounter. That wasn't so strange in itself, many attributes manifested in the mark. Agents had reported a tingling sensation when danger was approaching, or when witnessing acts of criminal behaviour, or even when listening to a conversation--although whether it was triggered by falsehood or truth seemed to depend on the topic and the parties involved.

But to the best of Kitty's knowledge, no one had ever used their mark to witness the crimes of an individual or to justify an execution.

Of course, it also tingled faintly whenever she was in the presence of Ric Barnes.

Kitty shifted her eyes to the glass and steel building across the street, and the white tigress found herself wondering how the lynx was handling himself.

* * *

On reaching the third floor of LBC World Press, Ric Barnes swam through a sea of desk clerks and ringing telephones. The major buzz around the office was about a break-in and murder at the old castle yesterday. A security guard and at least one suspect, most likely a member of a local gang, had been killed, and several priceless artefacts had gone missing.

Ric managed to insert some of the missing pieces himself, such as the identity of the young vixen Vince had been busy entertaining yesterday morning. The journalist didn't know much about Tiger's Stripe's "public restoration" program, but he suspected that the missing valuables served to cover up what really happened.

Ric was also greatly disturbed that a death had been involved. He was still mulling this information over when he reached the frosted glass door of Wilson Kneedy, Editor in Chief.

The lynx rapped on the glass, and a gruff voice told him to enter. A rough grouse with a gaunt frame sat behind the ancient oak desk, his brown feathers—ink-stained at the tips—blending into the grain the wood. Kneedy disdained the traditional leather executive chair in favour of a high-backed, unpadded wooden one with old-fashioned metal casters.

Wilson Kneedy was the kind of individual who seemed to live, eat and breathe printed media. There was even a long-running joke among the staff that the rhythm of the printing presses occupying the lower floors of the building was actually the old grouse's heartbeat, and that if you cut him, he would bleed ink.

The walls of Kneedy's office were lined with framed front pages of historical events throughout the paper's history.

Among them were the Queen's Golden Jubilee in 1990, written by Ric himself; the launch of Longear-1 in 1973, Amarthias' first digital telecommunications satellite; and the detonation of Amarthia's first atom bomb in 1952, with highlights on its lack of effect on Moana Kaitiaki. The paper's oldest entry was the discovery of the Arx Monstra in the mountains of Kolovania in 1888. Ric wondered if anyone would believe that the fantastic and disturbingly detailed images within that tome were actually real creatures and that he had met the people who hunted them.

The only departures from the gratuitous display of printed media were the bulky computer monitor on one corner of Kneedy's desk, and a graduation photo featuring the grouse's wife—who was a lovely robin—and their twin sons.

Kneedy's initial quick glance turned into a start of surprise. "Barnes?" he croaked, then quickly cleared his throat, "My God, man, where have you been? Sanders returned from assignment in Pytan without you, and then we heard terrorists had bombed the airport. Now that I know you're alive, why aren't you still in Pytan? I expected you would be all over that war business."

"I am," Ric said hesitantly, "It's a little complicated."

Kneedy set down his pen and stared at the lynx through tiny circular spectacles. "Sedic Barnes at a loss for words? Now, this is something."

The grouse rose and came around the front of the desk; he was several centimetres shorter than Ric.

"Ugly business covering a war," the editor went on, "I admit I'm surprised you made it out of the country. Sanders has been practically useless without you, especially since he lost his camera; which I see you recovered. We lost some prime coverage thanks to your little disappearing act."

"I'm fine thanks, how are you?" Ric said with a smirk.

Kneedy broke into a beaked version of a grin and grasped the lynx's furry paw with his scaly bird-hand. "It is good to see you, Barnes. I take it you stopped by to deliver your report? Sanders said you were right there in the market square when the ambassador's daughter was shot. Then he started rambling on about secret agents or some such nonsense." The grouse eyed him as if eagerly awaiting confirmation.

"I supposed one might think that in a high-stress situation," Ric replied carefully, "But it's a little less dramatic than secret agents. They were a private security team, bodyguards for some oil contractors. That in itself is a good story, we all had to fight to get out." He had carefully rehearsed this story with Mohan and Elder Tyrsus, but the lie still felt sour in his mouth.

"Of course," the editor said, sounding not at all convinced. He returned to his chair and sat down. "Well, glad you made it out safe."

Ric could hear the obvious disappointment in his boss' voice.

"I'm going back," the lynx said tiredly, "While I was stuck in Pytan I came across a few leads that should prove to be a good follow-up on our war correspondence."

Kneedy's eyes lit up. "Really? Tell me."

Here goes nothing, Ric thought. Aloud he said, "I'm going to make contact with the Soketh."

The grouse looked at him like he had grown another head, it was an expression Ric had received on many occasions. "The Scavengers?" Kneedy said, "Really? That's a bit unusual. But perhaps..." He trailed off for a moment then tilted his head down to look over the rim of his glasses at Ric. "I might take some convincing. Traders in ancient baubles aren't exactly the first thing people think about during a war. And do I even need to ask how long you'll be with them?"

Despite the editor's tone, Ric could tell the wheels in the old bird's head were already turning.

"How many bombed-out buildings do people need to see to get the point across?" Ric said, "The Soketh see the environmental effects of the war outside. Burning oil derricks, ruptured natural gas pockets, ruined sandworm silk farms..." He trailed off, letting his editor fill in the gaps.

"Yes," Kneedy said thoughtfully, "yes I suppose that could work. After all, you made the Queen's Jubilee sound interesting for all its grandstanding."

Ric let out an involuntary chuckle.

"I suppose this will be a rather long-term project?" Kneedy continued, "No matter. Alright, you've sold me. But I expect regular updates! As often as you can. If I don't hear from you in a month—"

"You'll assume I'm dead," the lynx finished for him. "Like you always do."

Kneedy smiled up at him "You're a damn bloody fool, Barnes. Maybe that's why I like you. I assume you'll be taking Sanders with you?"

Ric frowned. "I'm afraid I can't," he said slowly, "Just allowing me to tag along involved some major compromises. The Soketh are not very trusting of outsiders."

The grouse nodded. "Well, I'm sure I can find something for him to do."

Ric gave a final wave and left, closing the door behind him. Again, he swam through the ocean of activity on the press floor until he reached the pair of desks that he and Ed Sanders shared. A lanky orange fox with spiky black long-fur sat sullenly in one of the chairs, flipping idly through a camera magazine, no doubt pining for his lost Revolution 45 millimetre.

"Hey, you dropped this," Ric said cheerily as he deposited the camera and the folder of photos on Sanders' desk.

Ed looked up at him and blinked. "Ric? Bloody hell, I thought you were dead!" He rose and grabbed the lynx by the shoulders, the closest he would get to a hug in public. "When I heard the airport was bombed I assumed the worst."

"Believe me, Ed, I'm still trying to piece everything together myself. I hope that will earn your forgiveness?" He gestured toward the folder.

Ed picked up the camera first and carefully examined it until he was satisfied it was in the same condition as when he'd last seen it; then he sat and took out the photos, sifting through them one by one.

"No pictures of those weirdoes from the Kairran market," he said, "I expected as much. Still, they did leave us some nice shots. So, what happened?"

Ric looked at Ed for a long moment. "I need some coffee," he said at length, "Come on."

The lynx led his photographer down to the lobby, where they made a brief stop at a small café near the main entrance--the owner must have made a fortune after leasing space where his services were needed all hours of the day. Paper cups in hand, Ric proceeded to the patio area in front of the LBC World Press headquarters and took a table far from the door. The air was chill that morning, as if suddenly remembering it was still winter, and not many of the building's occupants had decided to sit outside.

Ed promptly took a seat while Ric leaned back against the tabletop.

"I have to go back out there, Ed," Ric said slowly, "And I can't take you this time."

Ed set his cup down slowly and looked up at him. "You're sure?"

Ric nodded. "I'm sure. I know, mate. We've been through hell and back, just like Mrs Grady's herb garden."

Ed couldn't suppress a smile. "Dodging bombs isn't quite the same as dodging dirt clods when you're seven."

"No, it isn't," Ric said, pushing himself off and taking the seat opposite Ed, "But this is big, Ed. Big! Probably the biggest story I'll ever cover in my entire life."

"So big you have to leave your best mate out of it?" Ed asked accusingly.

"Oh, come off it," Ric said, "You don't think I wish I could take you? This is like..." He paused and spread his hands helplessly. "It's like destiny or something."

"Destiny, huh?" Ed folded his arms on the table before him. "Are those freaks from Pytan involved?"

"That's a little harsh, don't you think?" Ric replied. "They did save our arses."

Ed just stared at him and waited for an answer.

Ric sighed. "Yes, they're involved," he said, lowering his voice, "Look, I've known you too long to believe I could hide anything from you, but it's just too dangerous to say anything else."

The fox leaned forward. "You mean this is like proper spy shit?" he asked in the same conspiratorial tone.

Ric didn't answer right away. His eyes had caught movement across the street, specifically, near a white Camp Wagon parked next to a newsstand across the street. The lynx watch as Mohan calmly purchased a copy of Ric's paper at the kiosk and proceed to casually review it while leaning against the truck and keeping one eye on the lynx and the fox across the street.

"Well, why don't we ask them?" Ric said, reaching up to rub the scruff on his chin thoughtfully.

Ed turned to look behind him as Ric waved.

"Ow!" the fox's hand went to his ear as his old friend flicked it with a finger.

Ric chuckled, "And I thought you'd seen enough spy flicks to know you never look around."

Even while the lynx chastised Ed, he could see Mohan tap on the side of the Wagon. Kitty seemed disinclined to remove herself, but eventually, her father managed to convince her to get out. The tiger remained with the vehicle as his daughter approached the table.

"What?" Kitty said sullenly.

"Ed?" Ric said, "This is Kitty. You remember her, right?"

Ed paused uncertainly.

Kitty gave a nervous smile, and a sat next to Ric, but she fixed the lynx with an icy glare as she did. "What the bloody hell do you think you're doing?" she whispered fiercely.

"Ed has been my best friend since we were cubs," Ric said quietly, "He seems to think I've gotten myself involved in some 'proper spy shit', so I'm hoping you can help explain the situation."

Kitty growled low, and Ed shrank back slightly as she turned her eyes on him. "We're private security," she said, "We were watching over some oil contractors in the region, but they scarpered when the war started."

Ed nodded sagely. "Oil speculation's still a dodgy business in Estan," he said, "It's no wonder you didn't want any photos getting leaked."

And then the fox did something Ric didn't expect. He smiled.

"I admit, it's a good cover," Ed said, "Did Kneedy buy it?"

Kitty turned her eyes back to Ric, curious to hear his answer.

Ric nodded. "I'm pretty sure he did," the lynx replied.

Ed's smile turned to a frown as if he suddenly remembered something. "Are you sure about this, Ric?" he asked, "I mean, when you quit the academy, you couldn't stop talking about how communication was so important. Haven't you always argued that lies and misinformation are the kind of shit that got your dad killed?"

Ric's ears folded back as he leaned forward on his elbows. "You think I don't know that?" he said, "Dammit, Ed, you don't know how difficult this has been. Dad always taught me never jump to conclusions; get as much info from all sides as you can, then assess the situation. I always thought that same principle could, and should, be applied to journalism. You give the people all the facts and let them decide."

Kitty cocked her head to the side. "But he never told you what to do if it turned out that information could get you or the people you care about killed," she said quietly.

Ric thought he heard a note of sympathy in the tigress' voice, but he couldn't pierce the frozen veil behind her eyes. She looked away uncomfortably.

"It isn't easy deciding what should and shouldn't be said," Kitty said, "But sometimes it comes down to what's best for the public and what's best for the people you care about."

"Proper spy shit?" Ed asked again.

Ric and Kitty nodded in unison.

The fox placed his hands on the table and leaned forward even further. "So, what's your cover story?" he asked Ric, a hint of eagerness creeping into his voice.

Kitty gave an exasperated chuff, but Ric couldn't hold back a chuckle. He wasn't surprised by Ed's reaction; his friend had always wanted to play secret agent when they were younger. The photographer must have been extremely jealous that his best mate was actually going down that path.

Ric spent the next several minutes going over the same story he had fed Wilson Kneedy. Ed listed intently, taking sips of his coffee at intervals but never losing a single word.

When the lynx had finished, Ed jerked his thumb at the tigress. "And Kitty here," he said, "She'll kill me if I say anything?"

Kitty growled in annoyance.

"I don't really think so," Ric said, "They're more the 'discredit you and leave you a laughing-stock' type. But it still wouldn't be a good idea."

"Destiny, eh?" Ed said, running a hand over the spiky tips of his own long-fur, "Can I help in any way?"

The lynx couldn't help but smile at the fox's enthusiasm. He was grateful Ed was taking things so well, but his friend had made a good point earlier. Ric became a journalist because he believed in the freedom of information, and now he was diving head first into a realm of lies and secrets. How many of his own principles would he need to compromise in the end?

He didn't realise that Kitty might be thinking the same thing until she answered for him. "Ric might still have time to write while he's away," the tigress said, "You can support his cover by digging up what you can about the Soketh. We'll make sure he gets the info, and in return, he'll have genuine material to provide the paper."

Ric looked at her for a long moment. He had always believed that his future with the Tiger's Stripe would involve learning to hunt monsters like Mohan and his Scrappers. It hadn't fully dawned on him that the scope of the Laohu Tiaowen was much broader.

Ed nodded to Kitty's response. "You'll have it," he said, "That is, of course, dependent on where Kneedy sends me while you're gone."

Ric grinned mischievously. "Oh, I think I know where he'll stick you. You know Drummond has been itching to get his hands on you!"

"Ugh," Ed groaned, "The sports pages? I could cover a real football match alright, but Drummond actually thinks people want to hear about Wook football." He used the slang term for citizens of the West United Kingdoms. "They don't even kick that often, they should call it handball."

"Yes, but wasn't that cute poodle working down there?" Ric asked with a wink, "Dana?"

"Denise." Ed flushed, but smiled. "You always could play the diplomat. Alright, have it your way; but you better bring back some good pictures. Don't go getting yourself killed out there, yeah?"

Ric grabbed Ed's proffered hand. "No promises, but you know me."

"We should get going," Kitty said brusquely and stood.

Ric followed suit, then he came around the table and gave Ed a brotherly hug. "I swear I'll be back," he said.

The fox patted the lynx on the back. "Bloody well right!" Ed said, "And I'm sure you'll have an even better story to tell when you do."

But will I be able to print any of it? Ric thought.

The lynx and the tigress returned to the truck and climbed in.

"Well, I think we're done here," Ric said, "Kitty seems to think you can actually help me maintain my cover legitimately."

"That shouldn't be a problem," Mohan said starting the engine, "You won't be anywhere near the Pytan, of course, but there are several Soketh agents you could talk to at the Sanctuary. I'm sure they'd be happy to filter you material. And you can always hit up Zed." The tiger pulled away from the curb. "What about your old chum, the fox?"

Ric paused. "I think he'll keep his suspicions in check for now," he said, "He didn't believe a word of the private security story, but he's smart enough not to press."

"I'll admit, I'm surprised he didn't try digging for more," Kitty said.

"He's known me too long," the lynx said, "He knows I'd only tell him what was safe to tell him."

"No worries, mate," Mohan said, "We'll keep an eye on him."

"I suppose the next stop is home," Kitty said.

Ric stared out the window as the LBC World Press HQ began to shrink from view. "Yeah, I suppose so."

9 – Home

As they pulled up to the row of two-story yellow brick dwellings, Kitty watched Ric's face change as memories of his cubhood came back to him.

"So much has changed over the years," the journalist said quietly, "And yet so much hasn't."

The lynx began pointing out where he and Ed Sanders would run along the lane and play in the dirt of the quaint little gardens on the long row. He saw that Old Mrs Grady the titmouse still tended beautiful rose bushes three doors from his own home, and how the Sanders, Ed's parents, still lived right next to the Barnes.

"It's all here," Ric said with a note of wonder, "Somehow it all seems so...ordinary."

His brow furrowed suddenly.

"Something wrong?" Mohan asked, suddenly alert for danger even though his mark wasn't tingling.

"No," Ric said, "And maybe that's the problem. I didn't become a journalist because of a lust for adventure or restlessness. I did it because this kind of ordinary living, this contentment, often leads to ignorance about the important things going on in the world around you."

"And that ignorance can breed apathy," Mohan said.

Ric nodded.

"That ignorance can also help them sleep at night," Kitty said from the back seat.

Ric turned to look at the tigress, but her attention was focused out the window. Kitty hadn't been wrong, Ric was facing the choice of leaving his own mother in ignorance or telling her things that might keep her awake at night. Then again, she already knew her son travelled to dangerous places as part of his regular job.

Mohan parked the truck, and the journalist climbed out. He stared up at the gathering clouds as a halo of light filtered down reflecting off the grey slate of the houses and framing the distant castle in a warm glow.

Maybe it's a sign, Ric thought as he removed his suitcase and backpack from the boot.

Mohan leaned out the window and asked, "You all right, mate?"

Ric nodded and sighed. "Yeah, yeah I think so. I won't be long. Mum hates long goodbyes."

"Take as much time as you need," the tiger replied.

Kitty also climbed out of the truck, but all she did was frown and walk toward a public dustbin, fishing a pack of cigarettes from the pocket of her jeans.

Ric watched her a moment. Of all the members of Mohan's Scrappers, the white tigress was the one who puzzled him the most. While on the hunt in the Valley of Nefrit, Kitty had been the consummate professional; calm, collected, and every inch a deadly weapon in and of herself. Ever since they had reached civilisation, she had become increasingly taciturn and sullen. Just having a conversation with him and Ed seemed to have put an inordinate amount of stress on her.

Her behaviour reminded Ric of a predator eager to return to the hunt. For a moment he wondered what her prey was, but something told him he already knew. Monsters weren't the only thing Mohan's Scrappers were hunting while in Pytan; but their other quarry, Jirair al-Seil, had gotten away. And Kitty had made it no secret that she wanted blood for the mouflon's misdeeds.

Ric filed this away in his mind for later and walked up to the door of his childhood home. He hesitated only a moment before knocking.

"Won't be a moment," a voice called from somewhere inside.

Ric heard the sound of a bolt and chain being drawn—a reminder of how things had changed. The female bobcat who answered the door was several centimetres shorter than him and several years older—the white on her face and paws began to show. She wore a long heavy skirt against the chilly air and had tied a floral-print apron around her waist. A matching headscarf covered feathered blonde long-fur that fell to the bobcat's shoulders, and she studied her visitor through startling emerald-green eyes. The journalist may have inherited his lynx father's height and jawline, but his eyes and high cheekbones belong to his mother.

When Elsabeth Barnes realised who was standing on her portico her smile broadened and she rushed forward to embrace him. "Oh, Percy!" She was the only one who called him by his middle name. "I thought you were still in Pytan? There has been such terrible news coming from there."

Ric returned her embrace. "Hullo, mum."

Mrs Barnes pulled away and looked at her son. "You seem to be eating well enough, no new cuts or bruises," she said and glanced behind him, "Your friends aren't going to join you?

Ric started in surprise. "They didn't want to intrude–"

"Nonsense!" his mother interrupted and waved to Mohan and Kitty across the street.

Kitty seemed even less inclined to move than at the LBC World Press HQ, but her father coaxed her along and came with her.

Mohan tipped his hat to Mrs Barnes. "G'day, ma'am," he said.

"A plainsman," Elsabeth said curiously, "You're rather far from home, mister?"

"Mohan, Mrs Barnes," the huge tiger replied, "And this is my eldest daughter Kittina."

"Kitty," the tigress corrected.

"Well, do call me Elly," the bobcat said.

Elly Barnes led them through the parlour and practically forced them to take seats in the living room. Mohan took up almost the whole couch, but Ric managed to find space on the end.

"I was just about to make some tea," Mrs Barnes said, "Would you like some?"

"Yes, please," Ric answered, "Lemon only, of course."

Mohan ordered the same, and Kitty asked for lemon and milk. It just wouldn't be proper to refuse.

"I am so sorry about this," Ric began after his mother vanished into the kitchen.

"No worries," Mohan said, "Sometimes things don't go as planned, and you adapt."

While Elly busied herself in the kitchen, Kitty took a moment to study the living room Ric had grown up in. The long narrow space was typical of the row houses in that neighbourhood. The tigress sat in an old wooden rocker set before a large bay window that looked out into the street. The couch Mohan and Ric sat on was just inside the double-wide entryway, set opposite a small fireplace and modest colour television; and upholstered armchair stood off near the entrance to the kitchen and dining room at the rear of the house. The mantle above the fireplace bore a standard variety of family photos and a vase of fresh daisies.

Kitty froze when she saw the daisies. Twice during their adventure in Pytan. she had seen memories triggered by daisy blossoms, and now it was happening again. She tried to look away, but her eyes locked on the photo next to the vase. The face of a puma gazed down at her, deep gold eyes boring into her sapphire blue.

No, she thought to herself, *No he can't be there!*

She looked again. and the vision was gone. In place of the puma was a lynx with a strong jaw and brown eyes. He was wearing a blue dress uniform with blue and gold epaulettes, a blue and white checkered police cap was tucked under one arm.

"That's my dad," Ric said, noting the tigress' gaze.

"Strong resemblance," Mohan said.

The kettle singing in the kitchen interrupted any further conversation.

"Have you been to the paper yet, Percy?" Elly Barnes called out to them from the kitchen. "Edward and Mr Kneedy call at least once a day to check if you've turned up suddenly without telling them."

She brought out a tea service with scones and jam and set them on the low glass-top coffee table. Ric helped her move the armchair closer to the couch, and she seated herself.

"Now," the bobcat said, "Do tell me how you got out of that mess in Pytan."

Ric was at a crossroads. What should he tell her? What could he tell her? Mohan and Elder Tyrsus had been vague when it came to this part. They explained that it was entirely up to Ric whether he told his mother the truth or not. Naturally, they had also stressed the danger she could be in. Somehow, having Mohan right in front of him made the decision harder.

The lynx sipped his tea gingerly and set the cup down.

"It's rather complicated, mum," Ric said, rubbing his chin in thought, "You're right, there are terrible things happening in Pytan right now. Even I can't say for sure what's really going on, but the catalyst was the death of the Barjan Ambassador's daughter. Not long after, Sultan Abdulkadir was killed in a terrorist bombing. Both sides hold the other responsible and are more than ready to blow each other up over it."

"And I take it your associates here help you get out of the city when they began to seal the borders," Elly Barnes said.

Ric glanced at the tiger and his daughter. "In a way." He paused. "They were working undercover as private security agents. But that isn't who they really are."

The lynx stopped again, and his bobcat mother set her cup down gently and looked at him. "Is that so?" she asked.

"I'm sorry, mum," Ric said, smiling sadly. "I thought I knew what I was going to tell you, and now I'm at a loss for words. But, I have to go with them. I can't explain it, but I know it's the right thing to do. I'm not quite sure where our next destination is, but it's vitally important that if anyone asks, including Ed, you tell them I've gone back to Pytan."

Elsabeth Barnes looked from Mohan to Kitty and back to her son. It was a long time before she finally spoke.

"Percy," she said, "Have I ever told you, you were special?"

Ric grinned. "Only every day."

His mother smiled back. "Well, it's true. From the day you were born, your father and I knew you were destined to great things. Especially with that odd mark on your arm."

Ric started. "You knew about that?"

Elsabeth Barnes glanced at Kitty again. "I don't know what it means, dear," she said, "But I noticed that young miss Kitty has a similar mark on her arm. Or at least a part of one. Your father used to tell such stories about a great-great uncle who had such a mark, but it was so very long ago."

Mohan leaned forward intently, a strange look on his face.

"You didn't know?" Ric asked.

"Swear to it, mate," the big tiger said.

Ric turned back to his mother. "And dad never mentioned him to me?" he asked

"It didn't seem important," Elly replied, "They were only stories passed down to him from his grandfather." She paused. "Oh dear, I've gone and upset you. Please, what's wrong, Percy?"

Ric sighed. "It's nothing mum. But your right, this birthmark does seem to be some kind of omen in our family."

"We can check our archives," Mohan said and turned to Mrs Barnes, "Do you have a name?"

She thought for a moment. "I believe it was Malory," she said, "Are you going to tell me what this is all about?"

Ric smiled and made up his mind. "These people work for an agency called KLAWS," he said, "They, well, it's not easy to explain. Mohan?"

Ric had provided the foundation by mentioning KLAWS, and for the next hour Mohan, explained the minor details of the organisation. Ric didn't want to reveal the truth about Tiger's Stripe but still wanted his mother to understand that her son was essentially going to become a spy.

The journalist only half listened. The news that one of his ancestors may have been an agent of the Laohu Tiaowen distracted him considerably. He was more eager than ever to reach the so-called Sanctuary and scan its records for the truth.

His mother eventually got up to cleaned up the tea service, and Mohan encouraged his daughter to help. Kitty flashed a look at her father, but she didn't want to argue. The truth was, Kitty was growing a little homesick sitting there in the Barnes' living, and she got a distinct impression that her own mother and Mrs Barnes would have become fast friends.

I can't stay, Kitty thought to herself, *There is still too much to do before I can go home.*

She heard Ric climbing the stairs and asked if she could excuse herself a moment. The white tigress found the lynx in his old room at the back of his house. His mother had kept the floor clean and the bed made, but the rest appeared to be exactly as the journalist had left it. Ordered stacks of books, newspaper clippings, and magazines occupied every conceivable surface except the floor and the bed. The window on the far wall looked out over the rear garden, and on either side hung a pair of movie posters; one was a spy thriller, and the other a science fiction space drama, which Kitty instantly recognised and remembered being quite good if a little campy. In front of the window was a long desk occupied by a personal computer and a typewriter; Ric must still like the feel and sound of traditional typing.

The lynx had set his luggage on the bed off to the right and was standing before a small cabinet on the opposite wall next to the closet door.

Ric looked up as Kitty entered. "I was just about to pack some fresh clothes," he said, "I suppose maybe I should get an extra suitcase."

"What?" Kitty asked, pointing at the cabinet, "You keep your longies in there?"

Ric reached out and opened the cabinet, revealing a carefully arranged memorial to his father. Newspaper clippings and photos covered the inside of the doors and the rear panel, each piece bearing some memory of the elder

Barnes' successful career, his death, and the debacle that followed. A centre shelf held a small glass-top jewellery box containing the pips from the elder Barnes' uniform and his twenty-year service ring.

"Still some unfinished business?" Kitty asked.

Ric shook his head and sighed. "His death was an enormous source of embarrassment to the department. Miscommunication, misinformation, the outright denial of indisputable facts, just one huge cock-up. It was the reason I quit the Academy. I spent years gathering every scrap I could, hoping I could force the department to make things right."

The lynx turned and looked at the tigress, and she saw a strange fire in his eyes that she hadn't seen before. "In the end, I realised that even if I did expose the corruption that got my dad killed, seeing the perpetrators brought to justice wouldn't bring him back. Eventually, I stopped searching."

Kitty turned away. She didn't know if the journalist meant to imply anything, but her thoughts were drawn to her own quest, and the murderous blood rage that had already resulted from it. No, she couldn't bring back the souls who had been lost, but they would rest easier with the ones who tormentored them dead.

Are you sure about that? the tigress said to herself.

Kitty brushed the thought away and headed for the door. "Hurry it up," she said, "We should be going soon. Mohan and I will be in the truck."

Ric watched her leave, uncertain what he had said to rub her fur the wrong way. Shrugging, he turned back to the cabinet and opened the top drawer. Inside sat a brightly polished cherry-wood box. Taking a breath, he opened the box and gazed at the polished blue-steel object inside.

As the police in Hempsford were so eager to inform the agents, firearms were a tricky thing in Locke. The prevailing sentiment of the Parliament was that only members of the constabulary should carry them—and even that was a matter of heated debate. The fact that Ric still possessed this pistol, without a permit, was a severe infraction. However, the Chief Inspector of his father's department had insisted Ric keep the weapon rather than having the elegant piece reassigned or melted for scrap.

The customised Forester 1914 .45 Calibre was his father's most prized possession during his career. Most officers preferred the standard issue 9mm Medoccian-made pistols, but his father wanted something with punch. The elder Barnes believed that if you ever needed to draw your weapon in the line of duty, it was vital that it be able to stop your attacker.

Ric's father had never fired a single shot in his entire career except at the range. The elder Barnes often jokingly referred to the heavy pistol as "The Negotiator", because he had never had to use it as such.

If only he had used it that day, Ric thought sadly. He closed the box and reverently picked it up and placed it in his suitcase.

"You're taking your father's gun?" a voice behind him asked. He turned and saw his mother standing in the doorway.

With a sigh, Ric moved forward and embraced her. "It's going to be very dangerous where I'm going, mum. If I take dad's gun I just...I feel like somehow he'll be looking out for me."

"Him and your new friends?" she asked.

Ric paused a moment. "Yes, them too. It's...this is something I need to do, mum. Mohan explained how this organisation works, and I think I can really make a difference there. I learned some things on my trip to Pytan that I think are going to have an incredible impact on both my life and perhaps the world."

"A brush with destiny," his mother said and smiled sadly.

"You know how corny that sounds?" Ric chuckled, despite having used the exact sentiment while talking to Ed.

"But it's the truth," Elly Barnes replied, "And it's what you do, what you've always done. Remember I told you, you were special."

Ric smiled. "I promise I'll let you know if it ever amounts to anything."

His mother went to the shrine and opened the jewellery box. She picked up the service ring and stared at it a moment, the large gaudy blue gem in the centre glinting in the sunlight. Then she removed a silver chain from the pocket of her apron and slipped the ring onto it. Returning to her son, she placed the trinket around his neck.

"There," Elly said, "Maybe this will help as well. I know you wouldn't be going away like this if you didn't feel it was important. Just...just don't forget to write."

Ric hugged her close again, the tears starting to well up in his eyes. "Of course I will, mum."

"And ask that tigress out. She's a bit uptight at first but quite lovely."

"Mother!" the lynx said in exasperation and chuckled.

But the thought ran through his mind all the same, *Yes, she is quite lovely. And deadly.*

They exchanged more hugs on the portico.

"Oh," Ric said as he picked up his bags, "Should you speak with Ed, humour him. We didn't tell him as much as you, but I kind of let slip that this was some proper spy thing, and he might get a tad looney."

"You mean wanting to talk in code and what not?" his mother replied.

Ric nodded. "Right. Sorry about that, but I knew he wouldn't buy that I was just going back to Pytan to cover the war."

"Don't you worry, dear," Elsabeth Barnes said, "I think I know him well enough to keep him entertained and out of trouble."

"Thanks, mum," Ric said and gave her another half hug.

Returning to the truck, Ric tossed his fresh baggage in the boot and climbed in.

The agents and their charge drove away in silence as a few spatters of rain began to fall against the windshield. A late winter storm was approaching, and as Ric watched his home vanish behind them, he couldn't help but wonder if it was another sign of things to come.

Unbeknownst to the lynx, Kitty was thinking the same thing.

10 – Field Commission

Zed was waiting for them in the lobby when they returned to the inn. He bore the same serious expression Ric had noticed on Mohan's face last night.

"Basira has called a meeting in her room," the badger said.

They followed him upstairs.

It was evident that the inn's builders had not intended their rooms to fit eight people at the same time, one of which was a badger as broad as the door and another a tiger over two metres tall. Mohan remained near the entryway, avoiding the simple chandelier hanging in the middle of the room.

Elder Basira Tyrsus stood beside a simple desk, on which sat an electric teapot. Ric couldn't tell what she was brewing, but it gave off a faint sickly-sweet smell, and it made him sneeze after taking a deep breath through his nose. Kitty recognised the scent instantly, and the implication of what was about to happen filled her with uncertainty.

Tyrsus folded her feathered arms across her chest and addressed the room. "What I'm about to tell you is difficult, but it is information that will profoundly affect your mission.

Mohan, as your commander, is already privy to this; but I am taking Elder's prerogative to inform the rest on you."

The eagle paused, judging each of their faces in turn.

"On Faerday evening," she continued, "as we were busy extracting you from Pytan, an unknown element moved against the De Palma family. It was a professional hit, hard and fast. Only Yursa De Palma survived the onslaught, the rest were eliminated. Not even Vigo's wife and children were spared." There was a note of sorrow in Tyrsus' voice as she said the last part.

A collection of gasps went around the room.

Kitty's eyes flashed with anger, and she blurted out, "Bloody hell! You mean you were actually debating whether or not to tell us?"

Elder Tyrsus nodded slowly. "Yes, agent Katral, we were. I know you have all have a vested interest in this mission, but with the recent attacks directed against us, the Elders were uncertain if you should proceed." She cocked her head to one side and gazed at the tigress with a large gold eye. "I want you to understand it was my opinion that you should."

Vicki sat on the edge of the bed, looking almost comical with her webbed feet barely touching the floor and her hands folded in her lap. "Do we know who did it?" she asked, "One of the other mafia families?"

"That is the current rumour circulating in the underworld," the eagle answered, "But we don't think so. The De Palma's were too powerful for any single family to take on, and most of them are too busy trying to kill each other to join forces. No, this...feels like someone new."

Ric's whiskers twitched as he noted the pause in the Elder's voice, and he rubbed at his chin thoughtfully; Kitty was starting to notice that he did this quite often.

"It doesn't make sense," the journalist said, almost to himself. "Wouldn't it be better to keep the relationship between al-Seif and the De Palmas strong? Their combined resources would be formidable."

Elder Tyrsus shook her head. "Again, we don't know. Our primary concern is how this will affect our next move. Al-Seif has gained control of most of the De Palmas' legal assets, but Yursa still retains a powerful hold on the illegal ones. And since al-Seif's business dealings are legitimate, the Medoccian government has no recourse to prosecute him. As far as they're concerned, al-Seif hasn't committed any crimes within their jurisdiction."

Kitty growled at this, but Tyrsus ignored her obvious displeasure.

Zed raised a clawed paw and spoke up, "They could try linking him through Syris Industries. I believe they are headquartered in Medocci."

Elder Tyrsus nodded. "That's our next target," she said, "We're flying to Medocci tomorrow to deliver the evidence you gathered in Pytan. Thanks to that fragment of fiend bone with the Syris Industries plate grafted on it, our intel assets still believe they can form a solid case of bio-terrorism against Assad Alabwaq that will leak over to his alter ego, Jirair al-Seif."

"Won't that expose the existence of the fiend creatures?" Ric asked.

"Hey, that's right," Vince said, "If word got out that fiends were the source for the disease, disreputable types the world over would jump at the chance to capture one. Not to mention numerous governments would demand to know who else knew about them. Bad enough they point fingers over trade deals, biological terrorism would add a whole new level of mayhem."

Elder Tyrsus shivered slightly at the thought, her feathers making a subtle rustling noise, but she shook her head gravely. "No. It's bad enough we must reveal that Daeminox Syndrome is being used as a catalyst for a biological agent, but we don't believe we need to reveal anything more than that. Bone marrow tests from the fiend fragment will prove Alabwaq was in possession of the disease, but we'll provide an altered version of the DNA printout you found to make it appear he used common predators to create it; there are plenty of well-known, highly-venomous creatures in the world. Our primary goal will be to prove Alabwaq is Jirair al-Seif, and for that, we have all the photographs, documents, and handwriting samples that your team collected during your time in Pytan."

"The icing on the cake, as it were, will be proving al-Seif owned Syris Industries," Mohan added.

"Precisely," Tyrsus said, "So you see, Mr Barnes, we have a strategy in place."

Ric pondered this for a moment. "I admit, that sounds like a good legal case."

"You don't sound convinced," Mohan said.

The lynx shrugged. "What if it turned out al-Seif wasn't behind this whole thing?"

The room was silent for a long moment.

"Oh, come off it," Kitty said, "You aren't really suggesting he was dragged into this involuntarily, are you? After all the people al-Seif's killed? After the slave auctions and gladiator arenas? We know he's run guns through Adrakar and Bozambwe. What's one more method of killing to him?"

"I am afraid our journalist friend has a point," Zed said, "We can tie Assad Alabwaq to Syris Industries, but this operation is not entirely in character for him."

"This is true," Rizzo said, "Alabwaq would be more interested in fiends as a showpiece for his arena."

"Maybe he's branching out," Vince said, "Didn't we rescue some science fellas from the Warren who admitted they were working for Alabwaq?"

"Yes," Tyrsus answered, "But they insist Assad Alabwaq only hired them to make a strain of super-heroin. They informed us there was a second faction working in that facility, and Alabwaq's men were under strict orders not to interact with them. None of the techs we rescued were aware of what was happening in the creature lab until the beast broke free." The eagle shook her head. "I'm afraid Mr Barnes is correct, Syris Industries may be owned by Assad Alabwaq, and by extension Jirair al-Seif, but there is no proof he was directly involved with the creation of that...Frankenbeast."

"Ha, told you it would stick," Vince said turning to Vicki.

Rizzo, standing behind the hare, cuffed him over the ears for interrupting.

Kitty chuffed in agitation. "So where does that leave us?"

"Exactly where we are," Elder Tyrsus said firmly, "Al-Seif has gotten himself involved with a major player, someone with powerful influence and resources. It is very likely that this third party is the one who eliminated the De Palma family and has started targeting our own operations."

"And al-Seif has outlived his usefulness," Kitty said.

Tyrsus shrugged. "Not necessarily. If this third party has woven itself so deeply into these affairs, it's possible they saw the De Palmas as an obstacle in al-Seif's path and were unable to move their pawn further with them in the way." The eagle paused, her golden bird eyes meeting each of theirs in turn. "With all this in mind, the Council has decided that whether we actually get al-Seif on trial or not has become irrelevant. If we want to know more about our new adversary, our best source of information is him. So, once we hand over our data to the intel assets in Medocci, our mission will be to capture and interrogate Jirair al-Seif."

Kitty opened her mouth and let slip a low growl, but it was lost in the expressions of disbelief from her fellow agents. Elder Tyrsus raised a scaly bird-hand to silence them.

"The Council has already voted on this course of action," the eagle said, "We will flesh out the details after we arrive in Medocci." She turned to Ric. "That just leaves what we're going to do with you."

The lynx looked around confused. "Am I not party to this?" he asked.

The eagle nodded. "Very much so, but as I've mentioned on numerous occasions, we really should get you back to the Sanctuary to start formal training. It appears fate has been working against us on that part."

Here we go, Kitty thought, and her eyes lit up in anticipation.

Tyrsus turned and poured a measure of the tea into a mug; the odour made Ric sneeze again, but it didn't seem to bother the other agents.

"*Labri'oot*," Tyrsus said, reverting to her native tongue. She held the mug in front of her. "I have conferred with the other elders, and they have agreed; you are being given a field induction into the Laohu Tiaowen. I hope you understand the gravity of this decision, it is a very rare honour, even for one who bears a birthmark."

Ric's eyes went wide, and he nodded solemnly.

"Raise your right hand," the eagle said, and the lynx did so. "Do you, Sedric Percival Barnes the Second, swear upon your honour to uphold the Pillars of the Laohu Tiaowen; to temper your strength with mercy and wisdom; and to remain loyal to the cause of justice?"

"I swear," Ric answered, and Kitty noted there wasn't even a hint of hesitation in his reply.

"Then let it be known that Sedric Percival Barnes the Second has become the Tiger's Stripe," Elder Tyrsus continued the invocation, "On the tip of his spear rest the scales of justice and honour. May his strength, his wisdom, his mercy, and his loyalty be the very foundations of Amarthia. So says Basira, daughter of David of the house of Tyrsus." She held out the mug of tea. "Drink."

Ric took the mug, breathing through his mouth to avoid sneezing again. Kitty could almost remember the taste of the tea from her own initiation, despite its sickly-sweet smell the liquid had a sharp sweetness with a surprisingly cool aftertaste like one had just sipped a piece of mountain ice despite the tea's steaming temperature.

Ric handed the mug back, and Kitty leaned forward slightly, eager to see what happened next. The Elder placed the mug on the desk, then turned and grasped the underside of Ric's marked arm at the wrist, being careful not to obscure any portion of the mark. She held him tight with her scaly taloned fingers and peered into the lynx's eyes with a peculiar intensity.

The gesture seemed to alarm the journalist, but before he could ask for a reason, Kitty saw his eyes widen as the effects of the tea overtook him. The tigress' mark began to tingle with the memory of her experience, and she knew that her companions felt it as well, but she could only imagine what Ric felt.

The lynx's forearm was on fire, and he staggered slightly at the sudden sensation of painless heat; Elder Tyrsus' firm grip kept him upright. Ric half expected to see the strange tiger's face on his arm start glowing, but the fur only stood on end as if charged with electricity. Ric's chest began to tighten, and the figures in the room shifted and swayed as if shimmering in summer heat. Then they vanished altogether, and the vision began.

* * *

Clouds. Endless clouds surrounded him, thicker than a Hempsford morning and masking indistinct shapes of varying size. Ric felt rock beneath his paws, and as the fog lifted, he found himself standing on the side of a mountain overlooking a fierce battle. The smoke from a thousand fires stung his eyes, but he could see that the armour worn by the soldiers was ancient and composed of tightly woven shafts of bamboo with forged iron chest plates bound in leather. The crowns of their helmets bore feathered pennants or fearsome crests that took the shape of dragon horns. In their hands, they wielded ornate swords, spears, glaives, and single-headed pole-axes.

It took Ric a moment to realise he must be looking at armies from imperial East Benai, at a time in history when the land was stilled divided between feuding emperors and councillors. He couldn't be sure if this was before or after the feudal shogunates and samurai of the Ku San Islands were added into the empire, but he didn't see any of their more familiar trappings.

Ric's vision cleared further and he realised that the soldiers were not the only participants in the battle. Great horned beasts prowled between the lines, their gold eyes divided by two vertical pupils like some mutant cat eye. Most had four legs, but some travelled on six, others on two, and still another on eight.

Cries went up from the soldiers who fought them, "*Roulin yeshou*! The devastating beasts have come!"

Ric recognised the creatures instantly. Fiends.

Except these fiends had riders! Broad dark shapes with armour covered in as many spikes as their mounts. One galloped close to where the lynx stood, giving him a better look than he actually wanted.

The rider's body seemed amorphous beneath its armour plates, but it had at least two arms and two legs. A narrow head attached to its broad shoulders, but Ric couldn't see any mouth or nose. Deep vertical furrows lined the face from chin to forehead, and although there were sockets for eyes, all Ric could see were dark voids that seemed to trail black smoke whenever the rider turned its head. The helmet atop this craggy skull-face had broad ornamentation along the crown that reminded Ric of a spiny crab or some other horned crustacean.

While this dread-knight appeared alien to the journalist, the beast it road upon was all too familiar. It was a fiend that Mohan called a grendel, five metres in length and three at the shoulder. Six gold eyes gleamed from the front edge of wings that gave the monster's face the appearance of a hammer-head shark with long horns curving outward from above each eye. There were no lips on the mouth to hide the terrifying bloodstained grin of the grendel's teeth, each as wide and sharp as a dagger blade.

The creature's chin ended in a long spike of bone, and two long horns jutted forwards from the sides of its jaw; a feature that had been missing on the beast Ric had encountered. A bridle was anchored to each jaw horn with fibrous cords running to the rider's harness; it was in this manner that the grendel's master controlled the beast. With a series of sharp tugs, the dread-knight ordered his mount to swing the spiked growth on the end of its tail and sent a dozen men sprawling broken on the ground.

Ric felt bile rising in his throat and quickly turned away. His eyes fell upon a bright rift of light on the horizon; through it poured legions of riders and their terrible fiend mounts.

Suddenly the lynx found himself next to the rift, looking at two figures locked in combat.

The first was a feline; tall, proud, with broad shoulders and a mane of reddish-black long-fur that ran down past his shoulders and stuck out from his head in spiky clumps. The style was so cartoonish that for a split-second Ric thought the warrior had leapt right out of one of the Ku San manga comics Ed was always reading, but he realised all too quickly that the outlandish hairdo was because the long-fur had become matted with blood. Ric thought the warrior looked like a tiger, but there was something odd about him.

And then it clicked: he didn't have any stripes!

The journalist had heard of stripe-less tigers, where the pigment of their markings was so pale as to be almost invisible, but this tiger truly had no stripes. There was only the white fur on his muzzle, chest, hands and feet, and the fiery orange fur on the rest of him.

Looking again, Ric corrected himself. The warrior did have a single stripe, a broad band that started somewhere under his long-fur and ran all the way down his back to the tip of his tail.

In his hands, the warrior carried a spear tipped with a long leaf-shaped blade. A tuft of red hair—probably from the mane of an ecquai—adorned the base of the blade. As he spun and twirled the weapon, the hair would create arcing patterns through the air that hung for a moment like the afterimage of a fire twirler.

Ric's gaze shifted to the tiger's opponent, a figured figure who appeared veiled in shadow. The journalist could tell that it was reptilian and that its scales were a dull red, but the head remained wreathed in smoke, making it impossible to discern what type of lizard the tiger was fighting.

The elegant sword wielded by the red lizard had a craftsmanship to rival the tiger's spear, but the glow that came off the blade was dark and ominous. In its left hand, the lizard carried some sort of tome.

Stripeless tiger and crimson lizard exchanged blow after blow. Sparks of brilliant light flew from the combatants' blades whenever they connected. Both appeared evenly matched, neither gaining ground on the other for long.

Then the lizard's blade cut deep into the tiger's side, and the tiger's spear pierced the lizard's chest just above the heart. Both mortally wounded, the tiger dropped his spear, grabbed onto the lizard, and hurtled the two of them through the portal.

There was a blinding flash, and now Ric saw himself standing on the peak of a pyramid in the middle of a jungle. It was a peculiar stepped pyramid from an ancient culture he wasn't familiar with. The trees beneath him began to sway, and he could hear the low coughing growls of fiend creatures lurking in the shadows.

A chill of fear crept over him.

Another bright flash made him look up, and there was the Tiger's Mark floating in the air before him. From its centre, a white hand reached down toward him.

He reached up to grab it.

* * *

Ric was back in Elder Tyrsus' room with the other agents of Tiger's Stripe looking at him.

"W-what the bloody hell was that?" he asked when his breath returned to him.

The eagle released her grip on the lynx's arm. "After three thousand years we still don't have a name for it," she said, "This tea is brewed from the fire blossoms that only bloom on the mountain of Huosheng, where the Tiger Temple once stood. What each member sees when they drink is different, but it is the seal that binds us together. From here, your life will proceed much as it always has, but you will never forget what you saw. It will guide you if you let it and lead you to your true place among our ranks."

"I honestly don't imagine how," Ric said.

Vince clapped him on the back. "All part of the journey, my friend. Even some of us more experienced types haven't figured it out yet."

"Is that what that vixen told you the last night?" Rizzo said mockingly.

Vicki stifled a laugh, but Mohan gave a harsh chuff that warned the basilisk and hare not to start up another of their tiresome arguments about Vince's nocturnal habits.

Kitty glanced from her father to Zed and Elder Tyrsus. Clearly, they had not told the rest of the team about the unfortunate fox's fate.

"Does every member see these visions?" Ric asked.

Zed shook his head negatively. "No, my friend. The tea is pleasant to the taste, but only those born with the mark experience the visions. I search for my own path."

"Well don't feel too left out, Zed," Mohan chuckled, "You still got all those Soketh's secrets up inside your head. That makes us even."

"Indeed," the badger replied with a grin.

Ric turned back to Elder Tyrsus. "Do you ever share these visions?"

"That is entirely up to you," the eagle said, "If you saw one of us in your vision, sharing it may offer some clarity; or it may cause strife. The Pillar of Wisdom can guide you here, but it is ultimately your decision. For many, the images can be very personal, and as an Elder, I would encourage you to try and discern its meaning on your own. As the days and years pass you may see this vision again, and you may see it change, or notice something you hadn't before."

The journalist nodded. "Well," he said, "I've never been one for spiritual journeys, but I love puzzles. This is one puzzle I might rather enjoy trying to solve."

Elder Tyrsus ruffled her wings slightly and addressed the room again. "Ok, show's over. I made a flight plan for eleven AM tomorrow. Feel free to relax until then."

"Somehow, I think the last thing I want to do right now is relax," Ric said.

A gleam came into Vince's eye. "Oh, I know how I can pass the time."

"What? Did you see a budgie at the bar that hasn't swooned over you yet?" Rizzo said, cuffing him over the ears.

The two left arguing and the others filed out after them.

"Agent Katral," Tyrsus said, motioning Kitty aside. "A word if you please."

Kitty obliged, and they waited until everyone had gone, her father closing the door behind him.

"Do you know why I asked you to come along yesterday?" Tyrsus asked.

Kitty shook her head negatively.

"It was a test," the Elder continued, "Despite what your father may believe, I knew our tail wouldn't divulge any information without sacrificing himself first. I wanted to see what you would do."

Kitty could only gaze at the elder quizzically.

"You have something in you," Tyrsus said gently, "A dark spirit that thirsts for blood."

"I didn't mean to kill him," Kitty argued, "My gun was aimed at his head when he lept at me, there wasn't time to aim anywhere else."

"Truly?" Tyrsus replied, "I know you were Elder Chang's favoured student, Ms Katral. He said your speed and accuracy were unmatched by anyone in his class. Save perhaps, Ms Rothschild."

Kitty bristled at this.

"Ah yes," the eagle said, "I know of your rivalry. I don't know how it started, but you've been most competitive. But that is beside the point. I know you have been more vehement about seeing al-Seif brought down than anyone here. But know that justice will come to him in his own time." Tyrsus jabbed a taloned finger at the tigress. "It is not for you to decide his fate."

Kitty curled her lip in a small snarl, but she bowed her head and said, "Yes, ma'am."

"Very good," Tyrsus said, "You're dismissed."

Kitty found her father waiting across the hall as she left the room, but he said nothing and went in to speak with the Elder himself. Kitty turned to see Ric at the end of the hall chatting amiably with Rizzo, Vicki, and Vince.

What did you see? she thought.

But the tigress already knew the answer. She knew because she had the same vision as the lynx, a vision of a temple in the middle of the jungle surrounded by fiends, and the bright light of a rift shining at its peak.

But do you see the river of blood that threatens to overflow and wash it all away? Kitty thought, *If you step through that rift, do you find yourself lying in a field of daisies on a bright spring day?*

A piece of that vision came to her then. The white tigress lay in the endless field of daisies, looking up at a blue sky. It was cloudless at first, but as she watched, puffs of white began to appear and gather right above her. When they had collected enough to form a solid disc, the face of a puma with copper eyes materialised in the centre of the cloud, the face of a lover long dead. Kitty knew this couldn't be a part of Ric's vision because that face was a torment of her own making.

And then, quite unexpectedly, the face changed. Now, she saw Ric.

Kitty felt something stir in her soul and quickly brought herself to the real world, turning to the elder's bedroom door. She thought about the tiger who had just entered, and it brought a wave of anger, which she used that to shut herself away again.

* * *

Inside the room, Mohan's ears twitched. He didn't know what brought on the strange sensation, but he sensed no danger and brushed it aside. He had other things to worry about right now.

Elder Tyrsus was cleaning up the tea by dumping it into a pitcher of water and carefully straining the fire blossom leaves. Once drained, Tyrsus carefully plucked out every speck of leaf and set them on a cloth to dry.

"You are curious, Mohan," she said as she performed this task.

The tiger crossed his arms over his barrel chest and leaned one shoulder on the wall. "Are you sure this is a good idea, Elder?" he asked.

"Elder? Please, my friend. I know I have more than a decade on you, but we birds don't show it like mammals."

"Basira," Mohan said, "We're hunters, not diplomats."

Elder Tyrsus picked up the pitcher and stirred the tea and water with a wooden spoon, diluting the blend. "It is also unwise to head directly for the Sanctuary. Medocci will give us a chance to draw them out."

"Or let them hit us again," Mohan said.

"Perhaps," the eagle said, "We cannot see that far."

Mohan scratched at an ear. "And the rest of the Elders are absolutely certain there isn't a leak?"

Tyrsus set the pitcher down and stared at the swirling water for a moment. "Beyond any doubt. There hasn't been a traitor in the ranks of the Tiger's Stripe since Aristo Dolvan, some five hundred years ago."

Mohan looked down at the eagle quizzically. He was used to the Elder Council playing things close to the chest, but he had always known Basira Tyrsus to more candid than the others.

The eagle passed the tiger the pitcher of water. "Dump this down the tub drain in the lavatory, would you?" Tyrsus said, "We'll need to gather more leaves soon. Perhaps Hati will be willing to put together an expedition?"

Mohan took the pitcher and made a polite bow to the eagle before turning to the door.

"General," Tyrsus said, using his field rank instead of his name, "There is a war coming, but we will weather it as we have before. The Laohu Tiaowen has not survived three thousand years without its own scars."

Mohan nodded without turning and left.

11 – Breaking Point

Saifullah El-Hashem eased the brand-new 1965 Restford Venturi Deluxe through narrow streets, silently thanking the lesser goat-god Nehbit for the invention of Air Conditioning. The merciless heat that pounded the city of Det that afternoon seemed determine to make the month of Geun the hottest of the year. Of course, there were still two months to go before summer surrendered itself to autumn.

The sea-blue Venturi was a prime example of WUK engineering at its finest, a mechanical beast of steel and chrome. Four chrome-ringed headlights glittered in the sunlight, and a convertible top of white canvas helped keep the heat outside and the cool of the A/C in. Small fins rose above the rear taillights, giving the vehicle a subtle resemblance to a rocket ship.

All eyes were on space these days. Ever since that damned atomic bomb over a decade ago it seemed everyone wanted a piece of the sky. But Saifullah knew it was only a matter of time before the whole thing collapsed under its bloated budget. There was nothing of interest out there anyway.

Saifullah carefully navigated a corner. The long automobile was far too big for a city like Det, but the mouflon liked to get out and flaunt the success of his antiquities business. Or at least he would on any other day, on any other errand.

Curse that boy! he thought, pounding out his frustrations on the steering wheel.

A small cluster of youths appeared on the next corner. They were hammering pamphlets into a wall. The papers bore a heavily stylized picture of a sun and a sword above a bold line of Netib script that declared:

RISE! FOR THE GLORY OF AYAD'NAHIM! CAST OFF THE
SHACKLES OF THE WESTERN INFIDELS!

Saifullah frowned and watched as a group of uniformed police spotted the hoodlums and chased after them. Ayad'nahim was the patron deity of the Nuadinites; the radical factions of which had grown increasingly hostile towards so-called "western" influences. They had also become increasingly violent, threatening to throw the country into civil war again.

This country will never know a moment's piece, Saifullah thought, *I can only hope that accursed offspring of mine hasn't fallen in with ruffians such as those.*

Even as he thought it, the mouflon knew it was unlikely. The younger mouflon, whom Saifullah grudgingly called son, had followed in his father's footsteps as far as his opinions on religion were concerned. Despite his brief prayer only moments ago, Saifullah doubted Nehbit even cared; that was assuming the lesser goat-god existed at all.

No, Jirair had no interest in the moral cause of the Nuadinites. But involving himself with their radical elements would provide precisely the kind of troublemaking opportunities Saifulah's son seemed to relish nowadays.

Saifullah pulled into the gravel parking lot of a long single-storied sandstone building fronted with striped blue and white awnings. Flags of the same colour hung limply in the humid air, hiding the crest of the Det police department within their motionless folds.

The heat hit the mouflon like a weight as he stepped out of the car. He only had to walk a few metres to the station's front door, but his fur was matted with sweat when he reached it.

For all the modern conveniences afforded to the Det police, A/C was not one of them. The stench of sweating animals—which generally went unnoticed by the anthropoid inhabitants of Amarthia—nearly caused Saifullah to gag as he entered. The station was crowded, and it seemed to get worse each time he had to come in. If it wasn't the Nuadinite radicals, it was gangs; if it wasn't the gangs, it was prostitutes—recently outlawed to appease said Nuadinites. On and on, a seemingly endless stream of minor felons, reprobates, and vagrants; and once in a while, a minor traffic violation.

And looming above it all, the ever-present lumbering monstrosity that was government bureaucracy. Perhaps western society *had* brought some troubles with it after all.

A short, overweight lion was dozing behind the front desk; he had shaved the hairs of his mane down to a few centimetres because of the heat. Saifullah wondered how he could sleep through the noise of the station.

The mouflon stepped up to the counter, amazed there was no line, and rang the bell.

"Ahmed," Saifullah said tersely, "Ahmed, I'm here for the boy."

The lion's eyes snapped open, and he yawned widely. "Hmm? Oh, Mr El-Hashem. Pleasure to see you again."

"Don't hand me that drivel." Saifullah fixed him with a withering gaze. "What's that damned spawn of mine done *this* time?"

Ahmed ruffled through some papers. "Let's see. Three counts of vandalism, possession of stolen property, and aggravated assault against an officer—that's a new one. His bond is six hundred carams."

Saifullah swore as he pulled out his billfold and paid the sum in cash. Ahmed called for the youth on the intercom, and they brought him out as his father was finishing with the paperwork.

Jirair stared at his elder blankly. The younger El-Hashem had adorned himself in faded jeans and a plain T-shirt and had tied a garish tie-dye headband around the base of his horns, which he had capped with tie-dye tassels.

Yes, there certainly were some negative influences from western society. The only thing missing from the outlandish outfit was that broken slanted "K" symbol that the Free Love crowd in the West United Kingdoms called a peace sign.

Saifullah's manner of dress couldn't have been a bigger contrast: smart powder-blue slacks—the matching suit jacket was in the car—a white short-sleeved shirt with wide lapels and a narrow pink power tie. It was the hight of fashion among businessmen in Locke and the WUK, and if his son had any sense he would learn that dressing the same would provide him with much better opportunities than...whatever style *that* was.

Saifullah handed the pen and documents to Ahmed, who promptly gave him a receipt for the bail. Saifullah turned on his hoof toward Jirair and returned his son's icy glare. He wanted to wring his offspring's scrawny neck, to take his thumbs and jam them through the pale eyes that painfully reminded the elder so much of his child's mother—whore that she was. Saifullah's balled fists shook with rage, and it seemed that maybe this one time he may actually strike Jirair.

But he didn't. His son was expecting that. It was all a game to Jirair, to see how far he could push his father until he finally did snap. Well, the little shit wouldn't win today!

"Let's go," Saifullah said quietly.

Jirair acquiesced sullenly.

They had barely stepped back into the sweltering heat when Saifullah turned to his son again.

"Next time I should just leave you to rot in there," he said, "Really, Jirair, the country is on the brink of civil war and your pinching dainties from storefronts. With all the money I spent on your tutors, I would think they'd teach you something."

"You certainly never did," Jirair retorted evenly.

The elder clenched his fists again, but it was still a game, and he wouldn't lose.

"I should send you to the military," Saifullah said, "maybe they can knock some sense into you. You better hope the Sultan makes some headway with the radicals. If the Nuadinite traditionalists had their way, you wouldn't have hands anymore."

"Let the pigs wallow in their mud pits," Jirair sneered.

Saifullah paled, a remarkable feat considering the amber fur on his face. While it was true that the sentient *Suidae* of Amarthia had a tendency toward slovenliness, to refer to someone as a "pig" was an insult of the highest order. It was slightly politer to use the term guingin; the wallowing non-sentient animals that had an unfortunate resemblance to a giant pangolin. They were also a forbidden food by the dietary laws of both the Nuadinates and the goat gods—not that goats ate meat anyway.

"You dare—" Saifullah began.

"Yes, I dare!" Jirair roared, cutting him off. "Look at us, *father*. We're animals, all of us! You think because we can walk and talk we're somehow better than the guingin that wallow in the mud? This whole country is a cesspool just waiting to boil over and drench the world in its filth. You speak of the current civil strife as if you actually give a damn, but in reality, all you care about is how this will affect your precious business."

Saifullah began walking towards the car, pretending to ignore his son's tirade.

Jirair continued undaunted, "I watch you, day in and day out, pouring bourbon down your throat and watching the stocks rise and fall, but not even a sideways glance for your own offspring. By the five hells, I bet you never even thought that I may inherit your business one day."

They reached the Venturi, and the elder mouflon whirled on the younger. "Like hell, you will!" Saifullah said, "You will *never* lay your hands on my assets, not a penny. You don't deserve it! I never asked for you, never asked that whore who bore you to—"

"Yes!" Jirair said with a sneer, "Yes, let's bring my mother into this! Who was she, *father*? You don't even know, do you? Just one more whore in an endless line that didn't even stop once I showed up. You grumble about my tutors never teaching me anything when the whole time they were too busy lying on their backs across *your* desk. You have forgotten my mother; drowned out her memory with—"

Now Saifullah struck Jirair. He thrust himself forward, lowering his head and smashing his horns across his son's face. Both mouflons were roughly the same size, but the elder was still the stronger, and Jirair toppled backwards onto the fine gravel that made up the parking lot of the police station. Only the curve of his own horns prevented him from cracking the back of his skull against the ground.

"Diana!" Saifullah cried, his voice a mix of rage and pain, "her name was Diana. And you, you little shit, you murdered her! Tore her soul out with your little strong hand." He collapsed against the bonnet of the car, heedless of the heat seeping through the fur of his hands. "You are not worthy to bear my name. Your name should be cursed and scattered to the sands."

Jirair stood up, blood dripping from his nose and the corner of his mouth. He stared at his father, breathing hard, his face a mask of barely subdued rage. And then he smiled. A horrible, grim smile without any trace of mirth or warmth.

"Seventeen years," Jirair said, "Seventeen years you have never raised your hand against me. I have been waiting for this moment; waiting to see what would push you over the edge. You call me weak, unworthy, but this day I have proven the stronger. I have broken you!"

Saifullah's eyes went wide, and his mouth went slack. He looked up into Jirair's bloodied face, saw the faint trace of the cut under his left eye. That had been his first mistake; he had never meant to hit the child, even as he threw the glass in rage. Originally, Saifullah *had* hoped the tutors would turn Jirair into something more, something he could turn his business over to without shame. But every time he saw his son's face, he saw the pale eyes of the mother who had died giving birth to him. Saifullah turned his grief into desire, seducing the tutors and leaving the child to fend for himself. And with each new mistress, his hatred for his son and himself grew stronger.

Now it had broken him completely; he had spilt his own blood. With a piteous wail, Saifullah El-Hashem collapsed to his knees on the ground.

"I do not want your name," Jirair said, staring down at his weeping elder. "Take it and bury it in the sands. This day I make my own name."

He turned and left.

Saifullah did not remember getting into his car or driving home, but he did remember waking with a start the following morning.

He was in his office, an empty bottle lying toppled on the green felt placemat. He didn't see a glass. A small folio lay open on the desk, stained with age and a few fresh splashes of expensive bourbon. The pictures within showed a young female mouflon with dark long-fur. A smiling Saifullah, many years younger, was never far from her side.

He reached out and traced the white markings of the woman's face with a finger, trying to remember what her cheeks felt like.

A soft knock interrupted his reverie. The new maid—an elderly mongoose with pudgy cheeks—poked her head in hesitantly.

"Mr El-Hashem, sir," she said in a wavering voice, "It's about your son, sir. I went to wake him for school, but he wasn't in. There's a large suitcase missing, it appears he took many of his clothes and a few smaller items. Should I phone the police?"

Saifullah gently closed the folio and sat back in his chair.

"No," he said softly, "I have no son."

12 – Clean House

Delshad al-Seif felt the kick of the plane's wheels hitting the runway and roused himself from sleep. He pondered the curious dream he had experienced during the flight. His father had told him the story of his final argument with Saifullah El-Hashem many times. The details changed slightly with each telling, but certain things always remained the same, particularly the heat of that day and how much Jirair detested the impracticality of the blue Venturi. Delshad's active mind extrapolated the rest.

As a child, he often wondered why his father continued to tell such a sad and violent tale to him. Eventually, he realised it was because his own father did not want to make the same mistakes.

That did not mean Delshad had had a carefree childhood. He was a mixed-breed, half mouflon and half ibex. Though taller than his father, Delshad had a similar bone structure and had inherited the mouflon fur markings on his head, arms, and legs. From his mother he had inherited a grey torso with a black ridge down his front and back and ribbed ibex horns, which grew out in a gentle curve to a length of about half a metre—slightly longer than his mother's.

Though it wasn't obvious to species outside the *Caprinae* family, to others of his kind Delshad's heritage was as plain as the nose on his face; and mixed breeding was often a source of prejudice and ridicule on Amarthia, even when it was difficult to tell a mixed-breed from a pure-blood.

They hid such prejudice well in Medocci, where Delshad was raised, usually masking it behind other sins outlined by the Aabanite Catholic Church.

Even were that not the case, Carmen Abbatelli didn't like the thought of her son being nurtured without a father.

It was several years before she eventually tracked down Jirair al-Seif. The mouflon was more than happy to reconnect with his lover, but he took to fatherhood uncertainly.

Those early years were rough. Al-Seif's ambitions kept him away in Pytan much of the time, and even when he was home in Medocci, the mouflon always seemed just the slightest bit harried; as if there were things that demanded his attention elsewhere.

Yet Delshad came to understand that Jirair was doing his best to be the antithesis of what his own father had been. Al-Seif never shouted at his boy, never taunted him, and he involved himself as much as possible with his son's education.

Eventually, father and son learned how to communicate with each other. Delshad learned the machinations of his father's legitimate business and its complex language of finance and questionable ethics. Once he could "converse" on the same level as his father, their relationship improved dramatically, and they learned to share their own individual hopes and ambitions.

Now Delshad al-Seif ran the legitimate business fronts, while Jirair al-Seif continued to work deep in the shadows as Assad Alabwaq.

The ibex-mouflon knew his father would have preferred things stay that way, that his son would never have to deal with the illegal side of the business. Jirair had made terrible enemies under the alias Assad Alabwaq, and keeping both Carmen and Delshad safe and seperate from them had always been paramount.

Fate had other plans, and Delshad, now in his mid-twenties, admitted he was all too eager to fill his father's shoes. He was in Kairran, the heart of Assad Alabwaq's criminal empire, with only one task before him: reassess his father's criminal enterprises and restructure them as necessary.

In Delshad's mind, this mission was the greatest gift his father could have ever given him. It was an act of unquestioning love and trust. He would *not* let his patron down.

The private plane taxied to a stop near the hangers at the south end of the Nayhadjin International Airport, and the twin props of the engines wound down. It was still mid-morning of the first day of Met, but the sun was already starting to bake the tarmac.

Delshad straightened himself as he stepped onto the gangway, smoothing out his expensive sky-blue silk suit. At the foot of the stairs, a tall dromedary waited dressed in an elegant white cotton thawb with gold embroidery. A tall turban adorned his head and perched on the end of his nose was a pair of circular sunglasses; the spectacles were specially designed to clamp snuggly to the long bony bridge of the dromedary's nose, but a chain connected them to the collar of his thawb should they be knocked loose.

Delshad shook the proffered hand and smiled. "You must be Rashid," he said in Netib. Unlike his father, it was not Delshad's first language and bore faint traces of his native Mecci.

"I am," the dromedary answered, bowing low. "It is a pleasure to meet you, sahib. Your father does not speak of you often, but when he does it is with great pride."

Delshad smiled. He was not surprised his father didn't speak of his family while toiling in the underworld. Such information could become a liability.

"Sahib?" Delshad said, "You are from Busawar?"

"Indeed," Rashid answered, "My family emigrated to Pytan many years ago, but some mannerisms die hard."

Delshad nodded and took in his surroundings quickly. To the north, cranes and construction equipment were busy repairing the south terminal, damaged in a terrorist bombing the week before. The war with Barju had done little to slow construction, and the terminal would soon be open again. Whether international service would be restored while the war was going on was another matter.

"I take it you have already passed us through security?" Delshad asked Rashid.

"Of course, sahib." The dromedary nodded. "Your father still retains some powerful connections. Speaking of which, I'm afraid his associates in the General Council are most insistent on speaking with you."

Delshad smirked. Of course they would be, but his father had taught him how to deal with politicians. "They will have to wait," he said, "My father has many business assets that must be secured before politics get in the way."

Rashid bowed again. "Very good, sahib. But I think you will find much of it has already been seen to, at least in Kairran."

"Please call me Delshad, or better yet, Assad Alabwaq. While I'm here, I carry my father's full authority, and it would be better if everyone knew my name holds as much weight as his own."

"Yes, sir. Do you wish to begin straight away, or retire for a few hours?"

"Best not to delay, I slept quite well on the plane." Delshad produced a small sheet of paper and handed it to Rashid. "Take me to my father's apartments and gather these lieutenants, assuming they are still in the city. There is a little matter of payroll to discuss."

An armoured limousine took Delshad into Kairran's Khalif Yashem District, northwest of the airport. The district was a far cry from the twisting streets and sandstone buildings of the Dahley markets, and the polar opposite of the Khamir slums on the northeast edge of the city. The ordered rows of skyscrapers, separated by bands of fresh blacktop, bore a much closer resemblance to urban city centres like New Port in the West United Kingdoms. This was the brain of Kairran's foreign trade and business, while the ports just to the east were the heart. It was also home to most of the city's more affluent populace.

The apartments of Assad Alabwaq were nearly as decadent as his villa in Medocci. It was a modern penthouse suite in one of the taller skyscrapers built along the Hutsepth Canal. Two walls consisted of towering floor to ceiling windows that looked out onto a large wrap-around balcony featuring a pool flanked by finely-crafted wooden deck chairs and wrought iron picnic tables. The windows provided excellent views from the dining area, lounge, and a living room with self-service bar. Post-modern artworks provided splashes colour against the stark white walls, which offset pieces of dark furniture with lines so sharp and cushions so thin they didn't look at all comfortable.

The back quarter of the first floor was composed of one large kitchen with stainless steel appliances and a walk-in freezer. Above the kitchen was a second-floor loft, reached via a glass and steel spiral staircase on the living room side—clear mats of thick plastic covered each glass step to protect them from sharp-hooved feet.

The loft served as an entertainment area with a pool table, card table, and a large screen projection TV connected to a hi-fi stereo. The master bedroom and bath were accessible through a short hall just off the loft, while the guest rooms were on the first floor beyond the living room, accessed via an entrance hall featuring a private elevator.

Overall, the apartments resembled a mini-resort designed for the comfort of a single owner. And yet it felt empty.

Delshad knew that his father rarely entertained guests, and his most prized artwork was at the Medoccian villa. The pool, though always cleaned and ready, had probably not seen use in many months. Delshad had often overheard his mother talking on the phone late at night, and he knew his father was on the other end, sitting in this vast apartment with only his bodyguard and wishing desperately that his mistress could be there.

Well if Delshad was going to reassert his father's influence in the region, he would make sure to celebrate appropriately. He could almost picture a few bikini-clad sheep lounging in the chairs, or maybe the exotic spots of a leopard.

He shook his head to clear it. Time enough for that later, he had preparations to make.

It only took two hours for Rashid to gathered the people Delshad had wanted to see. No wonder his father praised the dromedary's efficiency. From the loft railing, the ibex-mouflon examined the finely dressed men and women of varied species gathered in the living room below. They clustered uneasily around the bar or seated themselves on the collection of couches that attempted to fill the large space.

These were the people his father had chosen to run elements of his criminal enterprises, not only in Kairran but across Pytan and the other nations of Estan. They were smugglers, drug dealers, blackmailers, thieves, and murderers.

Delshad descended the spiral stairs, noting the looks of disdain some of the guests shot in his direction—apparently being the son of their feared employer did not bear the same weight as being the man himself.

Yet.

As he reached the floor, Delshad cleared his throat and addressed the crowd, "Ladies and gentlemen, might I have your attention, please. Many of you do not know me, but I am the son of Signor Assad Alabwaq, your employer. You may address me as the same, for obvious reasons." He gestured to the ebony horns sticking out beyond his carefully groomed black long-fur.

There were a few murmurs, but no one seemed to pay much attention. Delshad's father had warned him this might be the case, but that he should proceed with all the authority he could bestow on him. And not be afraid to set an example.

"I will not take up any more of your time than necessary," Delshad continued, "Your employer, my father, has given me the authority to restructure his assets while he sees to his expansion in Medocci. I am pleased to see that you have already done half the work for me. So, let me begin by congratulating you on surviving the first week of this unfortunate war with such *forza d'animo*. Ah, your pardon, I am slipping into Mecci. Your, uh, fortitude."

The murmurs had stopped, some of the sneers became more prominent while others faded to become looks of confusion.

Good, let them think the young upstart is clueless, Delshad thought.

Aloud he said, "To commend you for your perseverance, let us toast your health!" He motioned to one of the goat servants, who produced a tray of glass wine flutes filled with the bubbling liquid. "I planned to host a party here this weekend, but I concluded there was no reason to wait to open the wine stores."

The sparkling wine made its way to the hands of the guests, and a spotted serval cat servant handed Delshad a glass from a separate tray. The young ibex-mouflon was watching the crowd closely; only one of them—an old but heavily built frilled lizard—seemed to catch on that Delshad's drink did not come from the same source as the rest.

Delshad raised his glass. "May fortune smile on you and see us through trying times."

They all drank, except the lizard.

Delshad smiled coldly. "Did you know that champagne was invented by a Meccinai general? He was in charge of a garrison in Maris, which is why everyone assumes it's Marissian."

The crowd stared at him in confusion for a moment, then they began to react. There were a few coughs and groans, several guests suddenly doubled over clutching their midsection.

"General Champagne had a clever way of removing his political opponents," the mouflon continued, "He would invite them to lavish dinner parties and poison their wine."

Eyes began to widen, throats began to tighten.

"Really?" Delshad asked, placing his glass on the servant's tray, "Only a week after my father had left the country, and you sold out to Kristoph Weis or Mody Nahas? I told you my father gave me complete authority to restructure his assets." Delshad spread his arms wide. "Consider this your termination notice."

The guests gagged and wheezed as the poison worked through their systems, causing their tongues to swell and their throats to constrict, closing off the flow of air to their lungs. Glasses fell to the floor with a crash. A cyrax reached out in panic and tore at the dress of the elderly cheetah beside him; she was too busy clawing at her constricted throat to attempt to cover herself. A scrawny bull with blunted horns tore at his sealed larynx and toppled backwards over one of the couches. Soon, all of Delshad's guests were clawing at themselves and each other until their beautiful clothes were tatters and blood began to spatter on the floor.

Delshad frowned, he had hoped to avoid such a mess and would have to get it cleaned before the party.

The frilled lizard who had refused to drink had moved away from the melee, but a large mastiff bodyguard barred his exit to the balcony. The lizard turned toward Delshad and waited patiently. The bodies of his former co-workers twisted and writhed on the blood-stained carpet until their movements became faint twitches, and then stillness. Within moments it was just the frilled lizard and the ibex-mouflon.

"*Brava*," Delshad said, giving him a slow clap, "Very observant. A pity you did not use those brains before you betrayed my father."

"Naturally I assume you will not even allow a witness?" the lizard rasped, tensing.

The mouflon shook his head, "Perhaps if this were any other circumstance, but there are no second chances after such a betrayal. You must have known, must all have known, that this would ultimately be your fate."

"We shall see," the lizard replied, "Your father has not regained his throne yet. Things are not as they were before he left."

The lizard removed his dinner jacket and moved towards the empty space that divided the living room from the dining area and kitchen. He wouldn't have to contend with broken glass or the tangle of bodies here. Placing his left foot in front of his right, he hunched down and brought his fists up in front of him.

Delshad's smile grew colder. He drew out a small pistol from a concealed shoulder holster, pointed it at the lizard, then twirled it and set it down on the serval cat's tray next to his champagne flute.

"Were I my father, I would just shoot you," Delshad said, removing his jacket, "But I remember you. Solair the Golden Scale is what they called you. I've seen you in the arena. Granted, that was years ago, and your scales have wrinkled, but I will accept your challenge and allow you to regain some honour."

The ibex-mouflon moved to within a few paces from the lizard and went into a stance; arms up in front of his face, his weight placed firmly on his left hoof, and his right leg cocked in front of him with the tip of his hoof barely touching the floor. It was the basic stance of chut-ri, the Busawan martial art that Abar Kami had taught him.

Solair acknowledged his employer's acceptance of the duel with a nod. He didn't have any illusions about his chances, not at his age or against a disciple of chut-ri, but he had once been one of al-Seif's gladiators, and he would end his life by their code.

They faced each other in silence, neither making a move. Finally, Solair made a feint with his left foot and lashed out with his right hand, attempting to slash at Delshad's midsection with his long lizard claws. The ibex-mouflon dodged easily, stepping to his left and bringing his elbow down toward the centre of Solair's back.

The frilled lizard anticipated this and spun away to his left, taking the blow on his shoulder, but landing a strike with his thick tail across the ibex-mouflon's side. Delshad grunted and leapt back out of the lizard's range.

Solair faced him again and tried to bring his arms up, but shooting pain lanced through his right side; his shoulder was dislocated. The ibex-mouflon may not have his panther mentor's speed and fluidity, but he made up for it in raw power.

Delshad saw the flinch and moved in with a kick to Solair's right knee, but the lizard lept sideways and lashed out at the limb with a foot-claw. The ibex-mouflon did something the lizard did not expect, allowing Solair's attack to connect with his leg and using the momentum to drive it up towards the lizard's face.

Solair arced backward to avoid the sharp hoof while Delshad twisted and dropped to one hand, sweeping out his other leg at the lizard's exposed midsection. The blow connected solidly, and the ibex-mouflon heard the satisfying crack of a rib. Solair doubled over with a cough of blood.

Delshad finished his turn and spun to his feet, taking advantage of Solair's shock by swinging his arm out to deliver a blow to the side of the lizard's head; it connected solidly with his ear hole.

That was the end for Solair. The lizard staggered back, completely disoriented, and Delshad moved in to land several quick blows with his fists, elbows, and knees, finishing off with a vicious front kick that sent the lizard crashing into the square pillar that supported a corner of the second-floor loft. The impact sent a priceless Jake Ollaque oil painting crashing to the floor.

Solair hung there against the wall for a moment, his battered and bloodied face looking almost like the painting he had just destroyed. As he began to slide to the floor, he reached feebly to his right—and the gun resting on the servant's tray.

The serval cat moved the tray out of reach but raised a questioning eyebrow at his employer, wondering if the ibex-mouflon might actually want his opponent to retrieve the weapon.

Delshad snorted in disgust. "Even in seeking a warrior's death you reach for the coward's escape."

He rushed towards the lizard, head lowered. At the last moment, he dropped down almost to the floor and bent his head down into his stomach. Using his powerful legs for leverage, Delshad lunged upward, impaling Solair through the chest with his horns. Solair's eyes bulged, and the last of his breath escaped his lungs with a painful wheeze. He went limp against the wall.

Had his horns been angled differently Delshad might have left the lizard hang a moment longer, but he quickly grew uncomfortable. Putting his hands on the corpse he yanked himself free, blood spurting from the wounds and onto the floor. Already a servant was standing by with a towel and Delshad could hear water running upstairs as a bath was drawn. His father certainly did believe in hiring efficient staff.

However, slow clapping from the entry hall caught his attention.

13 – Business Associates

Two more guests had arrived, guests that Delshad had hoped to avoid at least a little while longer.

The first was a hart, and even without the uniform weighted down with ribbons, it would have been easy to tell he was a soldier. The sharp black eyes, the grey long-fur trimmed at a consistent three centimetres, and his erect posture all bespoke of someone who had lived a life of order and discipline. He had several battle scars including a half-missing left ear, a jagged white scar on his right cheek, and one of his long narrow horns was cut several centimetres shorter than the other.

"An impressive display," said Rousel Ach'eman, recently appointed Governor General of Pytan. "You clearly don't mind getting your hands as dirty as your father's."

"Yes," the markhor beside Ach'eman replied, "But I think your father would have handled it much cleaner as well as quicker."

Delshad bristled at this. The markhor was Agabe Hassan, recently self-appointed Regent of Pytan. Hassan was also a military man, but from his bearing—and the fact that he wore a suit instead of a uniform—it was clear that he had not seen combat in many years. He still kept his spiral-twisted horns polished to a bright sheen and had buzzed his grey long-fur to the same length as his body-fur.

It was Hassan's eyes that gave him away. The large brown orbs with their odd *Caprinae* pupils were deep-set under drooping brows and looked perpetually exhausted. They were politician's eyes.

Delshad took several breaths and let Hassan's comments go. Dealing with the Regent would be the biggest obstacle he had to get by during his stay. Delshad couldn't just kill him like he had his traitorous employees, and his political connections were far to valuable to lose.

"I was not expecting to see you so soon, Regent, General," Delshad said, wiping the blood from his horns with the towel.

"It was not *you* that we expected to see," Hassan said.

Delshad removed his shoulder holster and slipped the pistol back into it. For the briefest instant, he thought of using it against the meddling politicians, but he placed the gun on the tray and began stripping off his blood-soaked shirt. His father must have gone through the same feelings a hundred times, he could endure as well.

"Yes, I'm sure you didn't," the ibex-mouflon replied. "Well, spit it out. I'm sure you can see I'm quite busy. Downsizing is always such a tedious task." He gestured to the pile of corpses on the living room rug.

Hassan frowned. "Indeed. We understand you have come here to consolidate and liquidate," he glanced again at the bodies, "your father's assets in Estan."

"And to pay debts," Delshad said tiredly, placing the bloody shirt on the serval cat's tray and moving on to his slacks.

Hassan came forward into the room and helped himself to an expensive bottle of bourbon. He paused with the glass half to his lips.

Delshad waved absently as he began removing his pants. "Only the wine was poisoned," he said, "I didn't not wish to spoil my father's bar, even if he touches little of it." He placed his pants on the tray with his gun and shirt. A goat servant offered him a fresh towel, but Delshad waved him off and stood before his guests stark naked.

Hassan frowned in distaste. "Yes, well, getting back to the matter at hand. You are, of course, aware of the deal we have made with Assad Alabwaq. A deal concerning a new and particularly potent strain of heroine."

General Ach'eman folded his arms across his chest, eyes narrowed. "But the crop was destroyed," he said slowly, "By your father's own pet project, I might add."

Delshad hesitated only for a moment. The beast that destroyed the heroin farm had been the progeny of his father's mysterious partner, Freggs. But that was not information these politicians needed to know.

"*Come ti pare!*" Delshad threw up a dismissive hand. "That creature wasn't my father's design. He has done well enough without such abominations."

"Truly?" Hassan said, "Wouldn't such a creature be a rather interesting addition to his gladiator games?"

Delshad paused again. It was true that his father seemed less and less pleased with the spectacle of the arena of late.

But surely, his father couldn't believe that the creature grown in that jungle lab was meant to be a show piece?

Aloud the ibex-mouflon said, "*E allora*? So what? I'm certain my father would have wanted something on a more manageable scale were that the case."

"Hmm, yes," Hassan said, "Perhaps that was the shipment we heard rumours about making its way to Kairran. Then the entire ship mysteriously vanished!"

Delshad's eyes narrowed sharply. Throughout this entire conversation he had grown increasingly aware that the Regent and his Governor General knew more information than his father or he had given them credit for. But who could be there informer? His trip around the Medean Basin had given him plenty of time to examine the traitors within Alabwaq's old smuggling partners a dozen times over, and all his information on Hassan and Ach'eman showed that they only delt with his father directly, never with an underling.

Delshad cleared his throat. "The *Resthoven*," he said, and scratched at his chin, "Yes, that must also be addressed. But that does not concern you, nor was my father responsible for the vessel's disappearance."

"Indeed?" Hassan said, "Well, in any case, it appears we may have to start looking elsewhere for our...product."

"There is no need to act so rashly," Delshad said, "I will have someone sent to Jar-Geshim to take care of that cowardly snake, and we will have the plantation running again very soon."

"You needn't bother," Ach'eman said, "Our men are already waiting to proceed with taking back the city."

Delshad paused. "Take back?"

Hassan gave a derisive snort. "Of course. Surely you did not think we could let that band of murderous thugs continue on their merry way while we focus our forces on defending Pytan. The loss of the heroine is regrettable; waging a war is so expensive, requiring both time and resources. However, the hydroelectric damn we built back in the thirties is well overdue for an upgrade. I believe it could provide a much-needed boost to our energy supply in the coming months, or even years."

Delshad eyed the Regent and Governor General with renewed intensity. "The bandits will not surrender."

"Do not worry." Ach'eman waved a hand dismissively. "We don't expect them to."

* * *

The young crime lord and the two corrupt politicians held no concerns about talking in a room full of servants. They were some of Alabwaq's most trusted employees, and while Delshad's display had been more violent than his father, they were used to the customary weeding out of traitorous elements.

But there were two figures who observed and mentally recorded their conversation with great interest.

One was a tamarin servant who had kept dutifully out of the way as Delshad poisoned his traitorous employees and talked shop with the Regent and Governor General. Witnessing such a blatant display of criminal behaviour caused the odd birthmark on his left side—which looked like a tiger's face—to tingle with a peculiar intensity.

The other observer was the serval cat now holding a tray laden with Delshad's bloody clothing. He had neither birthmark nor tattoo, but his sharp ears hung on every word the *Caprinae* said. And every so often his eye would glance at the tamarin.

14 – The Siege of Jar-Geshim

The Marshal cracked open his eyelids and looked around his bedroom. It was late afternoon in his little jungle kingdom, and the sunlight drifted through thin curtains that rustled gently in a warm breeze.

It was unclear what purpose the circular chamber had once served in the ancient temple when the city was at its most grand, but now it resembled a brothel from the WUK's Western Expansion days in the mid-1800s. The wooden furniture was solid, carved with flowering vines that twisted up the edges, and had knobs and fittings made of heavy brass that was badly in need of polishing. Red banners bearing a ringed silver star hung from poles set in the alcoves on either side of the only entry, which had no door. At the centre of the room stood a four-poster canopy bed with several large cushions surrounding it. The Marshal was alone in the room save for a female pine snake lying beneath him, sleeping soundly.

The old cobra wished he could doze as peacefully, but he hadn't been able to get a proper night's rest since the Pytian army had arrived at the edge of his jungle. No, earlier than that, ever since those damn hunters from KLAWS came to his doorstep last week.

Rolling off of his concubine, the Marshal coiled his lower half on the stone floor, which the sun had made deliciously warm.

A sentient snake's appearance often drew the epithet "half-lizard", which, of course, most found highly insulting. The Marshal was five metres in length, but only half a meter wide at the shoulders. And he did have shoulders; they connected to a narrow anthropoid torso that—proportional to his head and slender arms—ended approximately where his waist would be. Taking his measurements into account, if he had legs like a lizard, he would have been just over a metre tall with an exceptionally long tail. At the end of each arm was a long-fingered hand with short claws at the end of each digit.

The Marshal flexed his arms to loosen sore muscles and slipped on the fringed leather vest hanging on the back of a chair. A ringed silver star was pinned to the left breast; he had scuffed and scratched the engravings to the point of illegibility, but they had once born the legend: WUK Marshals Service, Beauregard, Carlin.

The vest served as his only attire; sentient snakes seemed exempt from certain social norms, like pants. The Marshal mused briefly that sentient insects were the only other exception considering they were essentially giant talking counterparts of their tiny non-sentient cousins.

He shrugged indifferently at the thought, content that he didn't have to worry about wrapping up five metres of scales, which he only did if the weather got cool—an extreme rarity in the Valley of Nefrit.

The Marshal wondered what had woken him from his afternoon nap and slithered over to the window.

Jar-Geshim was an ancient city, a ruin built upon a ruin built upon yet another ruin, and slowly improved upon over long generations. The original buildings—if they still stood— rose in elegant tiers of stone and forged metal, their balconies requiring engineering skills that had sadly been lost to the ages; but that hadn't stopped the style from being endlessly copied by artists who dabbled in fantasy or science-fiction matte painting.

Shuffled between the original ruins were slightly newer buildings of sandstone and marble, the remnants of whatever empire had conquered the original builders— probably Meccinai from the style of the pillars and the temple the Marshal had turned into his dwelling.

In the 1930s, the Pytan government briefly occupied the city and reinforced the older buildings with concrete. They also brought electricity by building a hydroelectric dam into the ancient bridge spanning the nearby waterfall.

Finally, at the very edges of the city, were the bandits' contribution to Jar-Geshim's infrastructure: sheds and hovels made of corrugated tin plates, scraps of sheet metal, and even the broken fuselage of a crashed aeroplane.

To the Marshal, the hodgepodge of architecture was a testament to the resilience and adaptability of the people "civilised" society called "outcast".

Cocking his head to the side, the cobra listened to the sounds of his city: the bark of traders, angry shouts of drunken layabouts, gunfire, cries of both pain and pleasure. His forked tongue flicked out and captured the faint smell of opium dens, gunpowder, exotic spices, and hundreds of unwashed bodies. The perfume and incense of his bedchamber partially masked the stink, but the Marshal welcomed the raw stench of the city. To him it was the scent of life itself; life away from meddlesome laws and politicians. A life of true freedom, with him as its benevolent dictator.

His eyes wandered over to the cages and gibbets arranged on one side of the city square, some occupied by fresh victims of his harsh bandit justice.

Mostly benevolent anyway.

Still, the Marshal wondered how long he could hold it together. His deal with Assad Alabwaq had fallen through with the destruction of the super-heroin crop, and after the events that followed he was mildly surprised there hadn't been a revolt against him yet. Perhaps any rivals waiting in the wings were holding back until the Pytian army made their move?

Another sound made the Marshal turn. His concubine had awoken and stretched luxuriously as she sat up in bed. She was roughly his size, only a few centimetres shorter, with a rounded snout that characterised non-venomous snake species. The Marshal traced the subtle curves of her female upper torso and the intricate patterns of her dark scales against the cream-coloured ones. A new fire sparked in his eyes.

He began to slither toward her again when he suddenly noticed the figure standing in the alcove on the opposite side of the room. The intruder was not hiding behind the banner, and the Marshal wondered how he hadn't noticed the him before.

The figure was canine, a dark-furred greyhound with ears straightened to tall points that stood out from dark long-fur slicked back with pomade. The Marshal almost mistook him for a "greaser", the hoodlum crowd the cobra hung around in his teens before—well, before now. The image certainly fit with the greyhound's black biker's leathers. There was a red silk sash tied around his upper left arm and his right was in a sling.

"Who the devil're you?" The Marshal hissed in his heavy Carlin drawl, the cobra hood attached to his neck and shoulders flaring in agitation.

Before the figure could answer, there was a distant sound of thunder. Moments later there came a tremendous *crash*, and the building shuddered with the impact of an explosion.

The pine snake, whom the Marshal had completely forgotten, screamed and slithered out the door, abandoning what little clothing she had. The Marshal rushed to the window again. Black smoke was rising from the direction of the city gate.

"Bastards!" the cobra said, pounding his fist on the stone sill. "The Pytian bastards finally did it! We saw them park outside the jungle on Faerday. They've been waitin' all weekend to push in on us. Probably got the entire valley sealed, tryin' to keep us from sneakin' out. Why the hell didn't our advance guard warn me the attack was comin'?"

He slithered over to an antique bureau and threw the doors open. Inside were a bandolier and a brace of heavy revolvers. They were excellent weapons; single-action Peacemakers with wood grips and filigree along the cylinder and barrel. The Marshal had not worn them in a very long time, but he kept them cleaned and oiled despite some of the painful memories associated with them. He used his anger to thrust those memories aside now.

The figure in the alcove didn't so much as flinch as the Marshal slipped the guns on, not even when he loosed one and pointed it at the intruder.

"You, I recognize you," the cobra said, his eyes narrowing sharply. "Your one of them Scarlet Dream fellers that General Hassan sent to kill those damn KLAWS agents; the ones that caused the bloodbath in the square. We're still tryin' to clean the blood off the tiles."

The figure said nothing, he just continued to stand there staring impassively at the cobra. Another volley of artillery fire shook the palace, the Pytian army was shelling the city before moving their ground forces in. Why hadn't any of the Marshal's guard come to inform him about the situation yet?

"You come here to assassinate me personally? Is that it?" The cobra's eyes burned with rage, but the hand holding the heavy revolver remained steady.

The figure continued to say nothing.

The Marshal slithered closer slowly. He glanced down the hall, but even his concubine had vanished; the palace seemed deserted. Screams began to filter in from outside. He had to get out there, rally the troops. This was *his* city, and he'd be damned if he let the Pytian government have it. He wasn't going to lose another one.

The Marshal flinched slightly at the old memory, but the intruder either didn't notice or chose not to take advantage of the cobra's pause.

When the Marshal was barely a metre from the figure in the alcove, he struck. Even at fifty years old, he was lightning quick; in moments he would have his fangs buried in the interloper's neck and pump him full of deadly venom.

The stranger was faster.

The greyhound grabbed the banner pole behind him with his left hand, spun it around and jammed the top crossbeam into the cobra's mouth. Twisting the end, he jerkered the Marshal's head to the side and rammed the snake into the floor.

The Marshal hissed and squirmed in rage, fangs still bared, but the intruder was much stronger than he looked, even with only one good arm. Every time the cobra tried to whip his tail end around to trip his attacker, the banner was jammed further into his mouth.

The stranger placed a foot on the Marshal's chest, and the cobra felt the press of cold steel; the greyhound had capped his foot claws with razor tips, a common practice among warriors and dirty street fighters.

"*Non*," the canine said in a low voice.

The cobra stopped struggling, and the greyhound eased the banner gag back enough to allow him to speak.

"Marisian?" the Marshal asked, "You ain't one of the Scarlet Dream, are you?"

"Very perceptive," the greyhound said, "Now, if you wish to live, I suggest you follow *moi*."

"You expect me to abandon my city?" The cobra asked. The marshal had landed on one revolver but started edging his hand towards the other holster. A sharp warning from the greyhound's toe claws stopped him.

"I expect you to place your own survival above a doomed cause," the intruder said, "like you always have, Mr Sampson."

The Marshal's hood flared, and he hissed sharply, "Don't call me that. *Never* call me that! Where did you hear that name?"

"We know many things about you...Marshal," the greyhound replied, "But the most important right now is that your instinct for survival has brought you very far, and my employers feel they can still make use of it." The banner pressed into the cobra's mouth again. "But if you insist on no longer being of any use..."

The Marshal glared at his attacker, but as the banner pushed further into his mouth and the razor claws began to dig into his chest, his eyes widen in fear. Slowly he nodded.

The greyhound stepped back and allowed the snake to rise. The Marshal noticed his attacker remained tense and alert as he retrieved the fallen revolver, but the cobra was smart enough to figure out that if this intruder had wanted him dead, he would be.

Let's see were this leads to, the Marshal thought.

The barrage outside had increased in intensity, but the Marshal realised most of the shells were centred on the walls and outer rings. The bastards were trying to save the hydroelectric plant.

"My city," he said softly.

"Jar-Geshim is doomed," the stranger replied, "If you are wondering where your guard is, my colleagues—who actually *do* work for the *Alqarmizi Alhulm*—have dispatched with them already. Even now they are tearing through the rear ranks of the city's defenders to soften them up for the Pytian troops."

The Marshal nodded with grim acceptance. He had expected such a betrayal the moment the Scarlet Dream showed up at his gates. But he had to admit, he anticipated a little more warning.

There was an old-fashioned hat rack near the door, and from it the cobra retrieved a black gambler hat, perching it neatly atop his arrow-shaped head and securing the leather ties under his chin with a drawstring bead made of turquoise. He drew both revolvers and held them at the ready.

The greyhound led him out into the halls, and the Marshal gazed down into the open courtyard that had served as his throne room. He gave a slight shudder as his eyes flicked between the bodies that lay scattered throughout the hanging gardens and the small amphitheatre at one end. It appeared they put up little resistance and had met their demise with ruthless efficiency. A cold shiver ran through him as he suddenly realised it must have been their muffled death throws that had disturbed his afternoon nap.

The cobra's eyes moved to the trophy hanging on the wall above and behind the stone seat of his throne. The jagged skull was almost as big as his greyhound companion and had four eye sockets, two on either side. The crest at the back of the skull bore a wreath of twisted ebony horns and the mouth, mounted slightly ajar, displayed several rows of serrated teeth.

Perhaps that was the real root of his troubles. The creature had no name, but the Marshal had heard the KLAWS hunters refer to it as the "Frankenbeast". He had read Margret Kelly's *Monstroso* many years ago—and was a huge fan of the old black and white horror film—but it was a mystery why the hunters thought the name so fitting.

Of course, the terror was real enough. The hunters had warned him that the creature's blood was toxic, but the cobra had no idea it would turn out to be the mysterious sleeping plague known as Daeminox Syndrome. Two of the Marshals's favourite taxidermists had died while working on mounting the head.

The bones of the creature seemed harmless enough once stripped and dried, but the Marshal refused to go anywhere near the skull after seeing the taxidermists' fate. That was why he spent the afternoon in his bedchamber rather than basking in the sun on his throne, with those terrible eye sockets boring into the back of his head.

Looking at the scattered corpses of his guard again, the Marshal supposed that in some sick twist of fate the strange hunters with the tiger-face markings had actually saved his life.

The cobra's greyhound guide was moving quickly now, carefully checking the shadowed alcoves of the hall. The Marshal realised his rescuer was searching for agents of the Scarlet Dream, and that his escape from the city probably wasn't a part of the *Alqarmizi Alhulm*'s agenda.

This became obvious when one of their agents—a mongoose no less—stepped out of the shadows and confronted them.

The mongoose was dressed identically to the greyhound down to the red sash on the left arm. This was probably what caused the assassin to pause, but as he looked from the greyhound to the Marshal and back again, sudden realisation flickered in his eyes. He moved to draw a curved dagger from his belt.

The greyhound reacted with blinding speed, kicking out with his foot and slashing the mongoose across the stomach with his toe claws. The blow knocked the breath from the assassin's lungs, and he doubled over in pain. The ensuing struggle was a blur of motion that only lasted a few seconds but ended with the greyhound getting behind the mongoose and the Marshal hearing a sickening *crunch* as his rescuer snapped the assassin's neck.

The Marshal had sentenced many people to a gruesome death and had seen many brutal fights in the cage arena in the palace courtyard, but something was disconcerting about the manner this greyhound went about killing. It was cold, methodical, and carried out with such unnatural swiftness that the cobra had to turn aside.

His gaze travelled into the dark alcove from which the attacker had come, and he saw a form lying in the shadows. It was the pine snake from his bedchambers. Grim curiosity made the Marshal move closer, and he realised she was still breathing.

The Marshal didn't know what came over him at that moment but seeing her lying there suddenly brought a stab of pain from a past the cobra thought long buried.

A small voice inside him whispered urgently, *You can't leave her there. Not again.*

The greyhound watched as the Marshal lifted the pine snake up and threw her over his shoulder in a fireman's carry; it was less dignified, but he could move quicker with her tail dragging behind than if he carried her in his arms before him.

"Leave her," the greyhound said, "There is no time and no room in the boat."

The Marshal's hood flared, and he bared his fangs at the intruder. "No, goddamn you," he said with cold finality. "You say the city's lost; so be it. But if I can save one, just one, maybe I can deal with it."

The greyhound started walking again but continued to admonish him. "She means nothing to you. Just your latest whore of the week. Do you even know her name?"

The Marshal looked at the face swaying next to his as if for the first time. Aside from a few scars and bruised scales— natural effects of hard living in a city of bandits—he suddenly thought she was quite beautiful.

"No," he said, "But I'll learn it."

They spoke no more as the greyhound led them down through the palace and into the gardens by the river. Their party exited just in time, an artillery shell sang over their heads and slammed into the ancient temple. There was a creak of stone and wood as the second floor collapsed into the courtyard, burying the Marshal's throne and the trophy skull.

The Marshal couldn't see the panic and destruction that was marching its way through his precious city on the opposite side of the ruin, but he could hear it. The ground quaked as several of the elegant structures—which had stood for time immemorial—collapsed under the bombardment, killing and injuring who knew how many bandits as they ran through the streets below seeking an exit.

The Marshal's blood boiled. It was true that the citizens of Jar-Geshim were nothing more than the dregs of society; thieves, cutthroats, swindlers, the lowest of the low. But the Marshal saw people. He had banded them together, taught them to build, gave them their bread and circuses while keeping the bahngers of so-called "civilised" society at bay. For all their violent tendencies, they had created their own civilisation here.

And now it was going up in a cloud of smoke.

The cobra turned, looking for the side gate, but the greyhound tugged at his vest. When the Marshal turned, his guide gave him a curt negative shake of his head and continued through the gardens. With a resigned sigh, the Marshal followed.

As they drew near the edge of the lake, they spotted several bandits, mostly from aquatic or water-dwelling species, diving into the water. They began swimming furiously for the opposite shore, away from the burning city. They could make it! They were almost there!

Then the Marshal watched helplessly as a Pytian patrol boat came cruising around a bend in the lake. The bastards had actually shipped in water support to secure their containment area.

Instead of helping the refugees out of the water and arresting them, the forward gunner opened fire with a mounted machine gun, slaughtering them to the last swimmer.

The Marshal let loose a cry of anguish at the sight. His greyhound companion didn't even seem to notice.

The faux Scarlet Dream agent led the Marshal, still carrying the unconscious pine snake, down to the water's edge at the far end of the palace gardens. A few fishing boats sat tied to the stone quay, but most had rotted through long ago.

"What now?" the Marshal hissed, "You saw what that boat did to the swimmers. We can't get out that way, and we can't just sit here 'til nightfall."

The greyhound said nothing and reached down toward a patch of Lilly pads. And pulled them away like a canvas.

The Marshal had never seen such an ingenious netting, it seemed to shift patterns as the greyhound rolled it up, appearing first as the Lilly pads, then like the rocky quay, and then finally as its actual form: a series of tiny mirrors designed to mimic whatever environment it was laid in. The Marshal had heard rumours about the WUK military researching such tech but didn't know a working prototype existed.

The craft the greyhound revealed underneath was equally impressive. It was long and low, and the engine resembled something the Marshal had once seen on a jet ski rather than your standard outboard propeller. Two long tubes ran along either side of the narrow hull; they looked like torpedoes, but the Marshal realised they were fuel tanks for the jet motor. He wondered briefly how fast the boat could travel with the throttle open—and if it would fly if you put wings on it.

The greyhound climbed aboard and stood by the engine. "If you wish to take her, you must both lie in the bottom of the boat. I'm sure you will have no problem with that," he said with a cold, sardonic smile.

The boat was barely four meters long, but the marshal managed to lay the pine snake with her tail coiled beside her then put himself on top of her in a similar fashion. Had he been in any other situation the Marshal may have found himself somewhat aroused, but the damp bottom of the boat combined with the boom of artillery fire help dashed such thoughts immediately. The shells were falling so fast now they almost matched the rhythm of his heart, he was surprised the city hadn't been totally levelled.

The greyhound threw the amazing camouflage net over the snakes and started the engine. Or at least the Marshal assumed he started the engine, all he heard was a soft, high-pitched whine and he felt a subtle vibration through the hull of the boat.

They began to move.

The Marshal lay very still. He couldn't see what was happening, but as the boat moved further out into the lake, he could feel them pick up speed. The greyhound was throttling up to counteract the current pulling them towards the dam and the falls.

Eventually, the Marshal heard another sound, the heavy thrum of the patrol boat's diesel engines.

This was madness. Sure, they might look like a patch of Lilly pads, but wouldn't the soldiers think it odd for a cluster of river plants to be in the middle of the lake? And not only that but to be moving *against* the current? And what about their pilot? He wasn't hiding beneath the camouflage. Wouldn't they think it strange to see a greyhound just floating there along the surface of the water, like a miracle out of that damned Fosday School book his mother had tried to make him pay attention to as a kid? How the hell had he ended up like this, laying in the bottom of a secret spy boat on top of a cheap harlot he'd suddenly taken a fancy to?

And then the patrol boat passed them. Yes, they were beyond it now, their own craft was picking up speed, and the sound of the Pytian artillery was quieter. The miracle netting had worked.

What the Marshal couldn't see was that it was no trick of magic or technology. The greyhound had manoeuvred them to the far side of the bridge, in the shadow of the Warren. The Marshal wouldn't have liked to see them so close, but it was safer for the greyhound to make his approach from this side. The patrol boat spotted them, of course, but the greyhound stood and made a predetermined signal with his hand. The captain of the patrol craft ordered his ship to stay clear and ignore the smaller vessel and dismissed any questions from his subordinates with a curt recital of "that's classified."

When they were clear, the greyhound continued to keep their speed low, trying to make as little wake as possible. It took them almost an hour to reach the far side of the long lake. The artillery had finally silenced.

The Marshal felt the boat hit the bank and shift as the greyhound jumped out and pulled it further onto the shore. The netting came off, and the Marshal blinked in the sunlight. Fos and Druna were sinking toward the western horizon now; once they were gone the pale green disc of Midori would rise above the mountains.

"How did you do that?" the Marshal asked.

"Is she awake?" the greyhound answered, ignoring his question.

The Marshal looked down at the pine snake. She did not appear injured, but if she had only fainted when the Scarlet Dream agent attacked her, she should have woken by now. He smacked her cheeks gently, but there was no response. Then he noticed the dart in her neck; he had overlooked the tiny barb in their rush to get clear of the city.

Plucking it from her scales, the Marshal tasted the end and spat. "Ullayla root," he said, "Paralyzes but doesn't kill. That mongoose must have shot her, but we came along before he could finish her off."

"We don't have time for this," the greyhound said, retrieving two small backpacks from a clump of bushes. He tossed one to the cobra. "Clothes and food."

The Marshal let the bag hit the beach and slithered onto the shore. He began searching the river plants intently.

"You may know some things about me, point-ears," the cobra said, "But you clearly don't know half as much about the Valley."

The cobra plucked a bright orange blossom with triangular petals. Returning to the boat, he crushed the flower with his fingers and waved it in front of the pine snake's nostrils.

She gasped for air, and her eyes fluttered open; they were silvery white with black pupils. They widened further when she saw who was holding her.

"Lord Marshal," she hissed softly, "What has happened? Where am I?" She had an exotic accent the marshal couldn't quite place, perhaps from somewhere south on the continent of Mwungo.

"The city has fallen," the Marshal answered gently, surprising himself with his tone. "This unusual gentleman here has seen fit to rescue yours truly from the fray, but I couldn't leave you behind when I saw you hadn't escaped the palace."

Her eyes flicked to the greyhound, and she suddenly felt very uncomfortable, crossing her slender arms across her bare chest; despite her profession—and the fact that without true mammary glands there was nothing to hide—she still had some latent desire for modesty in her. The Marshal removed his vest, and after some hesitation, she put it on.

"*Arrête de traîner!*" the greyhound said impatiently, "We have wasted too much time as it is. The army has the valley sealed off, but there is a route over the mountain that will lead us to safety. We must get moving if we wish to meet the truck before sunrise tomorrow."

He started off into the thick vegetation, leaving the snakes staring after him.

"I do not like this man," the pine snake said.

"Neither do I," the Marshal replied.

Turning to the southwest, the Marshal gazed at the smoking ruins of his city. A few of his people may have escaped the army's net as they closed in, but something told him it wasn't many. The Pytian government had learned from their mistakes during the 1930s invasion and would have bolstered their unit with experienced jungle fighters as well as armour support. Few if any would be left to mount a counteroffensive; the army would slaughter every bandit down to the last man and woman—thank whatever gods might exist there were very few children in Jar-Geshim. The only way out for the bandits would be to flee into the Warren, and the Marshal shivered slightly at the thought of what waited for them inside.

No, the bandits of Jar-Geshim wouldn't be bouncing back from this one for a very long time.

The Marshal felt a hand on his arm and turned to see the pine snake staring at him intently. "We shall return, Lord Marshal. They cannot quash a spirit that is truly free."

The cobra smiled sadly, her youthful naivety was somewhat endearing. The Marshal knew better, he'd seen it all before. Despite their nearly lawless society, there were still politics in play here, and the Pytian government had won this round. But if there were any hope left, he would find it in such spirit as hers.

"Too true, my dear," he said, removing her hand and retrieving the pack from the ground.

Inside, the Marshal found a dark tube-shirt, an article of clothing specifically designed for his species which covered roughly half his body. He put it on quickly, slung the pack over one narrow shoulder, and turned to the jungle.

"The government is corrupt," the cobra said, "Eventually they will get lazy, and we will take Jar-Geshim back. But I fear this time it's gonna take a long while to regroup. Right now, all we can do is survive."

Which is exactly what point-ears up there knew I would do, the Marshal thought and started in the direction of the greyhound.

"Don't believe I caught your name, hon," the Marshal asked over his shoulder.

"It is Mavuto, Lord Marshal," she answered, following him into the foliage.

The cobra laughed dryly. "I think my days of being the Marshal are over now, Mav. Call me," and he paused, recalling another life, long ago. "Well, call me Dean."

15 – Dirty Deeds

The Lone Palm Bar seemed typical of a port city like Khet: low ceiling, lit be garish neon, smoke so thick you could barely see through it, music so loud you could barely hear your own thoughts, and packed almost to capacity with broad-shouldered men and floozy-looking women from a wide variety of species.

There were many more aquatic types here than in Det, and a nineteen-years-old Jirair watched them from a table set more or less at the centre of the room. He had taken the surname al-Seif now—in Netib it literally meant "the sands". Jirair considered it a sick play on Saifullah El-Hashem's admonishment that his son's name should be scattered and forgotten, like sand in the wind.

A female lionfish approached his table.

"Get you anything?" she burbled.

The slight gurgle in the lionfish's speech was the result of the water flowing over her gills, produced by the ingenious re-breather collar secured around what would classify as her neck. The bulbous device connected to a pair of tanks on her back and allowed her to remain out of water for several hours.

Jirair studied the barmaid. As a terrestrial being, aquatics always struck the mouflon as odd. At least the sentient insects of Amarthia had the decency to look like hom-an-sized counterparts of their tiny cousins. But aquatics on the other hand...Jirair got the distinct impression fish heads and fins were never meant to fit on an anthropoid body.

At least she was a lionfish, which were attractive even in a non-sentient form. It could have been worse, she could've had the beak and tentacled face of an arthropod.

"Just a beer, please," Jirair answered her before his staring became too uncomfortable. Although, in a place like the Lone Palm she was probably used to leering gazes.

The waitress shrugged and moved away, her fish-tail swaying hypnotically with each dip of her hips.

Jirair ignored the retreating distraction, preferring to go back to feeling very out of place in his environment. He hoped Tan would show up soon so he could get out of there.

Several minutes passed before the lionfish returned with his beer. Jirair took an experimental sip and grimaced at the bitter, watered-down draft that seemed to contain little if any alcohol. He laughed mirthlessly. Oh, how his father would gloat if he could see him now.

Jirair frowned angrily at the thought. Two years had passed since the argument in the lot of the police station, and despite his current circumstances, Jirair had no regrets. Life had forced him to grow up since then. He had even traded the T-shirt and jeans for a more sensible "turtleneck" shirt and tweed trousers. The shirt style, inspired by the shelled reptiles, had become surprisingly popular at the start of the new decade. Welcome to the seventies.

The mouflon took another gulp of the terrible beer and turned his attention to the room, hoping to spy his new employer or at least something that would distract him.

A group of patrons stood huddled around a small cage on a table, watching some sort of animal fight and betting on the outcome. The embattled creatures were small avians with bright blue plumage that ended in a fan of purple feathers at the end of a long lizard-like tail. The head was angular, almost like a gecko but the eyes were much smaller. Two black horns sprouted from the back of the skull.

Jirair recognised them as cauracua, a tropical avian found almost exclusively in the Valley of Nefrit. As he watched, one of the cauracua darted in and tried to strike at the other with its horns, but its opponent leapt out of the way and slashed at the attacker with the small talons on its feet. Both creatures were incredibly fast and appeared evenly matched.

One of the spectators blocked Jirair's view before he could see the end of the fight, and he shifted his eyes down the bar. They stopped suddenly on a melanistic female ibex, sitting alone with a glass of wine. The dark ringlets of her long-fur cascaded down past her shoulders, only a shade darker than the fur that covered her body. Her black and pink floral shirt left little to the imagination with its low neckline, very uncharacteristic for the style of the decade, and one side of the matching pleated skirt was split all the way to her hip, revealing a long shapely leg. But the ibex didn't carry herself like the cheap harlots that hung all over the rough dockworkers and sailors. She seemed more dignified, refined.

And she was looking at him.

Jirair had half a mind to wave her over when the man he had been waiting for stepped into his line of sight.

Ricky Tan was small for a leopard and practically swam in his baggy sports jacket and dark slacks, which flared out around his ankles in the popular "bell-bottom" style. His small green eyes were narrow and slanted at the corners, typical of Amarthians born in and around East Benai. There was a long smooth knife scar under his right eye that stretched almost to his ear, which also had a small chip cut out of it.

"You alone, *pheuxn*?" Tan asked Jirair.

The leopard's accent was heavy and broken, and the word he used sounded faintly like *fee-yen*. In the Benese dialect spoken in Bangkor, Chichu Province, it roughly translated to "buddy" or "pal"; but in this context, it would have been more accurate to say "partner in crime."

"Yes," Jirair said quietly, "I thought you would be here half an hour ago. I suggest we get moving if we do not wish to upset the transport team."

"You talk too good for a dockworker," the leopard said, "Talk like rich boy. You need office job. Maybe you run books for Ricky, yeah?" He let out a high-pitched cackle that sent shivers down Jirair's spine.

"Where ever you need me, Mr Tan," Jirair replied amiably.

Ricky Tan laughed unpleasantly again, he sounded more like a hyena than a leopard. Jirair felt dirty just being in his line of sight, but Tan's named had been bouncing around the docks for almost a year now. The mouflon rationalised that with the right kind of help, Ricky Tan could become a major player in the world of smuggled goods. And Jirair al-Seif wanted to be that right kind of help.

The leopard stopped laughing abruptly and jabbed a clawed finger at the mouflon. "Now you listen good, *pheuxn*, I need you where you are. You know the yard and you know the security. Now, if we running late, let's go."

As they got up from the table, Jirair glanced toward the bar, but the female ibex had vanished.

The Lone Palm rested along the shoreline right next to the shipyard, all the better to serve thirsty sailors and dockworkers. And since shipyards were international territory, they avoided the new alcohol ban put in place by the Sultan to appease the traditionalist Nuadinites.

More importantly, the bar was not far from the main container yard, where stacks of crates waited to be loaded onto flatbeds for transport across the country—trains did not fare well in the sands of Pytan.

Jirair led Tan to a chained service gate where they met a monitor lizard, a sheep, and a bull. All wore cloth masks over their faces and dark clothing. Tan greeted them with a prearranged signal and Jirair turned his attention to the gate. The mouflon had rigged the entrance earlier that day, wrapping the chain around the posts, but leaving the padlock open. The main office of the port was experimenting with analogue security cameras, but out here in the storage yard all the thieves needed to watch for were regular patrols.

Jirair checked his watch and scanned the yard for the tell-tale signs of an electric torch. He spotted one some distance to their left, moving away from them.

"The guard just made his round," he whispered, "I'd say we have another fifteen minutes before he swings back this way."

Tan nodded in response.

The mouflon led the way into the container maze, his eyes darting to the numbers and letters on the side of each steel box as he followed a carefully memorised route. Finally, Jirair stopped in front of a long blue container with markings stating its origin as Libris, on the far side of the Medean Basin.

"You sure this the crate?" Tan asked, pointing to the container.

"I checked it three times before my shift ended," Jirair said, "The materials are there, just like you ordered. As soon as the delivery team arrives with the truck, you will find yourself several hundred thousand carams richer."

"You better make good," Tan said, shaking a clawed finger at the mouflon, "Or I take your horns, yeah? Maybe mount them on my wall."

Jirair wondered if the leopard would make good on his threat; he had a suspicion that Tan's constant grandstanding was compensation for his small stature. The mouflon made a note that if he ever made a threat, he would back it up with immediate action.

The container latch stuck a little and made a horrible screech as Jirair opened it. His companion's cringed at the noise.

"Don't worry," Jirair said, "We should have plenty of time to get the cargo out to the truck before the guard arrives."

That was assuming the other team arrived in the next few minutes. Where were they? The truck needed to park outside the gate, but the delivery team was supposed to come in and help them carry the shipment out of the yard. The packages in question were large and long, requiring two men to move each one. Each bore a "Hastings Research Laboratories" logo on top, printed in large block lettering.

Tan produced an electric torch with a purple tinted lens. "You mark them like I showed?" he asked, flipping the light on and turning the faint beam to a corner of one of the boxes.

The blacklight torch revealed the small "RTX" Jirair had drawn onto each crate earlier that day.

"Hey, what's that?" Tan said, moving the light over the top of the box.

The torch revealed another previously invisible symbol next to the laboratory logo. It looked like the face of a tiger.

"That mean anything to you, *pheuxn*?" the leopard asked accusingly, "You make some other deal?"

"No, mister Tan," Jirair replied firmly, "I had no idea another party had marked these crates. They must have been branded elsewhere. Perhaps it has something to do with their destination?"

Tan popped the latches on the side of the box and opened it to inspect the contents. Inside, packed behind foam peanuts, were bolts of tough fibrous cloth. Jirair was not familiar with the manufacturer, but he knew that it was an experimental ballistic weave called Kevlar.

"Everything look intact," Tan said, resealing the crate, "Whoever other guys are, they out of luck. But I watching you, sheep. This deal go sideways and I tan your hide!"

Jirair nodded solemnly, but the extra mark had him worried. Kevlar was being tested by both military and police to make body armour. However, these particular crates weren't going to any military outfit Jirair had heard of. The manifest he had reviewed listed them as "CO: Belamy Research Labs, Zarazum Crater, Pytan".

As far as the mouflon knew the city of Zarazum Crater was primarily a massive academic facility focused mainly on geological studies—a true oddity among the other settlements of Pytan. Jirair couldn't begin to fathom what a bunch of rock-pickers would want with high-grade ballistic cloth. Not that it mattered; thanks to Ricky Tan they would have to order another shipment.

Tan's confidence is a strength, Jirair thought, *But his lack of knowledge or concern about his competitors is a weakness. I should keep an eye out for this mark in the future.*

Suddenly, Jirair heard the jangle of keys coming toward them through the container maze. He cast a panicked look toward his fellow collaborators, the guard should not be coming back so soon, and they had barely got the first few boxes unloaded.

"Everyone out of sight, get inside!" the mouflon hissed. Tan made to protest, but Jirair shoved him into the container. "No time! I work here, maybe I can chase him away. I swear this is not a double-cross!"

Just as Jirair closed the latch the beam of the guard's torch flashed across him.

"Hold it right there," a voice behind the light said, "Working a little late, aren't you?"

The guard was a zebra, pudgy around the middle, but active enough that he could chase the intruder down if he needed to. Jirair put on his most disarming smile, it wasn't uncommon for a worker to hang around this late in the container yard. He didn't have the right paperwork, but he did have his ID badge—and he knew the guards hated checking paperwork. If Jirair used just the correct jargon, all the guard would do was escort him off the premises. Then he would simply loop around to the side gate and let his erstwhile partners free.

Worse case scenario I have a knife in my belt, Jiriair thought, *but surely there will be no need to use it.*

Even as he thought it, Jirair al-Seif knew he was tempting Fate that night. Just as the mouflon opened his mouth to explain himself, an orangutan roughly Jirair's own age came plodding around the corner, followed by two canines, a cockatiel, and an ant. They were all dressed in dark clothing— although the black ant didn't need it.

"I think you're lost, Mody," the scrawny cockatiel was saying, "The container was supposed to have—" He trailed off as the guard turned to him.

The zebra looked from them to the mouflon still holding the latch on the container, to the four crates that had already been unloaded and stacked on the ground. A cold smile crept onto his long, striped face.

"Working late indeed," the guard said, "What is it? Narcotics? Bootleg entertainment? Pharmaceuticals?"

The orangutan took a step forward, but the zebra put a hand on his gun belt. "Ah, ah, come now, surely we can come to a...arrangement?"

A corrupt guard could be useful, Jirair thought quickly, *but they are also a liability. This one seems a bit too eager to make a deal, he's probably trying to put us at easy before turning. He's a fool to think he can handle us all on his own, but if he could, that would certainly be a story to tell around the watercooler.*

"Ok," Jirair said aloud, "how much? Ten per cent? Won't be much, this is a small-time haul."

"Six men, one an o-rang who could lift two of you?" The guard almost laughed. "Come now, I'm not stupid. You think we don't keep track of the type of contraband that comes through our port?"

Actually, I know you don't, Jirair thought, and another realisation came to him, *He's stalling us.*

Aloud the mouflon said, "It is only imported silks. Really, you caught us on a bad night." Jirair knew he wouldn't be winning any awards with his performance, but he needed the guard to think he was playing along.

"Bad in more ways than one," the zebra said and jerked his head to the container. "Open it up, let's take a peek. Probably more where those boxes came from."

Jirair was glad the darkness made it difficult to see the sweat matting the fur of his brow. Was Tan armed? He couldn't remember. They had more than enough men to overpower a single guard, but if there were gunfire, it would bring the whole yard down on top of them.

The mouflon made a show of tugging on the latch. "Damn sea rust," he muttered, "It's jammed shut."

The zebra drew his gun and motioned for the orangutan to step forward. "I'm sure he can get it open."

Jirair stepped to the side, turning his back to the guard and giving the orangutan a signal to make it look good. The simian wrapped his long fingers around the latch and tugged, moving the bar a fraction of an inch for effect.

"Hey watch it," Jirair warned, raising his arms over his head dramatically. "The cargo may have shifted. If it snaps free you'll go tumble—"

The orangutan threw the latch up and made a show of bumping into the mouflon, shoving him backwards. As Jirair stumbled Into the guard, he bucked his head back and caught the zebra in the shoulder with a curved horn. The equine bellowed in pain and dropped his gun; however, before he could retrieve the weapon, the mouflon was on him, knife in hand.

A strange feeling overcame Jirair at that moment. The stripes and wide eyes of the zebra melted away, and for a second Jirair was staring at another mouflon, the face of his father.

"You will never earn my name," the vision said in his father's voice.

Jirair went pale.

"Your tutors were my whores, and I deprived you of the future you deserve!" his vision-father went on, sneering in contempt.

Rage flooded into Jirair, and he plunged the long blade into the mouflon's chest; once, twice, thrice.

On the third strike, the vision faded and Jirair found himself straddling the fallen zebra. The last of the guard's breath came out with a strangled gurgle.

Jirair sat there panting, his knife buried to the hilt in the guard's chest. He stared at the blood seeping out of the wound and onto his hands, then turned his gaze to the zebra's eyes, staring unseeing at the night sky and the pale green disc of Midori high above.

Jirair staggered to his feet, stumbled off to the side of the shipping container, and deposited the contents of his stomach onto the ground.

Eventually, he recovered enough to stagger towards the delivery crew, now joined by the unloading crew and Ricky Tan from inside the container. They looked at him in silence, then Tan ordered everyone to get moving.

"You lucky that gun not go off," the leopard said grimly.

The orangutan came over to the still-shaking mouflon. "First time you've killed?" he asked simply.

Jirair stared at his bloody hands and nodded.

A giant red-furred hand rested on his shoulder. "It will come easier, but it will never be pleasant. Do not forget that. But do not forget that it was either him or us. That was quick thinking, catching him with your horns. I think he was expecting the knife first."

The mouflon nodded again. When he first joined Ricky Tan's operation, he knew what might be required of him. He wondered what might happen if he ever had to kill. Would he do it? Would guilt haunt him as he pondered what would become of his victim's family? Would he sink into madness as the voices he had silenced tormented his dreams?

But now he had done it. He had snuffed the life out another sentient creature. And he did not feel guilt, he did not feel sorrow. In fact, he felt elated! He had enjoyed killing. And the fact that he had briefly seen the face of his father, the one person he hated most in this world, only seemed to increase his jubilation.

A cold, almost ghastly smile crept onto his face. "I-I did it!"

The orangutan took a small step back, confused by the other's almost euphoric outburst.

"I did it!" Jirair repeated. "I hold the power of life and death in my hands."

The orangutan appraised him for a long moment, then smiled himself. "I believe you will go far, my friend." He reached out a long-fingered hand. "I am Mody Nahas."

The mouflon hesitated a moment. He didn't think it wise to give out his real name, not if he intended to continue down this criminal path. Nahas' comments about his quick thinking and his horns suddenly made him think of the cauracua fight in the bar, and the black horns that the nimble creatures used to strike at each other.

"Assad," he said, grasping the huge hand, "Assad Alabwaq."

16 – Ebony Angel

Jirair al-Seif shifted in his sleep, but his dreams were not finished with him yet. The viewscreen of his mind flashed ahead a year after the events he had just witnessed. He sat at a corner table in the Lone Palm again. The mouflon tolerated the atmosphere now, but the mouflon didn't think he would ever say he enjoyed the place.

It was high summer in the month of Colvus, and the crowd was as thick as the smoke. The A/C barely kept the room at twenty-three degrees centigrade, and it stank of old beer, sweating mammals, and cheap cigarettes. Al-Seif, now operating under the name Alabwaq, almost laughed at the stereotypical seediness of it all.

The cauracua fights were in full swing. One of the black-horned avians faced off against a much larger munski. The scaly rodent-like creature looked ridiculous with its rabbit-like ears and bulging luminous eyes, but tiny sharp teeth flashed when it opened its shrew-like mouth. It wasn't quite an even fight, the cauracua was more agile. It darted in to smack the munski with its sharp horns, stunning the larger creature and leaving it open to slashes from the avian's talons. Within moments the cauracua would be able to deliver the killing blow.

It was such moves that had inspired al-Seif to take the name Assad Alabwaq, and he planned to use similar tactics against his own opponents.

"There aren't any seats left," a soft voice interrupted his thoughts, "Mind if I sit here?"

Jirair looked up and found himself staring into the face of the female black ibex he had seen almost a year ago. She was young, almost too young, she couldn't be out of her teens yet; of course, Jirair himself had only turned twenty a few days ago. Her eyes were pale blue, like water in a pool, and framed by the dark ringlets of long-fur that matched the colour of her shining ebony horns. The melanism that turned her body-fur black was highly unusual and gave her an exotic appearance that Jirair found intoxicating.

She wore the same black and pink floral dress again, and this close to the hourglass figure it covered Jirair found himself struggling to keep his eyes on her face. Two glasses of amber liquid occupied her hands, and she kept them spaced strategically in front of her. He forced his eyes up, and she gave him a dazzling smile.

"Look all you want," the ibex said, "you're the only one who gets the privilege."

The Meddocian inflexions in her voice were like music to Jirair, but his brow furrowed. "I've seen you here before," he said, "but I know we've never met. Why do I get such an honour?"

"Because you are like me," she said simply, "We don't belong in a place like this."

She gestured to the chair again and cocked her head questioningly.

"Please," Jirair said, rising and pulling the seat out for her.

"My name is Carmen," she said, with another brilliant smile, "Carmen Abbatelli."

"Jirair al-Seif," he said before he could stop himself.

Carmen handed him one of the glasses, and Jirair took a tentative sip. It wasn't poisoning he was worried about, it was the questionable quality of the liquor. The brandy went down smooth, too smoothly to have come from the Lone Palm.

He downed the glass in a single gulp and raised an eyebrow at Carmen. The radiance of her smile turned mischievous, and she produced a small crystal flask from her purse.

"Colleté," he said appraisingly, "I doubt The Lone Palm has ever seen a bottle of Medoccian brandy in its life."

"I have a confession to make," Carmen said, swirling the liquor in her glass, "I stole it from *mi padre*, he owns the distribution house here in Pytan."

That got the attention of his Alabwaq side. "Dante Abbatelli?" he said, "Yes, I know that name. However, I was under the impression that outside lovely establishments like this, alcohol was strictly prohibited in Pytan." He leaned forward and placed his elbows on the table, lacing his fingers together in front of him.

"Since the sultan's decree three years ago, yes, it is." She tilted her head down and looked at him coyly. "Only licensed businesses within the international trade zones, such as this bar, may distribute alcohol." She leaned forward, the folds of her dress revealing just a little more. "And locals like you aren't supposed to be in here."

Jirair didn't fall for the distraction of her cleavage this time, he stared her straight in those stunning blue eyes and smiled.

"Perhaps that would be true if I were a Nuadinite," he said, "And even Tunish, the Caprinae god of delights, encourages moderation."

"An antheonist, then?" Carmen asked, raising an eyebrow.

"I have no patience for any of the gods," Jirair replied, sipping at his brandy, "Lately I've even found myself quite disassociated from my own countrymen. As for you, I am quite sure I've read that Aabanite Catholics are discouraged from getting drunk."

"So, between us we have learned not all Pytian's are Nuadinites and not all Medoccians are Catholic," Carmen said, her eyes dancing with light.

She reached into her bag again and produced a slim silver case. Snapping it open revealed a line of thin dark cigarillos. She offered one to the mouflon, and he sniffed it appraisingly.

"At least you acknowledge that Pytan grows the best tobacco," he said.

Smoking was a habit one couldn't avoid picking up when one worked at the dockyards, and Jirair produced a gold-plated lighter which he used to light both his and Carmen's cigarillos.

"Now, I doubt you came to my table to discuss religion," Jirair said, pouring another glass of the brandy and topping off hers. "And we both know our knowledge of quality liquor and tobacco is not what you meant when you said we don't belong here."

The ibex laughed, a musical trilling in her throat that Jirair found infectious. "How do two souls end up in a place like this, eh?" she asked, "Both too wise to be associated with such common rabble, yet seemingly doomed to wallow in society's mud pits?"

The mouflon's brows furrowed. "How indeed," he said, "but I'd still prefer a straight answer."

Carmen puffed on her cigarillo and studied him for a long moment.

"I've been watching you. You associate with that leopard, Ricky Tan. Everyone here knows who and what he is, and are wise enough to let him be. But you." Carmen paused and cocked her head to the side, judging him with her gorgeous eyes. "You show nothing but contempt for him and do not hide it."

"I wasn't trying to hide it," Jirair said, "Tan knows of my contempt for his behaviours. Has he sent you to test my loyalty, or to kill me?"

Carmen frowned slightly, but a mischievous grin quickly replaced it. "What if I were an assassin? This is a nice quiet table. I could leave your corpse propped in the corner like any other drunk."

"With your figure and that dress?" Jirair asked, grinning himself. "There is not one pair of eyes here that wouldn't see you do the deed. You said I was the only one who is allowed the pleasure of staring, but I can see others over your shoulder who did not get the message."

The ibex tapped ash into an empty beer bottle that served for an ashtray. "You could stop them, I know you command respect here. Why else have they refrained from accosting me?"

"You truly believe I have that much influence here?" the mouflon said, "I am not physically a match for half the ruffians at the bar."

"You fight with your mind," Carmen replied, "Go on. Stop them."

Jirair studied her through the smokey cloud between them, then he turned and gave a stern look to the burly patrons who cast leering gazes at the ibex. One by one they averted his gaze and found other distractions.

"You see?" Carmen said without turning, "They respect you. They will not dare to mess with a man whose weapon is intellect. Tan is too blind, and *es stupido*, to see the demon he has created."

Jirair took a final pull on the cigarillo and dropped the stub in the beer bottle. He admired the ease with which this young woman could discuss the use of mind over brawn, and even knowing he was a criminal did not seem to phase her. Yet there was a tone in her voice, one that implied she was both repulsed and excited by the nefarious power he wielded.

"And does this demon tempt this angel?" he asked.

Carmen put her elbow on the table, resting her delicate chin against a balled fist. "There are no angels in this world,

Jirair al-Seif," she said, "Only the demons we create for ourselves. And someday those demons must be paid."

The mouflon raised an eyebrow. He was no poet, but the curious saying was one he could understand. But surely the debt against him had only begun to build.

"Then did you come here to create another demon?" Jirair asked, "Perhaps you were implying earlier that your father has more than fine brandy to sell?"

The ibex leaned back with a huff. "Bah! Let papa dig his own grave with his smuggling. Poor mama would be heart-broken to see what he has come to; mourning that he has no sons to pass the reigns to."

Jirair shrugged apologetically. "Your pardon. Obviously, it is not business you wish to discuss, but I see in you someone who might one day do quite well for herself."

"Indeed?" Carmen said mockingly, "A woman running a business in this man's world?"

It was Jirair's turn to laugh. "That may be true, especially in Pytan, but even now the winds of change blow through Locke and the West United Kingdoms; the pinnacles of what they call western civilisation. This country may have regressed of late, but surely Medocci is not so backward? Did not their ancient armies once possess fierce female warriors? Surely the modern woman can do better than fill out a secretary's desk."

Carmen took a long sip from her brandy, and when the glass came down she was smiling again, but it was cold this time. "You see?" she said, "Different. Too intelligent for a seedy bar. A forward-thinking man, even among the sands. I've been stuck in this shithole since I was a girl. I have done more to help dear papa sell his grappa than he will ever admit to." She leaned forward again, and a fire was burning in her eyes. "But I'll tell you another secret: I'm already planning to get away! I will study business in Locke. Then *mi padre* will see what I can really do!"

Jirair looked at her gravely. "If escape is what you seek, I cannot help you."

Carmen laughed, bright and clear. "No, I have my own way. But if you are so eager to talk of the 'province of men', as *mi padre* would say, there may be something I can help you with."

The mouflon arched an eyebrow. "Is that so?"

"You want to gain an advantage on Ricky Tan, *si*?" Carmen's voice lowered conspiratorially. "Booze does quite well here. And when I am gone, mi padre might discover he needs a new partner."

The ibex leaned back and drained the rest of her bandy.

Jirair let his eyes wander down her body this time. "You are truly a remarkable woman."

Carmen set her glass down and leaned almost double over the table, beckoning him closer with a long finger. "There are no angels in this world," she whispered in his ear, "Only the demons we create for ourselves."

She grabbed him by the lapel and kissed him roughly.

The dream shifted again, flashing through the next several weeks like a movie montage. Those had been some of the happiest days Jirair al-Seif had ever experienced in his life. He spent every moment he could spare with the dark-furred ibex, talking most of the day, and loving deep into the night. He could hide nothing from her, and he discovered he didn't want to. Politics, religion, and especially business permeated their conversation; they even discussed the fact that he had killed a man in cold blood—and there had been more after the guard that fateful night. Nothing seemed to shake or shatter Carmen's desire for him, although Jirair's callous view of life and death did make her uncomfortable on occasion.

Every time he asked her why she endured their conversation she always had the same answer: he was different. They were opposites, drawn inexorably towards each other. If Jirair was to dwell in the province of Death, then she must be Life for him.

But as with all good things, his joy in her was not to last.

One morning Jirair sat up in bed and studied Carmen's figure in the soft light, listening to her breathing as it matched the gentle crash of the waves outside. Carmen's bungalow wasn't much bigger than his own apartment, but the furnishings were better, the walls cleaner, and their privacy complete. In fact, Jirair had already made arrangements to sell his place and take possession of the bungalow after she left. However, he was beginning to wonder if it might be too painful to sleep in the bed alone.

Carmen stirred and blinked up at him.

"Good morning," Jirair said quietly.

The ibex smiled that brilliant, beautiful smile. "Good morning."

He loved her one last time, but when they finally pulled away from each other, he sat on the edge of the bed and stared out the patio doors at the sun-drenched beach and the crystal blue water of the Medean Basin beyond.

Carmen curled up next to him, wrapping her arms around him and resting her head on his shoulder, one cheek nuzzled against the curl of his horns.

"You think these are the last of our days together," she said quietly.

"Perhaps so," Jirair replied, "You have your own path ahead of you. It might be best if your journey took you from here. Far from me."

The mouflon felt her shudder slightly and he turned, letting her fall into his lap. "In just a few days you have come to know me better than anyone in my entire life," he said, reaching down and stroking one of her horns. "But you know darkness lies in my future. With you I can be Jirair, but out there…" He nodded to the beach outside. "I am Assad Alabwaq. You told me you believe I am destined to greater things, but the road I must travel to get there is dark and full of death."

Carmen reached up and touched his face. "There are no angels…" she began.

Jirair shook his head vigorously. "Yes, yes. 'Only the demons we create for ourselves'. But I do not think you realise just how dangerous those demons can be, and the things I may be driven to do."

The ibex leaned up and kissed him, and he kissed her back.

"You will never harm me," Carmen said when she pulled away, "This I know. It may be many years, Jirair al-Seif, but we will find each other again."

That afternoon she was gone, waving from the deck of a liner headed for Locke.

Jirair watched the horizon until the ship vanished from sight. Then he waited until the bright disc of the sun also disappeared, followed by the pale orange day moon of Druna. When the last sliver of light was gone, so too was Jirair al-Seif. The mouflon who turned back to the city of Khet with the pale green night moon rising behind it was Assad Alabwaq.

17 – Stripes

Jirair al-Seif hoped that his dreams would end there, but Fate seemed to have one more vision to show him. Time flashed forwards again, but only by six months, to the beginning of the next year. He stumbled glumly into the smoky atmosphere of the Lone Palm Bar. It was the one place related to Carmen that he couldn't ignore completely; too many of his business dealings went down there. All around him the patrons drank and cheered, starting off the month of Caprus with a traditional binge.

Alabwaq took a table at the centre of the room and ordered a beer from the ever-present lionfish waitress that he still had not learned the name of.

"Damn, you look like shit, *pheuxn*," a voice said.

The mouflon looked up, mildly startled. "Tan," he said, "I didn't expect you back until tomorrow."

The leopard eyed him sideways. "You not get my note?" he asked.

"Apparently not," Alabwaq replied.

The mouflon studied his employer briefly. Ricky Tan had developed an annoying habit of wearing his wealth on his sleeve, and doing so poorly. His wide-lapeled suit was expensive but ill-fitted; apparently, he had paid no attention to his tailor's instructions on keeping the wrinkles out. The silk was also such a garish shade of shiny lavender that it hurt Alabwaq's eyes. Gaudy rings with large jewels decorated the leopard's fingers, and studs and gold hoops lined his earlobes in mismatched patterns. Last but not least, Tan had cut his black long-fur into a bowl-cut made popular by a rock-and-roll band from Locke.

Alabwaq would have laughed if he hadn't been so disgusted at the bizarre mishmash of styles.

"Very well," the mouflon said, "Since I did not get your note, remind me what was in it."

Tan's eyes lit up with a fire Alabwaq knew well. It was the look he got whenever he had just discovered some new enterprise. Even after several years in the leopard's employ, the mouflon was unsure if the look was a good thing or a bad thing.

"I'm bringing new stock, fresh from Adrakar," Tan said, the excitement building in his voice, "They got fire!"

Alabwaq's brow furrowed in confusion. "I don't understand. I thought you went to Adrakar to sell a shipment, not bring one back."

Tan laughed and finished Alabwaq's beer in a single gulp. "I show you!" he said, waving him on with a bejewelled hand.

The leopard led him out of the bar and toward the warehouses at the north end of the dockyards. The security guard saw them and let them pass without incident; Tan had several on his take by this point.

The building the leopard stopped at was a fair distance from the gate, but only two rows off the main avenue leading up to the piers.

"You don't want the clients getting lost, eh *pheuxn*?" Tan said as if by way of explanation.

Alabwaq's look of confusion only grew. He knew this warehouse, as Jirair al-Seif he had helped Ricky Tan purchase this building and several identical ones throughout the yard. Multiple locations made it more challenging to track contraband—especially if you never used the same building twice.

On the outside, it was a corrugated steel structure with wide glass windows on the upper levels and bore the faded brown logo of Crane's Song Industries on one corner. Crane's Song was a manufacturing company owned by Ricky Tan and used primarily to mask his illegal operations.

This particular warehouse was Tan's newest acquisition and was not yet a part of the smuggling rotation. In fact, all Alabwaq remembered about it was receiving the purchase order from Tan a few days after he met Carmen. At the time Alabwaq thought it unusual that his employer wanted yet another warehouse, but he was too preoccupied with Carmen to pay much attention.

Six months was a long time for a warehouse like this to remain off the smuggling roster, something that should have piqued Alabwaq's interest immediately. Even Carmen had warned him that he should not neglect his employer. And yet, all Alabwaq had done at the time was ensure that his own machinations remained hidden and unaffected by his employer, leaving the leopard to his own devices.

If Ricky Tan's excitement was anything to go by, clearly the leopard had been busier than Alabwaq thought.

Inside the warehouse, they passed through a standard arrangement of tall metal shelving units marching from one end of the vast space to the other, each one packed with crated goods of varying size. They stopped in front of one of the largest crates, at least four metres to a side and generically labelled as industrial machine parts. The leopard gave a curious knock on the side and after a few seconds, a quarter panel opened from the inside.

Tan stepped aside and motioned for Alabwaq to step through.

The interior of the crate did, in fact, contain machine parts, but cleverly arranged on moving racks. If customs attempted to pry open the crate normally, all they would find was exactly what it said on the label. But after Tan's clever knock, a pair of muscle-bound frogs inside moved the racks aside, revealing a small caged lift leading down through the floor.

"We change the date on the box every few months and make sure a real shipment goes out at the same time," Tan explained as they descended. "Customs check all they want, but they only find parts."

"Clever, but what are you hiding?" Alabwaq asked.

The murmur from below told the mouflon he would soon find out.

The stairway ended at a short hall with a metal door at the far end. Tan made another knock, and a slot in the door opened to reveal a pair of simian eyes. They took one glance at the two persons standing outside, then the slide shut and the orangutan bouncer opened the door.

Ricky Tan gestured his lieutenant to enter first, and Alabwaq found himself in a tall room plushly decorated in burgundy, gold, and bright pastel draperies with large circular patterns. The mouflon considered the trimmings garish, but after seeing how his employer dressed, he was not at all surprised. A stage with curtained backdrops stood off to one side, and a bar with coat check sat opposite. Low tables and chairs filled the space between, currently occupied by an assortment of richly dressed patrons. Alabwaq noted with interest that they varied in both species and country of origin; clearly, Ricky Tan's market was expanding.

But what drew his attention away from the patrons was the spectacle on the stage. It wasn't the type of show one would find in the nightclubs on the surface; in fact, gladiator exhibitions were widely despised in the so-called civilised countries across Amarthia.

The warriors paraded up and down the stage, bulging with more muscles than Alabwaq thought it possible for a sentient creature to possess. Their gesticulations showed off every inch of their physical prowess to the gawking crowd. And they weren't alone. Each gladiator paraded a scantily clad individual before them, bound with leather ties. Most of the captives appeared to be of half-breed species.

Alabwaq had heard Tan express an interest in slave trading, but he had no idea that his operation had gone so far, or so quickly. Seeing it in person, the mouflon wasn't quite sure what to feel. Surely any moral citizen would be outraged, but the mouflon felt nothing.

Lives meant nothing in the underworld; if Tan or Alabwaq could take them why couldn't they sell them as well? These were no longer people, they were a part of the business; objects whose value depended upon their appearance and usefulness.

In fact, Alabwaq almost admired the spirit of the event; the raw animal power of the gladiators as they pranced on stage, and the cowed timidity of the slaves in the face of that power. In a way, it was a physical manifestation of his own beliefs. The strong controlled the weak, whether through physical might or the shrewdness of intellect.

Alabwaq found himself mesmerised by the show, but Tan tugged at his arm and led him to a pair of double doors at the far end of the room.

Any confused emotions the mouflon may have felt with the gladiator exhibition vanished instantly upon entering the arena itself. His jaw dropped involuntarily as he shifted his gaze from one end to the other; he hadn't known it was possible to hide such a space underneath the warehouse.

The circular arena was at least one hundred metres in diameter. At the centre was a square sixteen metres to a side, and sunk five metres below the spectators, ringed with barbed fencing. Rows of stadium seating, offset by box seats for the VIPs, surrounded the pit. At least two hundred people sat or stood in their seats, revelling in the bloody spectacle below. The sound of cheers and jeers mingled with the clang of metal and the bellow of a ceravaag from the pit in the centre.

The warrior currently embattled was a young frilled lizard with a bright yellow patch on his back. Every time he scored a hit on the cervaag, which aside from the feathers around its neck looked like a distant quadrupedal cousin to the gladiator, the crowd would shout "Solair! Solair!"

Alabwaq took a moment to marvel at the engineering involved with such a venue. He hadn't heard the slightest hint of the cacophony when they were outside in the warehouse.

"Did you build all this?" the mouflon asked.

The leopard laughed, but fortunately, the harsh sound was lost in the din. "No," Tan answered, "This been here long time, before either of us. But old Tenafi, the owner, he retired. I got good price and redecorated."

Alabwaq nodded in understanding. That would explain why he never noticed any major construction and why Tan had not put the warehouse into the smuggling rotation. He still mentally kicked himself for not keeping tabs on what was really going on behind his back; Carmen had been more of a distraction than he thought.

Ricky Tan continued to lead him through the throng of bodies until they reach the owner's box right down next to the edge of the pit. Several low couches allowed them to recline and enjoy the show. Splash guards created from a new shatter-proof material called plexiglass kept the blood contained in the arena.

Alabwaq had to admit there was something infectious about that gory display, an electric feeling in the air that seemed to permeate the crowd. As the mouflon watched, he began to feel his heart race and found himself cringing every time Solair—whom they called the Golden Scale—missed and took a blow from the beast.

Minutes stretched into eternity as the frilled lizard and his distant semi-feathered cousin twisted and slashed at one another. Finally, Solair gained the upper hand and drew the blade of his shortsword across the cerevaag's thick neck. The creature let loose a gurgling bellow, staggered, and went still.

Neither Jirair al-Seif nor his new alter ego Assad Alabwaq had ever heard such a sound as the crowd rose to its feet and roared with triumph for the young lizard's victory. He found himself on his hoofs, clapping wildly and adding his own cheers to the chorus.

As Solair exited and they waited for the next event, Tan called for a few of the slave girls. They were young and healthy, but Alabwaq noticed the dull look in their eyes.

"Heroin," Tan explained, adding one of his hideous cackles. "They stay nice and supple, yeah?"

To demonstrate the leopard ran a hand over the one nearest him, a dreamy-eyed half-tiger, half-cougar with stripes only on her legs and arms. She seemed not to care as Tan put his bejewelled fingers in places they shouldn't be, least of all without her consent.

Then the cougar-tigress' eyes flashed, and Alabwaq realised that her blank stare had been a front. Tan barked in pain as she crushed his hand between her thighs and twisted. A boar bodyguard struck her across the face and yanked her away.

Tan was on his feet, seething with anger and massaging his bruised hand. "Faking, yeah?" he said, and a toothy grin spread across his face as he snarled. "You got spirit! We see you fight!"

The slave girl spat at him and said something in a language Alabwaq didn't understand. Tan merely cackled and waved for the bodyguard to take her away. The leopard found another feline girl—not faking this time—and drew her down onto his lap as he leaned back on the couch.

Alabwaq looked away in disgust and declined to take advantage of the other girls. But he admitted to himself that it wasn't because he despised the act, it was because none of them could compare to his beautiful Carmen.

Several minutes passed before a gong announced the start of the next round and the ringmasters shoved four figures onto the arena floor; Alabwaq was not surprised to see the cougar-tigress among them. They were naked and armed only with simple wooden staves. Three of the four were females, and all appeared to be slaves—they must have somehow displeased their masters like the cougar-tigress had.

Another gong sounded, and the far gate opened. A pack of six crocodile-headed, panther-bodied bahnger stalked into the arena. The brightly coloured feathers on their necks shivered as they shook their heads and hissed at their naked prey, now huddled back-to-back in the ring's centre.

Alabwaq noted with interest that the cougar-tigress seemed to be trying to organise the others, but it was evident that the language barrier was hindering her efforts. Two of the bahngers lunged forward, and one of the girls shrank back, knocking the only male in the group—a horse from one of the smaller breeds—out into the circling predators. The bahngers set upon him in an instant and the fervour of the crowd rose to drown out his death screams.

Assad Alabwaq looked away; not because he couldn't stand the grizzly display, but because he wanted to study the faces of the crowd.

Some he recognised from local business magazines or television commercials, others he couldn't place, but from their clothing, they must have been of some importance. And between them were ordinary people. When the sun rose tomorrow many of them would open shops and greet their customers with a plastered smile.

But Alabwaq saw something more in the wild-eyed crowd: opportunity. For the first time since Carmen Abbatelli left him, a smile crept across the face of Assad Alabwaq.

* * *

"Pleasant dreams, *mi amore*?" Carmen's voice entered al-Seif's dreams.

The mouflon blinked as his eyes readjusted to the morning sunlight. He was lounging on a deck chair on the balcony outside his bedroom, the crystal blue waters of the Medean Basin crashing below, and not far away, the purple and white hull of his private yatch, the *Star of Carmen*. He turned his eyes from the horizon to look into the black ibex's pale blue eyes.

"What is it?" Carmen asked, seeing the pain in his pale-yellow orbs.

"I was just thinking about the past," he answered.

Carmen stared at him silently for a long moment. Then she gently took his chin in one hand.

"The days when you became Assad Alabwaq," she said softly, "If I remember, it was not long after that fate brought us together."

The ibex leaned forward to kiss him.

Al-Seif shook his head and rose to stand by the railing. "That was exactly where I belonged, in the gutters. I'm a monster, Carmen. Dozens, maybe even hundreds of men have fallen before me. All for my empire."

"All for this," Carmen replied sweeping her hand across the villa and the fantastic view over the bay.

"For your prison?" al-Seif asked bitterly.

"You know it is my choice to stay here," the ibex replied.

Al-Seif turned from the sunrise to lean on the balcony railing and look up at the gleaming glass structure of the villa.

"A crystal palace for a fallen angel," he mused.

"You remember what I told you at our first meeting?" Carmen asked, wrapping her arms around him.

The mouflon nodded. "There are no angels in this world..."

"Only the demons we create for ourselves," Carmen finished.

"I distinctly remember a third part about the debt coming due," al-Seif said.

Carmen released him and turned back to the bay, the folds of her nightgown draping around her as she leaned on the railing.

"They may," she said quietly, then cocked her head to her lover, "But not today. Not for many days."

"I hope you're right," the mouflon said, putting an arm around her waist.

They stood in silence for a while. The natural beauty was not lost on either of them, but al-Seif still couldn't shake his anxious thoughts.

"What troubles you most?" Carmen asked without looking away from the view.

"What Freggs is really up to, I suppose," al-Seif answered. "He claims I'm still a valuable asset, but constantly throws objects into my path. Like promising me a spectacle for my arena, then stripping it away."

"Or eliminating the De Palmas just as you gain control of their assets?" she asked.

Al-Seif nodded.

"As I recall," Carmen said, "I advised against giving Freggs access to your warehouse in Kairran. That was supposed to be for legitimate trade, and the arena beneath it would only have tainted the business."

"Yes," al-Seif said, "But he didn't have to destroy half the bloody building to prove his point."

Images flashed in the mouflon's mind. A half tigress with stripes on her arms and legs, and a metal box baring the hidden tiger-face mark. He went rigid.

"What is it?" Carmen asked.

"Stripes," he said.

The ibex blinked at him in confusion.

"There were stripes on that container," al-Seif continued, "The one Tan and I robbed during my first major job for him. I always thought it was odd that a geology facility should be getting a shipment of ballistic fibre."

"I don't—" Carmen began, but her lover interrupted her.

"Those agents sneaking around the arena," al-Seif said, pounding a fist on the railing in triumph, "The ones I think Freggs was really after. They work for an agency called KLAWS, and their emblem uses stripes. I can't believe I never thought of it before!" He gave Carmen a quick kiss on the forehead and hurried towards the balcony door. "Thank you, my dear. I have some phone calls to make."

18 – No Good Deed

Mody Nahas had always had his eyes on Assad Alabwaq's smuggling operation between Medocci and Pytan. It came as a quite shock to the orangutan that Yursa De Palma offered up those assets in exchange for his services.

D'Verant Industries was the subsidiary set up by Vigo De Palma to handle his family's venture into Pytan. The operation primarily dealt in small arms; easily concealed, easily marketed. Despite the small scale of the operation, it had made Assad Alabwaq and Vigo De Palma a great deal of money.

Nahas was appropriately suspicious of the gesture, but the orangutan had to admit it was a smart move on Yursa's part; the operation's connections to the De Palma Shipping lines made it a liability for the wolfhound, especially now that her husband owned the controlling shares on the legitimate end of her company.

The obese simian sat in the back of his armoured Tracksman Hiker—a custom job with an interior as opulently decorated as his home—and marvelled at the plans given to him by the wolfhound. He had everything right at his long, plump fingertips: schedules, tonnage, security assessments, and, most importantly, clients.

The bitch was as good as her word. With all the details Yursa had given the orangutan, it would be no trouble to seize a sizeable portion of the D'Verant Industries fleet.

Nahas picked up a ream of spreadsheets, reading them over with a mixture of wonder and incredulity. It was a beautiful little arrangement, especially since political uprisings were a caram a dozen in Estan. Alabwaq sold the weapons through the D'Verant Industries front, and then quietly informed his friends on the General Council about the sale. The government put the revolution down, seized the arms shipment, and melted it down for precious scrap metal. Which Vigo De Palma then bought through legitimate contacts, shipped using his own freight line, and sold to the arms manufacturers in Medocci.

Eventually, the cycle would start all over again.

Of course, Mody Nahas didn't have Alabwaq's connections with the General Council. If and when the next group of revolutionaries got their hands on an arms shipment, it might have some interesting consequences; particularly with a war going on.

The orangutan chuckled. No, that would not do at all; he would make sure the operation was put on hold for the time being. But there were still advantages to obtaining these resources from Alabwaq, especially while his son was in town.

Delshad had made a bold move by removing those lieutenants that had betrayed him and his father. Without a doubt that would make the rest of his employees think twice before signing over to somebody else. Alabwaq's clients might start feeling the same, but if Delshad were smart, and Nahas *knew* he was, the ibex-mouflon would realise taking violent action against his customers was generally not good for business; a frightened buyer tended not to pay as well as a satisfied one.

And that gave Nahas an idea. Thanks to a little information from Yursa De Palma, the orangutan had learned that several of Alabwaq's clients would be meeting at the port city of Khet to inspect a final shipment from D'Verant Industries. If those clients bore witness to a change in power, like an assault against Alabwaq's hired thugs, Nahas could present himself with a counter offer and convince the smart ones to sign a new deal. Negotiations always went over better when you could prove first-hand that you had the means.

Nahas' chief concern was that Kristoph Weis had laid claim to Khet after Alabwaq fled to Medocci, and the Dolan fox-shepherd would not take kindly to the orangutan operating on his turf.

Nahas' driver pulled to the curb, and the orangutan checked his gold wristwatch. At his signal, six Tracksman Hikers would descend on the piers. The heavy, bread-box-shaped vehicles—built primarily for expeditions out into the wastelands—would discharge a whole platoon of Nahas' best mercenaries. Nahas expected them to overwhelm Alabwaq's guard with minimal casualties and whisk the clients away to a secure location, where the orangutan would meet them personally and present his offer.

Yursa De Palma had already reassigned all the D'Verant crew, there would be nothing to complicate Nahas' operation but the clients. And the orangutan trusted his men too much to believe they would allow them to get in harm's way.

Nahas leaned forward in his oversized seat and checked the horizon. As soon as the sun began to creep over the lip of Khet's outer wall, he picked up the bulky handset of the car phone and ordered his men in.

Khet was a busy port even with the trade season two months away, and the rumble of six diesel engines was lost in the early morning cacophony that was the life's blood of the city. Nahas' men used the rising sun to hide their approach, the steel stop-bars at the gate offering little resistance to the armoured plating of the lead Hiker. The drivers ignored the protests of the guard; they would be gone out a back entrance before the authorities arrived to investigate the breach.

Ten minutes passed. Then fifteen.

Nahas' purple lips drooped in a frown. Something was wrong, the orangutan should have been able to hear the assault on the ships. At the very least his commander should—

The phone rang.

"Yes?" Nahas answered.

"Mody, *mein freund*!" a thin, reedy voice screeched in his ear, causing the orangutan to jerk the handset away from his head.

"Weis? What do you—" Nahas broke off mid-sentence, a sudden realisation coming to him. "You took the ships, didn't you, you bastard?"

"Please, Mody," Weis feined a hurt tone, "I can't believe you wanted to leave me out of your little romp with the wolfhound bitch. Did she squeeze your grapes good?"

Mody Nahas held the phone away from him again as the line filled with a hideous cackling laugh. Once it subsided, he brought the phone back to his ear.

"You're right, Weis," the orangutan said, his voice assuming a placating tone. "Khet is your territory now, and it was presumptuous of me to try operating in it."

"Ah, now that's better," Weis said, "Your men are fine if you were curious. They simply arrived at the dock to find the clients gagged and rigged with stun grenades. It simply wouldn't do to have them interrupting our conversation with reports."

"What do you want?" Nahas was finding it increasingly difficult to remain patient.

Weis' mocking tone suddenly turned cold. "You know you aren't the only one Alabwaq has crossed one too many times, ape. If you plan on taking out his *jung*, I want in. Who knows, we might enjoy our time together."

Not likely, Nahas thought. Aloud he said, "And why would I even consider that?"

The grating cackle came over the phone again. "Because the stun grenades weren't the only thing I rigged on the ship; and while we've been talking, I've found where you parked. How would you like an RPG up your ample simian ass?"

Nahas frowned and leaned forward to gaze out the window. He had ordered his driver to park roughly a block from the gate. A chain-link fence separated the shipyard from city property. Outside the barricade, the nearest buildings were at least a hundred metres away, but on the inside, several large warehouses and cinderblock administration buildings crowded right up next to the fence.

The orangutang spied movement on a number of these roofs and realised too late that his vehicle was terribly exposed. As Nahas watched, he saw a gecko wearing the black and green colours of Kristoph Weis poke his head over the edge of a warehouse roof and balance a long tube-like object on his shoulder. A ferret and a horse followed suit from different buildings.

Weis was not bluffing this time.

Mody Nahas leaned back with a resigned sigh. "Alright, Kristoph. We'll parley."

The cackling triumphant laugh at the other end of the line made the ape wince.

19 - Schism

Georgio Luzetti pulled at the massive wooden doors fronting Saint Ethan's Basilica. The old Aabanite Catholic church was only one of many that dotted Medocci, but it was the most famous one in Pacé Acqua.

It was Aevrday, the middle of the work week, named after Aevira, the ancient Medoccian goddess of centre and balance; try as they might, the Aabanite Church had never been able to get the name changed once the calendar was established. There were few patrons at the church this early, and Met was always a slow month for tourists.

Luzetti always felt funny when he entered a church, especially when he did so to conduct "business". It just felt weird with all the icons of the Twenty-One Martyrs staring down at you from the statues and stained-glass windows.

The Basilica was cross-shaped, with seating for as many as a thousand people, and divided as evenly as possible into twenty-one sections around a central colonnade. The extra sections were filtered into the longest section of the cross, which also served as the entry hall. Each division of pews had a Martyr assigned to it to symbolise all Amarthian kinds, and the shining gold pillar at the centre of the colonnade represented Aaba, the single Deity.

Several points about the arrangement always struck Luzetti as curious. You were welcome to sit anywhere, the unity of all species under God was the heart of the religion, but since each section of pews was assigned a Martyr, it often felt like only that species should sit there. Canines and felines always got the front rows, all the various species of birds and reptiles got only one representative Martyr each, and aquatic and insect species always hung out in the back rows.

It was difficult to think of a single Deity treating all sentient Amarthians equally when His house of worship seemed so segregated. This went double for Luzetti, who was half stoat and half squirrel.

Despite the soft pads of his feet, Luzetti's steps echoed through the cavernous space as he made his way towards the central colonnade. He passed by the rodent section, Saint Tellemius, and made the proper signs as he went by.

He also thought it was funny they called them Martyrs. After all, the story was that some two thousand years ago an angry mob gathered the Twenty-One together with the intent of crucifying them for spreading the belief that Aaba could forgive all the transgressions of Hom-an kind with the sacrifice of a soul not born of Amarthia. Well, just before the Twenty-One were to be put to death, a supernatural being of light appeared and offered to stand in for them, thus fulfilling the very prophecy the angry mob wanted to kill them for. The Twenty-One then went forth into the world to tell of their miraculous salvation, and the Being of Light whom they believed was Aaba Himself.

The stoat-squirrel stopped at the section devoted to Saint Elias, patron Martyr of Canines. There was only one occupant in the row, a tall wolfhound with rust-coloured long-fur and dressed entirely in black.

"Ms De Palma," Luzetti said quietly.

His voice still seemed to echo in the hush of the church.

"Sit beside me," Yursa said.

Luzetti did so and discovered the sound suddenly deadened.

"It's amazing, these old churches," Yursa said without looking at him, "If you sit just right you can hear as much or as little as you want."

"The crews for three of your D'Verant ships are awaiting reassignment," Luzetti said, getting right to the point. "Mody Nahas made his move, and Kristoph Weis intercepted him just as you thought."

Yursa cursed then made a sign. "I knew they wouldn't be able to pull off a simple task without getting in each other's way."

"Not entirely, ma'am," the stoat-squirrel said, "Both have agreed that Mr Alabawaq has been, shall we say, detrimental to their livelihood. They have decided to work together for the time being; at least for as long as it takes to deal with Alabwaq's son."

Yursa pondered this in silence for a moment.

"Could they become a threat?" she asked.

"Not here," Luzetti replied, "Even together they don't have the connections to move into Medocci. But they may make it difficult for our businesses in Pytan."

"To hell with them," Yursa said vehemently and made another sign. "I loved my father, but I always thought it was a mistake trying to expand so far away from home."

"Speaking of which," the De Palma lieutenant replied, "there are rumours that the Forreza, Favera, and Costellianos will soon move against us."

"Together?" the wolfhound asked.

Luzetti smiled coldly. "No. In fact, we believe they will move on each other as well. They'll be trying to prove they have the balls to fill your father's place. I've already put your men on alert for any activity."

"Good." Yursa lifted her eyes to the vaulted ceiling of the cathedral. "What about the consolidation of my father's assets?"

"Things are progressing, but slowly. We've isolated some of the mineral trades with Libris, but I'm afraid al-Seif's acquisition of the entire shipping line has made it quite difficult to separate the foodstuffs from his control."

"I knew papa should have diversified more," Yursa said with a sigh. "But it won't be long before I hold the reigns again. We have only to remove al-Seif."

Luzetti frowned. "Ma'am, I trust you as much as I did your father. But this vendetta against al-Seif—"

"Don't go there, Luzetti," Yursa said, letting loose a low growl. "That bastard will pay for what he did to my father. He will have his hands full with the coming war between the families, but I will ensure he does not survive it."

"Can you also ensure he doesn't intentionally damage your father's legacy before you can restore it?" the stoat-squirrel asked.

Yursa turned to him now, and Luzetti shrank back from the fire burning in her eyes.

"I will see Jirair al-Seif's empire burned to the ground, even if it takes everything my father left me with it."

She rose and made her way out of the row, pausing only briefly to perform the signs before exiting. Luzetti listened to the click of her foot claws as they echoed into the distance.

* * *

Even as Yursa De Palma left Saint Ethan's, the wolfhound's enemies were making there moves.

The Knife—that was the only name he went by—drummed his thick scaly bird-fingers on the steering wheel as he patiently waited for his target. No one knew how a kookaburra had ended up in Medocci or earned his place as an enforcer for Rosco Forreza, but that was just how the Knife liked it. All he cared about at that moment was whether he could pull this hit and still make it to Gino's to catch the football game.

Taking over one of the De Palma's money laundering operations this close to the patriarch's death was pretty risky, but Forreza liked risk, and so did the Knife. After some light observation, the kookaburra thought he had staked a good claim for his boss.

A diminutive mouse exited the loan service across the street, and the Knife got out of his car. The kookaburra used his wings to launch himself across the street and set down right in the mouse's path.

The bespectacled rodent squeaked in alarm and put a hand to his chest. "Holy shit! Watch where you're flying!" he panted.

The Knife continued to loom over the clerk. "The De Palmas aren't coming back," he said.

The mouse's eyes, already large, widened. "I don't know any De Palmas. Who are you? What do you want?"

The Knife produced a lengthy version of his namesake from a vest pocket. "Don't play the fool. Forreza knows you ran books for Vigo De Palma, and now that he's gone, we're going to collect."

The mouse's eyes followed the blade as the kookaburra twirled it around his scaly fingers. "I-I need time," he stammered, "Yursa, she's pulling everything in tight. I can't just—"

The Knife spun the mouse around and placed a feathered arm around his shoulders. He gestured toward the loan service with his blade. "Now don't you worry about the bitch. We already have plans for her. But Forreza needs to move some capital quickly, and you seem like just the rat to do it."

The mouse stiffened at the apparent insult, but his eyes never left the blade in the bird's hand. Slowly, he nodded.

The Knife smiled. "See that wasn't so bad. I'll be back after closing time with further instructions. In the meantime, why don't you produce some of De Palmas old books so Forreza can get a better idea what kind of operation you're running here?"

Again, the mouse nodded. However, the Knife misinterpreted the gesture. The kookaburra was too busy intimidating the mouse to notice that at the end of the block, a ferret had flashed a signal to the clerk and crossed to the other side of the street.

"Remember," The Knife said, "not a word. Or I might have to write the next couple entries in your books with your blood."

He shoved the mouse away and flapped back over to his car. As the Knife got in and started the engine, he caught a blur of motion out of the corner of his eye and heard the crash of glass as the passenger window shattered. Turning to investigate, something hard struck the Knife across his beak.

"Don't fuck with the De Palmas, *stronzo*," the ferret said, jabbing the kookaburra with the blunt end of a wooden stud again.

The Knife struggled to get out of his seat, but the ferret jammed the timber against the driver's door, temporarily pinning his arms down. Two green grapefruit-sized objects thunked onto the floor at the Knife's feet, and the ferret darted into a nearby alley.

The Knife's car erupted in a fireball.

Across the street, the orange light gleamed on the mouse clerk's teeth and reflected off his round spectacles.

* * *

Being a rat wasn't the only reason Emmy Garza went by the nickname "the Rat". People knew the short, round-framed rodent got into some underhanded dealings and was what his cousins in the WUK would call a "cheapskate". Sure, he was reinforcing a negative stereotype for rats, but it kept him in linen suits and fancy restaurants, didn't it? Of course, a couple of smart plays with the Favera family had also helped with that.

And things were certainly looking up for the Favera now. With Vigo De Palma dead there were a lot of opportunities for a guy with connections. And Emmy the Rat was a guy with connections, especially in Scogliera Piatta, Medocci's capital.

Garza adjusted the lapels of his dark tailored suit and checked the traffic on Via San Baptiste. Nothing was coming, so he made his way across and turned up Via Cassini, headed for the Bella Venuva Hotel and Grego Favera's base of operations.

Oh yes, it was going to be fine times for the Favera. They just needed to get rid of Yursa De Palma and move in before the Forreza, or the Costellianos did, but Emmy had an idea about that too.

Drugs. Drugs were the answer. The De Palmas had always been soft there, some nonsense about keeping kids clean. Yet, the De Palma patriarch hadn't had any problem with weapons, gambling, and other illegal goods.

Better a thug than a junkie, eh Vigo, Garza thought, *Grego won't be so soft. Not after he hears what Emmy the Rat has to say.*

He was so preoccupied with his pitch to the Favera Mafioso that he didn't notice the black sedan gliding up behind him.

The last thought that Emmy "the Rat" Garza had before the Costellianos' gunman spattered his brains against the wall was: *I'm telling you, Grego, cocaine is the high of the future!*

* * *

Captain Leo Donetteli shifted his prodigious weight out of the police cruiser. A lion shouldn't have drooping jowls, but the captain couldn't avoid them thanks to his love of good food. The flaps of skin wobbled as he shook out his dusk coloured mane.

Another pleasant late winter day was forming in Illia, far to the north of Pacé Acqua and Scogliera Piatta in the foothills that marked the lower edges of the Sweisæ Alps, the dividing line between Medocci and Vösleis. There had been light snow that morning, but it had melted by noon, leaving the cobblestone streets damp.

Donetteli had been hoping that the day would remain as quiet as the week had started. Then this call came in.

A uniformed capybara greeted the captain at the door to the café. No fat jokes or jibes about his superior being named after his species today, in fact, the officer looked ashen underneath his tawny fur.

It didn't take long for Donetteli to figure out why.

The dining area had transformed into a war zone. Tables were overturned, glass and cutlery lie scattered every which way, and blood spattered the fresco along the back wall. A line of tightly spaced holes snaked its way from one end to the other, shattering the once beautiful artwork. The only gaps were where the victims had been standing. To the captain's practised eye, the bullets appeared to be medium calibre, but only an automatic weapon could have supplied the quantity.

Regardless, they had done their work on the bodies.

There was at least a dozen of them, mostly mammals. A fox family sat crumpled in a booth on one end, the mother leaning protectively over her cub and the father laying sprawled on the table. Down the line came a mixed table of four: a male dingo, a male iguana, and two female felines; from the age range and clothing Donetteli guessed they were students from the nearby university. On the opposite end of the café was the owner, a venerable old anole lizard; he was slumped over his til with at least three slugs in him.

But it only took Donetteli a moment to discern that the victims at the centre of the massacre were the primary targets.

The porcupine was Lieutenant David Narsi, the two otters were known as the Torrento Brothers, and the tall leopard was none other than Georgio Crosetti, second cousin to Freddy Costelliano, the half-brother of the big man Maccello Costelliano himself.

"Holy Saint Eraphas," the lion breathed, blasphemously invoking the patron Martyr of all feline kinds. He'd seek confession later, after seeing this mess he felt he would be swearing quite a lot in the coming days.

He turned to the nearest officer, another lion who was much thinner than Donetteli. "What happened?" he asked.

The officer produced the yellow scratch pad. "Eyewitnesses spotted a brown compact drive by at eleven this morning. The plates registered the vehicle to Carlo Favera. Naturally, he declared the vehicle had recently been stolen."

"Of course he did," Donetteli said, growling low in his throat.

"Isn't that Crosetti on the floor over there?" the officer asked.

The captain sighed heavily. "Yes, it is. Freddy isn't going to be happy to hear his cousin's dead."

"And it looks like IA was right about Narsi," the officer said.

The porcupine detective had been under investigation by Internal Affairs for taking bribes from the Costellianos.

"Seems that way," Donetteli said with a chuff, "But even a corrupt cop doesn't deserve to go out like this."

The other lion put his pad away in a breast pocket. "Think they were actually after Narsi and Crosetti?" he asked.

Donetteli took another long glance at the carnage. "No," he said flatly, "Not for Narsi, at least. This was the first strike in a war. Mark my words, this is only the beginning."

20 – Zarazum Crater

"As you can see, the crater, much like the Valley of Nefrit, is one of the rare locations in Pytan where jungle vegetation thrives. It is sixty-four miles in diameter, almost three miles deep, with a total surface area of almost eight thousand three hundred square miles. And yet, despite multiple borings near the epicenter we have not been able to recover a single meteorite, leaving the cause of the crater quite a mystery. We discovered traces of ancient ruins in the bowl, which we believe to be all that remains of a once great city near to the centre of the blast. The newer ruins along the lip were probably built by later civilizations who came to—"

"That's is all very interesting, Professor," Delshad al-Seif said patiently, "But I'm afraid I simply do not have time for a complete lecture."

The elderly chinchilla, one Professor Marcus Thomas, blinked and turned back to his guest. "I'm sorry?" he said, "Oh! Yes, I am sorry. It is all quite fascinating work, but I do get carried away."

The ibex-mouflon and the chinchilla stood outside the main hall of the Zarazum Crater Geological Institute. Despite the lush tropical jungle spreading out to the edges of the crater, the institute itself was a thoroughly modern university campus complete with lecture halls, grassy quads, and even a sports arena; all built along the southern edge of the large lake that flooded the centre of the crater.

Of course, just to get inside Delshad had to have his pilot land his father's helicopter on the rim of the crater, then pass through no less than three fortified security gates under the watchful eye of heavily armed patrols. Researchers they may be, but the permanent inhabitants of Zarazum Crater weren't stupid.

As an international research community, the University operated apart from Pytan's laws but tried to observe most of them out of respect for the host nation. Assad Alabwaq and his rivals left them alone because, beyond scientific curiosity, there really wasn't much of value in the crater. Or at least that was their excuse.

Had Professor Thomas gone on with his lecture, he would have revealed that there were actually several ancient ruins scattered around the bowl, and all of them were of particular interest to the Soketh tribe know as the Blue Feather—although not all of them were birds. The nomads were fiercely protective of ancient knowledge, and a substantial number of them had taken up semi-permanent residence within the Crater; even the researchers had to defer to them before proceeding with any excavations.

And the Soketh had an extremely low tolerance for thieves and smugglers like Assad Alabwaq.

The only reason Delshad was here now was that his father believed he had discovered a lead on the agents that had destroyed his facility in Kairran, and had hoped he could learn more about their operation.

Professor Thomas adjusted the pith helmet on his head, his large ears stuck out through holes in the crown. "Could you remind me what it was you were searching for?"

Delshad smiled ingratiatingly. "Many years ago, my father helped move some materials for Belamy Research Labs. It sparked his intellectual curiosity and mine. I was hoping to inquire about their latest developments."

"Belamy, you say?" the chinchilla asked, scratching at an ear. "Hmm, we get so many smaller labs that rotate through here. Never on a permanent basis, you understand. There is a Dr Simon Belamy who works over in Artefact Cataloging; perhaps he's related? Though I dare say, he's been here as long as I have."

"Thank you, Professor," Delshad said quickly, "If you could point me in the right direction I'll let you return to your own work."

"Yes, of course. Thank you."

It wasn't a long walk, and Delshad had an excellent sense of direction. He was momentarily distracted by a pair of female ferrets in lab coats crossing the quad and wondered if either of them would be interested in a helicopter ride over the crater. Regretfully, he turned his mind back to the task at hand; his father's work needed to take precedence here.

Tel'Nadi Hall was on the far eastern edge of the campus, an impressive building crammed with offices and large temperature-controlled rooms lined with row upon row of storage shelves. Each shelf was carefully labelled and laden with a variety of ancient pieces of stone, wood, and other material Delshad couldn't identify.

The ibex-mouflon was actually saddened that he couldn't take the time to learn more about the pieces. He might not be as enthused as one of the researchers, but he did have an appreciation for old civilisations; specifically, in the rulers and how they maintained their power.

The professor Delshad was looking for was a light-furred badger whose appearance immediately made him think of a beach ball. The multi-coloured shirt he wore under his wrinkled lab coat didn't help dissuade the impression.

The badger was currently fussing over a labelling machine and a large stack of pottery shards.

"Dr Belamy?" Delshad asked, "My name is Delshad al-Seif. I was wondering if I could ask you a few questions about one of the labs that use to operate here in the crater."

The badger looked up from his machine and adjusted a pair of round spectacles on his snout. He scratched subconsciously at his side. "I'm sorry, do I know you?" Belamy asked in a slightly self-important tone. "I'm afraid I'm quite busy, The Soketh just gave us permission to start cataloguing pieces from Site D."

Again, he scratched at his side.

"Is something wrong?" Delshad asked.

"No," the badger huffed, "a bit of poison ivy. Or something like that. Ask Daniels in the botany lab, there must be a hundred varieties of the stuff here."

"Sir," Delshad went on patiently, "I wanted to ask if you remember a research lab here that bore your name."

Belamy's eyes narrowed sharply. "Who are you? Insurance adjuster? You're a good twenty-five years late on my claim."

The ibex-mouflon held up his hands in a placating gesture. "Please, doctor. I'm afraid I don't know what you're talking about. I found some old papers in my father's study about materials he traded to—"

"That was it!" Belamy interrupted him. "Materials! They shut down my lab because of several thefts. When I couldn't perform my experiments, I lost my grant money. Fortunately, the University board of directors took pity on me and stuck me here."

"What sort of materials were stolen?" Delshad asked.

"Oh, that was the biggest insult," the badger said. He scratched at his side again then forced himself to stop by folding his arms across his prodigious front. "It was mostly small things; a few microscopes, some sampling equipment, Bunsen burners. I swear it was Doyevsky who did it, back in those days things weren't so pleasant between Mosvia and the WUK. They still aren't, really."

Delshad frowned. "That was all? No cloth materials of any kind?"

"You mean like tent canvas or tarps?" Belamy asked, taking a cloth out of a coat pocket and cleaning his glasses. "No, why would we need that? The University can supply such material if we need it. Still, it was twenty-five years ago. I can't recall us ever needing any specialized cloth materials."

"It wasn't canvas," the ibex-mouflon said, "I believe the old packing list mentioned it was Kevlar, or at least an early prototype."

"Kevlar?" Belamy grumbled, "What the devil would we need Kevlar for? The campus guard has their own supplier. This is a geology station, not a textile mill."

Exactly what my father thought, Delshad mused. Aloud he said, "I have one more question that might be a little closer to your level of expertise."

"Fire away," the badger said, growing a little friendlier with the change of subject.

"Have you catalogued any unusual fossils here?"

Belamy scratched at his nose, then his side again. "Unusual? My boy, this site is well over three thousand years old, maybe even closer to four; well before any of the ancient sultans rose to power. Everything we uncover here is unusual. But in terms of actual bone specimens, no, not that I can think of. The ancient city had a pretty broad population. Not as diverse as our modern world, of course, but still a pretty standard assortment of mammals, reptiles, and birds."

"Any animals?" Delshad asked, meaning non-sentient species.

"No, just people," Belamy answered, "We suspect the ancient Amarthians either hadn't grasped the concept of domestication or kept the farms far from the city. Before this crater appeared, the land was as arid as the Sultan's Drifts outside Kairran; too hostile for most of the predators that inhabit Pytan."

"So why build a big city way out here?" Delshad asked.

"Precisely!" the badger said giving an emphatic gesture, "Professor Thomas has some amazing theories on that. Of course, the Soketh just smile and nod when they hear them, and they won't tell us what they think."

"What about the native wildlife now?" Delshad asked.

"Oh, your standard mix of bahnger and ceravaags," Belamy said, "We never go outside the gate without an armed escort, usually in the form of a squad of Soketh."

From the badger's tone, Delshad guessed that the professor suspected wild animals weren't the only thing the guards were keeping an eye on.

Delshad couldn't sense any deceit on the part of Professor Belamy. His father would be disappointed, but Delshad knew he would understand the circumstances. The trail had been cold for far too long.

The ibex-mouflon checked his wristwatch. "Well, I believe I've taken up enough of your time, Professor. Thank you again."

"Not at all," Belamy said and turned back to his labelling machine, scratching at his side again.

Delshad found his own way out of the building and back across the campus. A University utility vehicle drove him out to the helipad, and as he approached the waiting aircraft, the pilot hailed him and held up the bulky handset of a satellite phone.

"Urgent, sir," the muskrat said.

Delshad took the phone. "Yes?"

"Tunis here, Mr Alabwaq," the hesitant voice answered, "You assigned me to the Nanca Fier transport."

Delshad acknowledged with some trepidation; the transport run in question was a shipment of arms for a guerrilla faction in Bozambwe, and vital for maintaining Alabwaq's hold in that region.

"Sir," Tunis went on, "It's the convoy. It's…my gods." There was something like a choked sob in the speaker's voice. "You need to see this. I know it will take time for you to arrange transport, but please hurry!"

Tunis gave a set of coordinates for his employer to plot the journey. Delshad did not need a map to know he would be heading into the middle of nowhere; that was the point of the convoy's route.

The ibex-mouflon handed the phone back to the driver and ordered him to make all speed for Tanahwi on the southeastern-most tip of Pytan.

* * *

Through the blinds of his office, Professor Marcus Thomas watched the speck that was Delshad al-Seif's helicopter fade into the distance. Once it vanished from sight entirely, he picked up the phone on his desk and dialled.

"Yes?" a mechanical voice answered.

"Uh, Mr Freggs, sir?" Thomas half stammered.

"Ah, Professor!" Freggs said as cheerily as the voice filter would allow. "How are we today? I take it you are calling because there's been a discovery?"

"Uh, not quite, sir," Thomas said, then quickly added, "But we are making great progress! As you know the Soketh are very protective, and without your generous contributions—"

"Marcus," Freggs interrupted tiredly, "Please get on with it. I know you wouldn't have called unless it was important."

"Oh, yes!" The chinchilla snapped to attention despite being alone in his office. "Well, I wanted to tell you we just had a visit from a Mr Delshad al-Seif, a businessman from Pytan."

"I've heard of him."

"Well, sir, he was asking some rather odd questions about Belamy and that research program he ran twenty-five years ago. The one that got shut down because his equipment kept getting stolen?"

"I am familiar with Dr Belamy as well," Freggs said, obviously waiting for a point.

"Well, I just thought you'd want to know when something unusual happened, sir. And asking about a research project that's been gone for twenty-five years is unusual."

There was silence at the end of the line for a long moment.

"I wouldn't worry about it," Freggs said at last. "I doubt his inquiries had anything to do with your project. How is Dr Belamy?"

"Oh, just fine," Thomas replied, "I admit I don't remember what his original program was all those years ago, but he was quite distraught when the funding dried up, and it looked like he would have to go with it. As you know, it was thanks to your donations that the board was able to pay for his tenure and keep him on. I'm sure he'd love to thank you himself if you want me to transfer you—"

"No," Freggs said, a little too quickly, "I'm sure the good doctor has enough on his plate. Carry on, Professor. We are very eager to see what you may discover at the bottom of the lake."

The line went dead, and Thomas stared at it blankly for several minutes before returning the receiver to its cradle. The professor could understand why some of their high-profile donors would want to remain anonymous, but he didn't know any that went to such great lengths as to use a voice filter.

Across the campus, unbeknownst to Thomas, Doctor Simon Belamy was also making a call; and scratching absently at the Tiger's Mark on his right side that made his fur tingle.

21 – Usurper

It started to rain again, not at all surprising for the month of Epris, the height of the rainy season in Bangkor. Mudslides plagued many of the jungle villages and made the roads treacherous. And as if that wasn't enough, nature also dictated that it was mating season for the river serpents and jawjaqus—crocodile-like predators with long toothy snouts and bristling with porcupine quills.

But the reason Assad Alabwaq had put together a convoy of three armoured utility vehicles wasn't that of the weather or the predators or even a chance encounter with the socialist radicals of the Khai Longshoon who controlled this region. The time had finally come for the mouflon to remove the final obsticle blocking his path to power.

His driver, a wiry jackal with the almost prissy name of Tarren, pulled to a stop at the bottom of a hill, the utility vehicles following them pulling in behind. A stone stairway with a wooden railing on one side snaked its way up the slope to a compound containing a handful of structures and one long house with two tall stories. Mortared stone walls surrounded the complex, but the main building itself was composed of open balconies and tile roofs that curled upwards at the corners. Everything was trimmed in gold leaf with banners of gold and sky-blue snapping in the wind; the emblem on the banners depicted the nude upper torso of Dhav'Tashi, feline goddess of pleasure and delight, with her hands clasped above her head.

Overall the compound reminded Alabwaq of pictures he had seen of a feudal Benese fortress. He would have expected nothing less from the home of Ricky Tan.

The leopard's organisation had grown considerably since a young dockworker named Jirair al-Seif had joined him four years ago. They had gone from textiles and guns all the way to a string of narcotics dealers and slave traders. Tan had even obtained a gladiatorial arena hidden under a warehouse in Khet.

The money had come rushing in, and Tan was eager to spend those ill-gotten gains.

The mouflon climbed out and stood in the driving rain; an umbrella would have been useless in this downpour. His jackal driver and two other men also exited, joined shortly by the henchmen from the other utility vehicles. All of them except Alabwaq carried compact submachine guns with large silencers attached to the muzzles. They also wore two-toned sashes of purple and gold around their waists, colours that Assad Alabwaq had decided would become his personal emblem.

Alabwaq didn't play favourites among species, he hired men and women who would get the job done. Those that surrounded him now were loyal only to him, and a few had very personal reasons for being part of this mission.

The mouflon paused, letting the rain soak through his silk suit. It plastered his dark long-fur to his head and gathered in his purple and gold horn tassels, causing the threads to clump together. He was actually dreading what came next. It had to be done, of course, there was no question about it, but Tan had been the one to get him this far. It was almost a shame to have to take him out.

Almost.

He motioned to his henchmen, and they split up; three went around the left side of the hill, and three went to the right, the rest started to climb the stairs.

The rain was actually a blessing, Tan's guards didn't see them coming until it was too late, and the heavy drumming downpour masked the muffled pops of the submachine guns.

Less than five minutes passed before Alabwaq saw Tarren the jackal step out the main gate and wave him up.

The opulence of the home's interior almost made the mouflon gag. Not because he didn't enjoy the finer things, but because their arrangement was so gaudy and mismatched that Jirair's own sense of taste found the display revolting. It seemed that Ricky Tan was embracing the 70s with as much gusto as his tiny frame could muster.

There were archways everywhere, and each room had so many geometric lamps and furnishings, Alabwaq felt he had stepped into one of Cornelis Mauresch's famous optical illusion paintings. The shag carpets had faux Barjan, Benese, and Pytian designs, not dreadful in their own right, but lined up on top of each other so that their colours and patterns clashed terribly. Gold and obsidian statuary—mostly naked feline women—lined the walls, backed by heavy maroon draperies. Vaulted ceilings arched high overhead, painted with graphic imagery from the fabled Vitallis Sumatra—again the lewd drawings depicted mostly felines. Alabwaq had to admit the artist was talented, but the subject matter was tasteless.

Ricky Tan lay on a kidney-shaped couch at the centre of the main room, arms raised, ears back, and teeth bared in a vicious snarl. One of his concubines—surprisingly, a fennec fox vixen—sat huddled in a corner, sobbing quietly.

Tan glared at the man he knew as both Jirair al-Seif and Assad Alabwaq. "So, this is it, yeah?" he asked, "You come for me in my own house? You got balls, *pheuxn*."

Alabwaq looked down his long nose at the leopard. Tan's silk suit was an excellent cut similar to the mouflon's own, but it had a bright green paisley pattern that hurt Alabwaq's eyes just to look at. Large gold chains hung about the leopard's neck, a few sporting symbols of virility from several cultures—the most prominent being Dhav'Tashi.

Yes, Alabwaq thought, *The world will be better off without this fop attempting to act high-class.*

"This is it," the mouflon said slowly.

Tan growled low. "You move quick, I give you that. I knew you come, just not now. Maybe another two year, maybe five."

"Are you familiar with the cauracua?" Alabwaq asked, stoking the purple feather he wore in his lapel. "You should be, as many times as you forced me to meet you at the Lone Palm in Khet. They move very quickly, using the black horns on their head to stun their prey so they can move in for the killing blow."

"Ok, I get it," the leopard said, starting to squirm in his seat; his arms were getting tired from holding them up, or maybe it was from supporting all the gaudy rings on them. "I'm stunned, you boss now. I still got contacts, can still help."

"Listen to you," Alabwaq said coldly, "mewling like a cub. All of your contacts are *my* contacts, they have been for the past two years. And it was your own doing. It was always me you sent to make the deals while you lived it up in your arena." He shrugged. "I just made a few of my own deals on the side."

The mouflon stepped forward and drew a pistol from a concealed shoulder holster. "I should thank you. I would never have got this far without you. This is all mine now."

Three shots cut Tan's final protest short. Alabwaq put two bullets through the leopard's chest and one through his head. The concubine screamed, and he turned the gun on her but paused.

"No," he said flatly, "You're too pretty. You'll go to auction."

Alabwaq put the gun away and turned to his driver. "Round up any slaves you might find," he said, "If any of the surviving guards seem like good fighters save them for the arena. Burn the complex. If you actually want anything, take it, but burn the rest to the ground."

Without another word he spun on his hoof and stepped back out into the pouring rain.

* * *

From the shadows, a figure stood patiently watching the mouflon's men slaughter the guards. The luminous gold eyes remained unblinking as they calmly watched the one called Assad Alabwaq deftly murder the small leopard, Ricky Tan. The black panther's tail wanted to twitch, but through a sheer act of will the watcher forced it to lie as still as the obsidian statue he hid behind.

He was most curious about the mouflon. He had displayed a will of iron while the watcher's former employer lay petulantly on the couch, trying to think of a way to save his hide instead of facing his doom. Perhaps this Alabwaq was the one he sought, a man truly worthy of his protection and devotion.

For now, the watcher would have to wait; but someday, very soon, he must confront this Assad Alabwaq and learn what sort of man he really was.

22 – Leads

Jirair al-Seif's eyes opened slowly. His dreams were more pleasant this time. Overthrowing Ricky Tan's organisation was undoubtedly a high point in his rise to power.

It was Taursday, the De Palma funeral was set for tomorrow, but al-Seif was growing increasingly restless waiting at his villa. He could only imagine how his beloved Carmen felt; his fear for her safety had kept her confined within the villa's walls for much of the last ten years. The mouflon wouldn't even let her attend parties without either himself or Abar Kami standing guard.

Maybe he could change that today.

After a shower and breakfast, he went into his study and picked up the phone.

"*Buongiorno, parla il signor* Torosian," a mild voice answered when the call connected.

"Ignatius, it's Jirair al-Seif."

"Al-Seif, *salam ya sadiqi!*" Ignatius Torosian replied, switching from Mecci to Netib without any obvious effort. "To what do I owe this pleasure? Another business venture, perhaps?"

"Not exactly," the mouflon answered, "But I would like to speak with you. Are you free for lunch this afternoon?"

"For you? Of course! But I would like to know a little more if you can spare details."

"Not over the phone, but it does concern shipments we both lost recently under very unusual circumstances."

There was a brief pause on the other end. "That is most cryptic, my friend, but if it concerns you that much, I will do my best to assist."

Al-Seif thanked Torosian and hung up. Carmen entered moments later.

"Good news?" she asked.

"A lead, at least," al-Seif answered, "How would you like to join me for lunch in Scogliera Piatta?"

"Is it business?"

The mouflon sighed. "I'm afraid so, but not the illegal kind."

Carmen came over and kissed him on the forehead, then rested his head against her chest. "I appreciate the offer, but I will decline. Besides, Yursa may have given you until after tomorrow to live, but the other families may not be so charitable. It would be much safer to stay here."

Al-Seif sighed again. "Yes, it would, my dear, but I can't stay here a moment longer. I'm afraid I've grown restless and feel the need to actually *do* something. I will take every precaution; with the exception of taking Abar with me, of course."

Carmen leaned down and kissed him passionately. "I can bare this house with either you or Delshad, but without either, it is very empty. Hurry back, and do be careful, my devil."

"No angels," the mouflon replied smiling.

Al-Seif had Abar Kami ready the graceful 1954 Baronville Regalia for the three-hour drive southwest along the coast, leaving orders with the panther to defend Carmen should anything happened—a distinct possibility as she had pointed out.

The Medoccian rail system could have gotten al-Seif to his destination in half the time, but driving made him feel more active than he had in the past week. Secretly he also hoped that he might encounter a bandit ambush; the adrenaline rush might help him relieve some stress.

Unfortunately, this was highly unlikely. The Medoccian government kept regular patrols on the primary coast roads, giving bandits little opportunity to set up roadblocks. They found it easier to waylay the backroads leading out to smaller settlements surrounding the larger cities.

About halfway through his trip, al-Seif did encounter a small pack of panther-like forest bahngers crossing the road, but a single blast of the Regalia's horn caused the reptile-headed predators to scatter, leaving brightly coloured feathers behind in their wake. The mouflon watched them vanish in the rearview mirror, then settled back into his seat. There was nothing for him to do but enjoy the view and think.

Delshad's exploration of the Zarazum Crater had turned up nothing. Jirair wasn't at all surprised; Ricky Tan's robbery of the Kevlar fibres was a long time ago, and there was no guarantee that any data from that far back would provide any relevent clues, to begin with.

The call from his lieutenant about the convoy was more troublesome. The Saran Waste between Nanca Fier and the northeastern tip of Bozambwe was one of the most hazardous regions of the southern continent, but his caravan wouldn't have gone without suitable protection.

Based on the time difference, al-Seif expected his son was already on site if not close by. Delshad would travel with full guard, but hopefully what he discovered would be nothing more than a chance encounter with a party of desert bandits.

And if it wasn't? the mouflon thought darkly.

Al-Seif forced the thought away. He suspected that Freggs possessed creatures other than the one he had promised to send to Assad Alabwaq as a centrepiece for his area games. It was what the mechanical voice planned to do with them that plagued al-Seif's mind.

In a way, that was part of the reason he drove to Scogliera Piatta now. If Freggs had more of these creatures, he needed some method of transporting them. That left the mouflon with just one question: where was the *Resthoven*?

Freggs had wanted al-Seif to use that freighter in particular, completely ignoring the fleet of De Palma Shipping vessels he had unlimited access to. Perhaps the mechanical frog had an ulterior motive that al-Seif was blind to thanks to his focus on his pet creature.

Al-Seif hadn't been the only one with cargo on that ship, but after a few inquiries, he had been surprised to find the name Ignatius Torosian on the list. Torosian was the CEO of East Wind Holdings and was entirely legitimate as far as al-Seif was concerned. In fact, it had been Carmen who suggested making a partnership with Torosian in the hopes that his lawful nature would rub off on her paramour.

Much as al-Seif had enjoyed the venture, he couldn't say he was eager to do it again. Legal trading could turn a profit, but it just didn't bring the excitement Assad Alabwaq's criminal enterprises did.

Al-Seif slowed as he approached the gate traffic heading into Scogliera Piatta. It was a beautiful city; really there were few in Medocci that weren't. *Scogliera piatta* literally translated from Mecci as "flat rock", so named for the wide plateau overlooking the Meadan Basin to the south. Below this cliff stretched a countless number of green vineyards. Naturally, al-Seif was biased towards Carmen's own family vintage, but he would be the first to admit that the wines of Scogliera Piatta were fantastic.

The traffic inched forward, and eventually, al-Seif found himself within the bounds of the city itself.

As the political capital of both the province of Pianure Rosso and Medocci as a whole, Scogliera Piatta bore a different structure from the more resort-based Pacé Acqua. The streets around the large municipal buildings and embassies were more haphazard, laid out in circular blocks that didn't quite fit together, and connected to each other via long, broad thoroughfares. Except for several large hotels along the plateau's edge and down near the beaches, most of the buildings where conversions and renovations of much older structures that had been there for two hundred years and more.

However, it was the business district on the east side that al-Seif made his way to now, and here the glass and steel of skyscrapers were the norm.

The Medoccian branch of East Wind Holdings Incorporated was unique from the tall rectangles. The curving white structure, with aqua-tinted glass that reflected the brilliant sky, looked almost like a cloud about to float away. Al-Seif hoped that if it did, it wouldn't take the café on the ground floor with it. He was almost ashamed to admit it, but lunch at Pearl de'Sain Jean was at least part of why he wanted to meet Torosian on his home turf.

The mouflon left his keys with the valet and found his lunch date was already waiting for him at a shaded table on the fenced-off portico. The tall Kikuyu three-horned chameleon—also called a Jackson's Chameleon, but nobody knew why—stood head and shoulders above the mouflon and gave him a pleasant businessman's smile as he shook his hand and offered him a seat.

"*Salam* again Jirair," Torosian said in perfect Netib, "It is a pleasure to meet with you again. I do hope you are doing well; I heard about what happened to Signor De Palma, such a tragedy."

"Thank you, Ignatius," al-Seif said, "It has indeed been a most difficult time."

The mouflon was pleased to be able to speak his own tongue again. However, he was well aware that Ignatius Torosian could speak several languages fluently, and all without any trace of accent or the tell-tale reptilian rasp typical to his species' relatives.

Torosian seated himself again and straighten the pant legs of his immaculate grey suit, which matched well with his pale blue-green scales. "Tell me," he said quietly, "is it true what they're saying about Vigo De Palma's mob connections?" He kept both eyes trained intently on his guest.

"Even almost a week after the fact I could not say for certain," al-Seif lied, "I was as shocked about the allegations as anyone. Unfortunately, I cannot deny that mob-related violence has risen following Vigo's unfortunate demise. I hope it is only because they seek to obtain his shipping business as a front for some nefarious operation."

"Even so, I would hate to think that you willing married into such a predicament." One of the chameleon's eyes flicked off to the side then back again.

"Perish the thought."

Al-Seif had always had trouble reading Torosian, maybe it was the way his eyes twitched every which way. The chameleon was a bit reclusive, but most people attributed that to his tragic and well-publicised past. Anyone was bound to be a little reserved after surviving a plane crash on the edges of the Aizlgeist and having only the company of dead loved until help arrived, which had taken over a month.

"What of the shipping line?" the chameleon asked, "Doesn't the business now pass on to Vigo's daughter, Yursa?"

Al-Seif bristled a little. "Not exactly," he said, "I'm afraid I recently purchased a large number of shares in the company before Vigo's death. It effectively put me in control of De

Palma Shipping, but I'm afraid it may also make me look suspect."

Torosian's eyes continued to flick this way and that without any noticeable pattern, but he always kept one on his guest. "Well, I hope it turns out for the best," he said amiably, "For you and your wife."

Al-Seif had to force a smile.

The chameleon waved a waiter over and ordered a bottle of the local wine, then he focused back on the mouflon. "Tell me, Jirair, why did you suddenly want to get in touch? Our last venture was, oh, at least a year ago. And what was that cryptic bit on the phone about recently lost shipments?" Torosian cocked his head to the side and gave a half smile. "Unless you have plans for another venture, I fail to see how that may concern you."

"Perhaps not me directly, but the ship you commissioned. The *Resthoven*."

The waiter returned with the wine and poured them each a glass. Torosian lifted his drink and breathed in the heady aroma of pressed grapes. He took a delicate sip and set the glass down. "Nineteen seventy-one, excellent year."

Al-Seif paused a moment, just that morning he had been dreaming of the year 1971. He tasted the wine; it was quite good, but he preferred harder liquors, like Carmen's grappa or her father's Colleté brandy.

"That ship troubles you," the mouflon said, "I've never been good at reading you, but this time I can tell."

Both eyes locked on al-Seif, tiny muscles making them squint slightly. "You have checked the manifest?"

Al-Seif nodded.

Torosian sighed and let one eye stare off into the distance. "Then you know we had a shipment of computer parts on board," he said, "You should look into that, by the way. Computers are getting quite big you know. Ah, financially speaking; the parts themselves are getting smaller and more delicate."

"Was there anything special about these parts?" the mouflon asked. "Or dare I venture that they weren't parts at all? A new trinket perhaps?"

The chameleon locked both eyes on him and blinked. Like his life-altering plane crash, Torosian's penchant for ancient artefacts was well known. He often decorated his offices with them, and if one wasn't careful, they might fall for the trap of asking about them, causing the chameleon to gleefully dive into tales of his much younger days when he would go treasure hunting himself. All the tales ended the same way: he got old and decided to focus more on his business.

"No, it was nothing like that," Torosian said, but al-Seif thought he heard a faint quirk in the usually measured voice. "Seriously, Jirair, I urge you to drop this matter. You know how paranoid the government can be when running shipments for them."

"So, it *was* government hardware the thieves were after," al-Seif said as if that was the theory he had been formulating.

"Is that truly your theory, Jirair?" Torosian asked, "That would be quite a prize, but hardly enough to make a whole ship disappear."

The mouflon paused, the time had come to drop some bait. "I had heard rumors that weapons might be involved," he said, "Highly specialized weapons, perhaps even new delivery platforms."

Torosian eyed him curiously. "You mean biological," he said, "My dear sir, I am afraid I have never heard anything so ridiculous."

He reached into his suit and withdrew a piece of paper, carefully unfolding it on the table before his guest.

"Look, here is the insurance forms for my claim on the cargo," Torosian said, "All above board and all perfectly normal. And there is a copy of the ship's manifest."

Al-Seif looked over the papers carefully. There couldn't be any mistake, it was a claim for a large number of servers and business machines. The contract was military, but as far as the mouflon could tell it was nothing more than workstations for one of the many bureaucratic offices that did nothing more than push payroll around.

Al-Seif shook his head and handed the papers back. "Maybe I am getting too paranoid," he said, "But I think something about that ship still troubles you."

Torosian's face was more neutral than worried. "Of course it does. They put into port at Kalegos after declairing a medical emergency, then whole ship vanishes into thin air. And more than that, someone went through a great deal of trouble to remove the records of the ships passage through the region. If it hadn't been for my contract, and the fact that I supervised the loading in East Benai myself, I might think I was going mad."

The chameleon accepted the papers back from al-Seif. Setting them on the table, the chameleon tapped the papers with a clawed finger. "The entire cargo, including my own investment, was worth several million Locke pounds," Torosian said, "It was exceedingly difficult to get the insurance company to settle when they couldn't be one hundred per cent certain the ship even existed."

"Well, if I were them, I wouldn't want to face your lawyers either," al-Seif said, attempting a gracious smile.

The chameleon chuckled. "Indeed! Well, I don't know about you, but talk of conspiracy makes me hungry. Let's eat."

The next several minutes pasted in near silence with only the slightest hint of polite small talk. The food was as excellent as al-Seif remembered, and the mouflon pushed his salad bowl away with a contented sigh. His chameleon companion locked both eyes on him and started chewing on a toothpick.

"Aside from your conspiracy, you still haven't told me of your investment in the ship," Torosian said patiently.

Al-Seif sighed. "Well, unlike you, I'm afraid I did have an artefact on board. Not as ancient as those ones you collect, but a lovely statuette from East Benai. It was going to be a gift for...Yursa." He had almost said Carmen but managed to catch himself.

"Really?" Torosian said, one eye flicking away, "I do not mean to pry into your affairs, Jirair, but while the whispers about the mafia may only be rumour, it is well known that you and Yursa De Palma are, shall we say, not on the best of terms?"

Al-Seif gave a derisive laugh. "Indeed. Ten years is a long time to hate someone, especially a spouse. Maybe I'm getting sentimental, but I had hoped maybe this gift would help change things. Now that her father is gone I'm wondering if it would have made any difference."

The smile on the mouflon's lips was more to congratulate himself on a masterful piece of bolvinshit than anything else.

"But I would not expect a bachelor like yourself to understand," he finished.

The chameleon chuckled. "Perhaps you are right, my friend."

Al-Seif rose and rebuttoned his jacket. "I do wish I could chat longer, Ignatius, but as you know, I must attend a funeral tomorrow."

Torosian nodded. "Again, my deepest sympathies. But I would like to leave you with a word of caution. Legitimate businessmen like us are much better off without the mafia."

"Perhaps," al-Seif replied. "But you should not underestimate Yursa. She is a spirited woman, and quite determined. Mafia or not, I think she intends to come out on top."

Al-Seif left the café feeling more confused than enlightened. Freggs had done a masterful job convering up the transport of the creature, even an overt hint at smuggled cargo had got a sneer from Torosian, a partner al-Seif was certain would carefully vet any ship he used.

Had Freggs and his associates really been after that shipment of computer parts? If so, why had they jeopardised the cargo by transporting the creature on the same vessel?

The valet brought the 1954 Baronville Regalia up to the curb. It wasn't customary to tip in Medocci, so al-Seif didn't bother.

Just as the mouflon climbed in, the car phone rang.

Al-Seif picked up the bulky handset and listened intently to the caller. The colour drained from his face, then swiftly changed to a vision of such cold fury that the valet—waiting at his stand for the next customer—shrank away from him.

"I shall return at once, Abar," the mouflon said, his voice dripping with ice, "These bastards will pay for their folly."

Al-Seif slammed the handset down and threw the eight-cylinder engine into gear.

At the screech of rubber, Ignatius Torosian looked up from a spreadsheet an assistant had brought him moments ago. He saw the long, graceful Regalia speeding away and hoped nothing untoward had happened to make his business partner so reckless.

23 – Reunion

Carmen.

It seemed an eternity since he watched her board that boat, seeking to further her education in Locke. He still saw her in his mind, waving from the aft deck. But the mouflon who had turned away from that empty horizon six years ago was Assad Alabwaq, a man she could never and must never know.

Now it was 1974, three years after Alabwaq's violent overthrow of Ricky Tan's empire. There had been the expected fight between several of Tan's old lieutenants, but Alabwaq dispatched with them as quickly as he had the leopard. Word got around, and the rest fell into step behind their new employer.

Alabwaq weeded out the ones who were only playing, of course, the ones who thought they could blindside him and usurp power for themselves. The Black Horns made it quite clear he was watching his back much closer than his predecessor had been.

But underneath the mouflon's cold exterior was a man who didn't want to hide in the shadows anymore, a man named Jirair al-Seif.

It was time he resurfaced.

Jirair al-Seif appraised the new warehouse with an anxious eye. The ink on the lease agreement in his hand was still fresh, and he took no small amount of pride in having signed using his given name. This would be his stepping stone out of the cesspool he had sunk into. From this warehouse, he could begin to move legitimate trade goods, and hopefully, create a gap between the man who was Assad Alabwaq and his true self.

The words of his lost lover echoed in his ears, "There are no angels in the world, Jirair, only the demons we create for ourselves." And Assad Alabwaq had created many demons in a short time. In the corners of his mind al-Seif hoped this enterprise would be enough, that he had not fallen too far into the pits of whatever hell existed.

The painters finished up their work on the new logo and began carefully peeling the masking away. Al-Seif watched as a stylized avian carrying a wrapped parcel was slowly revealed. Block lettering underneath it—in Locken instead of the traditional Netib—read *Golden Seas International Trading Co.*

Al-Seif beamed as bright as the paint drying in the early spring sunlight. Yes, here in Kairran, the capital of the nation, he would begin to finally make things right.

And yet he felt something missing, a pang deep in his gut that refused to go away. He knew what it was but couldn't bring himself to admit it. Instead, he told himself he was just worrying that he was growing too fast.

Al-Seif had enemies everywhere now. Just last year he had a falling out with Mody Nahas when they tried to claim the same smuggling route out of Gat-Bahar. His once friend and business partner had proven much shrewder than the mouflon had anticipated, creating his own little empire to rival that of Alabwaq himself. The orangutan had reciprocated for their parting-of-ways by moving his base of operations into Kairran ahead of al-Seif.

The mouflon knew the risks of purchasing a legitimate business on enemy territory, but he did it anyway, intent on showing the obese orangutan that he wasn't afraid of him.

In hindsight, al-Seif should have tried to recruit Nahas long ago. Or killed him.

The strange feeling of emptiness got bigger.

Al-Seif ordered his driver—the same jackal who was with him at the home of Ricky Tan—to take him back to his newly acquired penthouse. Tomorrow he must take up the mantle of Alabwaq again and oversee renovations on the arena in Khet; his clients would appreciate the addition of a parking garage, it made admission to the venue much more inconspicuous.

But that was tomorrow. Al-Seif felt himself fatigued by his responsibilities, and wanted nothing more than rest and a good glass of bourbon.

The big block V8 of the brand-new Regent Motors Crosswind rumbled to life, and Tarren the jackal eased away from the curb. The Crosswind was a narrow, boxy vehicle, painted white with a black roof of treated bolvin leather. The square headlights and steel grill up front combined with the sharp slope of the boot in the back gave it the appearance of a wild beast, crouching low before the pounce. It was a vehicle sharp enough to let people know that the owner had money, but the wheelbase was practical enough to squeeze down the narrow streets of Kairran.

Most importantly, it was very unlike the massive land yacht that was the '65 Venturi al-Seif's father had owned, or perhaps still owned.

Al-Seif leaned further back into the red leather seats and forced the thought from his mind. It had been almost ten years since he last saw his father, there was no reason to bring him up now.

He felt the empty spot in his gut grow again.

The apartment building was close to the waterfront between the market district and the port along the Hutsepth Canal. The neighbourhood was a little more touristy than business-like, but it had an excellent view and was close to al-Seif's new warehouse.

Tarren pulled into the underground garage and parked in his assigned space on the first level—roughly halfway between the entrance ramp and the elevator. The jackal got out and opened the rear door for his employer, and together they walked to the lift.

A sign hung on a chain across the doors. It read "Out of Order".

Al-Seif frowned. There were only eight flights of stairs up to the apartment, but he didn't feel much like walking. He made for the stairwell and climbed to the lobby; perhaps the desk clerk knew what was going on.

At a glance the lobby appeared empty, not surprising considering most of the building's tenants were still at work this late in the afternoon. However, the attendant was not at his post either.

The mouflon stepped brusquely up to the lobby counter and slammed the bell in agitation. What the hell was going on? He had chosen this building because the staff was usually prompt.

"Jirair?"

Al-Seif paused. The voice was soft, musical, and achingly familiar. He turned to discover the lobby was not as empty as he thought.

The woman stood tentatively next to one of the low benches and al-Seif's breath caught in his throat at the sight of her. There was no mistaking those faint markings on her melanistic face, the dark ringlets of her long-fur, just a shade darker than her body-fur. And, of course, the ribbed ibex horns.

It was Carmen Abbatelli.

The ache in al-Seif's gut seemed to swell until it felt like it would consume him. He couldn't deny it any longer, he knew what he had been missing all these years. Her, and it had always been her. Even in his darkest, most violent moments, he could feel her watching him, feel the brush of her hand against his fur, hear the musical trill of her voice in his ears. She had promised to return to him, and now she was here.

Al-Seif made as if to reach for her, and paused.

No, he didn't deserve her. Not after everything he had done. Assad Alabwaq was not the man she had fallen in love with, and that was the identity that had consumed him in the past six years. He should turn her away, keep her from the filth that he dealt with every day. He should...

His thoughts trailed off as a second, much smaller figure poked its head around Carmen's skirt.

"Mama?" the quavering voice asked.

Jirair al-Seif looked at the boy. He could not have been more than six years old. The markings on his face were that of a mouflon, *his* markings, but it was evident that his horns, though still underdeveloped, were that of an ibex. Al-Seif's eyes shifted to Carmen's.

Tears were streaming down her cheeks, but she smiled. That brilliant, dazzling smile that he knew so well. "Yes," she said, "This is Delshad. Your son."

Al-Seif stood there, dumbstruck. Suddenly, all the memories of his childhood came flooding back. The heartless tutors, the cruel caretakers, the drunken rage of his father. His hand unconsciously went to the scar under his left eye.

The words of Saifullah El-Hashem came echoing out of the past, *You murdered your mother, you little shit. You tore her soul out with your little 'strong hand'. You are not worthy to bear my name!*

No.

The mouflon clenched his teeth and balled his hands into fists. No, he would not be that man!

Al-Seif stepped forward, and the child shrank back behind his mother. Carmen placed a protective hand on his shoulder, shocked by the sudden pained look in her lover's eyes. Then al-Seif's face softened, and he got down on one knee.

"Come here, boy," he said gently.

The kidd came forward slowly, his little hooves clacking on the tile floor. Al-Seif reached out and gently stroked the tuft of black long-fur between his horns. Delshad gave him a tentative smile.

Al-Seif opened his arms, and the child climbed onto him, wrapping his small arms around the bigger mouflon's neck.

"I will never hurt you," al-Seif whispered, holding him tight. His eyes began to moisten, but he fought back the tears.

Carmen came forward now and embraced both father and son. The father stood and shifted the boy to one arm, wrapping the other around the mother and kissing her gently on the forehead.

"I will never hurt either of you," al-Seif said. "But what are you doing here?"

"We tried my bungalow in Khet first," Carmen answered, "but you had sold it."

"I'm sorry," al-Seif said hesitantly, "there were too many painful memories there."

"I understand," she said and smiled, "Afterwards, we went to my father. I am glad to see you left him alone, but he knew all the tales of the dreaded Assad Alabwaq." She caressed al-Seif's alabaster horns and smirked at the paradox of his criminal pseudonym.

Al-Seif's face darkened, and he turned his eyes away from her. "I'm not the same man you left."

She took his chin and gently forced him to look at her. "Yes, you are," Carmen said, "And you could never be any other man."

"I've...done things. Terrible things. All in the name of my ambitions." His voice had gone quiet, almost pleading.

"There are no angels in this world," she said.

"Only the demons we create for ourselves," he finished, "And hell has never seen such a demon as I."

"And you will become greater still," Carmen said and kissed him.

Al-Seif held her close for a moment, then stiffened and pulled away, setting his son down on his hooves. "You aren't safe here," he said to both of them, "I have too many enemies in Pytan."

Carmen leaned back on one leg, cocking her hips to one side and crossing her arms. Her lips curled into a half smile, and she arched an eyebrow at him. "You think I did not consider that, *mi amore*?" she asked, "I told you I was going to school to learn business. Delshad and I have been quite happy with my little vineyard in Pacé Acqua."

Delshad raised his hands in front of his face and made a squeezing gesture. "Squish, squish," he said with a smile.

Al-Seif could not help but smile in return. "And I thought you were averse to following in your father's footsteps," he said to Carmen

"In part," the ibex said, "I promise you Abbatelli brandy is superior to Colleté." She placed a hand on her son's shoulder. "But Delshad needs his father, Jirair. I'm sorry it took this long to come find you, but there is still time to make up for it."

Al-Seif nodded. "You're right. You were always right. But you must return to Medocci for the time being. I will be with you again soon, I promise. I will build you a house there, a place where you can be safe."

The adult mouflon turned to his jackal bodyguard, who had been standing patiently off to the side while his boss went through this very uncharacteristic display of emotion. "Tarren, call the airport and have my plane schedule an emergency flight to Medocci. We can drive to Khet tomorrow."

The jackal nodded and picked up the lobby phone. His face soured immediately, and he pressed on the cradle button several times. Tarren hung up the handset and said, "The line's dead."

The lobby lights went out, leaving only the late-afternoon sun filtering through the glass doors.

"The garage, quick!" al-Seif ordered.

Tarren led them down, pausing when they reached the door to the first level and peering out cautiously. The emergency lighting was still working, but the lights were spaced so far apart that great pools of darkness separated them from the stairwell door and the safety of the car.

As his eyes adjusted, Tarren scanned the few cars already in the lot. The jackal motioned for his charges to move out of the entryway and off to the side. They would be the proverbial sitting ducks if they remained in the stairwell, and there was more cover among the parked vehicles.

Of course, that could also work against them. Tarren held up a hand and stepped slowly into the blackness, staying out in the open to distract any would be attackers from his charges.

The jackal needn't have worried. A metallic scraping sound issued from the direction of the ramp and six burly figures began strolling casually into the garage.

Two were warthogs dressed in jeans with matching longshirts, one had both conical ears pieced with so many studs it was amazing he could keep his head up. Figure number three was a rhinoceros in a sleeveless T-shirt who was short for his species but still built like a tank. Four and five were canines from the mastiff breed, one of which was female, and wore a loose tie-dye shirt cut-off at her midriff with a matching headband to tie back her sandy long-fur. The final thug was a muscle-bound tigress with small hoops marching up the inner lobes of her ears and wearing a fish-net tank-top.

Al-Seif had no doubt that all six of them were probably gladiators, even the two women were physically on equal footing with their male counterparts.

In their paws, the assailants carried heavy clubs, lead pipes, and the tigress dragged a length of chain along behind her—that was where the scraping noise came from.

Al-Seif didn't need three guesses to learn who sent them, each had a tattoo on their arm of a banana piercing their skin and dripping blood; the emblem of Mody Nahas.

The rhino, presumably the leader, called out to Tarren, "We gonna give you one chance, *rafiki*." Neither Tarren nor al-Seif understood the word, but they guessed it to be from the Kowo language, putting the rhino's origin at somewhere on the coasts of Bozambwe. "You can walk away, right now, and leave your employer to us. Maybe you join us and Mody Nahas pay you nice."

The jackal drew two long knives from within his jacket. "Like hell," he said, "Nahas would probably use deserting my employer as an excuse to kill me."

The group stopped within two metres of the jackal and spread out in a rough semi-circle. The tigress swung the chain up and grabbed the loose end with her other paw, pulling the length taut in front of her with a menacing clash of metal. The rhino hefted his lead pipe.

"You can't take us all, *rafiki*," the rhino said, his small piggish eye narrowing.

"I can try—"

The jackal never finished his sentence as the tigress lashed out with her chain. Tarren ducked to the right and stabbed toward one of the warthogs, who was attempting to use the diversion to brain the jackal with his club. The blade cut across the warthog's arm and he dropped his weapon, but the rhino charged in before Tarren could finish him off. The jackal fended off his clumsy blow with an offhand strike across the rhino's horn, but now one of the mastiffs was lunging toward him, braying as if rabid and using both hands to swing her pipe.

Al-Seif knew his lone bodyguard would lose the fight, Tarren was tenacious and loyal but severely outnumbered. The mouflon drew a small pistol from within his suit jacket, but in the dim light, he couldn't pick his driver from the tangle of bodies struggling in the garage lot.

Tarren ducked beneath the tigress' chain and kicked her in the gut. The male mastiff quickly took her place and swung his free hand at the jackal. Tarren dodged left and slashed at the arm, adding another scar to the already colourful assortment on the canine's muscled appendage. The jackal then made a feint at the pierced warthog, but his brother brought his pipe up under Tarren's chin and jerked his head up.

The tigress swung her chain around the jackal's neck and yanked back. Al-Seif squeezed off a round at the figure choking his bodyguard, she grunted in pain and relaxed her grip but did not fall—it must have been a graze.

Tarren used the slack to lash out with both feet at the rhino and the un-pierced warthog, but it wasn't enough to save him. The male mastiff swung his club into the jackal's gut, and he gasped and fell to his knees. The rhino brought his pipe down on Tarren's head, and al-Seif heard a sickening wet *crack* as his skull split. His bodyguard was finished, but the group continued to beat on the jackal's body mercilessly.

Overcome with rage, al-Seif levelled the pistol at the group and squeezed off several rounds. The rhino, one of the mastiffs, and both warthogs fell under the barrage. Then the slide locked open with a dull *click* as the pistol's magazine emptied.

The tigress and the female mastiff stared at the mouflon and the two figures huddled behind him. There was a groan, a gasp of air, and three of the four thugs who had fallen began to rise.

"Eeyow!" the pierced warthog said, "That hurt like a mutha."

The rhino staggered to his feet and grinned at al-Seif, the emergency lighting shining dully off his flat blood-stained teeth. "Mody's no fool. He want us to take care of you nice and close, but he knew you be packing." He slammed an open palm against his chest. "Latest body armour, courtesy of your old textile trade."

"Oi," the tigress growled angrily at the rhino, "Thanks for telling us, you bastard."

The rhino gave a dismissive shrug. "Not enough to go around," he said.

The tigress' retort was interrupted by an agonised wail from the mastiff bitch. "He's killed Bosco!"

The other mastiff had not risen with the rest of them. The rhino leaned over and saw a neat bloody hole right between his eyes.

"Lucky shot," the rhino said, "Or maybe not. Bosco and Dolly, they littermates. You paste now, Black Horns."

The group moved toward the huddled *Caprinae*, and al-Seif placed himself in front of his son and mistress.

"Back up the stairs," he ordered, but he wasn't sure if that was wise, Mody Nahas may have sent more thugs to come in through the lobby. "I'll cover you, just get to safety."

When the gang was less than two metres from the trio, al-Seif saw a sudden blur as a shadow detached itself from the darkness and leap upon the rear flanks of the thugs. The mouflon would never forget the incredibly brief struggle that happened next.

Something struck the rhino hard across the head, and he staggered to his left, driving his horn into the eye of the bejewelled warthog. Nearby, the other warthog suddenly had his arm twisted behind him. There was a sickening *snap* as the limb broke and the shoulder was dislocated. The mastiff bitch turned to face the dark attacker, but her legs were swept out from underneath her before she could even raise a fist.

The tigress, having fair warning, broke away from the group and dodged the blow meant for her. She lashed out with her chain, but the shadowy figure caught it in his paw, pulled her in, and delivered two quick jabs to her chest, finishing the combo by driving his elbow up under her chin. She crumpled senseless to the ground.

The rhino yanked his horn from the gored warthog, who crumpled to the ground thrashing and screaming and holding his bleeding eye socket. The rhino stared at his companion dumbly for a moment, then turned and charged towards the shadow with a bellow of rage.

With a flick of the shadow's wrist, the chain lashed out and wrapped itself around the rhino's snout. The figure kicked out with his left foot, connecting with the rhino's shoulder, and spinning his body to the right while the shadow yanked on the chain in the opposite direction. The rhino's neck snapped with a loud *crunch*.

The mastiff bitch was on her feet again, and leapt on the shadow's back, attempting to pummel him with blows to the head and shoulders. The figure dove backwards, slamming her into a support pillar. Her grip slackened, and the shadow rammed his head back into her snout. She yelped in pain and fell off.

The warthog with the broken arm was feebly trying to drag the one with the gored eye back towards the ramp. The tigress moaned feebly from the ground, blood streaming from her broken nose.

The shadow turned to the mouflon, and al-Seif could sense the question in his posture even if he couldn't see his eyes. Al-Seif turned to Carmen.

She pulled her son in close and buried his head in her chest. "Spare the women," she said quietly.

"They're dangerous," al-Seif argued.

"For me," she replied.

Al-Seif nodded then turned to the shadow and motioned with his snout toward the warthogs.

The figure glided like a ghost towards the retreating *Suidae*. It was over so quickly, neither one had the chance to beg for mercy. Then the shadow grabbed the tigress and the mastiff by the scruff of their necks and dragged them up the ramp into the waning daylight. Moments later the figure returned and stepped into the light.

The black panther was tall and rail-thin, with straight black long-fur that fell before his golden eyes. He wore a conservative black suit in a style that reminded al-Seif of a movie poster he had once seen for a Benese martial arts film, it had small black buttons down the front from neck to waist, and the cuffs and collar were trimmed with white. Al-Seif was amazed to discover that despite the brutal contest that had just occurred, there was barely a speck of blood on the panther.

"Are you well, sir?" the cat asked in Locken. The voice was soft and faintly tinged by a Benese accent. It reminded al-Seif of Ricky Tan's, but with a better grasp of grammar and vocabulary.

The mouflon nodded warily but kept himself between the panther and his family. "I thank you for your assistance, though I wish you had arrived sooner."

"Your driver was a good man, he died with honour," the panther said, "I would have saved him, but more of Mody Nahas' thugs were attempting to flank you through the stairwell from the lobby and the lower level. Had I not dispatched them, you would not have survived."

"Does our rescuer have a name?" Carmen asked.

"I am Abar Kami." The panther made a curt bow with one hand to his chest. "I was formerly in the employ of Ricky Tan."

Al-Seif was on his guard again. "In his employ? I sifted through his entire staff, and you were not among them."

"As it should be. Perhaps it is more accurate to say I was his indentured servant. He kept me in his personal guard, and I fought in private exhibitions solely for his amusement. It was my duty to remain unseen."

The mouflon cocked his head and eyed Abar Kami curiously. "Do you seek my death, knowing that it was I who killed him? If so, spare my son and his mother, they are still innocent of my crimes."

"That is true," the panther answered, "But, I do not seek revenge. No, indeed you have freed me from my debt. I am loath to speak ill of the dead, but Ricky Tan was a coward and a truly feckless man. I watched your men move on the home of Ricky Tan. Had he faced his fate with honour, it would have been my duty to intervene. But even in defeat, Tan sought a way to save his own hide, pleading for his life like a helpless kitten. I let him die, which is to my shame. You, on the other hand, showed strength. A will of iron I have never seen before."

To al-Seif's surprise, the panther got down on one knee.

"As penance for my shame I must offer you my service," he said, "To defend your honour."

The mouflon frowned. "I am not a man of honour," he said.

The panther continued to kneel. "Indeed? You know I could have killed you and your family as easily as these thugs, and yet you place yourself before them, and offer your life in exchange for theirs." Kami bowed his head even lower. "This is an act of honour, small though you may think it. Until the end of my days or until such time as you release me, I will defend you and your family."

The mouflon stared at the large cat with wonder. Al-Seif had heard of such proud warriors in ancient tales but did not believe any of them still existed. To have one pledge himself to him was something out of legend.

Al-Seif nodded to Kami. "I accept your service, but only if you offer it as a free man. There is no shame in allowing cowards to be snared by their own traps."

The panther rose and nodded. "Then I offer it as a free man. And I accept the truth of your words. I believe your woman would say Tan succumbed to the demon he created."

Carmen eyed him shrewdly but nodded and said nothing.

"One more thing," al-Seif said, "The man you saw kill Ricky Tan was Assad Alabwaq, but I accept your service as Jirair al-Seif, my true self as it were. I believe you understand this."

Kami nodded again. "Many are those who travel with two souls, especially in the dark corners of the world."

Al-Seif felt Carmen shiver as she huddled close behind him. He turned to her. "No angels, remember?"

She held her son close and nodded.

Kami retrieve the car keys from the body of Tarren the jackal. As the panther drove them out into the waning daylight towards the airport, al-Seif saw the tigress and mastiff bitch limping down the sidewalk. They were battered and shaken but did not weep. He believed his new hire would call them true warriors for their behaviour.

The mouflon also made a note to sell the penthouse as soon as possible and purchase a new one further away from the market district.

From the back seat, Delshad al-Seif watched these events with wide eyes. His mother never wanted him to witness this violent side of his father's world, but he would always remember the strange manner of the panther's speech and the ease with which he had overcome the thugs who tried to kill them. Nor would he ever forget the way his father had placed himself before them, knowing he would die if the panther willed it.

As Delshad huddled with his mother in the rear seat, he stared at the profiles of Abar Kami and Jirair al-Seif riding in front, and his eyes gleamed with profound admiration.

24 – The Defender

Slowly, Abar Kami roused himself from his meditative state. The ancient technique passed down to him from generations of Chong Ryu monks in East Benai, allowed the panther to witness events of the past, the consciousness of all nature filling in the parts he had not personally experienced and sharpening those he had.

Kami had focused specifically on the day he offered his services to Jirair al-Seif; it had been much on his mind lately. He saw that his employer's criminal empire was crumbling, but still, the mouflon maintained the iron will that had drawn the panther to him. Jirair was more prone to outbursts of rage now, but he had never forgotten the debt he owed to Kami and often begged his pardon should he appear weak. The panther saw this thread of humility as a strength; only a wise and strong man could admit his limits.

Heed thy own advice, sensei, he thought to himself.

Kami rolled his shoulders slowly and noted a few more aches and pains in his joints. Even maintaining a disciplined routine of diet and physical training, he could not mask some of the injuries he had suffered in the tournaments.

Heed thy own advice and fear not your own limits.

Kami was at the upper end of thirty now, his long-fur trimmed down to the length of his body-fur and he had let the scruff on his muzzle grow out until it formed a small neatly brushed beard—best viewed in profile because it was the same colour as his silky black fur.

He came awake fully now, and slowly took in the room around him. Though his employer had no need to make such concessions, the panther had been pleased to find that al-Seif had commissioned a private dojo strictly for his bodyguard's use. It connected to the main house, but the rice paper walls and doors, combined with the solid cherry-wood beams created a pleasing, almost timeless environment when compared to the remainder of the ultramodern villa.

An extensive collection of martial weapons lined one wall, and over the years, the panther had used them to train the house guard and disciple al-Seif's son, Delshad. Kami also continued to focus on his own training, ever improving his skill to better serve his master.

Of course, perhaps master was the wrong word. He and Jirair al-Seif would never use the term friends, but there was a trust between them that stretched beyond the bounds of a mere employer-employee relationship.

Abar Kami did not follow any traditional concepts of right or wrong, there was merely what was. He felt al-Seif knew this as well, but the mouflon's own upbringing still caused him to judge his activities on a preconceived moral scale.

For Abar Kami, it was the bands of Fate that tied him to al-Seif, and he would never do anything to harm those whom Fate had decreed he must protect. Al-Seif understood this, which is why the mouflon had the utmost confidence in the panter's ability to defend his beloved Carmen while he drove out to Scogliera Piatta.

Kami rose gracefully to his feet and stood on the thin grey mat at the centre of the room. He was naked to his waist and wore a pair of grey cotton shorts that served as his exercise uniform. His arms, legs, and torso bore scars from numerous battles. Not as many as one might expect based on the number of fights he'd been in, but enough to show his experience. Each scar was a calculated risk he had made in the ring, and each one was worth the pain of victory. There were none on his face.

Slowly, he began to move his hands in a rhythmic pattern before him. First, he jabbed at the air with his right paw, then his left. Then he added an upward elbow strike. After a minute he included kicks; short, sharp blows that would break his imaginary opponent's legs if they connected.

The strikes and stances were all part of chut-ri, a brutal and particularly deadly martial art commonplace on the streets of Bangkor in Busawar. But it was different for the panther, Kami had spent his cubhood in the home of Khmer Rook, one of the last great Chong Ryu monks to journey south from the mountain monasteries of Thaanit Por. For Abar Kami, the art of chut-ri was his entire being.

The motion came faster and faster, Kami's mind randomly counting off the names and numbers of each stance and strike as he flowed effortlessly from one to the next. He was moving so fast now that an outside observer would see only a tall blur of shadow that seemed to have separated itself from the wall.

The panther moved towards a wooden practice dummy and prepared to unleash a new set of kata on it; he would need a new one once he finished, the third one he replaced this week.

But as Kami brought his arm around to strike the dummy's "head" he stopped his elbow mere centimetres from contact.

What was that sound from the gardens?

The double rice paper doors leading outside stood open, and Kami peered out across the small pools and sand gardens that he tended as part of his training. Nothing moved except the gentle sway of the trees in the late winter breeze.

That was the problem.

Al-Seif's guards were excellent, especially with Kami's training, but they still could not remain hidden from the panther's eyes. And at this time of the day, there should always be one near the perimeter wall outside his dojo.

The panther crept as gracefully as only a feline could out into the gardens. The trees between him and the outer wall were thin on the bottom but had broad boughs—the better to provide shade while strolling. A guard could stand just right to remain hidden from a casual glance, but there really wasn't much in the way of substantial cover, and none of the shrubberies along the ground was higher than Kami's knees.

There was a statue of a female hart pouring water from a jug at the far end of one of the pools—it was one of Ms Carmen's favourite pieces. Kami crept as stealthily as he could towards it and crouched low behind a stone bench.

Something lay in the bushes off to his left. Approaching it, Kami discovered the body of a marten, his throat slit. The tracks on the ground nearby were faint; as if someone were trying to make as little impression as possible.

Bandits do not come quietly, Kami thought, *Damn me for a fool, I have let this fortress make me soft. I should not have allowed Ms Carmen from my sight.*

The weather was pleasant, most likely the mistress of the house would be down on the beach. She wouldn't be alone, there were always at least two guards patrolling the shore at all times. Kami made his way in the direction of the lower footpath.

Not five metres from the body of the marten the snap of a twig brought the panther up short. Hushed voices, barely more than a breath, came from the trees on Kami's left. One of the house guards came around the corner on his regular route. He saw Kami crouched behind another statue—a frolicking sheep—and was about to stop when he realised it would probably be best if he acted as if nothing was wrong and continue onward.

The panther made a mental note to praise the ferret's initiative, he only hoped the intruders had not caught the slight hesitation.

They had not. The rustling in the trees went still, and the guard passed between Kami and the point he believed the voices had come from. Moments later a finch and a skink, both dressed in dark green tracksuits, crept out from the trees and moved on the guard. The panther was on the skink instantly, tearing his neck open with his claws. The finch looked around, startled by the sudden blur of motion, giving the ferret guard time to draw his knife; he carried a submachine gun but didn't want to raise the alarm with gunfire. More points from Kami.

The finch thug managed to parry the ferret guard's blow, but the panther kicked him in his knobby knees from behind, and he toppled forward, giving the ferret a clean strike at his neck.

The ferret cleaned his knife on the finch's feathers and shook slightly from the adrenaline; Kami hadn't even begun to sweat. The panther motioned the guard to make a sweep of the gardens, and to quietly alert the remaining house guards, then he continued towards the beach.

To reach the private strand, one first had to pass by the generator shed and down a narrow tunnel carved into the cliff face. There were no signs of tampering on the door to the generator, but Kami saw that at least two more thugs had tracked dirt down the path leading to the beach.

The stairway was a narrow series of doglegs zigzagging down the cliff to the beach below. The walls and arched roof were of natural stone, but the steps were made of flat, evenly spaced sandstone. Every ten steps a window cut into the seaward side—on Kami's left as he stood at the top—offered a breath-taking view of the Tharsian Sea and Medean Basin. However, Kami could not see the narrow beach below until he reached the final dogleg and the last flight of stairs leading to the beach gate.

Five figures stood on the beach: Carmen, her two guards, and two intruders. At the bottom of the stairs, the panther found the body of a third guard just inside the gate; his neck was broken.

There was no time to plan. Kami dashed out through the open gate and onto the beach. Carmen's guards fought bravely but fell before Kami could get within five metres of them. He noted that these intruders wore grey tracksuits instead of green.

The largest one, a bulldog with a jagged scar on his left cheek, leapt on Carmen. She didn't cry out, but she fought vigorously, attempting to gore the canine with her horns. The bulldog managed to get her arms behind her and held her fast while his companion—a stereotypically greasy-looking rat—came forwards wielding a long bloody knife.

The bulldog saw the panther leap and shouted a warning. Kami thought it was too late for the rat, but the rodent ducked sideways and slashed out with the knife. The panther was surprised to feel the cold burn of the steel across his left side, but he sealed the pain away behind his rigorous training and rolled back to his feet. The sand beneath his paws brought back memories of battle in the arena, and Kami bared his teeth in a wicked grin that made the rat and bulldog hesitate.

"Leave him, Tony!" the bulldog shouted, still firmly grasping the struggling Carmen. "Do her and the jobs done."

"You crazy, Giorgio?" came the reply. "You might have a death wish, but we turn our backs on this guy and we're done."

Giorgio growled and shifted Carmen's wrists to one paw, raising the other to wrap it around her neck. That was the opening Kami was waiting for. He kicked out at the bulldog's knee. Had the panther hit squarely, the bulldog's leg would have broken in half. Unfortunately, it was only a glancing blow, but it caused enough pain to loosen the canine's grip and allow Carmen to tear free. The ibex butted her head back, striking her captor across the face with the side of her horns before darting away towards the water.

Tony, the rat, hadn't been idle during this exchange. He lunged forward and scored another deep slash across Kami's back. The panther snarled and took the pain, placing himself in the assailants' path until he was sure Carmen was clear.

The pair tried to break apart and flank Kami, but he lashed out with his foot and caught the rat in the side. He felt a satisfying snap as several of the rat's ribs broke. Tony had the presence of mind to stab at the panther's leg but only managed a superficial cut.

Giorgio, the bulldog, faltered a moment, caught between his desire to fulfil his contract and helping his colleague take down the deadly panther. The job won out, and he turned to race after Carmen. He should have heeded Tony's earlier warning about turning his back on the panther.

Kami was on the bulldog instantly, delivering a sharp kick to his side that spun the bulldog around, and then he found himself lifted off the sand as the panther brought his elbow up under his jowls.

Tony tried another stab at the panther's back, but Kami was ready this time. A swift back kick to the rat's chest broke more ribs and knocked the air from his lungs. The knife dropped from Tony's hands, and he sprawled out on the sand, gasping.

Kami calmly walked up to the rat, bent down, and delivered a vicious punch to his throat, crushing his windpipe.

The bulldog staggered to his feet again and chucked a handful of sand at the panther. It got into his wounds, but Kami just grit his teeth against the pain and strolled forwards with murderous intent.

The panther was pleased to find that this warrior was facing his defeat with honour. Instead of falling to his knees and begging, the bulldog put up his fists and started circling to his left.

Kami knew what he was doing, he'd seen the knife lying on the sand. He brought up his own fists, heedless of the blood still streaming from his wounds.

As the panther had expected, once the bulldog had forced his opponent to circle away from his fallen comrade he leapt for the knife in the sand. Kami allowed him retrieve the weapon, curious what the bulldog would do next. Instead of rising to his feet first, Giorgio foolishly attempted to lunge upward from a kneeling position.

The panther made him pay for his mistake.

Kami grasped the knife hand and bent it back until he felt the wrist snap. The bulldog cried out in pain, but the panther quickly silenced him by shoving Giorgio face first into the sand and bringing his foot down on his neck.

Abar Kami stood victorious once more on bloody sand.

Carmen approached slowly. "Are you all right, Abar?" she asked.

"I will be fine, Ms Carmen," came the soft reply, "Are you at all injured?"

The ibex shook her head negatively.

Three figures were running up to them from the beach gate. Kami recognised one as the ox who was the chief lieutenant of the house guard.

"Sir," the ox addressed the panther shakily, "We dispatched two more intruders by the main house. All clear."

"How did they get in, Shalzar?" Kami asked coldly. He was pleased to see the ox, who was nearly twice his size, shiver slightly at his tone.

"A service gate at the opposite end of the compound. It was originally for a garden extension, but sir al-Seif cancelled the project."

"I do not care what it was for, commander," Kami said with a low growl. "All I care about is that there is a hole in your perimeter. A hole which, if not for my daily exercises, would have caused my charge great pain or even death."

The ox's tail was swishing back and forth in agitation now.

"However," Kami continued, "there is some fault to be placed on me as well. I know both of the gate you speak and that I should have been with Ms Carmen all along. I could have performed my meditations on the beach as easily as in my dojo."

He turned to the bodies on the sand. "Who were they?"

"No IDs were found on them," Shalzar answered, "but I recognised two of them from Mrs De Palma's security files; they were top hit men from the Costelliano and Forreza families. I would not be surprised if the third pair came from the Favera."

Carmen let a snort of agitation slip. "I suppose we have something to thank that bitch for now."

"Indeed," Kami said, "I expected the other families to try something like this. However, I also expected that our security was solid." He turned a meaningful eye to Shalzar who stamped nervously.

"The guard will be doubled, and the gate welded shut," the ox said, clearly shaken. "And I will personally see to the installation of a new camera by the gate as a precaution."

"See that you do," the panther said, "But also know that I will be bringing this matter up with Mr al-Seif. He may not be as forgiving as I."

The ox nearly fainted under the panther's withering glare.

Carmen regained some of her composure. "Please, Abar," she said, "Shalzar has done everything he could. Let me speak with Jirair."

Abar Kami nodded. "As you wish," he said. He gently took Carmen's elbow in his paw and led her toward the villa.

25 – Nanca Fier

Even in late winter, the deserts of Nanca Fier were a sea of blistering yellow sand broken by occasional pillars of misshapen brown rock. A lucky traveller might find a few scrawny shrubs or a stunted tree growing in the shade, signs that water was nearby; if not, one could only find death in that scorching heat. Pytan had deserts, but Nanca Fier was the mother of deserts.

It amazed Delshad al-Seif that such an inhospitable landscape somehow managed to support a population large enough to call itself a nation, and yet a flourishing coalition of city-states had risen from the sands. The Ferriers were incredibly independent people, you had to be in an environment like this, but they were far from bandits. A simple common law kept the peace between the cities and gave them the respectability they needed to trade with the outside world.

Of course, the law only applied *within* the cities; ouside, you were on your own. Bandits and smugglers couldn't resist the lawless wastelands, but the Coalition didn't worry too much about them, only fools dared to challenge the desert.

If the scyllian sandworms or a pack of desert rix didn't get you, thirst and flesh-ripping sandstorms would.

There were also the Soketh to deal with. Several large tribes of the nomadic treasure hunters called the wastelands home, and they tolerated neither bandit nor smuggler.

Delshad sat in the back of a Tracksman Landscout— smaller cousin to the Hiker—hoping none of these dangers crept up on him, but well prepared for any of them. Tracksman designed the tough, compact four-wheel-drive specifically for this environment, and the ibex-mouflon had no less than four of his father's most highly trained gladiators as bodyguards.

And yet somehow Delshad knew it was neither bandit nor scavenger that he would have to worry about at their destination. He knew it from the moment he answered the phone in Zarazum Crater.

This was one call the ibex-mouflon couldn't ignore. The weapons smuggling portion of his father's operations had faltered significantly after he fled Pytan, and it was partially Assad Alabwaq's own doing. When the elder al-Seif offered Vigo De Palma the opportunity to expand into Pytan, the deerhound made astounding headway into the trade. After De Palma's death, many of Alabwaq's competitors snatched up most of the old supply routes before the mouflon could reassert his control.

The war between Barju and Pytan didn't make things any easier. Many of Alabwaq's rivals were frothing at the mouth over the conflict, but in Delshad's opinion trading arms to both sides was a high risk, low reward situation. The war was too close to home, and with every crime lord in both Pytan and Barju trying to sell such a hot commodity, most of them would end up spending the majority of their earnings just trying to undermine the competition.

Assad Alabwaq needed a high risk, high reward gambit to keep his reputation intact, and that meant pushing further away. Fortunately, a territory dispute had surfaced in Bozambwe, far to the southeast.

The convoy route crossed Nanca Fier, and after that, a broad uninhabited section of the Saran Waste that didn't suffer from the 'dead zone' effect that plagued the rest of the region. However, something had interfered with the convoy several kilometres northwest of the Ferrier city known as World's End. Delshad thought it a fitting and rather ominous name.

A speck appeared on the horizon and soon resolved itself into a small camp of three tents. A pair of boxy Landscouts and one monstrous Tracksman Hiker expedition vehicle parked nearby. From the antennae and satellite dish on the roof of the Hiker, it was evident that it served as the communications truck. Several armed guards, mostly of desert-dwelling reptile species, wandered about the camp dressed in sand coloured robes and turbans to protect them from the environment.

As Delshad's vehicle pulled up to the largest tent a tall dromedary with an equally tall turban stepped out. His white cotton thawb, trimmed with gold embroidery, seemed rather ostentatious for the desert, but then again, so was Delshad's silk suit.

Delshad paused as he climbed out of the Landscout. "Rashid. I do not recall summoning you here," he said.

The dromedary bowed low. "Indeed, you did not, sir," Rashid replied, "When the convoy did not check in at its appointed time, I took it upon myself to investigate."

The ibex-mouflon continued to eye his assistant warily. "Where is Tunis?"

"Dead, sir," Rashid replied simply.

"I trust you will explain why and how?" Delshad asked.

Rashid bowed again and motioned his employer to follow.

The camp rested at the base of a large escarpment of rock partially buried in sand. As they rounded the dune the remains of a second camp, twice the size of the first, came into view.

Delshad stopped dead in his tracks, dumbstruck by the devastation before him.

The convoy vehicles—eight Hikers and four Landscouts in total—formed a rough semicircle with the half-buried pinnacle at their back. Canvas enclosures extended out from the side panel of each Hiker to provide shelters, and a single free-standing canopy stood at the centre of the camp near the base of the rock.

It was a classic tactical setup, ideal for a party on the move. During the heat of the day, the camp occupants could rest with the rock to their backs while the Hiker's formed a rough wall on the outside.

Despite the defensive advantage, something had torn the entire unit to shreds.

Four of the massive hikers lay on their sides, the heavy exploration vehicles pushed over like toys. Deep gashes raked the side panels, created by claws much more substantial than any on a ceravaag or desert bahnger; and neither of those common predators could have torn through the hardened steel anyway, it was virtually bulletproof.

The silvery divots of bullet impacts riddled several of the vehicles, but as near as Delshad could tell they all came from inside the camp; the mercenaries had been shooting at something within their perimeter. Two of the Hikers had suffered massive explosive damage, possibly from grenades, and the resulting fire from their fuel reserves had spread unchecked across the camp.

The central canopy, which must have served as a temporary canteen, was nothing more than a pile of tattered canvas and metal poles.

Mingled throughout the debris were pulpy bloody masses that Delshad could only assume were the remains of his mercenaries. The blood had run so thick across the ground that every inch of sand within the interior of the camp was a dull red. The stench of charred and rotting flesh hung in the air along with clouds of small biting desert flies.

There had been over two dozen men on this trip, all armed with the best assault rifles and side arms that Assad Alabwaq's dirty money could buy. None had survived.

"The shipment," Delshad eventually managed to say, his voice little more than a rasp in his own ears. "What happened to the shipment?"

Rashid gestured toward some of the less damaged vehicles. "We have recovered eight of the forty-four crates. The rest were unsalvageable."

"But they are all accounted for?"

Rashid nodded.

"What did this?" the ibex-mouflon asked. "What in the name of all the goat gods could possibly have done this?"

Rashid motioned for him to follow.

At the opposite edge of the camp, near a deep cleft in the escarpment, lay a large, humped object covered by a tarp. Delshad noticed that patches of bright orange began to appear mingled with the dull red blood stains. Rashid led him around these.

"Do not touch it," the dromedary said. "You asked me what happened to Tunis; it was this. He was splashed with the blood during the attack. Last night he started forgetting tasks I had just assigned to him. This morning he slipped into a coma. Before you arrived, he was dead."

Delshad shrank away, careful to watch his footing. He recognised the symptoms of Daeminox Syndrome; and an extremely potent strain, at that.

Three men in hazmat suits stepped out from the cleft as they approached. The trio had been keeping watch from the shade, where it was much cooler. The bulky, mirrored facemasks made it difficult to tell what species they were, but at least one was a reptile because his suit was modified with a tail sleeve—most mammals could slip their tails, albeit uncomfortably, down one baggy pant leg.

Rashid motioned to them, and they moved toward the tarp. Grasping a corner each, two of them carefully lifted and pulled the covering away, the third gathered up the centre portion. They had to move cautiously because the hide of the massive grey-green shape underneath bristled with a veritable forest of bony yellowish spikes; yanking the tarp aside would have torn it like paper.

The creature was eight metres in length and had six legs, each with a large four-fingered hand-like foot tipped by serrated claws. Each of the claws was as long and broad as Delshad's own hand. The hide between the spikes was a tight-knit web of diamond-shaped scales.

"My men broke two folded-steel bayonets trying to poke through the hide," Rashid said, "Experiments with rifle fire managed to chip small chunks of its flesh away, but the wounds were shallow."

"Well, whatever this beast is," Delshad said, "it isn't explosive proof."

The creature had no head because one of the doomed mercenaries had jammed a grenade down its throat. The beast then dragged him several feet before his arm tore from its socket and the grenade did its job seconds later.

"This is one of the creatures my father wanted for his arena, isn't it?" Delshad said flatly, pointing to the beast.

Rashid hesitated before he answered. "I cannot be certain, but that is my assumption, yes. There are many tales and legends about the unexplored regions of the Saran Wastes. We did not expect to find one out here."

The lizard member of the hazmat team spoke up, "It is a *bhairavi*, one of the Terrible Ones."

Delshad raised an eyebrow. "And what would a creature from the legends of Nhiavi be doing so far from Busawar?" he asked mockingly.

"I was not a religious man until I saw this, sir," the lizard replied, "The *bhairavi* are the hounds of hell, demons sent by the dark goddess Rhavi to cause great evils upon all hom-an kinds. Even as a child I did not believe. But now..."

There are no angels in this world, only the demons we create for ourselves. And someday the demons must be paid.

His mother's favourite poem flashed briefly through Delshad's mind. Had someone called upon this demon to bring ruin to his father?

He shook his head to clear it. "I have no time for religious nonsense," he said, giving the lizard a dismissive gesture. "If it were truly a demon I would not expect conventional weapons to have had any effect, even after stuffing a grenade down its gullet."

Yet despite his admonishment Delshad glanced around the carnage again, finally realising the destructive force his father was attempting to harness. And this was just one creature. Or was it?

"How many sets of tracks were found?" the ibex-mouflon asked.

Rashid raised a quizzical eyebrow.

"How many?" Delshad pressed.

"Three, sir," the dromedary answered.

"And only one dead." Delshad looked out into the desert. "How is it that the others have not attacked our camp, seeking vengeance for their pack member?"

Rashid seemed to be formulating a reply when a jackal mercenary—the son of al-Seif's old driver Tarren no less—hailed them from the other side of the camp. "The radio, sir," he said, "They're calling for Assad Alabwaq by name."

Delshad frowned and took one last look at the monster's corpse before departing.

The interior of the communications Hiker was mercifully cool. Despite his recent flippancy about religion, Delshad found himself muttering a silent 'thank you' to Nehbit, the lesser goat god of weather. It never occurred to him that his grandfather had once done the same thing in the interior of a blue 1965 Venturi.

The horned lizard operator passed him the handset, nodded, and stepped out.

"Alabwaq speaking," the ibex-mouflon said.

"Please, Delshad, allow me to use your true name."

Delshad al-Seif went rigid. The voice was cold, mechanical, obviously masked by some kind of filter; but it couldn't entirely mask the faint trace of a Locke accent or the glottal clicks that were common to the speech of all amphibians, particularly frogs and toads.

"You are the one my father has been dealing with," the ibex-mouflon answered coldly, "The one called Freggs."

The mechanical voice chuckled. "Guilty as charged. No doubt your next question will be why I'm calling you, so I will simply get on with it. I wish to inform you that you are treading very dangerous ground, my boy."

"Did you unleash this monstrosity on my men?" Delshad asked through clenched teeth, his free hand balled into a tight fist.

"Why no, perish the thought." The tone in the mechanical voice was flat. "We had heard rumours such creatures were in the area. Clearly, we were too late to warn you before you sent your convoy through."

"They were bait for a trap, then," Delshad said, "That's why the remaining two haven't set upon our camp."

"A bold accusation. And were the other two in my possession, what makes you think I won't unleash them on you?"

"You still need me," the ibex-mouflon said, "and my father."

"Tch, tch." Fregg's mechanical tongue clucked. "Both of you? Maybe. But surely you must know we're powerful enough to thrive without either of you."

"It's the blood, isn't it?" Delshad said, "That's what you want. It carries Daeminox Syndrome."

"Carries?" the voice asked mockingly, "My dear boy, the blood of these creatures *is* Daeminox Syndrome! Could you imagine the possibilities should you be able to synthesise that?"

Delshad's eyes widened. Could it be possible? Daeminox was the most dreaded sleeping sickness across Amarthia. It ravaged whole communities on the frontier borders. A cure would be worth millions, but a weapon...

"You're insane!" Delshad said hoarsely, "Tens of millions would die in the epidemic. How would you turn a profit if there's no one left to collect?"

"Oh, and you were doing so well," Freggs mocked, "You're as single-minded as your father, never seeing the bigger picture."

Delshad bristled. "Very well," he said quietly, "I'm listening."

The voice chuckled again. "That's the spirit! We're aware you've spent an inordinate amount of time in Libris and Gat-Bahar. Your interest in the salvage business has also been noted. The Basilisk Ocean has claimed many ships, and we can help you reclaim them. And beyond that, your brief time in you father's shoes has proven you are more than capable of taking on the mantle yourself."

Freggs continued like this for several minutes, piecing together various enterprises that the son of Jirair al-Seif had established on the side. Some were mere distractions, but others had become more than passing fancies.

Delshad al-Seif stood in the cool of the Hiker's rear compartment staring at the handset. What the mysterious mechanical voice had told him appealed to ambitions he had long thought hidden, even from his mother and father. Logically, Freggs must have weeded the information out through some sort of psychological profile, gathered over long years of observation. But for some reason, Delshad was having a difficult time getting the logical part of his brain to function at that moment.

"Well, Mr al-Seif? What do you think of my offer?" Freggs said.

Delshad hesitated. He had always known that one day he would surpass his father; that the borders of Medocci and Pytan couldn't contain the scope of his ambitions. What Freggs offered was a jumpstart on those aspirations.

But at what cost?

Finally, his analytical side was beginning to reassert itself. Despite Delshad's personal goals, he couldn't deny that he loved his mother and father and would never do anything to hurt either of them. It seemed strange that a family with as ruthless a reputation as theirs could hold such bonds, but they were there none the less.

Then Delshad thought of the thing under the tarp and the ruin it had left behind. His sanity won over his ambition.

Delshad took a deep breath. "No."

Freggs was silent for a moment. "What?"

"I said 'no', Mr Freggs," Delshad repeated, "What you're asking me to do...I do not claim any false sense of altruism, but this is madness. I would slaughter hundreds in the name of my ambitions, but I could never risk the lives of millions, especially when it may endanger the empire of Assad Alabwaq or the lives of my mother and father."

"I assure you they will receive every protection," Freggs said.

"Yes, just like you promised my father you would get him one of those, what was it, *bhairavi* for his arena? And let's not forget you used one of my smuggling convoys as bait to trap more of them."

"You are making a grave mistake, boy." The mechanical voice was obviously less than pleased. "Your father was warned to stay out of Pytan until we were finished. You complicated matters, but we assumed you could be reasonable. I hate to think we made a mistake."

"You did," Delshad said flatly and disconnected the call.

He stood in silence, contemplating what he had just done. After composing himself, he stepped out of the Hiker into the blistering sun.

Rashid looked at him with alarm. Beneath the dark markings on the ibex-mouflon's muzzle, Delshad was very pale.

"Is everything all right, sir?" the dromedary asked.

"Yes, Rashid," Delshad answered, adjusting his suit and placing a pair of sunglasses over his eyes.

He stared northward for a long moment. "Pack everything up and burn that...*thing*," he said at last. "I want no traces we were ever here. Make it look like bandits fighting each other if you can. Then I want you to return to Khet and gather the remaining gladiators; we need to close the arena for a while."

"Very good sir," Rashid said, "Shall I inform your father about this incident?"

Delshad looked up at the sky and squinted at the pale orange disc of Druna, the day moon, trailing the sun.

"No, I'll inform him myself," he said, "In fact, I think there will be a very lengthy talk between us."

26 – Parente Defunto

Vigo De Palma raised a bushy dark-red eyebrow as he watched the long maroon and white car through the window. The Regalia was an exceptionally graceful vehicle, and the tall deerhound admired the sweeping curves of the fenders and the shining chrome of the exhaust pipes as they threaded out of the bonnet covering the eight-cylinder engine.

Vigo scratched thoughtfully at the steel grey fur on his long muzzle. "You can tell a lot about a person by the car they drive," he said whimsically.

"How does he get it through the streets?" asked the young wolfhound standing beside him.

"I'd imagine very carefully, *mia cucciola*," Vigo replied. The word he used literally translated as "puppy", even though his daughter Yursa was well into her twenties now.

He wagged a clawed finger towards the car. "That is a man of taste and refinement, but also a man of ego. I am most curious how our business ventures will turn out."

"I don't trust him, papa," Yursa said, letting slip a low growl.

The deerhound turned to her and smiled. "I admire your spirit, Yursa, but you have much to learn. Assad Alabwaq is a dangerous man in his own country but remember that it is the De Palma family who holds the power here." He turned back to the window. "Besides, his interests in Medocci seem to be only in legitimate trade; why else would he approach us as Jirair al-Seif and not his underworld pseudonym? Now, go into the other room and sit quiet. I will leave the speaker on so you can overhear us."

"Yes, papa," Yursa said sullenly.

She stepped out of the office, pausing briefly by the calendar to fix the date in her memory: Colvus 23rd, 1982.

From the window of the neighbouring office, she watched as her father exited the raised double-wide trailer that served as the main office for the De Palma Shipping Company. He strode over to the Regalia, a friendly closed-lip smile on his face. The driver was just getting out, and both she and her father studied the black panther dressed in a sharp driver's suit and cap; here was a man who served double duty, clearly both servant and bodyguard to his employer.

The panther opened the door, and Jirair al-Seif climbed out of the back. The mouflon was dressed in an expensive white linen suit with a purple feather stuck into the lapel. The ensemble appeared ostentatious next to her father's khaki slacks and striped polo, but the deerhound was on the job; around the docks, it was best to wear something you wouldn't mind getting a little smudge on or smelling of fish and sea salt at the end of the day.

Al-Seif offered a polite smile and his hand, which Vigo took in a firm grip. They exchanged several pleasantries that Yursa couldn't hear, but from their gestures, it was clear that the mouflon was admiring the De Palma's operation and her father was impressed with the car.

Vigo led his guest back to the office. Despite his wealth, De Palma believed in functionality over substance. The faux wood panelling and thin brown carpets seemed almost like a joke compared to the finer trappings found in Vigo's home, but both he and his guest understood the need to cut costs where it didn't matter. At the very least, Vigo had wisely invested in a central A/C system, and the cold air was refreshing after the blasting heat of summer out on the pier.

From her seat in the second office, Yursa heard her father and his guest enter.

"I'm afraid I can only offer you water or lemonade," Vigo said, "I keep a dry work site."

"Water if you please," al-Seif replied, "But I had hoped we could get to the heart of the matter quickly."

Yursa heard the chug of the glass-bottle water cooler as Vigo filled a pair of paper cups.

"Not at all," her father said, "It appears we both have a lot in common, in more ways than one."

There was a shuffling noise as he pulled his chair around from behind his desk; her father always preferred sitting in front of his guests rather than hiding behind furniture during a conversation.

"Pytan has always been difficult to get into," the deerhound began, "Please pardon me if I offend, but your government is quite volatile. I am amazed that the sultan has remained in power so long."

"Abdülkadir is popular among the citizens, even if the traditionalist Nuadinites still cause trouble now and then. But he is, shall we say, naive to certain business transactions that occur within his borders."

"I had heard otherwise," Vigo said, "In fact the last I heard, he was causing quite a stir among some of the more...questionable practices in Pytan. He seems particularly adamant about stamping out the slave trade and curbing gladiatorial events; for which I wish him all the best, it is a despicable enterprise."

A slight snarl crept into her father's voice at the end and his guest was silent for a long moment, probably nursing his water as he pondered his next words.

"This is true," al-Seif said evenly, "But the sultan is very gullible. One positive spreadsheet and he believes his measures are working. However, I assure you, Mr De Palma, that my interests with you here are strictly legitimate. I wish I could tell you that the names of Jirair al-Seif and Assad Alabwaq are as far apart as the breadth of the Serenity Ocean, and as unknown to each other as the shores of Kudai are to whatever lies across that same ocean. But we both know that is a lie."

How poetic, Yursa thought derisively.

"Then why do you seek my help in arranging a trade partnership with you?" Vigo asked.

"For the same reason any man does anything against his nature. For love. I do this because my beloved Carmen believes having more legitimate business in Medocci will help distance me from the empire I created as Assad Alabwaq."

Carmen Abbatelli, Yursa thought, *Yes, his mistress. That is a weakness we should consider.*

"I think you understand this better than you let on," al-Seif continued.

Vigo let slip a wistful sigh. "Francesca, my wife, is a strong woman; as are most Medoccian women, I should say. She understands the dirty nature of this business, but I agree that it is her love that keeps me from becoming a complete monster." He paused, and Yursa could almost picture her father's eyes narrowing as he judged his guest. "She is also part of the reason I do not deal with drugs and slavers."

There was another long silence. Even through the intercom, Yursa could almost feel the tension building in the room. Her father and Jirair al-Seif were engaged in a battle of wills, each carefully testing the defences of the other.

"And yet I believe you know what I can offer in return for your partnership," al-Seif said, breaking the silence, his tone acknowledging that this was De Palma's turf and he would respect it.

Vigo said nothing, waiting for the mouflon to continue.

"Your influence with the mayor has undoubtedly given your family a great deal of leeway," al-Seif said, putting special emphasis on *family*. "But there are other families you must compete with; the Favera for example. And despite mafia influence, there is still honest law enforcement in Medocci. If you could establish some international interests in Pytan, you may create a haven should things take an unexpected turn for the worse."

"Extortion is not your forte," Vigo said darkly, "Do not try it."

"You misunderstand," al-Seif said, "I am not threatening you. I am the stranger here, and you would be a stranger if you decided to expand into Pytan. In these areas, we can both benefit. My goods and your ships throughout the Medean Basin, and in return…" He paused letting the thought hang for a moment. "You said yourself Pytan is such a volatile region. Weapons are a good investment there, and the Medoccians make some of the best firearms."

"To defend our homeland and protect against bandits," Vigo said, "The latter are quite persistent and resourceful. Particularly in a country where the wealthy tend to take up residence outside the city walls."

"Very true," al-Seif said, "If weapons do not appeal to you, the Sultan has also declared Pytan to be free of inhibitions, particularly alcohol. This is mostly to appease the Nuadinites, but they sip fermented bolvin milk when no one is looking. There are many avenues where an intelligent canine such as yourself could invest a little capital."

"And signorina Carmen Abbatelli does make such a fine vintage," Vigo said.

"More than that," the mouflon replied, "Her father still owns a distillery in Khet that distributes Colleté brandy. He wants to retire soon and will need someone to pick up the reigns."

Clever bastardo, Yursa thought, *He knows which of our enterprises have been faltering.*

She listened intently as another silence grew. She didn't want to admit it, but it was a reasonable offer. Many of the De Palma's money laundering businesses were currently under close observation, and what the Mouflon proposed was precisely the kind of relief they needed to take some of the heat off. There was also a genuine threat that Medocci's honest authorities would decide they needed to "get tough" on the mafia families; they were long overdue for such a culling. Pytan was a nation of moral ambiguity, the perfect place to move ships and assets when the hammer finally came down.

Yursa decided it was time to make an appearance. She went out into the lobby and knocked on her father's door.

"Come in," Vigo called.

Al-Seif watched as the stunning female canine entered. She returned his gaze through eyes as pale grey as her body-fur and brushed a strand of rust-red long-fur back behind her shoulder.

Vigo smiled. "Ah, Yursa! Please, come in. You might find some of this interesting. Let me introduce Jirair al-Seif. Jirair, this is Yursa, *mia figlia*. My daughter."

The mouflon rose and bowed. "A pleasure," he said, "This seems a good sign, Vigo. *Yursa* is a Pytian name. In Netib it means *wealth*."

"Indeed, it does," Vigo replied, "I cannot deny Pytan and the other nations of Estan have fascinated me for many years."

Yursa eyed her father quizzically but said nothing.

"However," al-Seif said, "I had assumed my business was with you, Vigo."

"Nonsense!" Vigo beamed. "Yursa has proven quite adept at learning the family trade. Although there are still a few things she could learn from her brother Tito."

"Indeed?" al-Seif replied.

The mouflon sat again and repeated his offer for the young wolfhound. Yursa listened attentively as if it was the first time she had heard it.

"Well, what do you think my dear?" al-Seif said when he had finished.

"Well, I find it a terrible idea," Yursa said flatly.

Al-Seif frowned.

"Signor Alabwaq already owns many of the markets he suggests we move into," she continued, "It would be far better if we followed our cousins into the WUK."

Vigo nodded thoughtfully. "True, *mia figlia*," he said, "but the families in the West United Kingdoms operate much different from us. And the expenses we would incur moving across the Basilisk Ocean would likely be greater than the returns we would get through Jirair's offer."

Yursa folded her arms across her chest. "And what about these legitimate trade deals?" she asked, "What guarantee do we have that you will not simply try to overtake our enterprise?"

"None," al-Seif said rising to his hoofs and buttoning his jacket in preparation to leave. "I informed your father that I wished to engage in more legitimate business for the sake of my son and his mother."

Yursa arched an eyebrow incredulously.

"I thought that would be your reaction," the mouflon replied, "Well, Vigo, I believe I have said all I need to say. Take as much time as you need to think things over. If I should I need to return to Pytan, my manservant, Abar Kami, can tell you how to reach me."

Al-Seif bowed to both canines in turn, but let his eyes linger a little on Yursa. It was not a lustful or appreciative gaze, but one that a fighter might give when measuring an opponent. She returned the same look.

The mouflon left the office and returned to the Regalia. Abar Kami had remained standing dutifully by the door despite the heat of the day.

Father and daughter watched from the office window as the Mouflon climbed into the back seat of the long Regalia. The panther driver gave one brief look towards the office, got in, and drove away.

"I don't trust him, papa," Yursa repeated with a low growl.

"That is good, *mia cucciola*," her father replied, "He is very dangerous, but so are we. I think he has much to offer us, but we must be cautious."

"Perhaps there is a way of keeping a closer eye on him," Yursa said, "You honestly believe his story about wanting to do right by his unwed whore?"

"Yursa!" Vigo growled, "Please, he may be many things, but al-Seif is certainly a man in love. How many times have I told you about the opportunities that have gone by because your mama disapproved?"

"What would such a man do for his love?" Yursa asked slyly.

Vigo glanced over and noticed that although she looked at the warehouses across the way, she no longer saw them. Her gaze had turned inward in thought.

Yursa turned to him suddenly. "I want to be present in all your dealings with him," she said, "He knows I have your best interests at heart and will most likely welcome the chance to keep a closer eye on me. But perhaps we can convince him my interest is more than professional?"

Vigo frowned. "Is it, *mia figlia*?" he asked, taking a seat behind his desk again. "He sounds too devoted to his mistress to take another."

"He is a man of ego," Yursa said, a twisted smile curling her lips. "And a stranger in Medocci. There are a few customs we might invoke that would allow us to keep an eye on him and protect us from betrayal."

Vigo's bushy brows furrowed. "I'm afraid you may have out-thought your papa this time, *mia cucciola*. Such practices have not been used in Medocci for generations."

Yursa smiled warmly and ruffled the greying dark-red long-fur atop her father's head like she used to when she actually was a puppy. Then she bent down to hug his narrow shoulders and kissed him on the cheek.

"You will see, papa," she said, "I will shadow him for a couple years; and when the time is right, he will be bound to us like *family*."

* * *

Yursa De Palma didn't even hear the minister's words as he recited the funerary rites which seemed to permeate all such events regardless of religion. At that moment she cared very little for expressions of pity or religious encouragement.

Her mind had drifted to the past, and now it returned to the present. It was Faerday, the fifth of Met, nineteen ninety-four by the Colvan Calendar. And her father was dead.

A full week had passed since her family had been mercilessly slaughtered. It felt like an eternity. The partnership between the De Palmas and al-Seif had indeed been profitable, but if Yursa had known what it would eventually cost her, she would never have gone through with it.

The sky was a light patchwork of grey clouds and rays of sunlight. Winter attempted to hold on to its fleeting grasp, but instead of snow only a light rain washed the coasts of the province of Pianure Rosso; a gentle drizzle that cast odd rainbows across the ancient Santo Aquilla graveyard.

The De Palma mausoleum rested at the peak of a modest courtyard shaded by a small grove of cypress trees and overlooking the cliffs of the city of Pacé Acqua. It was a beautiful location to be laid to rest, but the last remaining De Palma matriarch could not give in to its lull.

The large turnout for her family's funeral was not surprising in the least. The heads of almost all of Medocci's remaining crime families had shown up to "pay their respects", mingling with the celebrities and power-players who had been her father's friends and clients. But Yursa knew that their eyes were carefully trained on her and not the row of caskets before them. She stood resolute in the rain, proud and fierce, keenly aware that even the slightest show of weakness would mean the utter collapse of her family's legacy. She trained her doleful eyes on the mouflon at the back of the crowd and let the hate renew her strength.

How dare that bastard show his face here! She thought, *And what's worse, he brought along his ibex whore. If their bastard son wasn't away in Pytan, I'm certain he would be here as well.*

Yursa noted the fire burning in their eyes. She had heard about the attempted assassination yesterday. Those idiots in the Costellianos and Favera had moved too soon, it was poor form to strike against al-Seif this early. Her father would understand the need for patience against a man like Assad Alabwaq. Now her own plans for him were in jeopardy.

However, Yursa also noted that the mouflon's panther bodyguard stood not far behind them instead of waiting at the car. Al-Seif showed he wasn't afraid just by making an appearance, but he also showed he wasn't a fool by keeping his guard close.

Yursa took some comfort in knowing that the enemies surrounding her were also the enemies of Jirair al-Seif. Despite his clever manoeuverings a week ago, which granted him almost complete control of the De Palma's business holdings, al-Seif was now faced with having to defend those newly acquired assets against the other families just as she did.

And Yursa would not make it easy for him. She would bury him just like he buried her father and her mother and her brothers and her sisters. She would see him squirm like the worm he was as she placed him on the hook, bait used to lure out the ones who had really ordered the attack on her family. And then she would watch his bones bleach in the sun as she left him in the giant sandbox that he called home.

The wolfhound's gaze shifted to the petite ibex. But first, she would make al-Seif feel loss as she had.

The priest ended his sermon, but Yursa only heard the last bit of the verse in Mecci: *Parente defunto.* The dearly departed.

The service ended, the caskets were interred, and the throng began to disperse. Al-Seif and company vanished shortly afterwards, not willing to stay any longer than was necessary. Some remnants of the other families hung back to observe the De Palma matriarch. Yursa continued to stand alone by the iron doors of the mausoleum.

Eventually, even the spies of her competitors left, and the wolfhound was truly alone. A Medocci funeral was a sacred occasion, despite the violence that had broken out over the past week, none of the other families would dare to make a move against her that day.

And still, the tears would not come. Yursa had spent all of them on the day she cradled her father's head in her lap.

She felt a presence behind her and turned. Not three metres away stood a tall canine wearing a tan trench coat. His ears were straightened to points, and they stuck out the top of a black beret perched on his narrow head, strands of dark long-fur protruded from beneath the cap. His natural coat was a magnificent silky blue-grey, and from his features, Yursa instantly identified him as a greyhound; however, he had a slightly bulkier build than usual for his breed. She also noted that his right arm was in a sling.

She raised a questioning eyebrow but said nothing.

The greyhound bowed slightly. "Madame De Palma," he said in a resonant Marisian accent.

"Mademoiselle," she corrected him, "I plan to have my marriage annulled tomorrow."

"May I suggest that that would be a mistake?"

Yursa's eyes narrowed sharply. "Did he send you?"

"No. However, if you would allow me to explain, I believe you would find your marriage to Jirair al-Seif can still be most advantageous to your future goals."

"And those might be?"

"Why, revenge, of course." The greyhound offered an ingratiating smile. It felt very cold. "You see, I represent certain parties who are...shall we say less than pleased with Monsieur al-Seif's recent behaviour?"

"I have no time for this," Yursa said with a dismissive wave of her hand, "You're right, I do want *my* revenge. And I'm going to devote what remaining resources I have to accomplishing that."

"We don't wish to rob you of your sport," the greyhound said, "You've earned it. However, we only ask that you consider our offer. Revenge is a costly endeavour, we would hate to see you...overextend yourself." He smiled coldly again. "Once your vengeance is complete you will no doubt ask yourself where to go from there. We can put the De Palmas back in their proper place."

"What is your offer?"

"Please, Mademoiselle, not here among the dead. This is an offer for the living. I know of a wonderful Marisian restaurant in the city. Won't you join me this evening?"

Yursa judged him coolly. For a moment she regretted that she had never been as discerning as her father. The De Palmas never dealt with the Marisian crime families, but from this greyhound's mannerisms, she was fairly certain those were not his connections; he was much too refined. He was also quite handsome.

"Very well," she glanced at the crypt, "You can leave instructions with my driver, Mr—"

When she turned back, the stranger was gone.

* * *

The greyhound had already known what her answer would be. In fact, he had left instructions with Yursa De Palma's driver even before approaching her. Such was the benefit of an extensive psychological report and observation.

The thought brought a brief frown to the greyhound's face. And yet there was that minor hiccup with Delshad al-Seif. It was not enough to shake his confidence in his superiors, but it was quite an unexpected turn of events.

As the greyhound left the graveyard, he heard a chirp from his pocket. The dish for the satellite phone was stored away in his bag, that meant it was a local call. He plucked the bulky handset from his pocket.

"*Oui*?" he answered.

"She accepted our proposal?" the mechanical voice asked.

The greyhound paused. It was not Freggs on the other end of the line, but he recognised the voice instantly. Unusual to get a call from the Master himself, but the greyhound didn't think he had anything to fear.

"I didn't wish to discuss the matter in the graveyard," the greyhound said carefully, "She has agreed to meet me for dinner this evening."

"And that is all?" There was an almost accusatory edge to the filtered voice.

"We shall see," the greyhound smiled wistfully, "few women can resist my charms."

"She is an asset, nothing more. I trust you will remember that."

"But of course."

"If she does not accept our proposal then we have no further use for the De Palma family. But I have another task for you."

The greyhound got into his rented sedan, and the rain began to pick up. The signal got fuzzy but held. "I am ready to serve," he said.

"The hunters have been skulking in Medocci since Aevrday. They are waiting for their assets to acquire an indictment against al-Seif's pseudonym, Assad Alabwaq. We want to keep them entertained while they wait."

The greyhound grinned coldly. "What did you have in mind?"

"They have learned that al-Seif made a visit to East Wind Holdings yesterday and decided to make an appointment for this afternoon."

The greyhound paused. "I do not mean to question you, sir, but is this wise? What about Torosian?"

"You sound unsure of yourself. Never fear, the chameleon will continue playing the fool, and you will not lose your precious restaurant, I will see to it. The fact that al-Seif went snooping around there was more than they needed to get their noses twitching, it was inevitable they should investigate it as well. Naturally, they will find as much of a dead end as the mouflon did. If we're lucky, they'll be even more discouraged afterwards."

"*Pardon*, sir, but I thought we didn't do luck."

The mechanical voice chuckled, an eerie crackling sound like live electrical wires scraping on metal. "No, not luck. But chance is in everything. Should they survive our gauntlet, it is of no consequence. They will fall eventually, as will the rest of the Nameless Ones."

The greyhound shivered slightly at this, but he controlled the burning fury that suddenly sparked deep inside him; he probably wouldn't have been able to do so had the voice actually spoken their accursed name.

"Do it by this afternoon," the voice continued.

The greyhound frowned at this, it would push back his dinner plans, but he acknowledged.

"One final thing," the voice said, "Did you get the snake taken care of?"

"*Oui*, but I couldn't prevent him from bringing along a concubine."

"Really? How interesting. Traces of his old life, perhaps?" There was a musing tone to the voice, and the greyhound knew the question was rhetorical. "Yes, very interesting. I trust they are enjoying their new surroundings?"

"As well as can be expected," the greyhound answered, "It is colder than his plush palace, but he is grateful to be alive."

"Yes, and we must keep him that way. Perhaps this rescued concubine will awaken the man we need from his scaly hide." The voice paused for a moment. "Did she have a name?"

"I believe she said it was Mavuto."

There was another pause, much longer this time. "That means 'trouble' or 'problem' in the Kowo language. But whose problem, I wonder? Regardless, you have your orders. Get to it."

The call disconnected.

The greyhound tossed the bluky handset onto the passenger seat and listened to the rain drumming on the window for a moment. Then he turned the car on and put it in gear. It would take him ten minutes to return to Pacé Acqua, and from there he would board the next train to Scogliara Piatta. He had plenty of time to make a few strategic phone calls.

27 – East Wind Holdings

Kittina Katral puffed on a cigarette and stared out at the beautiful city of Scogliera Piatta. It was the only thing she could think to do without driving herself completely mad with boredom.

Mohan's Scrappers, their recent recruit, and Elder Tyrsus had spent the last two days in Medoccian capital enjoying the comforts of a rather pleasant suite at the upscale Darlington Hotel. The accommodations were provided in large part by the generous coffers of Vince's security systems business—a private venture which he left in the care of an old schoolmate while the hare gallivanted around the world playing secret agent.

There had been a sense of urgency to get to Medocci and deliver their evidence on Jirair al-Seif, but now that it was done all they could do was wait. Rizzo, Vicki, and Vince took the opportunity to go sight-seeing, as only Vince had ever visited the coutry before. Tyrsus, Mohan, and Zed connected with the local assets supporting the Tiger's Stripe. There weren't many operations in the region aside from the Scrapper's fellow hunter team, TS Five, but they didn't want to step on any toes while they were visiting.

Only Ric and Kitty were left to hold down the apartment, and the tigress got uncomfortable hanging around the journalist.

Kitty leaned forward and sighed, flexing fingers that longed to hold a gun instead of a cigarette. Spending a few hours at the range was her method of choice to relieve stress at the Sanctuary, but it was almost as difficult to walk around with a firearm in Medocci as it was in Locke. She was tempted to abandon her teammates and take a trip outside the walls; a little dust-up with some bandits would help her ease the boredom.

The white tigress turned at the sound of the balcony door opening, and immediately turned back when she saw it was only Ric. Her wearisome charge had also been feeling the strain, but his answer to the lack of activity was to engage his companions in conversation about their lives as agents of Tiger's Stripe. Bloody journalists.

And yet, Kitty couldn't blame him. Mohan and Tyrsus were frequently promising to deliver the lynx to the Sanctuary, but events continued to conspire against them. Kitty could tell Ric's curiosity about Tiger's Stripe's headquarters was eating him alive, and she wondered if the journalist would ultimately end up disappointed when he finally did walk through its doors.

Admit it, you weren't, she chastised herself.

Even now, the thought of walking through the thick blast doors into the Dome and seeing the statues of the Seven Founders sent a slight shiver up Kitty's spine. But it was not the shiver of excitement she had experience on her first visit. In her mind's eye, she saw the stone eyes of the Founders of the *Laohu Tiaowen* glaring down at her, feeling nothing but the weight of ancient judgement crashing upon her shoulders.

The tigress shrugged off the feeling and tried to focus on the city below her.

Ric coughed behind her. "Basira and the others are back," he said, "The Elder called a meeting. Looks like something might actually be happening."

Kitty nodded an affirmative and stubbed her cigarette out on the iron railing of the balcony. She hoped it wasn't just another news update. They had heard all about the fall of Jar-Geshim, Delshad al-Seif's emergence as Assad Alabwaq in Pytan, and the mafia attack on al-Seif's villa in Pacé Acqua.

And still, the agents had done nothing. If the same thing happened again, Kitty swore she was going to take a cab to the airport, grab her rifle, and go hunting in the woods overnight. Maybe she could find that miraj den TS Five had been working on? She had a standing rivalry with Terry Rothschild, TS Five's sniper, and would relish the chance to score a few kills over the ferret.

The agents of the *Laohu Tiaowen* gathered in the common room of the hotel suite.

Elder Basira Tyrsus made a quick headcount and began as soon as they were all present. "Jirair al-Seif visited with a former business colleague in Scogliera Piatta yesterday," she said without any fanfare.

Vicki's eyes widened. "How did we not hear about that?" she asked.

Elder Tyrsus shook her head and ruffled her wings in agitation. With all the other small hints that someone was hunting the *Laohu Tiaowen*, it didn't escape the golden eagle's notice that there had been a hiccup in their intelligence service.

"Could it be because of your allocation of resources?" Ric asked, "Like your lack of assets in Locke?"

The eagle shook her head again. "Not this time, I'm afraid. This mission was a part of the Scrapper's primary objective, so we had assets made available. More than that, we have another hunter team based here in case anything from the Aizlgeist wanders into Aerenia. However, our intelligence network has been so focused on the recent mafia activity that al-Seif's visit went unnoticed until the last possible minute." Tyrsus leaned against the bar of the small kitchenette and folded her arms across her chest. "We're one hundred per cent certain this was intentional; the mafia uprising is being used as a screen."

The room was silent for a long moment.

"You mean there's someone else out there," Kitty said quietly, "Someone with the knowledge and power to keep us blind."

The eagle nodded slowly.

"So, what do we do?" Ric asked.

"The only thing we can," Elder Tyrsus replied, "Jirair al-Seif went to East Wind Holdings for some reason, and we need to find out why."

The lynx nodded. He had expected as much, but he was new to this spy game, and the only way to learn was to ask.

"We still have details to flesh out," Tyrsus said, "I've made an appointment with Torosian for this afternoon, but certain details were purposely left vague."

Vince practically leapt at the news. "At last! A chance to do some real spy work." The hare grinned, displaying large front teeth. "I could even use a code name. How does Theseus A. Nalias, esquire sound?"

Despite the mood of the room, Vicki began to laugh uncontrollably, holding her sides as if wounded.

Rizzo screwed up her face in thought, then groaned. "*Mon Déesse.* 'This is an alias'? Really?"

With her Marisian accent, the first two words actually did sound close to Theseus.

The basilisk would've cuffed the hare across his long ears if he hadn't been across the room. Both Mohan and Elder Tyrsus rejected the hare's idea out of hand, and Vince set himself to the task of inventing something much less obvious, and silly.

"Kitty," Mohan said, "You and Vince will take point, again. You get to make the meeting."

"Gee, thanks," the tigress muttered.

"You can thank your computer science degree," her father said, a hint of a paternal smile on his lips.

Ric raised a quizzical eyebrow at Kitty.

"What?" she asked, clearly embarrassed. "I like computers. Don't get to use them much when hunting monsters, but it's a useful skill."

"There's also the fact that the Tiger's Stripe placed you on the payroll of United Plains Business Machines," Elder Tyrsus said, "We've learned that East Wind had a shipment of computer parts on board the *Resthoven* when it vanished. That's likely al-Seif's connection to his visit. Since you actually know what you're talking about in that area, you get the job."

Kitty chuffed in annoyance but nodded her consent.

"So why am I goin'?" Vince asked.

"Oh, you have it easy," Mohan said, "You're an insurance adjuster hired by UBM to investigate the lost shipment."

The hare frowned. "That sounds kinda thin."

The tiger nodded. "Yeah, but with your charming good looks, you'll make it work. And if things go Rollaroo in there, you're the one that will need to crack the security lockdown while Kitty provides fire support."

Kitty chuffed angrily. "Thanks for the vote of confidence, and here I actually believed that bit about using my brains for once."

"What?" Mohan was genuinely shocked. "No, I didn't mean—"

Tyrsus interrupted the tiger before the argument could continue. "If Torosian sees through your ploy it's more likely he'll just throw you out on your ears," she said, "Based on what we know, East Wind is just another pawn in this game. But it's always best to play things as if there is a supervillain working behind the scenes. If someone is expecting us, they could override the building security and send their own goons in. You're a better shot than Nieves."

"Now it's my turn to feel dejected," Vince said.

"It's settled," Tyrsus said with finality. "We'll position the rest of you once we're on site. We still need to gather equipment, so let's get moving."

The group broke up, but Ric noticed the long look that passed between father and daughter before each turned to make preparations. Mohan's was one of concern and apology, but Kitty's was a blazing sheet of ice.

* * *

The Scrappers prided themselves on being able to work on the fly, and within three hours they had outfitted themselves for a light reconnaissance mission. They had decided to appropriate the gear from KLAWS, Tiger's Stripe's child organisation, and the operative who signed it out to them had protested furiously.

He shut up as soon as Elder Tyrsus uttered a code phrase.

"What did you tell him?" Ric had asked.

"Essentially, we're taking this, and you don't have clearance to know why," Tyrsus had replied, the trace of a sardonic smile playing at the soft corners of her beak.

They parked their new van, adorned with the innocuous logo of "Salvano's Heating and Cooling Co.", at the end of a street only a block away from the headquarters for East Wind Holdings Incorporated.

For the second time in as many weeks, Mohan found himself wearing a set of headphones in the back with the radio equipment. His ears itched as they pressed against the sides of his broad head, but he resisted the urge to scratch.

Rizzo sat in the driver's seat with Tyrsus riding shotgun. Vicki and Zed took up positions on the opposite end of the street, forming a loose perimeter outside the sweeping glass and steel building.

After being dropped off a block away, Ric approached the café and was shown to a seat near the main entrance for East Wind Holdings. He ordered a coffee and picked up a menu, pretending to browse its contents.

The journalist was barely able to contain his excitement; for the first time since his recruitment, he felt like he was actually fulfilling a role on the team. Tyrsus confided in him earlier that he may have a future with their intelligence department.

The lynx's keen hearing kicked in almost instantly as he casually sipped on the tiny cup of strong Medoccian coffee. The talk of the town, even here in Scogliera Piatta, was the massacre at the De Palma villa in Pacé Acqua last week. Organized crime wasn't normally the subject of gossip, but such a high-profile assassination and the grandiose manner in which it happened was hard to ignore. As were its results.

There was a surprising amount of disbelief that the De Palmas were actually once Medocci's most powerful mafia family. Apparently, Vigo had done an excellent job of keeping that side of his business out of the public eye. Unfortunately, there was also no denying that mafia violence had escalated significantly since the De Palma patriarch's death.

And after the attack on the villa of Jirair al-Seif, Yursa De Palma's husband, many of the well-to-do café patrons were wondering if they might be next, especially if they had been linked with Vigo De Palma in any way.

The second most talked about news was the war in Estan, not quite as urgent in the minds of most Medoccians, but still felt. Air travel was more difficult now. Kirque continued to offer a neutral landing strip, but the only way to reach Busawar and points east was either across the battlefield between Barju and Pytan or north through Mosvian airspace, and the Mosvian Communists guarded their borders viciously. There wasn't even the slightest thought of attempting to cross the Aizlgeist. The mysterious Land of Ghosts was a dead zone, not even orbiting satellites could get a clear picture of its interior.

Ric drank all this information in as he watched Kitty and Vince stroll purposefully towards the main entrance of East Wind Holdings. The hare wore a fashionable tweed suit, although it was not as expensive or attention-grabbing as some of his other outfits. The only thing that clashed was the faded white fedora, his ears poking out the crown as always.

When Ric saw Kitty, his breath caught slightly. Gone were the faded blue jeans and the band T-shirt, replaced by a simple knee-length navy skirt that hugged her hips and a conservative long-sleeved blouse; it was just sheer enough that Ric could make out the dark stripes on her arms, but she wore a white undershirt to conceal her torso and mark. A pair of horn-rimmed glasses replaced the dark shades that normally slipped into the black gauges in her lower earlobes; if anyone actually looked through them, they would discover the lenses didn't offer any kind of vision correction.

The journalist couldn't take his eyes away from the tigress. Despite her obvious attempt to look frumpy, Ric thought she looked absolutely gorgeous.

Fortunately, Vince's chattering broke the lynx's train of thought. In addition to the van, they had also loaned some top-notch surveillance equipment from KLAWS. Kitty, Ric, and Vince all had radio receivers that looked like stud earrings and wore tiny microphones inside their lapels. The audio quality wasn't as good as any of Tiger's Stripe's equipment—which Vince was quick to point out—but it was certainly better than nothing.

"I'm rather curious about this Torosian fellow," the hare said, "I mean, who is cruel enough to name their kid Ignatius?"

"And look who's talking," Mohan replied from the van, "Vincenzo Abner Horatio Nieves."

Near an alleyway somewhere at the end of the street, Vicki laughed. "Horatio?"

"Now that ain't fair," the hare said defensively.

"Stay on point, Vince," Elder Tyrsus chimed in. "At most Torosian has only been involved with a few custody battles over ancient artefacts. He is something of a collector."

"You mean thief," Zed growled, a sound so vicious Ric almost tried to shrink away from his earpiece. The badger could be very stern, but this was the first hint of raw anger the journalist had ever heard in his voice.

"Torosian is well known to the Soketh," Zed continued, "We have warned him many times to keep off the ancient Tetzuma ruins. It is true, he has not gone exploring in recent years, but he has plundered many artefacts from Amarthia's past. Fortunately, we are certain he has never gotten hold of anything dangerous."

Vince was about to make a response when Kitty stopped him. "Hush," she breathed, "There might be fewer people here than at the Kairran market, but wouldn't you look good on camera wagging your gob to nobody."

Ric was able to track them through the lobby windows until they reached the lift, then they were on their own.

Kitty rode up in relative silence, but Vince couldn't stop himself from striking up a conversation with a mouse whose curvy frame seemed eager to make up for her species' small stature. On the thirtieth floor, she hastily grabbed a scrap of paper from her purse, scribbled something on it, and handed it to the hare before she stepped out. Kitty just gave him a look of disgust as they rode alone up to the thirty-sixth floor.

The reception outside Torosian's office was impressive. The vast space was enclosed by high beige walls adorned with modern paintings from local artists. Large clay planters held either tulips or tall snake plants. Instead of recessed fluorescent lighting, incandescent bulbs provided a much softer light, which drifted down from gold-capped fixtures that hung from brass stanchions affixed to the ceiling. The sea-foam carpets were plush and soft on Kitty and Vince's unshod feet.

Behind a sturdy half-moon-shaped desk of cedar wood lounged a female red wolf, her feet propped on the top despite wearing a skirt that barely came to her knees. If she stood up, she would undoubtedly be several centimetres taller than Kitty, and possibly Vince as well. Coffee-coloured long-fur fell in layers down past her shoulders; her bangs were cut straight across her forehead, just above her sharply angled eyebrows. A pair of blazing gold eyes gazed at them curiously, and her lips seemed curled in a perpetual grin. To Kitty she had an almost devilish look, with her pointed ears doubling as horns.

The wolf's low-cut blouse left little of her buxom frame to the imagination—a fact Vince picked out immediately—but there was little doubt in Kitty's mind that the secretary's looks were not the reason she sat behind the desk. It wasn't just the muscular tone of the wolf's arms and legs, it was the way she held the nail file she was using to manicure her claws. The grip was loose and fluid, even while she tried to look bored dragging the file lazily across the tips of her fingers.

It was the grip of an expert knife thrower.

The brass plaque on the desk read *S. Devereux*.

Vince strode up to the desk and put on his most winning smile. "Ms Devereux, we—"

"Reed," the wolf said in a bored, flat tone, "Ms Reed. Sylvia's out sick, yeah?" The inflexion of her last word made the statement sound like a question.

Kitty felt a prickling in her left arm, very faint, but there, all the same. It wasn't strange for a high-level CEO to use a receptionist that could double as a bodyguard, but the fact that the wolf didn't appear to be the usual receptionist set Kitty's mark tingling. On top of that, Reed had answered in Locken with a very distinct northern WUK accent, as opposed to a Medoccian one.

Still, Vince hadn't seemed to pick up on it; and flirt that he was, Kitty knew the hare well enough that if they were in any real danger, he would feel the same as she did.

Vince tipped his fedora to Reed and smiled again. "Terribly sorry, darlin'," he said, using the same tones he had used on the mouse in the elevator. "As I was sayin', Ms Reed...uh, you have a first name, darlin'?"

"Pris."

Vince grinned wider. "Lovely. Well, Pris, we have a two-thirty with Mr Torosian. I believe it's under UBM."

The receptionist remained in her seat, dragging the file lazily from one claw to the next. Eventually the intercom buzzed. "Show them in, Ms Reed," the voice was firm but tired.

Kitty flicked her eyes up to the closed-circuit TV camera in the corner above the desk.

With a surprising display of dexterity, the wolf stretched out one of her long legs and flicked a button on the desk console with a manicured foot claw. She kept her eyes on Vince as she did so, but the hare looked away when she moved; he might not be a prude, but he was still something of a gentleman. Kitty looked, and was not surprised to see a brace of knives strapped the Ms Reed's thigh.

With a brief mechanical buzz, one of the tall wood doors next to the reception desk cracked open. Vince grabbed the vertical brass bar and held the door open for Kitty. She scowled at him as she passed but gave one last glance at the receptionist. Reed was back to filing her nails, but the tigress was almost sure the wolf had given them both the faintest of appraising glances, and not the friendly kind.

If the reception area had been impressive, it couldn't even begin to compare to the office of Ignatius Torosian.

The same incandescent light fixtures from the reception area hung from the ceiling, but that surface was now twice as high above them, tall enough that a few small trees actually grew in little flowering gardens at the corners of the chamber. Every few lights, a sun lamp replaced the incandescent bulb to create a warm patch below it, no surprise considering the reptilian occupant—fortunately, Torosian kept the humidity low. Small potted palms lined the walls, separated at intervals by priceless bamboo paintings from East Benai's Fujiko Dynasty, roughly 2,500 years before the establishment of the Colvan Calendar. The floors were of expensive and very high-quality white marble laced with veins of emerald green. A long plush carpet, the same sea-foam colour as in the lobby, created a path from the door to the massive desk at the other end.

As Kitty and Vince moved towards the desk, they passed display cases that made them feel like they were walking through a museum instead of an office. Earthenware pots, both whole and fragments, nestled on brass-edged pedestals. If they had taken the time to read the neat plaques on each one, they would discover they dated between 10,000 and 7,000 BC, and came from the Fahir'Jin and Aa'kari peoples, two of Amarthia's oldest known civilisations—not counting the Tetzuma according to Zed and the legends told by the Soketh.

Rows of arrowheads, also from the Fujiko dynasty, were arranged around a collection of spearheads of Cedonian origin—the ancient people that would eventually evolve into the Medocci Empire.

And at the end of the display walk, closest to the desk, were a set of intricately carved metallic devices of varying size and shape lying on a velvet cloth; parts of them appeared to have melted. The hare and the tigress could only assume these were some of the fabled Tetzuma relics that the CEO of East Wind Holdings had stolen from the Soketh. Their craftsmanship was indeed very like that of the bracer Zed wore on their hunts. The purpose and design of the display devices were wholly unknown to Kitty and Vince, and they assumed only Zed could tell if they were merely parts of a whole or had some individual function.

The far wall of the office was a series of floor to ceiling glass panes that offered a stunning view of the city below. With the sweeping white curves of the building's lower roofs along the bottom edge, it looked very much like they were standing above the clouds.

The enormous desk in front of the windows was fashioned of black oak, with a thick top of black marble veined with gold. Behind it, in a very comfortable looking leather wing-chair, sat Ignatius Torosian, his striped chameleon tail sticking through a custom designed hole in the backrest.

"Ah, Mr Hammond and Ms Drowse, I believe," he said in fluent, unaccented Locken. He favoured both of them with an eye each, it was slightly unnerving. "Admiring the collection, I see. Believe it or not, this is but a fraction of what you could see at my main office in East Benai. And please excuse Ms Reed. She is from a temp agency while Ms Devereux is home sick with a stomach bug. I would ask for another replacement, but Ms Reed has got surprisingly few complaints against her, and my schedule has remained on track for the day. It's just that damned lazy wook attitude of hers, pardon my language Ms Drowse, and no offence meant to either of you."

"None taken," Vince replied.

"I'm a Plainsman," Kitty said, "And I completely understand. Good help and all that sort of thing."

After listening to the pale blue chameleon's calm voice, Kitty actually felt the tingle in her arm lessen. Torosian was appropriately polite but still tired. The tone in his voice said

I'm a busy man, but you scheduled your time so let's get on with it.

Torosian nodded and turned head and both eyes to Vince. "Mr Hammond, I understand you wished to speak about a missing shipment of computer parts. We, that is the board of directors, have already spoken with our insurance adjusters, so I am not entirely sure why you're here."

The hare smiled ingratiatingly. "Oh, I'm not here about a claim, Mr Torosian. I represent UBM's interests in this case. Ms Drowse could probably explain better."

Kitty almost shot Vince a dirty look for placing the burden on her, but she cleared her throat and did her best to appear very business-like. "I'm sure by now you have investigated our claims that UBM had a few parts mixed in with your own shipment." Torosian nodded. "Well, there were a number of server parts we are somewhat concerned about. TX-800s, multi-data file-share systems. Not that this means anything to East Wind Holdings, it's all proprietary to UBM."

Torosian held up a hand to stop her. "My apologies, Ms Drowse, but I am already aware of this. If I am not mistaken those servers were to be installed at one of my partner companies, Carneby Investments in Locke. We both lost money when the *Resthoven* disappeared. What is it you really want?"

His head shifted from the hare to the tigress and back, but he had one eye on each of them again.

Here goes, Kitty thought and took a breath.

"Ok," she said, "What we want to know is about the ship itself. How does somebody lose a thirty-metre freighter grossing sixty thousand tons?"

Torosian's eyes flickered. "A very good question, Ms Drowse. But I'm afraid I have no more answers for you today than I had for a fellow associate only yesterday."

The chameleon leaned forward and folded his hands in front of him. "I don't know if you really work for United Plains Business Machines or not, but I must inform you I find this method of amateur detective work highly irregular. You went to great lengths to schedule this appointment on short notice, and after the week I've had, I agreed to it because I found it highly amusing. But I'm afraid you've run into as much of a dead end on this matter as I have, and let me assure you, my investigation was quite thorough, Now, if you will excuse me, I have important matters to attend to." He reached for a button on the desk console.

"Please, Mr Torosian," Vince spoke up suddenly, "Ok, you got us. We're actually working with the INA."

Kitty stared at him in bewilderment, she had no idea where this announcement came from or where the hare intended to go with it.

The muscles above the chameleon's bulbous eyes contracted, giving the appearance of furrowed eyebrows. "The INA?"

"International Narcotics Association." Vince fished out an officious looking badge and flashed it just long enough for Torosian to see the raised seal and large, important letters before stuffing it back in his pocket. "We're working with the Medoccian government because we believe the *Resthoven* was involved in a major smuggling operation."

Torosian stared at him with even more bewilderment than Kitty. "Well, this is most irregular. I was aware the WUK and several Aerenian nations were attempting to create such an organisation, but I didn't know they succeeded. And to think, I rather pride myself on being up to date with international relations; it helps when you run a large trading company like East Wind."

"If everyone knew about it, the smugglers could find out we're coming," Vince replied seriously.

"And you, Ms Drowse?" the chameleon asked.

Kitty's eyes flicked from the hare to the chameleon. "I'm as surprised as you are," she said, figuring it was best to tell the truth this time.

"I'm afraid Ms Drowse is only a means to an end here," Vince said officiously, "I do beg your pardon ma'am, but it was necessary after we learned Jirair al-Seif visited Mr Torosian yesterday."

"Jirair?" Torosian was thouroughly alarmed now, "I admit he mentioned something about it during our conversation yesterday, but his theory was a conspiracy of weapons smuggling, not narcotics. In either case, you must be mistaken. I had heard rumors that Jirair's father-in-law, Vigo De Palma, might be involved with the mafia, but I've worked with al-Seif personally, and I can assure you our business is strictly legitimate."

"We're aware of that, sir," Vince answered, "However, our investigation has revealed Mr al-Seif may have ties to Assad Alabwaq."

"I've heard the name," Torosian said, "Every self-respecting trader who runs through the Hutsepth Canal is aware of the country's less reputable elements." The chameleon steepled his fingers. "It helps in avoiding them."

"Are you aware that your business partner might very well *be* Assad Alabwaq?" Vince asked.

Torosian seemed to be considering how to respond when the intercom buzzed. "Mr Delany to see you, sir," the voice of the wolf droned, but even with the mechanical buzz of the intercom, Kitty thought she detected a hint of actual excitement. Her Mark began to tingle again.

Torosian smiled. "Mr Hammond, I have no idea what you or this supposed INA hoped to gain from these absurd accusations or this interview, but the least I can do is send you away with a good meal. Think of it as gratitude for providing me with a few minutes entertainment in an otherwise dull day." He pressed a button on the intercom. "Send him in."

The doors opened, and a tall greyhound stepped through. He wore an expensive grey suit that wonderfully complimented his blue-grey fur. A tan trench coat lay draped over his right arm, but Kitty thought she saw the strap of a sling peeking out.

"Gregory!" Torosian said with unexpected cheerfulness, "A pleasure to see you again."

"The pleasure is mine, *mon ami*," the greyhound said in a strong Marisian accent.

Torosian came around the desk and made to shake the man's hand, then noticed the sling. "Oh dear," he said in surprise, "When did that happen?"

"Last week," the greyhound replied, "while gathering some rare ingredients in Pytan. It is only a scratch." He cast a brief glance at Kitty.

The tingle in the tigress' mark flared.

The chameleon gestured to his other guests. "Allow me to introduce Mr Hammond and Ms Drowse. They were just leaving, but I thought I would send them your way before they go." Addressing Vince and Kitty, Torosian said, "This is Gregory Delany, he owns the Pearl de'Sain Jean café on the ground floor. I highly recommend it and insist that you stop there before you leave. My treat, of course."

Gregory Delany flashed brilliant white canine teeth and bowed.

Kitty's blood froze.

It was *him*! The sniper from the Kairran market and leader of the group of Scarlet Dream bikers that had tried to run them down in Jar-Geshim. The tigress had her suspicions when the greyhound first walked in, but the bow, that pretentious, graceful dip of his torso with one hand to his chest and the other sweeping out to the side. She would never forget that bow, first delivered to her from the back of a retreating speedboat and then from the back of a dirt bike on the streets of Jar-Geshim.

Kitty's mark was on fire now, a fierce blaze that spread from her arm and left breast all the way to her very soul. She almost feared it would manifest in a visible glow that would burn away her shirt. It was the same feeling she experienced when she had realised who the biker was, and her fury had spilt over into the bloodlust that drove her through the ranks of the Jar-Geshim bandits on a bloody rampage.

It took everything the tigress had to contain the burning rage that boiled inside. This was not the place for a confrontation. The greyhound was goading them, goading *her.* Somehow, he had learned that she would be there and had wormed his way up to the office to provoke a reaction.

"Are you alright, my dear?" Torosian asked with genuine concern.

With deliberate coolness, Kitty replied, "Fine, thank you. It's a pleasure to meet you, monsieur Delaney, and a generous offer. But I'm afraid we've wasted enough time here. Come on, Hammond."

Kitty practically dragged Vince out of the office and into the lift. As the doors closed the tigress glanced at the wolf receptionist. Kitty didn't like the grin that spread across the bitch's face.

"What was that all about, darlin'?" Vince asked as they descended.

"This was a trap," she said, and spoke directly into her lapel mic, "Fall back, we've been set up."

* * *

Back in the office, Ignatius Torosian gazed at the entry doors in mild confusion. The look on Gregory Delany's face was far different. The greyhound's eyes narrowed as if in a dream-like state of euphoria and a toothy grin spread across his face.

"Iggy," he said without turning to the chameleon, "might I borrow your phone, *mon ami*?"

28 – Tiger by the Tail

"Kitty, what's got your fur up?" Mohan asked from the van.

"Gregory Delany," Kitty answered as the lift descended, "He's the sniper I chased over the roof in Kairran. He's here!"

Mohan cursed.

"Did Torosian know?" Elder Tyrsus cut in.

"Not as far as I could tell. Apparently, Delany's a smug enough bastard to hide in plain sight; he owns the café here at East Wind." Kitty paused as the doors opened on the twenty-sixth floor, but she shot a withering look at the tabby cat who wanted to get on and convinced him to change his mind.

Kitty continued once the doors closed. "If he's an assassin for hire, operating out of a café is actually pretty ace. He can meet with high-class clients and have half the town enraptured by his *foie gras*."

There was a brief clatter over the radio, it sounded like a fork hitting ceramic. "Sorry," Ric muttered.

"What about the receptionist?" Vince said, "Rather convenient that she had to step in for the day. And she handled that nailfile pretty handy."

Kitty stared at the hare. "If you knew something was off, why didn't you bloody say so?"

"And miss all the fun?" Vince grinned.

The tigress almost cuffed him over the ears, but the lift slowed to a stop in the lobby. They stepped out as casually as possible. It appeared building security hadn't been alerted to anything untoward, but who knew what the greyhound—and most likely the red wolf—had planned for them.

"Anyone see anything yet?" Kitty asked.

The other agents reported negatively.

"Could it be a blind?" Ric asked, "Make you paranoid so that you don't see something later?"

"Good on you, Ric," Mohan answered, "But we're already on it. Everyone, just stay calm and make your way back to the van. Vicki and Zed, converge at the end of the block and make sure the others clear the café."

The main lobby of East Wind Holdings had a separate entrance for the café and patio dining area. Kitty and Vince made in that direction and met up with Ric at his table outside. The tigress glanced at a half-eaten plate of aukie liver on the table and frowned. The lynx pushed the plate away guiltily.

"I was only joking, Ric," Kitty admonished.

The journalist just shrugged helplessly.

The tigress jerked her head towards the valet stand and the café exit, but as soon as Ric's back was turned, she stole a quick taste with the claw of one finger. The *foie gras* actually was excellent.

Turning back, Kitty saw that the lynx journalist had barely taken three steps before stopping suddenly.

"What now?" she asked, irritated.

Ric gestured subtly to his left. "The brown stoat in the silver seersucker," he said quietly, "That's Raphelo Lougotti. He's one of the Favera's lieutenants. And he's watching us."

Sure enough, the stoat's beady black eyes stared unabashedly at the trio of agents. Kitty nudged Ric forward, but Lougotti's gaze never left them.

As the agents approached the valet podium, they found their path blocked by three hulking members of the primate family. Each of the gorillas wore a grey suit and dinner jacket that barely fit over their broad shoulders and bulging arms. The one on the left seemed slightly thinner than his companions, and the one on the right had a head with the oblong shape of a rugby ball. The centre one, whose brow was much taller than either of his companions, had four long scars across his face.

The agents measured their options. A knee-high metal fence enclosed the outdoor portico of the café; its purpose was to mark the boundaries of the eatery rather than to keep people out. It wouldn't take much just to hop over and dart down the street, but they didn't want to cause a scene just yet.

The centre ape said something in Mecci. Kitty and Ric only caught half of it, but they understood the word "Favera".

Vince, on the other hand, was fluent in the language. "It appears these gentlemen believe we're tresspassin' on Favera turf," he said quietly.

There was a clatter of cutlery, and the agents didn't need to turn around to know that the patrons dining outside had begun to move inside the café.

Ric fought the urge to turn and see if the stoat was still at his table behind them. The mark on his forearm began to burn. He was starting to realise the sensation was a kind of early warning system and assumed both Vince and Kitty felt it as well.

"Steady," Mohan's voice came to them over the radio, "Remember the mafia's in turmoil here. They might make big claims, but high-profile businesses like East Wind won't tolerate them, and have the security to back it up."

"Unless Torosian's made a deal," Kitty whispered.

"Vince, you're the talker," Mohan said, "See if you can convince them they made a mistake."

The hare was already putting on his best comradely smile. "Now don't be in a rush, *amico*," he said addressing scar-face, "We were in the process of leavin' when you seemed to step in our way."

The rugby-headed ape cracked his knuckles while the thin one cracked his neck.

Scar-face said, "We just wanted to make sure you found the quickest way out."

Over the shoulder of the thin ape, Kitty could see Vicki and Zed watching the standoff from the opposite side of the street.

* * *

The badger and the bullfrog had seen the thugs making their way towards the café. As they listened to the exchange between their comrades and the gorilla squad, Zed examined their avenues of attack. He was about to order a flanking manoeuvre when he felt a tug on his shirt sleeve. He looked down at the diminutive bullfrog next to him, then over to the alley Vicki was pointing at.

Roughly half a dozen figures, mostly canine, were moving towards them. Their leader was a scruffy rat with a chip cut out of his left ear. They all wore identical green coveralls and carried long knives.

Zed turned to face them, squaring his broad shoulders and preparing for a fight. Vicki shrank behind him; she would defend herself if she had to, but as a medic her own personal code detested violence. Her bulbous speckled eyes darted around looking for a way to scare off the gang.

Vicki spied a row of metal dustbins lined up along a wall. The trash hadn't been collected yet, and they gave her an idea. She started rummaging in her pockets.

The thugs began to bunch near the entrance to the alley, but Zed would not let them spread out into the street. The first of the thugs lunged at the Soketh with his knife and the badger easily sidestepped the attack, grabbing the knife arm and spinning the hound-mutt back into the group. The thugs scattered and let their companion fall to the ground, but he lay only a moment before picking himself up.

Zed's unique brand of martial arts was ideal for small groups like this. Every time one goon attempted to strike, the badger sent him back into the troupe, using him to trip up half his companions and leaving only a few able to mount a counterattack. And when they did, they quickly ended up in the same predicament as their fellows.

Meanwhile, Vicki found what she was looking for in her pockets. After their confrontation on the streets of Jar-Geshim last week, the bullfrog had got together with Rizzo to build the medic some small defensive weapons. Vicki pulled out a handful of cherry bombs and a small box of all-surface-strike matches and hopped over to the dustbins.

The bins were the simple, round, metal ones that seemed ubiquitous to every city—in a pinch, the metal lids made for excellent shields. With the right materials, like a handful of cherry bombs, they also made great urban mortars.

Vicki selected the one with the grimiest looking trash and started dragging it toward Zed and the alley entrance.

The badger continued his careful balancing act with the thugs, but he wouldn't be able to keep it up much longer. Soketh martial arts were all about using an opponent's strength against them, but unlike the undisciplined bandits of Jar-Geshim, the Favera henchmen had excellent command of their weapons. The badger had managed to avoid getting cut himself, but he was unable to get the goons to injure their fellow ruffians. Once they had caught on to the badger's strategy, several of the thugs actually dropped their knives and just tried to pummel Zed with their natural claws and teeth.

The rat leader ordered his men to regroup and prepare an all-out rush on the badger when Zed heard Vicki whistle behind him. The badger stepped out of the way, causing one of the felines in the group—a wiry lynx with a face much heavier than Ric's—to stumble past him and sprawl over the lid of the dustbin Vicki had propped up against another. The lynx looked confused for a moment before the cherry bombs inside exploded and sent him flying back into the alley along with a shower of refuse.

The thugs baulked as greasy papers, scraps of food, and other unpleasant bits of detritus coated their fur, but Zed didn't give them a chance to recover. The badger swept into their midst and began cracking heads and breaking arms; he left their legs alone, he wanted them able to walk away.

* * *

Over at the café, Kitty watched the fight across the street and smirked when one of the gorillas looked up at the sound of the explosion followed by the shrieks and brays of pain.

"Hear that?" Kitty asked, "That's just *one* of us. But you have to face *three*."

Rugby-head started to back off, but scar-face turned to him and bared his teeth. "Where do you think you're going, Marty? That's Carlos' gang over there, you know he's as dull as a bent knife. We can take these three."

The one called Marty looked uncertainly at the three agents. The lynx in the pocketed khaki vest looked like one of those sappy international news correspondents, and the rabbit in the fancy suit was grinning like a bucktoothed idiot. Honestly, Marty wasn't worried about those two. But the tigress...she was trying to look like a stuffy librarian, but the fire burning in those sapphire eyes was colder than the Sweisæ Alps in winter.

Or maybe like gelato, which would be the only thing Marty'd be able to eat after the tigress broke his jaw and knocked all his teeth out.

Whatever Marty the gorilla's final response was, he never got a chance to say it.

A squeal of tires made them all turn to the far end of the street—the end where Mohan, Rizzo, and Tyrsus sat huddled in the van. But it wasn't the agent's companions that came roaring around the corner.

The black sedan had no plates, and the windows were so dark that the occupants were barely visible. As the vehicle approached the café, the rear window began to descend.

"Eat dirt!" Kitty cried, and yanked Ric to the ground with her. Vince needed no such assistance.

The sputtering crack of an automatic weapon split the air as the sedan screamed past the front of the café. Ric felt hot blood spatter on his neck and the back of his hands as they covered his head. Three heavy *thumps* followed as the gorillas crumpled to the ground, riddled with large holes. Half of Marty's rugby-shaped face was gone.

Dazed, Ric looked up to see Raphelo Lougotti crawling away from his fallen henchmen; apparently, he had seen what was happening and also dove to the ground. There was another screech of rubber, and Ric turned to see the van skid to a stop in front of the café. Mohan was out and helping Vince to his feet. The sound of sirens already filled the air.

Someone must have called them from the café, Ric thought, *Pity they didn't arrive sooner.*

"Come on, nutter!" Kitty cried, lifting the journalist off the ground and shoving him towards the van.

Zed and Vicki came running from across the street. Once they were all inside Rizzo spun the wheel and made for one of the alleyways.

But it was too late. Compact blue and white checker cars with the word *Polizia* emblazoned on them came from every direction, cutting off their escape. Rizzo threw the van into reverse, but Elder Tyrsus put a hand on her arm.

"No, Emperatriz," she said calmly, using the basilisk's given name. "It's over. They won this round."

Rizzo's brows furrowed in dismay. Then she nodded, put the van in park and batted at the Buru'nadi prayer beads she always hung over the rear-view mirror.

Ric watched the beads swing back and forth then focused on the uniformed peace officers approaching with guns drawn.

"So," he asked, "Now what?"

29 – Delshad's Folly

There were two elements traditionally associated with gladiator games: the fighters and the slaves. As far as Jirair and Delshad al-Seif were concerned, slave trading was just a means to draw in their patrons; a pretty, often temporary, souvenir to entertain the guests when blood and passions ran high. Slaves were weak, petty things; often easily ensnared by their own addictions.

But not these ones.

The collection of ragtag figures who glared dolefully at the ibex-mouflon through the bars of their cells were all that remained of Alabwaq's once thriving trade. They were the survivors of the auction in Kairran last week, which was also their last needle.

Contrary to popular belief, Assad Alabwaq kept his slaves healthy by only doping them when presented in public. The low dose of heroin was enough to keep them docile, but still mobile. Oh, they were addicted of course, only one taste had been enough to ensure that; but doses were handed out in small quantity and many days apart. Long enough that their bodies could actually recover from the withdraw, but their minds still remembered the bliss.

The high was gone now, and the eyes of a myriad of species burned with a mixture of hatred, need, and despair.

"And beasts?" Delshad asked.

The dromedary Rashid checked a clipboard. "Barely a dozen, sir," he said, "Eight desert bahngers, a trio of ceravaags from the Valley of Nefrit, and a hargaer we captured in Kolovania. Your father planned to hold an exhibition the day after his auction last week, but circumstances being what they are…"

Rashid trailed off, there was no need to recount the elder al-Seif's recent misfortune.

"We should fix that," Delshad said, "It is only fitting that this arena see one last grand event before we close it."

The ibex-mouflon turned from the cage and began strolling leisurely towards the lifts that would take him from the bowels of the underground arena up to the main lobby.

"Arrange a new event for Setaurday," Delshad continued, "No, make it Fosday. We should give the guests time to recover from my party tomorrow night. Any beasts that survive will have to be slaughtered, of course, but I think we can avoid that with a good roster."

The doors to the lift opened and Rashid followed his employer in. "And the slaves, sir?" the dromedary asked.

Delshad was silent as the lift started to rise.

"Let the gladiators have them," the ibex-mouflon said at last, "If any survive grant them freedom, they'll have earned it."

The lift stopped and Delshad took a sharp right upon exiting to enter the kitchens that served the VIP lounge. He could hear the murmur of a crowd beyond the far door, even above the clatter of the kitchen staff. He took a peek through the diamond-shaped window of the kitchen door.

Roughly sixty warriors gathered in the Khet arena's VIP lounge; a large space tastefully decorated with purple and gold drapery and crystal chandeliers. Most of the combatants were twice Delshad's size, and half of them looked very uncomfortable in suits and ties. The females carried themselves with more grace but could still crush their employer's head between forearm and bicep if they wanted to; Assad Alabwaq played no favourites with gender, a fighter was a fighter.

Delshad had always enjoyed the gladiatorial games, they were one of the rare opportunities the young ibex-mouflon got to spend time with his father outside of Medocci, much to his mother's disappointment. Carmen loved both men dearly but had always hoped that as time wore on, they would find other means to satisfy their desires; she felt the violence of the arena was unbecoming of herbivore species, especially since they comprised the majority of those enslaved.

But both father and son revelled in the spectacle of combat. The truth was that every sentient being on Amarthia had a deep-seated bloodlust hidden within them. Jirair and Delshade saw no wrong in keeping their desires satiated by watching others give into them. Society might consider herbivores to be more peaceful than predators but put two rabbits in a room with only one knife and tell them only one is allowed to leave alive, and you will quickly see how the instinct for survival takes over.

Besides, after learning of the attempt on his mother's life yesterday, the last thing Delshad al-Seif wanted was to be less violent.

However, he couldn't lose control; not today, and not in front of his father's gladiators. There would be plenty of ways to release some of his frustrations once he took care of this vital piece of business.

The facility would find other uses until they could reopen but Delshad had yet to make the announcement of its closure to the gladiators themselves. He was unsure how they were going to take it.

Squaring his shoulders, the ibex-mouflon pushed open the door.

No one seemed to notice him exit at first, but Delshad noticed with a little apprehension that one lioness, in particular, was giving him much more than a casual glance. He purposefully averted his gaze and stepped up onto the long stage occupying one wall of the lounge. Primarily it was used for the gladiators to show off themselves and their slave accompaniment before matches, but today there was a microphone set up in the centre.

"Your attention please," Delshad said, clearing his throat. The murmurs died down. "Attention. Thank you all for coming. Some of you may recognise me as the son of your employer, Assad Alabwaq. While operating in his stead, you may address me as the same."

Delshad spoke clearly and firmly, as his father would have. These men and women may be little more than animals inside the ring, but outside they had at least some amount of sentient reasoning. Enough, at least, not to mindlessly slaughter the man who would provide them with their next taste of combat and fresh slaves to serve other needs.

"Though I don't know you personally," the ibex-mouflon continued, "I consider myself a fan, and I have witnessed many of you fight in the arena. Garik." He gave a perfunctory nod to the massive rhinoceros who was the current champion.

Delshad paused to let his words sink in a little, allowing the gladiators to bask in the praise they so strongly desired.

"No doubt you are all wondering why I asked that you get dressed up for this occasion," he continued, "Some of you may even have heard about how several of my lieutenants met an untimely end. I assure you I have not come to deliver you to the same ignoble fate. Nor must you face me as one of your former champions, Solair of the Golden Scale did."

Fresh murmurs rippled through the gladiators, this news had definitely reached them. Delshad hadn't thought about it at the time but defeating one of the gladiators' old guard in single combat, even if he had grown old and slow, had netted the ibex-mouflon a great deal of respect among Solair's younger peers.

"However," Delshad said, "The news I bring is still not good, and may distress some of you greatly. I am afraid that with the current state of foreign affairs in Pytan, I must close down the arena."

Gasps of dismay and not a few angry roars rose from the hulking guests. Delshad raised a hand to calm them.

"Do not think I have forgotten you. You are men and women of action." As he scanned the crowd, Delshad's eyes came across the lioness again. She winked and blew him a kiss, and for a moment he realised that, muscles or not, she wasn't half bad looking.

Delshad cleared his throat again and continued, "You will each receive a standard sum equal to what you would have earned this season had the games continued. Please see my assistant, Rashid, to arrange how you want to receive this payment or whom should get it in your stead."

Delshad thought he saw the dromedary's ever-present tall turban at the back of the room, mostly hidden by the massive figures staring up at him.

"But money is not enough," Delshad said, "You should be paid in blood!" A hearty cheer began but the ibex-mouflon spoke above it, "On Fosday there will be one final grand event to celebrate this venerable venue. May you fight and die well!"

Despite only occupying a third of the room, the roar of the gladiators rose to deafening in the space of the lounge. Delshad let it continue for a while before raising his hands to calm them.

"Hoprefully, not all of you will meet your end at this event," the ibex-mouflon said, pausing a moment, "because I have a reward for you as well. For those who survive and wish to continue training and fighting, I have made arrangements for you to do so on the Isle of Thyropolis!"

The tone of the gasps was very different this time.

According to legend, the island of Thyropolis was the birthplace of gladiatorial combat, where an ancient order of monks secretly recorded every battle and weighed the deeds of the contenders. This was all rot of course, but the island's tenuous legal status further propagated the myth. Though technically residing in Medocci waters, a private owner had purchased the island over a thousand years ago. The deed continued to pass down from one generation of mysterious owners to the next, keeping the Medoccian government from laying any claim to it.

Regardless of who really controlled the island, Thyropolis was indeed the site of a large gladiatorial training school; and every year, they hosted an extravagant series of competitions for all comers. Abar Kami himself held champion status in several events.

It had cost Assad Alabwaq a great deal of money and favours to make such an arrangement with the school; but of all the assets he needed to secure, the gladiators were the most valuable.

Delshad let his guests marvel at the news before continuing. "I knew that would get your attention," the ibex-mouflon said, "Now please, try to enjoy yourselves." He waved to a line of tables at one end of the lounge. "And do not forget that tomorrow I will be hosting another party at my apartments in Kairran. They have seen too little use in these past months."

The gladiators eyed the expensive spread on the tables with a great deal of suspicion. Delshad sighed in exasperation and went to the table himself. He had to sample at least one of everything, especially the various bottles of liquor, to put the fighters more at ease. Satisfied there was no poison, they descended on the booze and food like the beasts that they were.

The ibex-mouflon shrank back from the most uncivilised display, and for a moment he was concerned about how well the gladiators would mingle with the more refined guests at the celebration tomorrow. Delshad brushed the thought away; he wanted the last big bash at the penthouse apartment to be something worthy of a decadent crime lord, and a bunch of drunken, muscle-bound fools in ill-fitting suits dancing to a DJ was exactly the kind of spectacle he was looking for.

His father wasn't pleased with that part of Delshad's plans, and in the back of his mind, the ibex-mouflon knew he was right to think so. Delshad tried explaining that it was all about keeping up appearances, about letting others play the fool while knowing you were above them, but the elder mouflon still hadn't approved.

In fact, Jirair al-Seif had practically demanded that his son wrap things up and return to Medocci as soon as possible. He was proud that Delshad had resisted the urge to further his ambitions by making a deal with Freggs, but now that the mechanical toad knew his influence with the al-Seifs was waning, they would become his targets.

Delshad's train of thought was derailed as the lioness brushed by him. He turned to her, studying the curve of thighs almost as big around as his waist; she had purposely torn the seams of her dress just so she could walk. The lioness flexed one arm, then made a gesture like she was hugging something to her chest, presumably his head.

Delshad looked her in the eye and raised a questioning eyebrow. The lioness motioned for him to follow her to the edge of the crowd where they could hear each other speak.

"You were bold to take Solair alone," the lioness said, "Even at his age, he was a seasoned trainer."

Delshad's eyes narrowed sharply. "A pity his mind wasn't as sharp as his claws," he said cooly, "I hope it is clear betrayal is not tolerated."

The lioness took a sip from her champagne flute and grinned above the glass. "Indeed, in mind he was weak," she said, then leaned toward his ear and whispered, "But not all of us are pure brutes. Perhaps before you send me away, I could show you?" She reached up to run a finger along one of his ridged horns.

Delshad grabbed her wrist reflexively and was instantly wary of the lioness' movements.

The lioness hummed in approval. "Oh, such reflexes," she said, "Perhaps you would be willing to give me a *full* demonstration. Somewhere more comfortable?"

The ibex-mouflon's dark cheeks turned very red. Somewhere in the back of Delshad's mind the voice of his father was trying to tell him that this exotically tall feline had stepped beyond her bounds and should be put in her place. That was precisely what Delshad wanted to do with her, but not in the way the scolding voice in his head meant.

Maybe it was the booze the gladiators forced him to sample, but Delshad's vision began to swim slightly. The lioness really was a vision of physical perfection. Naturally, she didn't have a mane like male lions, but she still had long-fur. The golden locks were shaved on the sides below her round ears, but down the middle it fell in a tightly braided mohawk that reached beyond her neck; if Delshad recalled correctly, the style had its roots with ancient Norsen warrior women. Her arms were almost as big as her thighs, but the sky-blue dress she wore also showed off a tantalising torso;

everything about this lioness seemed proportioned just right, a symmetry of beauty and power.

Delshad looked around almost guiltily, but the other gladiators seemed much more interested in the food and drink. Gaining control of himself again, the ibex-mouflon looked up into the feline's dazzling blue eyes and nodded.

Delshad didn't know what had suddenly made him feel and act so childish, but he shrugged it off and squared his shoulders before leading his new date to the door. He was the master here, and he would act the part. His father may keep a strict policy of not getting involved with his employees, but Delshad was not his father. Of course, his father also devoted himself to only one woman.

Secretly, Delshad admitted that he'd often watched the female fighters in the arena and wondered if they were half as vicious in bed; this lioness seemed more than eager to let him find out. Abar Kami would have struck his pupil upside his head for the lack of discipline, but Delshad was already thinking about which holds he might like to try on the lioness in a most improper manner.

Assad Alabwaq's white limo sat parked in the underground garage. The driver, a lanky green anole, held open the rear door for Delshad and his companion without question or even the slightest tilt of his head; what his employer wished to do and with whom was none of his business.

"The bungalow," Delshad told the driver as he climbed in after the lioness.

The anole nodded, and climbed into the driver's seat, making sure the privacy screen was up. Delshad didn't even notice when the vehicle started moving, lions couldn't purr, but as she leaned against him she let out a series of low growls that reverberated through him like a series of shockwaves.

The bungalow in question was the very one al-Seif had sold after his beloved Carmen moved away. The mouflon had repurchased it at his mistress' request, although they rarely stayed there. Delshad had made the most use of it after he came of age, often taking long vacations at the beach and enjoying the fruits of his father's ill-gotten gains.

The bungalow was only a twenty-minute drive from the arena, but neither the limo nor its occupants ever reached their destination.

It was rush hour on a Faerday afternoon, and traffic was naturally heavy. The car entered into a construction zone, and a traffic officer waved the long vehicle down a side street. The anole cursed the ancestry of the cop as he carefully manoeuvred through streets barely able to permit the limo.

The driver turned a corner and entered into a makeshift market that had been set up along the narrow lane. He didn't notice that the street appeared deserted because soon after making the turn he slammed on the breaks to avoid a heavy cart laden with produce that was blocking the road ahead. The anole laid on the horn and spouted curses at the cloaked figure trying to urge on the ghuskas attached to the cart. Naturally, the humped, almost buffalo-like pack animals wouldn't budge.

The limo driver threw the vehicle into reverse only to discovered he wasn't able to navigate in that direction either.

While cursing out the cart driver, the anole hadn't seen the large military-style transport truck pull in behind them.

The anole's employer barely felt the lurch of the car when it stopped, and the blare of the vehicle's horn was somehow distant in Delshad's ears. He was far too preoccupied with the lioness.

She kissed him roughly, stroking his horns with her strong hands. The rapid vibration of her growling sent shivers up and down Delshad's spine, and he let his hands roam across the bulging muscles of her arms. Her hands moved down to his pants.

Up front, the cloaked figure moved towards the driver's window, one hand clutched to his chest in a gesture of apology. The anole scowled and rolled down his window.

The cloak came down to reveal a narrow-faced jackal and his other hand, hidden by the folds of the robe, came out carrying a small pistol. Before the anole could even react, the jackal calmly shot him between the eyes.

Delshad al-Seif's pants were on the floor now, and the lioness, still clothed, straddled atop him. The gunshot was enough to finally startle the ibex-mouflon out of his lust, but when he tried to push the lioness off, he found her massive hands around his neck, the claws of her thumbs pressing into the soft flesh beneath his jaw. The weight of her body was suddenly heavy against him, and he discovered that in his aroused state, he had allowed himself to become hopelessly pinned to the seat.

"I really do wish we could continue this," the lioness said, "but I'm afraid your offer to send me to Thyropolis just wasn't good enough." She bared her teeth in a wicked grin.

"Of course, it never really applied to me anyway, I never worked for you. You really should check your roster more carefully."

She opened her mouth and drew her rough tongue up across his muzzle and between his eyes. The claws at his throat tightened slightly.

Inside Delshad's mind, the primitive herbivore side of his being was screaming in panic. He was all but certain the lioness intended to eat him, breaking one of the most sacred unspoken laws of Amarthia. Even sentient fish and insects—who ate non-sentient fish and insects—would never dream of committing such a barbaric act as cannibalism.

Outwardly, all the ibex-mouflon could do was fix the lioness with his most defiant glare.

The door opened from the outside, and the lioness relaxed her grip. She dragged him half-naked from the car and threw him to the ground. A crowd of men and women as butch as the lioness encircled the limo now. Half carried assault rifles in their paws, the others carried long blades.

"Oh, but isn't he a pretty *jung* now, *ja*?" a high and reedy voice said. It carried the distinct sharp strains of a Dollan accent.

Delshad turned his head to see a short figure leaning against the truck with one foot on the front fender. At first, he thought it was a fox from the shape of his head, but the colouring was all wrong, it was more brown and black almost like a shepherd dog; his ears and tail were also more shepherd-like than fox-like. The left ear bent out at an odd angle in the middle, almost as if someone had cut a chunk out of it and it re-healed poorly. A plume of scraggly, platinum-coloured long-fur flowed down his back, tied in a ponytail.

Blazing orange eyes winked back at Delshad. There was the faintest hint of madness behind them, madness that made Delshad al-Seif very wary of the large pistol he held in his hand.

"*Ja*, a pretty *jung* indeed." The fox-shepherd slapped his knee and strode over with long almost tottering strides. "But not so much soon."

He made a sharp gesture to the lioness, and she summarily stripped off the rest of Delshad's clothes, leaving him stark naked except for his body-fur.

"We wouldn't want to get blood on those nice threads, *ja*?" the fox-shepherd grinned. His own clothing was a pair of khaki shorts that his lanky legs practically swam in and a very loud flowered shirt.

"I may not kill you, Weis," Delshad said with a growl, "But when my father learns what you've done—"

A series of sharp barks interrupted him as Kristoph Weis erupted in a fit of laughter. He waved the gun around carelessly, causing his henchmen to flinch every time it pointed their way.

"*Ja*, you *reiche jungs* all the same," Weis cackled. Delshad spoke little Dollan, but he thought the phrase meant rich boys.

"You get in trouble and it's always, '*mein vater* will hear of this!'" Weis went on.

Delshad continued to glare at him. On reflection, he had made a poor choice of words, but his threat had not been an idle one. Based on the madness in the fox-shepherd's eyes, the ibex-mouflon was wondering if Weis even cared.

"I'm still better off than you, half-breed," Delshad said coldly, playing on what he knew of Weis' ancestry.

Weis stopped laughing abruptly. He bent down before the nude ibex-mouflon, resting his hands on his bony knees. "*Ja*? Who you calling half-breed, half-breed?"

He knocked on Delshad's horns with a knuckle, then stood up and began pacing between Delshad and the truck, waving his gun for emphasis. "You, your *vater* is a sheep, a, a mouflon they call it, *ja*. And your *mutter*. Oh yes, dear sweet *frau* Carmen. She is an ibex, *ja*? You're as much a half-breed as me."

"But my country hasn't made me an outcast."

Delshad grinned so viciously that the lioness, who had been looming over him, shrank back; although in hindsight, that may also have been in preparation for the outburst she knew was coming.

Weis' back was to Delshad as he made this insult and the fox-shepard hunched his shoulders and scrunched down in a cartoonish fashion. He whirled on his prisoner and practically leapt on top of him. A stream of curses flowed from his lips as he kicked Delshad in the side again and again.

Delshad grimaced at the pain, but he smiled inwardly; he had struck a nerve. The Dollan Empire, nestled within the valleys of the Zeichlind Mountains in the country of the same name, was extraordinarilly fascist and placed a high degree of fastidiousness on breeding lines. Weis could never set foot in his homeland again, and most likely neither would his father or the bitch that sired him, if they were still alive.

Weis struck Delshad across the face with his canine foot, the short claws raking the ibex-mouflon's cheek. Delshad felt the blood start to well in the fresh cuts.

Then, almost as suddenly as the outburst had begun, the fox-shepherd was calm again. "You think I planned this on my own?" he asked, cackling softly, "*Nein,* much as I would like to take credit you must know I couldn't have done this alone."

The thought had crossed Delshad's mind, but the question was who? Freggs most likely, but he thought the mechanical voice would want someone less unhinged and flashy to be his assassin.

"*Nein,*" Weis continued, "Here you see both my men and some of Mody Nahas'. But how did we know you were here? How did I know that Reneta," and here he gestured with the pistol to the lioness, "would be just the kind of girl to give you a hard-on and drag you away from all those big gladiators?"

Weis bent down, sticking his face so close Delshad could smell the reek of his carnivore-breath. "Your mother-in-law."

Delshad's eyes widened involuntarily, and Weis cackled again.

"*Ja, frau* De Palma. She told us what we needed to trap you. And even now she plans to take care of *frau* Carmen and *hier* Jirair al-Seif herself."

Delshad realised with horror that Weis hadn't used his father's criminal pseudonym. Then his brows knit in anger and he spat in the fox-shepherd's face.

Weis wiped it away carelessly. "I sent men to help her. Maybe *frau* De Palma will let them have fun first. Your *mutter,* she's nice, *ja*? Very pretty. Nice big—"

Delshad wouldn't let him finish the thought. He lurched toward the fox-shepherd, biting with his flat herbivore teeth and swinging his arms wildly. But the wily Weis darted out of the way and Reneta the lioness leaned her weight against the ibex-mouflon again. Her growling took on a much different tone now.

"Ah, ah," Weis cackled, wagging his gun around again. "You can hit a sore spot and so can I, *ja*? But enough playing. Bye, bye, *reiche junge*."

Weis pressed the barrel of the pistol to Delshad's head.

* * *

Mody Nahas' eyes wandered delightedly over the veiled giraffe woman as she gesticulated on the raised platform at the centre of his audience chamber. The dance was an old tradition dating back generations, and it was building up to the best part; she only had a few shear coverings left on her slender bejewelled body.

Unfortunately, the sharp bells of his antique telephone cut his enjoyment of the dance short with their harsh ring.

Nahas pounded heavily on the arm of his chair, and the dancer and musicians stopped suddenly. They prepared to continue at the obese orangutan's command, but instead, he gave them the gesture to take a break and answered the phone.

"What is it, gods damn you?" the orangutan bellowed into the handset.

"Aw, Mody, *mein freund*," the reedy voice of Kristoph Weis answered. "I am interrupting something, *ja*? One of your concubines straddling your fat ass?"

Nahas' purplish lips frowned in disgust, the fox-shepherd had no taste at all. He would miss Assad Alabwaq when he was gone, at least the mouflon had class.

"I trust you are not interrupting my afternoon just to regale me with your juvenile imagination," Nahas said, scratching languorously at the bulk of his belly protruding beneath his silk vest.

"*Ja*, always quick to get down to business," Weis said sulkily, "Call the bitch in Medocci, tell *frau* De Palma the deed is done. Got some pretty pictures to back it up if she wants them."

"I have a better idea. We'll send them along to Alabwaq's right hand, I believe his name is Rashid. His word alone should be enough to make Assad faint dead away."

Weis cackled, and Nahas flinched away from the phone handset. "And dead he will soon be! But don't forget our bargain, ape!"

Nahas frowned again. "Yes, a truce between us. At least as long as this war is on. But depending on how long that is we may both need to apply pressure to the Regent and his Governor General before long."

Mody Nahas fervently hoped this would not be the case; the thought of having to work with the fox-shepherd a second time was truly revolting.

"*Ja, ja*," came the reply, "Now I will leave you to your dancing girls and hookas."

"Ass," the orangutan snarled and hung up the phone.

He turned to the giraffe dancer, waiting expectantly on the stage.

"Please, my dear," Nahas said, motioning with a long-fingered hand. "From the top, if you will. I find this dance must be played out in its entirety to be truly enjoyed."

The giraffe bowed and retrieved the veils she had discarded during the dance. It would take a few minutes for her to re-dress, but Nahas could be patient, and he needed a moment to think.

In the shadows behind the orangutan's stone throne, seemingly forgotten for the moment, stood a tattooed rhesus monkey. She had one very special tattoo on the small of her back, one that looked like the face of a tiger. And through the earpiece concealed beneath the veils covering her head, she had heard every word that Mody Nahas had exchanged with Kristoph Weis.

30 – Pawn Queen

Rays of morning sunlight crept through the thin curtains of the bedroom. Its lone female occupant let the beam's warmth bathe her for a moment before opening her eyes.

Yursa De Palma was alone. She knew she would be, but she let her thoughts drift back to the evening before.

The dinner last night had been excellent; whoever Gregory Delany really was, he had superb taste in dining. However, it was their conversation that had interested Yursa the most.

Delany was charming, of course, but it was a cold charm, almost cruel. He offered his condolences for her family, but there was a flat frankness to him that made Yursa feel as if it was merely a formality.

"You seem fairly detached for one so interested in my family," Yursa said after they had ordered drinks, "One may even be tempted to think *you* were their murderer."

"And what if I was?" Delany asked her.

Yursa looked at him for a long moment. "I would cut your heart out and make you eat it," she answered.

Delany smiled coldly. "That is good. That is the spirit my employer wishes to harness."

"Do not make the same mistake as my *husband*." She spat the word. "I am not a treasure to be displayed, a conquest to be made, or a power for anyone to master."

The greyhound studied her, stirring a martini with the tip of one finger and resting his cheek in the palm of one hand. "No," he said at last, "No, you are a queen, commanding all you see with a rod of steel."

Yursa's eyes narrowed sharply. "You did not deny my accusation," she said, "I am no longer amused by games. Does your *king* believe he can move this queen like one of his pawns?"

Delany didn't so much as blink. He just kept staring at her, his narrow black eyes burning like coal. Yursa spoke fiercely, but she realised she was losing herself in those eyes.

"If I am but a pawn myself, *chéri*, how would I know?" he asked.

"You are not a pawn," Yursa said, and took a long sip of her wine. "You are a knight, with armour black as pitch. Pawns do your bidding just as you obey your master's."

The greyhound said nothing, he didn't need to, it was all there in his sardonic smile.

"Is al-Seif one of those pawns as well?" Yursa asked.

Delany nodded. "*Oui*, but not one of mine. However, your husband has become a...liability to the one that chooses to move him."

Yursa bristled at the word "husband", and Delany seemed to take pleasure in reminding her of her self-imposed attachment. However, her demeanour changed to amusement once she caught the implication of Delany's words. Perhaps her greyhound suitor didn't intend for her to bear the shackles of matrimony much longer.

"Well," Delany said after a moment, "You are not a woman who wastes time so I will give you our offer, and we can enjoy our meal, *non*?"

Yursa said nothing.

"The De Palmas must, of course, rise above the glory your father once held. We can help with this, but you must work for us. Your assets can only stretch so far, and al-Seif still has control over the shipping lines."

"And if you were to remove him," Yursa said, "I could only regain De Palma Shipping if I remained married to him."

Delany shrugged noncommittally. "*Oui*, but we must also make sure you are not involved should anything... unfortunate happen to him."

"That is where we have a problem," the wolfhound growled, "I want to be *very* involved. I want to bite down on his throat and tear it out myself, then mount his bleached skull on the wall."

The greyhound frowned. "Please, *Mademoiselle*, though the fire of vengeance burns so brightly in you, we must keep those beautiful hands clean."

Delany reached out and stroked one of her paws. Yursa didn't pull away.

It was a tempting offer. For all her boasting, Yursa knew that her devotion to bringing al-Seif down would eventually leave her spent. What resources she had were powerful, but they were also irreplaceable.

As to the issue of her marriage, she suspected there was more to Delany's proposal than her eligibility to reclaim what was rightfully hers. She only wished she could figure out what it was.

The devilish greyhound that sat across from her had been appropriately vague about his involvement in the murder of her family. But why had he approached her if he was guilty? Did his own employers intend to intimidate her with their warped display of mercy?

Suppose I do roll over like a good bitch? she thought, *Wouldn't that be the perfect way to bring the real killers down? From the inside?*

Aloud Yursa said, "If I stand down and let you handle al-Seif, you'll restore my family's stadning?"

"And more, *chéri*," Delany replied. He took her paw in both of his now, stroking the grey fur gently. "We can give you the whole Medean Basin if you desire. However, I think we can let you have one little bonus. You can have al-Seif, but you must do it our way."

"I accept," Yursa said, rather more huskily than she intended. What else did she agree to?

The rest of the evening was spent with small talk. Once the deal had been sealed Delany would not talk about his real work, but he was more than happy to admit he was a successful restaurateur. She had heard of the Pearl de'Sain Jean but had never eaten there. It also didn't surprise her to learn he was a partner in the very restaurant they dined.

And all the while she continued to drink in those dark eyes. They sparked to life when he spoke of his businesses, but it was still a cold light, springing up from somewhere deep within him.

She wanted to dive in and channel those depths. She knew that what she found there would be as black as the deepest trenches of the oceans, but she didn't care. The abyss had caught her now, and the only place to go was down.

When they had finished, Delany saw the wolfhound out to her car. On impulse, Yursa grabbed the collar of his shirt and kissed him roughly.

"I want you," she whispered when she pulled away, "I shouldn't, you probably had some hand in murdering my father. But all the same."

The greyhound gave that cold smile again and held the door for her. Delany drove her to her apartment, and she didn't have to give him directions.

Marrying Jirair al-Seif had been Yursa's idea. It had worked, for the most part; the businesses of De Palma and al-Seif had flourished together, and Yursa had been able to gather insight on the mouflon's operations that would have otherwise remained hidden. But the wolfhound was never happy with the arrangement.

Yursa had never shared a bed with the mouflon, even on their wedding night. Naturally, al-Seif had his whore, Carmen, to keep his bed warm, but Yursa was always alone. She was a good Catholic, and even at the expense of her happiness, she wouldn't break her vows. Not for him.

But for Delany.

That night, Yursa De Palma felt her soul burn as deeply as the lust that had grown within her while watching the greyhound's eyes. It burned like the fires of hell itself. As the two of them fell together on her bed, she suddenly realised why Delany, not his employer, had asked her to delay the annulment of her marriage.

This was the ultimate insult, the ultimate cry against the vows that she knew meant nothing. Yursa was a prisoner, chained in a cell of her own making. She had lied to herself, believing that by keeping up her end of the marriage she would somehow prove al-Seif's better; and in all that time she never realized how much her desire to hold the moral highground was holding her back.

After this night, Yursa would be truly free of the bonds that had tied her to the hateful mouflon. The fires that consumed her this night would burn away the grime, refining her like silver, leaving nothing but the burnished edges of the woman that was her true self, the queen of an empire.

And the queen could do whatever she damn well pleased.

Now it was morning and Yursa De Palma was alone again, naked in her bed. Greg Delany had used her, but she had also used him.

And it had felt good.

Yursa doubted al-Seif would even care that his wife had cheated on him, he had done it to her since their wedding night. But it mattered to her, and Delany had known that. Their lovemaking was meant to shatter the prison she had entrapped herself in for ten years.

And what if he is the enemy? The thought suddenly occurred to her, unbidden.

Yursa shook her head to clear it and swung her feet to the floor.

The phone rang as she was slipping on a silk robe.

"*Sì?*" she answered in Mecci.

"Good morning, Ms De Palma," came the voice of Mody Nahas.

"I trust you have good reason to call?" Yursa asked.

She strolled to the balcony doors and threw them wide, heedless of the fact that she had not yet secured the robe around her.

"Indeed, I do," the orangutan said, "Delshad has been taken care of."

The wolfhound paused for only a moment. "That is very good. But where is your half of our bargain?"

"Close now," Nahas replied, "They should be arriving within forty-eight hours. By then, you will have the best that Weis and I have to spare."

"I hope you realise how much I have riding on this," Yursa said.

"Of course, my dear. They will be ready. I only hope you are."

The line went dead.

Yursa returned the handset to its cradle and returned to the balcony doorway. She stood as motionless as a statue, gazing at the rising sun. But the light of Fos no longer felt warm on the wolfhound's fur. The burnished figure Yursa De Palma had become was not of refined silver as she had believed, but of solid grey ice.

31 – Guns and Legends

Mohan's Scrappers weren't in in the Medoccian lockup long. The only difference from their incarceration in Locke was that Medocci had a larger staff of agents from Tiger's Stripe's Public Restoration division on hand to clean things up.

Their primary PR contact was Sergeant Delano, a broad female hippo. She gave them a decent faux interrogation, linking Mohan's Scrappers and their surveillance van to *Loro*, the Medoccian secret police—the name literally translated as "Them". Afterwards, they were free to go, minus the equipment they had borrowed from KLAWS.

The incident at East Wind Holdings had shaken the agents of Tiger's Stripe more than they allowed themselves to show. So much so that shortly after returning to their hotel suite, Elder Tyrsus ordered Mohan, Rizzo, and Zed to return to the airport and retrieve the small arms they had left with the plane.

Medocci's firearms laws were only slightly less strict than Locke's, but with all the mafia chaos it proved disturbingly easy to smuggle the guns in. They left their larger hunting weapons—like Mohan's belt-fed machine gun and Kitty's

.308 rifle—with the plane, but each agent was now armed with a pistol or revolver. Vicki was the only exception. Since there were no fiends to fight this time, the bullfrog steadfastly refused to carry any weapon other than the smoke bombs Rizzo had made for her.

Kitty kept a careful eye on their new recruit when Tyrsus made the announcement that they should arm themselves. During the monster hunt in the Valley of Nefrit, Ric had no difficulty shooting at the Franken-creature trying to eat him, but the tigress noticed that he had done very little shooting when they faced the bandits during their flight from Jar-Geshim. The lynx seemed to believed the age-old adage that the pen, or in his case the typewriter, was mightier than the sword, but the tigress hoped he was smart enough to know that even a Fosday edition wasn't thick enough to stop a bullet.

When Kitty awoke early the next morning, she immediately set herself to the task of cleaning her personal firearm at the dining area table. It wasn't long before her father joined her, but he sat at the far side of the table and didn't offer anything more than a brief "Morning", which Kitty promptly ignored.

And then Ric woke up.

The lynx strolled into the kitchen area and plucked an apple from the fruit bowl on the counter. "Will we really need those?" he asked, referring to the weapons.

"Hopefully no," Mohan answered, "But never hurts to be prepared."

Ric took a bite of the fruit, then gestured with it. "You know," he said around a mouthful of apple, "I'm worried things will get shambolic now that we're all armed."

The big tiger gave a half smile. "How's that?"

Ric swallowed and said, "It's like a plot device in a movie. You know, Fate will actually give us reason to use them now that we actually have them."

Mohan chuckled. "You sound like Vince."

Ric watched them work for a moment, munching his apple slowly.

"You're worried if you could actually do it," Mohan said, putting his gun aside for a moment, "You don't know if you could pull the trigger."

"I'm a journalist, not a warrior," Ric replied, "But the two of you." He trailed off and motioned to the tigers.

"Years of monster hunting will do that," Mohan said, "Although there's still hope for some of us."

Kitty paused for only a moment but did not look up.

Ric wasn't so sure of the tiger's assessment. From what he had observed, Mohan's daughter was every inch the warrior her father was. It was her motivations that made the journalist wonder. She was holding on to an emotional pain somewhere, something that both connected with her father and drove them far apart.

"Have a seat," Mohan said, breaking the lynx's train of thought. "I know you brought a lead-slinger of your own from home."

Ric nodded and went back to his room. He returned carrying his own cleaning kit and the polished wooden box containing his father's .45.

Mohan nudged his seat over so the lynx could have more room. Out of the corner of her eye, Kitty watched Ric seat himself and lay out his kit, but it wasn't until the journalist brought out his pistol and started stripping it down that she allowed herself to take an interest.

Kitty didn't raise her head, but the tigress' eyes rose to examine Ric's actions. There was a peculiar gleam in her sapphire orbs, like an instructor checking the progress of a student to make sure they got all the steps right.

Ric had seen that look before, just after the tigress had lent him a submachine gun during their fiend hunt. Kitty had clearly been impressed that the journalist knew how to properly clear and check the weapon and observe proper firearms safety. Honestly, it made Ric a little uncomfortable. He had never used his father's gun, but he kept it clean all the same. Having somebody judge his technique made him feel like maybe he was somehow doing it wrong.

"It's a fine weapon," Mohan said, breaking the silence. "Custom tooled, not really a cop's gun."

"It serves a dual purpose really," Ric replied, "The forty-five has more stopping power than your standard issue nine millimetre, but dad believed that just looking at it should make the other guy think twice. For almost twenty years he was right; he never had to draw it. He even jokingly called it his 'negotiator'."

The journalist hesitated slightly, remembering how negotiating didn't work the day his father was killed. "Of course, yours is pretty impressive as well," he finished, changing the subject slightly.

Even dismantled, the big revolver was intimidating to look at. The cylinder only chambered five rounds, but each cartridge was almost as big as Ric's little finger. The rubberised black grip was cushioned and moulded to the tiger's massive paw. But the most curious thing Ric noticed was the lettering etched into the long silver barrel.

"Babylon?" the lynx read aloud.

"It's from an old Busawan legend," Mohan said, "Remember when you guessed my heritage back at your hotel room in Kairran? My great grandparents were originally from Marbarresh in the Gunnesh province before immigrating to the United Plains. The old tales are something of a tradition in my family. If anyone bothered to listen."

The tiger glanced at Kitty as he said this, but only the slightest twitch of an ear signalled that the white tigress had heard him.

"I'll admit I can't remember all of it myself," Mohan continued, "but my favourite verse goes: *'O hear the lightning's crash, Quake at Babylon's thunder, Look upon the hills and fear!'*"

He grinned and held up the frame of the revolver. "This is a Chesterfield Model Five-Hundred. It fires a long-five-hundred, four-forty grain cartridge; essentially a fifty-calibre pistol round. And it packs a kick fit to knock the horns off a bolvin bull if you're not careful. Holding thunder in the palm of your hand."

Ric whistled appreciatively. He had heard that thunder in Jar-Geshim and the memory of it made the lynx's ears twitch a little. He also remembered that while the revolver had saved Mohan from becoming monster lunch, it had taken a mounted cannon to ultimately stop the creature.

Ric turned his attention to Kitty's pistol, and the tigress swiftly went back to the task of cleaning it and ignoring any comments the journalist might try to make.

The semiautomatic was much larger than Ric's .45. He wondered briefly how the tigress' slim hands managed to handle it, but watching her work with the parts gave him his answer: she handled it very well. Based on the bullets neatly arranged next to the magazine he guessed the chamber was probably a .357, yet the design was almost entirely alien to him.

The top assembly was two pieces: the barrel, which ended in a thick piece tapered to a triangular shape along the top; and the slide, which covered the bolt and extended forward to enclose the sides of the barrel. The barrel was affixed firmly to the frame and had an integrated rail system along the top, ideal for fitting accessories like the scope resting in Kitty's case. This was unique because most Amarthian handguns, like Ric's .45, had free-floating slides requiring accessories to be attached "under-barrel" on the frame.

But the most interesting feature to Ric was that the weapon was plated white gold instead of the traditional gunmetal black or stainless-steel. Like her father's revolver, there were characters engraved along the side, but they were not in Locken or any other language Ric knew.

"Does your weapon also have a story?" the lynx asked.

"Every gun has a story," the white tigress answered, not looking up from her task.

Ric frowned slightly when she didn't continue, so he tried another tactic. "That symbol on the grips, the wheat sheaves around a ram's horn, that's the Kirgue Arms brand. But I've never seen that weapon in the standard Kirque army."

Kitty stopped and raised an eyebrow at him, clearly both impressed and curious. He decided not to tell her it had taken an effort to dig that small scrap of information out of a dusty corner of his memory.

"No," Kitty said, "Nor are you likely to ever see it in production."

"Oh?" Ric asked.

"Let's just say sometimes there's hardware TS thinks would be better left in our hands alone. In fact, Elder Tyrsus was the one who helped us secure the plans for it, a *gift* from her motherland. Its project code name was 'Desert Hawk'."

She held up the frame, barrel towards the ceiling, and used her free hand to point out features as she spoke. "It uses a gas operated blowback mechanism up here in the barrel, similar to a rifle. Your forty-five has a more recoil-based system, like a majority of semi-autos. The extra gas pressure allows mine to chamber a larger round without excessive wear on the parts. Also, I can switch between three fifty-seven and fifty as easy as changing the bolt—I prefer the three fifty-seven for the extra ammo. Unfortunately, I've had problems with jamming; I need to get our smiths to take a look at it when we get to the Sanctuary."

"I'm afraid you lost me there. I know the basic mechanics and use, but not the science."

The tigress eyed him curiously. "A hunter should make an effort to know the tools of her trade. But I'll admit, I'd like to go over the blueprints with Ally again and try to reduce the weight. She's one of our Playground lab techs, handles most of our equipment research."

Ric smiled, this was the most he'd been able to get out of the tigress in almost two weeks. "I don't recognise those characters on the side," he said, "What does the inscription say?"

Kitty suddenly seemed to realise she was opening up and the ice-cold gates snapped shut again. She looked away and hurriedly started reassembling her pistol.

Ric was about to apologise for upsetting her, but she cut him off. "It's Benese Sanskrit," she said, "*Saifa*. Roughly translated It means 'lightning'. I have the Playground working on a second one, but I don't have a name for it yet."

"Is naming guns normal in Tiger's Stripe?" Ric asked, raising an eyebrow.

Kitty paused. "Well, no. But all the great legends have named weapons, right? *Grymmsil*, *Excelsior*, *The Blade of Elasar*."

"Wait a minute," Ric interjected, "Those first two are from epic poems in Norsen and Locke literature. But that last one is from John R Kelstien's *Trial of the Ring* trilogy."

Kitty's face flushed beneath her black and white fur, but with anger or embarrassment, Ric couldn't tell.

"Could we...talk about something else?" she said.

Ric studied her a moment. Obviously, the tigress was embarrassed about her geekdom, but there was something else there too. Pain? Resentment? An old memory, perhaps? He wondered if his conversation about her geeky side reminded her of someone else, someone she wanted to forget. The journalist in him was intrigued, but something in Kitty's body language told Ric he should let her be.

Surprisingly, it was her father that came to her rescue. "Many great warriors throughout history have named their favoured weapons," he said, "I think there's even some in TS that carry legends of there own."

Ric had a sudden flash to his vision the day of his initiation. He saw the battlefield and the ornate weapons wielded by the single-striped tiger and his shadowy lizard opponent.

"I'd very much like to hear some of those stories," the lynx said, "Maybe you can enlighten me about a few. Such as a Benese spear with a leaf-shaped blade and a plume of red ecquai hair tied around the gilded shaft; or a jewelled Benese straight-sword with a large square ruby in the hilt."

Both tigers stopped what they were doing instantly.

Kitty slowly set her reassembled pistol down on her cloth, and Mohan finished reassembling his revolver. He gave the cylinder a good spin out of habit, then set it down as well.

"Was this in your vision?" the big tiger asked.

Ric nodded slowly, the change that had come over his companions was both curious and terrifying. Carefully, he explained the battle he had seen to the tigers, omitting only the pyramid in the jungle that came after he stepped through the vision portal. The journalist's apprehension grew when he saw the dark look on the agents' faces as he described the shadowy lizard fighting the stripeless tiger.

Mohan took a deep breath. "Those are the weapons that began our order. They don't really have names, as far as I know, but the spear belonged to Singh Fang-Ruo, the creator of the *Laohu Tiaowen*. The sword." He paused for a long moment. "I can only imagine that the shadow you saw wielding it was the sorcerer Zhu Gan."

Ric's eyes narrowed at this. "When you say sorcerer, is this like when you told me that the Foresight of the Twilight Moon were into divination magic?"

The tiger shook his head negatively. "I wish I was. With the Foresight, their whole organisation was little more than a religious cult. Their so-called divination powers were smoke and mirrors combined with a brilliant use of technology and illusions."

"And a lot of hoodoo bolvinshit about ancient philosophy that they mistook as prophecy," Kitty mumbled as she carefully packed her pistol into its stainless-steel case and started cleaning up her kit.

"Yes, that too," Mohan agreed, "Zhu Gan was Fang-Ruo's greatest enemy during the War of the Four Winds in ancient East Benai, nearly a century before the Empire even existed. Our scholars have combed our histories for the smallest details, but as far as we can tell, what Zhu Gan had was very real mystical power."

Ric picked up the barrel of his pistol and a pipe brush. "Really?" he asked, "Could he call lightning like a wizard, or was it something more subtle?"

The big tiger chuckled dryly. "Nothing like what you might find in a fantasy novel, but it was dangerous. For one, he had an unusually savvy grasp of tactics and machines. The siege engines he designed for Emperor Singh-Yun were like nothing anyone had ever seen before, or since if history is any indication. Black-powder cannon wouldn't officially be invented for another thousand years, yet Zhu Gan was using things that could almost be described as laser beams. He also had the uncanny ability to manipulate people; some kind of brainwashing. But the real clincher was when he built an entire army of assassins and had them strike out at the allied generals."

Mohan's gaze went far away as if he was seeing the events he described play out before him. "That was what got Singh Fang-Ruo involved. He was a man of humble origins, but he believed in the honour of fair combat. The dirty trick Zhu Gan was using went against everything Fang-Ruo believed was honourable. So, he built his own army of assassin hunters, the *Laohu Tiaowen*, and set them upon the armies of Zhu Gan. What you saw in your vision was probably the Battle of Mount Guan Jing, the final confrontation that only ended after Fang-Ruo sacrificed himself the throw Zhu Gan into the portal and seal it for good."

Ric looked through the barrel of his pistol, checking for traces of dirt his pipe brush might have missed. "That doesn't really explain why the weapons seemed so prominent in my vision."

Mohan laughed bitterly. "No, I suppose not. You think you're going to figure out your whole journey only a few days after discovering the path?"

Ric frowned. "Well, when you put it that way I guess you're right."

The tiger reached over and patted him on the shoulder gently; it still almost knocked Ric out of his seat. "She'll be right, mate," Mohan said, "You've got a lot to learn, and patience is just the first lesson."

Ric nodded and went back to the pistol. "Well," he said, "You can't ignore the existence of mythical monsters when you've almost been eaten by two. I suppose magical weapons isn't much of a stretch beyond that."

"Perhaps they were not as magical as you believe, Sedric," a low voice spoke up from the entryway.

The three felines at the table turned to see Zed, Vince, and Elder Tyrsus had entered while they were talking. Vince promptly threw himself down on one of the deep-cushioned couches and propped his large furry feet on the glass coffee table, gently nudging aside the centrepiece of real fruit.

Zed walked over to the table. "The Soketh have scavenged many ancient ruins along the borders of the Saran Waste and elsewhere," he said, "Many of the wonders we have discovered would boggle the mind."

"Such as that bracer of yours?" Ric asked.

After a long absence, the archaic-looking device had returned to its place on the badger's left wrist; the golden top plate bore the raised image of a winged serpent eating its own coiled tail. On several occasions during the last week, the lynx had seen Zed use the device to generate a blue force field to protect his fellow agents.

"Indeed," Zed said with a nod. "Many of those ruins are from the Tetzuma, the first civilisation to rule Amarthia before mysteriously vanishing thousands of years before the War of the Four Winds was even an argument between two petty magistrates. It is quite possible that Zhu Gan found some of these artefacts and turned them to his own use."

"Well that's one theory," Vince said idly.

Ric turned in his chair to look at the hare. "You think it really was some kind of magical force?"

"More fun that way!" Vince replied grinning.

Mohan shook his head and started packing his revolver away. "Well, he's half right. Zed's theory is only part of it. Remember that portal you saw in your vision, Ric? We think the Tetzuma created that technology. Somehow, they mucked up and opened up onto, I don't know what to call it, another dimension or plane of existence. Maybe even onto a bloody other planet. Anyway, the fiends came through, and the Tiger's Stripe went from hunting assassins to hunting monsters."

Ric reassembled his own pistol and began cleaning up. "And if people like al-Seif got their hands on them it would be chaos."

"Precisely," Zed said.

"Just one more question," Ric said, "If these fiends have been running wild for so long, how is it that they haven't had a larger impact on Amarthia's ecology?"

"We are unsure," Zed said with a shrug, "There are two things that attract fiends: chaos and technology. Why technology is a factor is still unknown, but one can always find them around Tetzuma ruins. Perhaps there is some kind of lure in these cities that draws them."

"Like the grendel in Jar-Geshim," Ric said.

"Indeed," Zed replied, "Also remember that the Frankenbeast did not travel far beyond the lab in which it was created. Once a fiend has staked a territory, it tends to stay there as long as it is not disturbed."

"And they've never adapted to our ecosystem?" Ric asked.

"Not in three thousand years," Mohan said with a low growl, "All fiends do is destroy their environment. Remember the Warren? An area where a fiend takes up residence for a while is often very sickly. Plants die or mutate to become more carnivorous; wild beasts, if any actually manage to survive in fiend territory, are often more vicious than normal."

Ric nodded. He hadn't forgotten the alien feeling at the heart of Jar-Geshim's Warren where the grendel had been living for well over a thousand years. There was a heaviness to the air that threatened to choke the agents as they drove through. Its effect had clearly been visible on the feral Wildmen and their monstrous pet bahngers and ceravaags, which were twice the size of any other beast Ric had seen. Wherever these fiends came from, they seemed intent on converting their territory into something else, perhaps something that resembled home.

Ric was about to put his pistol away when Kitty chuffed suddenly. He looked at her, she looked down at the cloth in front of him. Distracted by their conversation, the journalist had forgotten one of the smaller pins.

That intimidated feeling crept over the lynx again as he carefully disassembled the pistol. It didn't take him long to figure out where the missing piece went, and he reassembled the gun correctly.

Using two fingers, Ric held the weapon up by the barrel to show the tigress. Kitty nodded satisfactorily, and the lynx put the pistol back in its wooden box.

The ruffle of Elder Tyrsus' wings brought their attention to her.

The eagle leaned against the kitchen counter with her arms crossed over her chest, but she was looking at the expansive view of Scogliera Piatta beyond the balcony. The sun was above the horizon now, painting the old buildings in vibrant light.

"Did our orders come through yet, Basira?" Mohan asked.

Tyrsus' wings shuffled again. "No," she said quietly, "A special session of the court will be reviewing our evidence today. I would say we'll know what's what within the next twenty-four hours."

"Do you think al-Seif might try to stop us?" Ric asked.

"Him, or someone else," the eagle said, "Keep those guns handy, my friends. You may need them."

The other agents joined her in looking out the window and the uncertain dawn of a new day.

32 – Special Delivery

The ports of East Benai's Imperial City bore witness to the nation's growth from feudal shoguns into the prosperous economic empire it was today. Gigantic freighters berthed along the busy piers while junks and fishing trawlers vied for space in the crowded waterways.

Generations ago, one could enter the bay of *Lóng de Zuĭbā*—the Dragon's Mouth—and see the tiered roofs of the Imperial Palace in the distance. Today, glass and steel skyscrapers hid the luxurious seat of the Emperor from view, but they also separated the venerable structure from the ramshackle huts and faded warehouses that lined the shore.

One of these warehouses, bearing slightly fresher paint, was the distribution centre of Kaulsk Shipping International.

The building buzzed with activity, and not just because several of the employees boasted insect wings. The morning rush was just getting started, and the Benese Empire's White Festival—the celebration of the end of winter—was only days away. And after that, the spring trading season would begin. The sheer number of packages coming through the centre would only increase as the new year moved on.

Despite the warehouse's geographic location, roughly half the employees were Locke citizens working on temporary visas. This was not surprising considering the origin of the company's corporate HQ, and Kaulsk believed a multinational workforce was a great way to bolster international relations.

It also provided an excellent cover for a certain clandestine organisation to rotate foreign agents into and out of the country on a regular basis.

In this case, the said organisation was KLAWS, the more "public" face of the *Laohu Tiaowen*. Every employee at this particular distribution centre was an agent, even if their assignment was simply to carry out the legitimate day-to-day operations of the business. This arrangement made it much easier to hide the secret of their clandestine operations because they didn't have to worry that a "normal" employee might see something they shouldn't have.

Peter Hensley, a red squirrel with a pronounced paunch above his beltline, grunted as he shoved a flat box off a trolly and onto the concrete floor. Most packages addressed to the business itself were office supplies, sent in care of the HR department. However, this parcel bore only the curious addressee of "Kaulsk Shipping, East Benai. To whom it may concern". That meant Hensley, as the distribution supervisor, would have to figure out where it needed to go from there.

The box was roughly two meters long and one wide and about fifteen centimetres thick. An odd size to say the least, especially if it was only more office supplies. It could be a framed painting or poster, but the damned thing was much heavier than any similar package Hensley had handled.

The squirrel thought he detected the faint scent of chemicals coming off it. Not enough to raise any alarms, old paintings were often packaged with some kind of repellent when shipped this way, but it was enough to make Hensley bring the box to a back room away from the other employees.

It also made the odd birthmark on the back of Hensley's left arm itch.

There were only a handful of Tiger's Stripe agents left at the distribution centre, mixed in among the KLAWS agents; not nearly enough, in Hensley's mind. Gang activity had recently skyrocketed in East Benai, aided by no less than three major crime syndicates: the Red Eagle, the Hikigaeru, and the Fire Dragon Star. The agents really needed the manpower, but for some reason Elder Takeshi had pulled nearly two-thirds of their operatives away after the Blue Wing emergency line went dark.

Samson Weathers was another that had stayed behind, and Hensley called him over as a precaution.

"Something amiss, Peter?" Weathers asked. The tall crane held a clipboard in one taloned hand.

"Not sure," Hensley replied, "but me mark's givin' me a fit, and somethin' about this package has me shook."

The crane nodded and looked worried. Weathers was one of the rare agents who bore a tattoo instead of a birthmark, but he had learned from experience that if one of his birthmarked comrades started to itch, it generally wasn't a good sign.

The squirrel reached into the pocket of his faded coveralls and took out a box cutter. Extending the blade, he carefully broke the packing seals on the cardboard. Inside was yet another box, a metal case with rounded corners roughly the same size as the cardboard it was shipped in.

The chemical smell was much stronger now, but Hensley still couldn't place it. Despite the warm latitudes of the Imperial City, the case was ice cold to the touch, and Hensley's chubby furred fingers brushed away a thin coat of frost from its top surface.

"Get Jameson down here right away," the squirrel ordered.

Weathers did as he was instructed, and within minutes the short, broad-shouldered lion who was the company's regional manager—and chief Tiger's Stripe agent—had joined them. Tyler Jameson took one look at the case and started scratching absently at his right side, where his own mark was. Without a word, the lion nodded to the squirrel foreman.

Slowly, Hensley unsealed the latches and lifted the lid. The smell of formaldehyde washed over the three agents, but it couldn't completely mask the stench of decaying flesh. Weathers took one look at the grisly contents, dropped his clipboard and immediately turned to wretch his guts all over the floor.

Inside the case, stretched and pinned like an artefact in a museum display, was the pelt of a ferret.

"My god!" Hensley breathed.

"It's Hideki Kensai!" Jameson said.

Pinned to the pelt was a yellow note. The lion retrieved it. "Here is Agent Two Forty-Nine," he read aloud, "We are watching. We are waiting."

Jameson crumpled the note and growled deep in his chest.

"Who in the bloody hell would do such a thing?" Hensley asked, his eyes still riveted on the tanned ferret pelt.

Weathers recovered enough to turn back to the grisly scene. "Look at his mark!" the crane said in a harsh rasp.

Hideki Kensai's Tiger's Mark, located just below his left shoulder, had been scratched through. The tears were not deep enough to be from a wild beast, most likely they had come from a long-clawed sentient species—a bear, badger, or even one of the many lizard or bird species.

Hensley gave a sharp bark of anger. "Who the bloody hell are these monsters?"

Jameson's brow furrowed in thought. "Whoever they are, they know who *we* are," he said patting his birthmarked side for emphasis, "Jeong was the last one to call Blue Wing before it was taken offline, right?"

"Aye," Weathers said, still unable to tear his eyes from the pelt, "He was down in the Quan-Sung District."

"Did our agents find anything?" the stocky lion asked.

The crane thought for a moment, running a scaly hand along the almost comical curve of his long neck. "Aye, there was something. Couple o' prostitutes claimed to have seen him run past their corner. They were contracted with the Hikigaru, so who knows if they told the truth. There was a pay phone not much farther along; we think that's where he made the call from. Hold up one."

Weathers went back into his office, and the other two agents heard the sound of metal file draws opening in sequence followed by a hollow *click*. Moments later the crane returned with a small pin in his talon.

"We found this taped under the phone." He held the ruby emblem up. It depicted a sentient eagle in flight, wings out, arms and legs stretched straight out behind it. "It's the emblem of the Red Eagle," Weathers explained.

Jameson motioned for the pin, and Weathers handed it to him. The lion pinched it between the claws of two fingers and held it up to the light. "Anything special about the pin?"

The crane shook his head negatively. "Just costume jewellery, but it's authentic to the syndicate. The leaders wear versions fashioned from real gold and gems, but they commission cheap glass ones like this for lesser members."

"So, it could be a lead." The lion tossed the pin back, and Weathers caught it.

"Or not," Hensley spoke up suddenly. The other agents turned to the red squirrel. "Why would the Red Eagle come after us? We're just a shipping company."

"A shipping company that's a front for covert agents," Weathers argued.

"No, hear me out," the squirrel said, "Remember that incident about two weeks ago? When the hunter team in Pytan had to clear out of our warehouse there?"

Jameson folded thick arms over his chest and shook out his mane. "You think they're trying to fold our world-wide operations?"

Hensley nodded, his tail starting to twitch with excitement. "Estan was our link back to Aerenia and parts west. With our operations cut off there, we're essentially on or own here. And since we've been focused on the gang problem here in Benai, it's only logical that's where we'd start our search."

"But why start us on a wild aukie chase after Red Eagle in the first place?" Jameson asked.

"It could be a double fake," Weathers said. The crane's companions turned to him. "A 'they know that we know that they know' kind of thing."

Jameson put a paw to his forehead. "Too many damned moving parts in this machine," he said, "We need to get the Elder Council in on this as soon as possible."

The lion moved forwards and gently replaced the lid of the metal box containing the pelt of Hideki Kensai, Agent 249.

"Strength and Honour, my friend," Jameson said, choking a little.

"Wisdom and Justice," Hensley and Weathers replied in hushed tones.

The lion turned back to his fellow agents. "No time to grieve, gentlemen. We have work to do."

33 – Best Laid Plans

Setaurday in Medocci passed without incident. The agents of Tiger's Stripe rotated through the lobby and grounds of the Hotel Darlington in four-hour shifts, keeping up the illusion of tourists on vacation.

Despite the crumbling ruins across the large courtyard fronting the classically designed Darlington, the hotel rested in a newer section of the ancient city. The paved roads were wider, and the buildings not so crowded together—this was in part to protect the landmarks they had been built around. The environs offered the agents a large number of escape routes, and their enemies a large number of entry points.

Kitty and Ric drew the graveyard shift, midnight until 4am. Despite her obligations, Kitty insisted the two of them split up, placing Ric in the hotel lobby while she headed to the bar.

Scogliera Piatta was known for its nightlife, but there were still rules about Fosday nights, especially since Medocci was the seat of Aabanite Catholicism. Fortunately, Hotel Darlington was a respected international chain across the continent of Aerenia and could operate under its own rules. The bar remained open, but It wasn't crowded.

Two hours passed.

Despite her training, Kitty's mind kept drifting back to Gregory Delany and his stunt at East Wind Holdings. The tigress wished she knew more about their opponent aside from his obvious arrogance. It was a coin toss on whether Delany would try something now and hope to catch the agents sleeping or wait until just before dawn when they were presumably just waking. That was assuming he tried anything at all.

And I have to sit out this life-or-death situation with the rookie, Kitty thought bitterly.

It was Ric's inexperience that bothered the tigress, or at least that's what she told herself. But per the *Laohu Tiaowen*'s traditions, Ric was her charge. When you found a birthmark, it was your duty to see the bearer safely to the Sanctuary.

The prevailing belief was that the journey served as a bonding experience between the old agent and the new. It wasn't uncommon for the more experienced agent to become directly involved in the rookie's training and develop friendships that lasted long into both agents' careers. Kitty's father and Zed were a prime example, even though the badger didn't receive his mark tattoo until after their first perilous adventure.

This was not a bond or responsibility that Kitty wanted. Not with a man whose inquisitiveness, whose candour, whose overall positivity reminded her of—

Stop it! her internal voice raged.

She took a swift sip of the gin in her hand and let the fire of the alcohol burn away the feelings that threatened to surface.

Kitty hadn't chosen the bar to drink away her problems, but she had to admit that the gin, served straight up, was helping. It was the activity that brought her inside. She had hoped the mental exercise of tracking all the bodies and exits within would free her from thinking about the lynx in the lobby.

The white tigress' body language spoke clearly of a woman who wanted to drink alone, although more than once Kitty had to deliver a curt growl to patrons too drunk or overconfident to get the message.

She took another sip of gin and glanced out into the lobby. Her charge was handling himself pretty well for his second observation mission, but the café at East Wind Holdings had been a different scenario. The agents were hunted now and operating in hostile territory. If their adversaries could pull off a drive-by at the café, they could very well storm the hotel.

Currently, the journalist—presumably feigning a bout of insomnia—was browsing the tourist pamphlets and asking random questions of the desk clerk. Once in a while, his eyes darted towards the hotel's main entrance, taking note of the patrons who came and went; mostly tourists returning from a night on the town. More than once Ric would spare a glance towards Kitty.

Not this way you bolvin ass, the tigress fumed silently, *I have the bar covered, you stick with the lobby.*

To Kitty's credit, even while she gave the lynx a stern look, she did not miss the movement from a booth at the back of the bar. The pair of wallabies had been flirting heavily most of the night, and finally decided to slip away and find more suitable environs for their activities.

Ric got the hint in Kitty's stare and went back to perusing a magazine rack. In the process of looking away, he missed the bellboy coming out of the service lift with a trolly. Kitty sighed in exasperation. There was nothing wrong with the parakeet bellboy, of course, just the fact that Ric hadn't seen him was enough to trigger the tigress' disapproval.

The sooner we dump him at Sanctuary, the sooner I can be rid of him, Kitty thought, nursing another sip of gin.

But you know that won't happen, don't you? her own internal monologue argued. *He's appeared in your dreams now, entwined with your destiny. Where he goes, you go.*

She drained the last of the gin and smacked the glass on the counter.

"Boyfriend troubles?" the bartender, a grizzled but kindly elk asked.

Kitty was tempted to give him a withering glare and tell him to leave her alone, but something stopped her.

"It's my fault," she said, adopting a hopeless tone, "I passed him at the Arcularium this afternoon and gave him a compliment. I had no idea we'd end up at the same hotel."

"And that was a bad thing?"

Kitty shrugged. "I may have come off as cross as a frog in a sock."

The elk raised a confused eyebrow.

"Sorry, I'm a Plainsman. I was a bit miffed, er upset. Think I scared him." Kitty's eyes strayed out to the lynx in the lobby again. "For the best, I think. He really shouldn't get involved with a girl like me."

"That is the sound of a woman who has been very hard on herself," the bartender said sympathetically.

Kitty felt her anger starting to rise. Her personal feelings weren't any of his business, but that seemed to be the penchant of bartenders the world over. She held her tongue and her emotions in check.

"You saw me chase away those other fellows," she said.

"Yes, and each time, you stole a quick glance to that lynx in the lobby to see if he was watching."

Dammit. Kitty thought she had been more careful than that.

"Let me get you something special," the bartender said.

Kitty watched as he took a fresh glass and added a finger of gin, something with a green tint and the scent of mint, and another finger of Locke bitters. Then the elk turned to the tigress and studied her as if trying to solve an unspoken mystery. Coming to a conclusion, he produced a lime and squeezed it into the cocktail.

"On the house," he said, sliding the green drink over to her.

Kitty sniffed it experimentally, it smelled strongly of mint, bitters, and citrus. She had no thoughts of poison, she'd been watching the bartender too closely for him to slip anything past her.

Kitty took a sip.

"Hm, sorry," she said with a slight grimmace, "Bit strong with the bitters. What's it called?"

"In Medocci we say *angelo caduto*," the bartender said, "In Locken, I believe it's called a 'fallen angel'."

Kitty hesitated slightly in mid-sip, but it wasn't enough for the elk to notice, and thankfully not enough to make her choke on the drink.

More like the Angel of Death, she thought.

Aloud Kitty asked, "So, is that me, signore? A fallen angel?"

"This is Medocci, signorina," the elk said smiling, "Poetry, it runs in our blood, *sì*? It is from our ancient legends of Romare and Juno that we get the word *romance*."

Kitty smirked despite herself. "You saying I should try to make it up to him?" She cocked her head towards the lobby.

"I am saying that Scogliera Piatta is a place where many things can happen," the bartender replied, "And it is a terrible thing to drink such good gin alone."

Kitty was about to reply when the bar phone rang. The elk moved to answer it and spoke rapidly in Mecci. He turned towards her holding the phone.

"It is for you," the elk said, slightly puzzled.

Kitty left the remains of her drink and swiftly put the phone to her ear.

"The room, now," Mohan said and hung up.

Kitty wasted no time. "Think I'll take your advice," she said to the bartender.

The tigress moved swiftly out of the bar and grabbed Ric by the arm.

"The suite, now," she hissed in his ear before he could say anything

Without another word, she dragged him toward the lifts.

The bemused elk watched them go, reflecting on the impulsiveness of youth and wondering if perhaps he had added a bit too much bitters.

* * *

Mohan, Elder Tyrsus, and the rest of the agents were waiting for them when they arrived in the common room of the hotel suite. Kitty and Ric were surprised to find that agent Delano from the *Polizia* was also in attendance. The hippo police sergeant was not in uniform, and her demeanour was far from the cheery woman who had processed them only a little more than twenty-four hours ago.

Both Delano and Elder Tyrsus gave the tigress a serious look as she entered, and Kitty knew why.

If Delano could slip by you, who else could, you drongo, the tigress chastised herself.

Kitty took her usual spot leaning against the wall while Ric sat on one of the curved chairs in living area.

"The plane is being prepped as we speak," Tyrsus began calmly, "We must leave as soon as possible, Kaulsk Shipping has been compromised."

"By Mbektar!" Zed gasped.

The agents of Mohan's Scrappers voiced similar expressions, that is except for Mohan himself, who was already privy to the news.

"Kaulsk?" Ric asked, "The packaging company we used in Kairran?"

Elder Tyrsus nodded. "Primarily it is a front for KLAWS. We use them sparingly to move Tiger's Stripe agents and equipment. We knew something was wrong when the Kairran authorities raided the warehouse at the Nayhadjin Airport just after the bombing. But now there's been an incident at the distribution centre in East Benai. Less than an hour ago they received a package that forced us to suspend operations in the region."

She paused, eyeing each of them gravely.

"The package contained the pelt of agent Hideki Kensai. He was skinned and tanned like a wild beast."

There were no expressions of shock this time, but every one of the agents paled visibly. Vicki actually had to grab the back of a chair to keep from fainting. Vince helped her steady herself, although it appeared he needed her support as much as she needed his.

When Mohan recovered, he growled deep in his chest. "What happened?" he asked, "Did anyone claim responsibility?"

The eagle shook her head negatively. "No," she said, "They left only a simple message: 'We are watching. We are waiting.' It is clear we have seriously underestimated our opponent. In fact, it is quite likely they are the reason our operation here failed."

Tyrsus motioned for Delano to explain.

"The legal inquiries have finished," the hippo said, "There was every reason for a case to be drawn against Syris Industries. Unfortunately, it appears the company no longer exists; Assad Alabwaq, a.k.a. Jirair al-Seif dissolved it several months ago."

Another round of dismayed outbursts circled the room, but none were more vociferous than Kitty, who crossed her arms in front of her and growled deep in her chest.

"Months?" Ric asked, "How is that possible?"

Delano shrugged. "That's according to the papers filed with the civic business bureau by al-Seif's lawyers. Granted, those papers didn't exist until a week ago, but bureaucracy being what it is, all the court sees are the effective dates. At this point, Syris Industries is a non-entity, and with it goes any case we might have brought against Assad Alabwaq."

"What about that other company we saw in the Foresight base?" Vicki asked, "Uh, Terrapin I think it was called."

"Another dead end," Elder Tyrsus said, "That company went defunct months before Syris did."

Ric rubbed at his chin. "Let me back up a moment, these papers were filed one week ago? As in, around the time of the De Palma assassination?"

Tyrsus nodded. "It appears al-Seif had set up quite a gambit. There were rumours floating around about a merger between Terrapin and D'Verant Industries; the subsidiary the De Palma's used to run smuggling operations in Pytan. We think al-Seif may have been attempting to blackmail Vigo De Palma by threatening to tie him into Terrapin and Syris. Both of them being defunct was probably a backup should things go awry."

"Like the assassination," Ric said quietly.

Delano nodded. "You've seen the chaos that erupted between the other mafia families," she said, "With them trying to fill the void left by the De Palmas, al-Seif has been keeping his head down. After getting rid of Syris Industries, all his business interests in Medocci were legal, or at least as legal as the De Palmas had set themselves up to be."

The hippo shook her large purple head sadly, there was no need for her to continue. The Medoccian courts had no recourse to move against al-Seif, and the De Palma assassination made it appeared that Vigo had paid for whatever illegal business he was involved in.

"So that's it," Kitty growled, "We're done. Two years all gone to shit."

"It appears so, yes," said Tysus, seemingly oblivious to the tigress' disrespectful tone.

Ric was in almost as much shock as Kitty. "But we've come this far," he said, "After all this, the entire adventure means nothing?"

Elder Tyrsus nodded gravely. "I am sorry, Mr Barnes, but that happens," she said, "This isn't a movie where the heroes always win. The *Laohu Tiaowen* is powerful, but not infallible."

Kitty closed her eyes as if doing so might contain the rage boiling inside. "And al-Seif?" Her voice almost cracked from the effort to keep it even.

"No longer your concern," the Elder said evenly, "After what happened at East Wind Holdings we know he is closely watched and more highly connected than we originally perceived."

"And if we tried to take him like you had planned?" Kitty asked, eyes still closed.

"We couldn't be sure that wasn't exactly what our mystery opponent wanted," Mohan answered.

Tyrsus nodded. "Thanks to the growing war in Estan, most of our Medocci resources are focused towards Kirque. Aside from the intelligence assets we needed here, we have no protection. Our best recourse is to regroup and reassess the situation."

"That isn't the only thing we can do," Kitty said quietly. The tigress' eyes opened to narrow slits, and they could all see the fire burning in those sapphire pools. "We could remove al-Seif ourselves. Take the pawn off the board. Cleaner for the public, and a lot cleaner than that bastard deserves."

"No," Tyrsus answered flatly.

Kitty's lips turned up in a snarl.

"The Council has not issued a sanction on Jirair al-Seif," Tyrsus continued, pointing an accusing talon at Kitty. "And until they do, we can do nothing. Our plan failed, and now your orders are to proceed with getting Sedric Barnes to the Sanctuary."

Kitty started to argue again, but the Elder cut her off, her wings spreading slightly in her agitation. "That's enough, Agent Katral. If you keep this up, I will have no choice but to suspend you from duty, pending a disciplinary review from the Elder Council." She turned to the rest of the group. "Now all of you pack your things, we leave immediately. Dismissed."

34 – Falling Apart

Sergeant Delano was needed back at her post and left as soon as the meeting adjourned. It took less than ten minutes for the agents to pack their belongings and gather once again in the common room.

Mohan checked the outer hall, one hand on the butt of his revolver. Nothing moved.

Silently they exited out into the hall and entered the stairwell. They went down one floor, two, a dozen. Nothing happened. Yet none of them dared to speak, as if the very mention that they might be a little paranoid would prove them horribly wrong.

They reached the door to the lobby, and Mohan brought them to a halt. The tiger concealed his revolver with the tails of his long coat, and the other agents followed his example.

"Delano was able to supply us with two sedans," Mohan said, "They're parked near the rear entrance; that's left as we exit this door. Zed and I have to squeeze in the largest one, but the rest of you should be fine." The tiger passed a key to Rizzo. "You get to drive this time."

The basilisk tried and failed to suppress a smile.

Mohan checked the lobby. "Ok, leave in twos. Vicki, you and Basira go first. Wander towards the main entrance and pause, that way we don't all look like we're going the same direction."

The pair acted as instructed, the eagle and frog stopping in the middle of the lobby as if they were inspecting their belongings before checking out and catching an early morning flight—reality often provided the best cover. Rizzo and Vince followed, pausing near the lavatory. Kitty and Ric were next and made straight for the rear entrance.

Finally, Mohan and Zed exited the stairwell, making their way casually in the direction Kitty and Ric had taken.

"Cover!" Vince's shout reached the tiger and the badger before they had gone more than a few steps.

The hare's sharp ears had picked up the whine of an engine before Mohan's had, and the tiger saw a dark shape swooped in above the ruins across from the hotel. The tall windows lining the entrance of the Hotel Darlington vanished in a fireball as a pair of rockets impacted on the sweeping driveway. Mohan felt the wind knocked from his lungs and Zed barely dodged one of the lobby chairs as it flew past him, embedding itself in the wall with the force of the explosion.

Smoke billowed through the shattered windows. The ringing in their ears eventually subsided into the whine of a helicopter as it hovered at the edge of the courtyard. Car alarms shrieked nearby, set off by the blast.

"Clever bastard!" Mohan growled, picking himself up off the floor, "One hell of a pilot to fly in low like that. Everyone to the cars! Now!

Ric had been knocked flat on his back, and Kitty grabbed him by the scruff of his neck and hauled him to his feet. There was a line of vehicles parked along the curb outside, but it was easy for the tigress to pick out the unmarked police vehicles. The grey sedans were the same make—Altameda Motors L380s—but one had a taller roof than the other; obviously a model made to accommodate larger species.

Kitty shoved her charge in the direction of the vehicles and turned to see her father standing in the now glassless doorway.

"Status!" Mohan barked as he ushered his team out of the lobby.

"I caught some glass in the arm," Vince said, clutching the slashed and bleeding appendage.

"Basira and Vicki are hurt!" Rizzo's voice called out.

The basilisk appeared pulling the bullfrog beside her. Being an amphibian, the stalwart Vicki had no teeth to grit, but the expression on her face was the same. Blood ran in torrents down her left leg, and she was unable to put any weight on the limb. Tyrsus limped beside them on her own power, but it was obvious that her left wing was broken and the eagle's face was streaked with blood from a shallow cut above her left eye.

Mohan and Zed were relatively unscathed and helped their injured comrades out into the street. The tiger squinted into the smoke that seemed to get thicker by the minute. The lobby attendant was dead, a shard of glass had caught the canine in the throat. Mohan couldn't see into the bar, but if there was anyone left inside they were probably huddled behind the benches in fear. He could hear the helicopter hovering patiently above the ruin, but no other explosions came.

Elder Tyrsus gingerly leaned against the wall. "Either our attacker is...waiting for a clean shot," she breathed through the pain, "Or his job was to soften us up."

"Well, he's doing a bloody good job of it!" Kitty growled.

The tigress assisted Rizzo with Vicki's wounds, rummaging through the bullfrog's medical bag for bandages and medication. She also produced a collapsible stretcher.

"God bless you, you overprepared genius," Kitty said and gave the frog a friendly peck on the forehead.

Vick smiled through the pain, "You bet."

Kitty glanced up at Rizzo. "You came out pretty good."

The basilisk hesitated. "Vince got in front of me."

The hare accepted a bandage from Kitty and tipped his battered fedora. "Think nothin' of it, darlin'."

Zed studied the alley and the buildings surrounding them. "We cannot outrun a helicopter, Mohan," he said.

The tiger nodded. "And we don't have the firepower to bring it down. We need to lay Vicki on the back seat of one of the cars. Going to be a tight squeeze to fit everyone."

"S-sorry about that," the frog murmured.

Mohan smiled down at the injured medic. "No worries, Vicki. You just rest."

Rizzo glanced around the vehicles parked on the street. The police sedans were armoured, but that wouldn't do much against a rocket strike. What they needed was a distraction, but most of the other cars were urban vehicles and not designed to leave the protective walls of the city. The blast had shattered many of the vehicle windows and those with alarms had their headlights flashing erratically.

Then the basilisk's eyes came to rest on a sleek red Menzetti Freccia. It seemed untouched by the nearby explosion.

"I've got an idea!" Rizzo said.

Kitty followed the basilisk's gaze and turned back to her with an evil grin. "I think I can help with that."

"Kitty..." Mohan started to say, "Oh, bollox. No time to argue. Vince, you think you're ok to drive?"

The hare finished binding his wounded arm. "Yeah, Mo, I'll manage."

"Right." The tiger motioned to the frog now lying on the stretcher. "Take Ric and Vicki in the smaller car and follow us. Ric, you're shotgun—I bloody well wish you had one now, but the job's the same. You see anyone tailing us, you shoot. Clear?"

Ric nodded, drew his father's .45 and checked the magazine. For the briefest of moments Kitty's eyes gleamed.

The whine of the helicopter's engines shifted slightly. The pilot was attempting to circle around to the side of the hotel.

"Bloody hell," Mohan muttered, "We're lucky there isn't room for him to fly down the street, but he could certainly get a clear shot at us out here. We have to move!" He turned to Kitty and Rizzo. "Go, go! You're the decoy, get moving."

Rizzo tossed the sedan key to Vince and jogged off towards the Freccia. The tigress turned to follow her.

"Kitty," Mohan called after his daughter. She turned. Mohan raised his fist and said, "Strength and Honour."

Kitty frowned and said nothing.

Mohan shook his head and helped Ric and Vince get Vicki situated in the rear of the smaller sedan.

* * *

Like most expensive high-performance vehicles on Amarthia, the Menzetti Freccia---Mecci for "arrow"—was armoured, and the blast from the explosion had done little more than coat the wedge-shaped automobile with fine dust. Rizzo and Kitty's first thought was how to get into the car, they obviously couldn't shoot the windows out.

As luck would have it, the owner had forgotten to secure the latches on the roof windows, which had a T-bar configuration.

It was the work of ten seconds for the basilisk to crawl under the steering column and pull the ignition wires. The fuel-injected V12 engine roared to life, and as Rizzo situated herself behind the leather-wrapped steering wheel, the expression on her face was pure euphoria.

"Mmm, you hear that?" the basilisk said, producing a satisfied thrum that sounded almost like a feline purr, "Four-thousand-two-hundred-sixty cubic centimetres of raw Medoccian engineering!"

"You can root it later," Kitty growled as she tossed the detached passenger-side roof window behind the seat.

Rizzo locked her own roof window back in place to protect herself but Kitty was going to stand on the passenger seat, it would be much easier to shoot at the helicopter that way instead of leaning out the side window. The tigress only wished she had something with more punch than her pistol.

On impulse, the tigress rummaged around in the glovebox and pulled out the registration. Her eyes widened.

"Oi, open the boot a sec, Riz," Kitty said.

Rizzo pulled the latch and pointed to the front of the car. The compartment was barely large enough for a mid-sized suitcase, but that was not what the tigress found inside.

Kitty let out and excited whoop and Rizzo arched a curious eyebrow. She leaned over and read the registration card.

"Isn't that lucky!" the basilisk laughed, "This just happens to be the property of one Nico Favera. Isn't he Grego's cousin?"

"Too right!" Kitty said and lifted something from the compartment, "And he does all of Grego's gun-running in Medocci!"

When the tigress slammed the boot shut she was holding a large assault rifle in her paws. The magazine extended from the butt behind the grip in what was referred to as a bullpup design.

"It seems old Nico likes to keep some product handy!" Kitty said with a toothy grin, "A Cavallieri em sixty-four with extended mags!" She slapped the tubular attachment beneath the barrel. "And grenade launcher! Only two rounds, though. Need to be careful."

The tigress climbed into the passenger seat, cradling the large weapon carefully. "This will even things up a bit!" she said, "Punch it!"

The basilisk didn't do so immediately. First, she reached into a breast pocket of her shirt and withdrew a strand of

Buru'Nadi prayer beads, which she carefully wrapped around the rearview mirror.

Picking up the end she kissed them and whispered, "Watch over me, father."

Kitty spared a glance towards the sedans, loaded and waiting for the decoy to spring. Her own father nodded to her from the driver's seat of the large one. The tigress couldn't decide if Mohan had been watching her too closely, or not enough.

The helicopter buzzed overhead, breaking her thoughts. Kitty watched it circle around, trying to find an angle to launch another rocket down the street. It was a light, single-pilot aircraft, probably a modified Pelican H-36, which was popular among flight enthusiasts across the globe. Two barrel-shaped objects were strapped to the landing skids.

Kitty rose until she was kneeling on the seat and raised the rifle to her right shoulder. This wasn't going to be as easy as she thought, she was left-handed but didn't want to catch hot brass in her face.

The first three-round burst raked the bubble cockpit of the helicopter, causing the pilot to veer away from the unexpected counterattack. Kitty's next two bursts went wide.

"Dammit, armoured!" she said, "Knew it would be, but I think that got his attention!"

Bracing herself between the dashboard and T-bar, Kitty nodded to Rizzo. The basilisk needed no further prompting, she threw the Freccia into gear and with a screech of rubber the sleek supercar launched from its parking spot like its namesake projectile from a bow.

Kitty felt the adrenaline hit her as the air came rushing over the Menzetti. She let loose a wild cry as they raced past the idling sedans. For the briefest of moments her eyes locked on Ric's as he sat next to Vince, and then they were speeding down the next block and into the maze of streets that was Scogliera Piatta.

The tigress turned back, not to see the lynx but to see if the helicopter was taking the bait.

It was.

"We got him, Riz!" Kitty shouted above the wind, "Come get us, you bloody bastard!"

She raised the rifle and let loose another burst. Even with the blood running hot through her veins the tigress was careful to aim high and wide to avoid hitting the buildings, which might be occupied.

The helicopter pilot was not so conscientious. A pair of flashes from the tubes on the skids precipitated the launch of two more rockets into the streets below.

Rizzo saw them coming in the rear-view mirror. She reached down and yanked on the handbrake, jerking the wheel to the left. Kitty braced herself against the T-bar as the Freccia drifted gracefully around a corner. The rockets exploded further up their previous path, and the helicopter swung wide to the right, attempting to loop back onto its target's new course.

"Careful, Riz," Kitty said, "We don't want to lose him yet."

Rizzo eased off the accelerator. The basilisk did most of the driving for Mohan's Scrappers and made it a point to memorise maps of each city they operated in. She scanned the road ahead and picked out landmarks, matching them to the maps and plotting their position relative to the airport. They were headed northwest, away from the destination of their companions. Good.

But they still needed an exit for themselves.

"We need to get him away from these populated areas," she said to Kitty.

"Easier said than done inside the walls," the tigress replied, "Ace! He's back on us. Give it some gas!"

Rizzo obliged.

It was rare that the basilisk got to have this much fun with a car. Most of the time, she was driving a utility lorry, and the streets were far too crowded to properly manoeuvre at speed. To really open up with the Freccia brought Rizzo back to her days driving the Neuf Maris Grand Prix; that is before she was expelled because her late father was connected to the anti-monarchy rebels, which she later joined herself.

During the day, the streets of Scogliera Piatta bustled with tourists and traffic. But now, at three AM in the morning, it was Rizzo's playground. She stuck to the wider streets, making sure that the helicopter always had a good view of them but never staying in a straightaway long enough for the pilot to get a good shot.

Rizzo slammed on the breaks as they zoomed around a corner, nearly colliding with a garbage truck coming the opposite direction. The basilisk threw the Freccia into reverse and sped down the opposite lane backwards.

"Rizzo," Kitty said nervously, watching the helicopter swoop in over the intersection they had just left.

The basilisk grinned. "I have this."

They entered into a roundabout and Rizzo yanked on the handbrake again, effortlessly spinning the car ninety degrees and shifting back into first gear. She was in second by the time they hit the next turn off, and then third as they rocketed northwestward again.

The helicopter cruised in seconds behind them.

Kitty harrassed their tail with several bursts from the rifle and wished she could try one of the grenades. There were still too many civilian structures around, and her training wouldn't allow her to endanger innocent lives, even if the same couldn't be said of their opponent.

The helicopter pilot also didn't have any thoughts about damaging the ancient monuments as his target raced below. They approached the spacious circular courtyard of the Priupas Arch, and as Rizzo drifted expertly around this larger roundabout, the helicopter let loose another pair of rockets. They struck along the mantle of the nearly two-thousand-year-old structure and blew the statue of Emperor Tanilius mounted on a decorated ecquai clean off the top.

"Bastard really won't let up," Kitty said.

"How much does he have left?" Rizzo asked.

The tigress understood that the basilisk was referring to their pursuer's armament. "I can't say really," she said, "We know for sure he doesn't have guns because he would have opened up on us by now. The pods attached to the runners aren't that large, but I can't tell if they're five rounds or six. He's loosed three volleys at us, so either he's only half done or running low."

"We'll be at the wall soon," Rizzo said, "Maybe they'll take care of him for us? I seriously doubt those fireworks inside the city went unnoticed."

Kitty looked up at the dark walls, intermittently lit by bright floodlights. They were coming up on the northwest edge of Scogliera Piatta, but there wasn't a clear space in sight. Unlike the cities of Pytan, the Medoccians kept most of their agricultural plots outside the walls; the fertile nature of the land made it easily replenishable should it be ruined by packs of wild beasts or raided by bandits. Unfortunately, that meant nearly all the available space inside was occupied by businesses and residences. Even if the border guards took action against the helicopter, collateral damage would be high.

"Head for the Gymnasium," Kitty said suddenly.

Rizzo looked at her sideways.

"Do it!" Kitty insisted, "It's the only open space close by. Even if we lost him in the city, he'd go right to the airport and shoot Tyrsus down as she took off. We need to take him out."

The basilisk nodded and yanked on the handbrake, spinning the Freccia into a 180-degree turn and racing back underneath their pursuer. The pilot did the same, demonstrating the manoeuvrability of his craft by pivoting in place. Kitty peppered the armoured underside of the aircraft for good measure, but she made note that even with the extended magazine she was running short on ammo.

Rizzo retraced several kilometres of their path until they reach the Micine Fountains, an elaborate collection of statues depicting the legend of Bathyus Mice, a crab who was Medocci's first and only aquatic emperor. Almost as soon as the basilisk entered the courtyard, she made a sharp right and headed down the Via Libra, headed for the southern beaches. Rizzo understood what the tigress wanted now. There were more glass and steel hotels along those beaches, but there were also many wide parks; including the Gymnasium.

The word had come to have a much different meaning in the modern world, but in ancient Medocci, the Gymnasium was the chief festival grounds for many classical sporting events and celebrations and was still used as such today.

The sleek Freccia screeched around a corner, and Kitty immediately began to scan the tree-lined courtyards. The park was far from flat and scattered with the crumbling remains of buildings and colonnades that had once served as market stalls, public baths, and gardens. Numerous twisting pathways wound through the park, all culminating at a large central point.

"There!" the tigress said, tapping Rizzo on the shoulder and pointing to the far side of the park.

The basilisk could just make out the black backdrop and latticed steel rigging of a semi-permanent stage erected at one end of a grassy amphitheatre. The venue saw much use for plays and concerts, no doubt Kitty planned to make the demise of the helicopter the latest attraction.

Their pursuer rounded one of the hotels behind them and found a clear shot. Rizzo saw the flashes in her mirror as it let loose another pair of rockets and jerked the wheel to the right, veering down a wide walking path. The rockets blew a public fountain and nearby newsstand to rubble.

The Freccia sailed over a short stairway and Rizzo cringed as the low vehicle slammed back onto the path with a shower of sparks. Menzetti normally outfitted their automobiles with superb suspension, but this was still a racing car and not an off-road vehicle. The wobble coming through the steering wheel was not reassuring.

Kitty rose in the seat and launched one of the grenades at the helicopter. It dodged easily, and the tigress' projectile excavated a chunk out of the landscaping, bursting a water main in the process. However, the manoeuvre distracted the pilot long enough to buy them the seconds needed to reach the stage.

"Circle the platform!" Kitty ordered, reloading the launcher.

The Freccia's speed had slowed considerably, due both to the gravel that made up the floor of the amphitheatre and the damaged suspension. Kitty watched as the helicopter moved to hover in the centre of the amphitheatre, evidently divining the car's path. The tigress threw open the door and turned to Rizzo.

"Give me a three count, then floor it past the other side of the stage," the tigress said and waited as the Freccia began to pass behind the backdrop for the stage platform.

As soon as they passed out of sight of the helicopter, Rizzo tapped the brakes and Kitty dove from the car. She hit the ground on her side and rolled with the impact, it stung like hell, but the tigress was on her feet in an instant. Kitty dashed for the corner of the stage they had just passed, counting off in her head and raising the rifle to her left shoulder. She couldn't miss this shot, better use the correct hand.

Kitty reached the corner of the stage right as her count hit three. Rizzo jammed her foot on the accelerator, making for a copse of trees on the far side of the theatre that would do very little to shield the Freccia from the helicopter's vision.

At that moment two things happened at once. Kitty, having reached the corner and taken aim at the helicopter, launched her only remaining grenade. The helicopter, having guessed the trajectory of its target, let loose another pair of rockets aimed at the copse of trees on the far side of the theatre.

It was too late when the pilot realised that half of the Freccia's occupants were missing. The grenade impacted along the upper edge of the bubble cockpit, the blast sheering clean through the exposed mechanisms of the rotor assembly. The cockpit itself shattered, sending multiple shards of superheated ballistic plastic right through the helpless pilot. Bereft of control, the small aircraft spun wildly several times before crashing to the ground in front of the stage. The rocket pods must have had at least one more load in them because the rounds ignited on impact, creating a spectacular pyrotechnic display worthy of any concert.

Kitty's shout of glee was interrupted as she ducked back behind the stage to avoid a chunk of flaming debris and turned in the direction Rizzo had gone. The basilisk had done everything she could, but the gravel offered no traction for the Freccia, and the supercar slid sideways directly into the path of the last rockets the helicopter had fired.

They struck the ground beneath the Menzetti Freccia, blasting it into the air. The supercar tumbled end over end until it came to rest—right-side-up—on the steps of one of the many ancient archways that dotted the park.

"My God!" Kitty gasped, dropping the rifle and running headlong for the Freccia.

The tigress skidded to a stop not three metres from the wreck as the door popped open and a long-clawed hand gripped the upper edge of the window.

Battered and bleeding, Rizzo climbed out of the wreckage.

The basilisk smiled wearily at the tigress. "A-Always...buckle up," she croaked painfully and collapsed on the ground.

* * *

Mohan was not surprised that no one else had appeared to molest the escaping agents. The helicopter was a warning. If it killed them, so be it, but the message was clear: *get out!*

"They are still toying with us," Zed had said as they approached the airport, watching the rear-view mirror as the fireballs lit up the city going in the opposite direction.

That was over an hour ago, and the eastern sky was beginning to lighten.

Mohan checked his watch for the hundredth time.

They should have been back by now, he thought, and the first dark tendrils of dread began to creep over him.

If Rizzo and his daughter didn't show in the next five minutes, he knew Elder Tyrsus would declare them lost. The Corvair 882 sat outside the rented hanger, and Mohan could hear the engines whine as Tyrsus warmed them up. Despite her broken wing, the eagle insisted she was good to fly, which was good because Mohan certainly didn't know anything about flying a plane. Zed might, the badger was full of secrets.

The Soketh poked his striped head out the rear hatch and looked at his leader standing on the tarmac with the ground crew. The tiger didn't need the badger to say anything to get the message: it was time to go. The airport was going into lockdown because of the explosions and if they wanted to make a break for it the time was now.

Mohan turned to one of the ground crew agents. "We still have people out there," he said to the banded lemur, "If they show up after we leave, you know what to do to get them to safety."

The lemur nodded and waved to the other members of the ground crew to take their positions around the plane. Mohan grabbed onto the boarding handle, but something made him pause before pulling himself into the plane. The drone of the Corvair's twin engines was loud in his ears, but he was almost certain he heard something else. He turned.

A pinpoint of light appeared in the darkness and soon materialised into a motorcycle and sidecar. Mohan held back a cry, but his heart leapt when he recognised the black stripes against cream fur. The figure in the sidecar must be Rizzo, but from the way she slumped in the seat, the tiger could instantly tell that something was wrong.

Kitty made a wide arc around the wing and brought the motorcycle to a screeching halt by the door.

"Riz is hurt!" the tigress shouted above the plane's engines as she unstrapped her helmet. Scooters were popular in Medocci, finding a motorcycle was luck, finding one with a sidecar was Providence, but finding helmets that fit a feline head and a rpetile one had been a pain in the ass. Oddly enough, it was Rizzo's last words about wearing a seatbelt that had suddenly made Kitty safety conscious even in such dire circumstances.

Zed was at the sidecar instantly and gently lifted the unconscious basilisk in his arms. "I will see to her," he said.

Mohan stared at his daughter for a long moment. He wanted to hug her, but such displays of affection between them had become uncomfortable recently.

"I—," he began, pausing uncertainly, "I'm glad you made it back."

Kitty tossed her helmet into the sidecar next to Rizzo's. "Yeah," she said and walked past him to the plane.

Mohan chuffed irritably, but it was lost in the drone of the engines. With a resigned sigh, he followed his daughter and boarded the Corvair.

Elder Tyrsus ran through her pre-flight checklist, but before they could taxi out, a messenger flagged them down. The red panda had a Tiger's Mark plainly visible in the markings of his face—it must have been annoying explaining the odd combination of white stripes to coworkers.

Kitty opened the rear door for him, and he poked his head into the cabin.

"Elder Tyrsus," the panda said breathlessly, having to shout over the drone of the twin propellers, "a message for you from the Council."

"Let's hear it," the eagle called out, not wanting to move now that she had found a comfortable position for her wing.

The red panda recited from memory, "Urgent from agent sixty-one, Nahas residence. Intercepted communique between Nahas and Kristoph Weis. Delshad al-Seif assassinated. Men from Nahas and Weis arriving soon to assist Yursa De Palma in the assassination of Jirair al-Seif. PR is readying a response, continue on mission."

The agents appeared to take this information in stride, but Kitty was genuinely distressed. Ric watched as the tigress' grip tightened on the door latch; had her fur not already been white the journalist was sure it would have turned thus.

"Things will get messy," Mohan said.

"Yes," Tyrsus agreed, "Thank you, Bastion."

The red panda nodded and left.

"Well, you get your wish, Kittina," Tyrsus called back, "Al-Seif won't live to see the end of the week."

Kitty said nothing.

The white tigress dogged the hatch and took the seat nearest to it; Ric noticed that she secured her bag near the door instead of in a bin closer to her. He also noted that her eyes flicked to the long case containing her rifle at the top of the pile in the rear of the compartment. The journalist didn't know what she might be thinking, but as the plane started to roll forward, he told himself it was too late for her to do anything now.

Ric didn't know anything about Kittina Katral.

Tyrsus lined the plane up and throttled up the propellers. The passengers felt themselves forced back into their seats and the wheels lifted off the ground. The eagle made a long bank to the right, climbing steadily.

As soon as Elder Tyrsus straightened out at an altitude of six hundred metres, Kitty was out of her seat. The aircraft was still ascending, but despite the angle, the tigress managed to secure a parachute over her shoulders with lightning speed and began tugging on her rifle case in the equipment pile.

"Kitty!" Mohan roared from his seat near the front, "Don't you fucking dare!"

The tiger rose and started staggering towards her, but it was too late; the tigress abandoned the rifle, grabbed her bag, threw open the door and was gone.

Mohan rushed to the portal and saw the white plume of the chute disappearing into the darkness.

"Bloody hell!" the tiger said with a snarl. "The rest of you stay here. Tyrsus, level off, I'm going to get her."

The eagle performed as instructed while the tiger strapped on another parachute and secured his own bag.

"Agent Katral," Tyrsus called from the cockpit.

Mohan turned.

"You know what this means?" the eagle asked gravely.

The tiger nodded. "Yes, Elder," he said and leapt out the door.

With a great effort, Zed and Vince managed to secure the hatch behind him. Ric wanted to ask Zed what the Elder had meant, but the question was silenced when he saw the grim look on the badger's face.

The journalist turned to the window to see if he could catch a glimpse of either Kitty or Mohan's chutes, but all he saw was a carpet of clouds turned pink by the sun rising in the east.

35 – The Demons' Due

"You'll wear a hole in the carpet eventually," Carmen Abbatelli said.

Jirair al-Seif kept pacing across the plush Pytian rug in his office. "I can afford another one," he said, "For now at least."

Carmen boosted herself off the corner of the desk and forced her lover to stop by taking his dark muzzle in her hands. She kissed the white patch between his nostrils and smiled.

"Don't think like that," she said. "My vineyard is still thriving, and Delshad has been making good progress in Pytan—"

"Delshad is what I'm thinking about right now," al-Seif said, "It's been almost three days since I heard from him."

"He is protected by your best men," she argued gently, "And you know that Yursa will not be so hasty after the stunt the other families tried to pull."

The mouflon sighed and took the dark ibex in his arms. "I wish I could share your optimism," he said, "However, Delshad's last report mentioned Mody Nahas and Christoph Weis might be close to joining forces. I know that fat ape won't like working with the fox-shepherd, but Delshad could still be in danger. Beyond that, I was informed this morning that the Syrus Industries files I had placed in the records office were accessed. Someone thought to try bringing a court case against me, and we both know that is not the style of any of our new mafia rivals."

Al-Seif took Carmen's hands in his and kissed the glossy red tips of her fingers. "I must confess, I have been thinking much about your favourite verse." He looked into her soft eyes. "And how the demons must be paid their dues eventually."

Carmen's face suddenly turned grave, but before she could respond, the chime of the doorbell interrupted their conversation. In the hall, Abar Kami answered the door, and the *Caprinae* in the office heard a muffled conversation.

Moments later the office door opened and Rashid stepped in followed by the panther.

The dromedary had changed up his ubiquitous white robe for a dark blue one, although the gold trim and embroidery was still present. He had also replaced the tall turban with a simple blue headscarf, the white gauze of a bandage peeked out from underneath.

"Rashid?" al-Seif said, the surprise in his voice balanced by an equal measure of dread. "Why are you here? What's happened?"

"Sir, madam," the dromedary said, bowing low. "I am afraid I bring terrible news."

Carmen rushed forward and grabbed him by the shoulders, lifting him up to look into his eyes.

"Where is Delshad? Where is my son?" From the tremble in her voice it was obvious she had already answered her own questions.

"H-he's dead," Rashid managed to get out.

The silence weighed heavy in the office for several moments, then the room filled with a keening screech that only a grieving mother could supply.

Carmen sank to her knees, still clutching tight to the dromedary's robes and forcing him down to one knee as well.

Al-Seif knelt and put his arms around his mistress, transferring her grip to his own. She collapsed against him, unable to stop the tears.

The tears in al-Seif's own eyes only helped to magnify the fire burning in them. "How?" he asked, his voice hoarse with rage, "Who were the bastards that did this?"

Rashid remained kneeling. "It was a collaboration between Mody Nahas and Kristoph Weis. After Delshad informed the gladiators of your arrangement to send them to Thyropolis, I assisted with their payroll. Then I went to the Khet airport, where I expected to rejoin Delshad. It was only then that I discovered he had made an unexpected detour to the bungalow, but never arrived. I spent more than a day making inquiries to find out what happened. That was when Nahas himself called and informed me that Weis had ambushed him."

The dromedary scratched absently at the bandages beneath his headscarf. "I was boarding the plane to come here and give you the news personally when Weis' men decided to attack me. As you can see, I did not escape entirely unscathed."

Carmen's sobs lessened enough for her to choke out, "How could they have trapped him? We warned him about the attack on the villa. He should have been more vigilant. You should have been with him!"

Rashid shook his head. "I know," he said, "It is to my great shame that I was not there, and I accept whatever punishment you see fit, even my own life. As to how they trapped him, I do not know. Delshad played things very close while operating in your stead." He nodded to al-Seif. "You would have been proud. I can only assume Nahas and Weis received inside information about your son's habits and...possible weaknesses."

The dromedary was obviously hesitant to speak this last part, but al-Seif knew what he meant. Try as he did, the older mouflon had never been able to completely expunge the playboy mentality from his son.

"It was her," Carmen breathed.

Al-Seif looked down and saw the ibex's pale blue eyes looking up at him, a fire even more intense than his own burning in them.

"It's that bitch, Yursa," she said, more confident now. "Only she knew as much about Delshad's habits and vices. And even if we never told her, she would have guessed that we'd send him back to Pytan."

The mouflon nodded. "Yes," he said, but his mind instantly went to a different source.

Freggs had warned al-Seif to stay out of Pytan while his associates operated in the area. The mouflon had been proud of his son for refusing the mechanical toad's offer, now al-Seif wondered if it had been Freggs' last attempt to avoid making good on his own threat.

"We must kill her," Carmen said, and the vehemence in her voice almost made al-Seif shrink back. "That bitch must pay for what she's done to us!"

Al-Seif thought quickly. If Freggs was ultimately responsible for his son's death, the mouflon had no illusions that the toad would use Yursa De Palma in some way. Killing her would alleviate both his own pain and Carmen's.

"She will be expecting that," al-Seif argued aloud, "She wants to hurt us; to avenge what she believes we did to her."

He winced as Carmen gripped his arm tighter than he believed possible.

"Let her believe it," the ibex said hoarsely, "I will impale her on my own horns for this outrage!"

Rashid stood now, but he kept his head bowed. "I understand your grief," he said, "Forgive me for speaking out of turn, but I believe it would be best if you went into hiding."

Carmen turned on him fiercely, but al-Seif shushed her and stroked a hand along the ridges of her ibex horns.

"He is right, *mi amore*," he said gently, speaking in her native Mecci to emphasise his words. "Even now, Yursa could be moving against the villa again. We are vulnerable, and she knows it."

Al-Seif gently stood and raised Carmen to her hooves, then turned to the dromedary. "Get down to my yacht, tell the captain to make ready for immediate departure. We will head west, perhaps to Libris."

Rashid bowed and left out the office's garden entrance.

The mouflon turned to the panther. "Abar, inform the guard and staff to keep up routine for at least two days. They are to act as if nothing is wrong. After that…"

Al-Seif paused. What was after that? Would he ever see his Medocci home again? He knew he could settle himself elsewhere, and even Carmen had said the physical amenities of the house held little value as long as…as long as she had her son and al-Seif.

In all his chaotic life, the villa was the one place where he had actually been able to find peace and even happiness. And now, he may be losing it forever.

"After that," he continued, "tell them they're free to go. Their services will no longer be required. They can have the house for themselves if they want. Go to the safe and distribute their payment in advance, with a bonus."

Abar Kami looked uncertain. "Are you sure, sir?"

The mouflon nodded. "I know it isn't like you to question my decisions, but I am sure. Until Yursa is dead, this place will never be safe. Perhaps someday we will return, but until then…maybe they should just run it like we were still here. Besides." He gave Carmen a firm hug with both arms. "This villa has been my dearest's prison for too long. It is time she saw more of what is beyond its walls."

Carmen started sobbing again, but al-Seif led her to their room at the top of the house and ordered Abar Kami to bring their suitcases. They would pack light, al-Seif always kept spare clothes on the yacht and Carmen loved shopping for new ones.

He instantly felt a twinge of regret. Shopping would do little if anything to relieve his lover's grief. Delshad had been their only child, and although Carmen was still of child-bearing age, nothing could ever replace her first born.

So what of it? al-Seif thought, *Another child may be the only thing to restore the joy she has lost. Perhaps a daughter? My empire is ruined, but Carmen need not share in my own despair. Perhaps it is time for the line of El Hashem and al-Seif to die out.*

Half-way through the task of packing, the phone on the end table buzzed, and al-Seif picked it up.

"Sir," the voice of Rashid said, "I have reached the yacht. Something feels...wrong. There was no crewman to help tie the launch off when I pulled alongside."

Al-Seif stepped out onto the bedroom balcony. He had a magnificent view of the sea from here and could see the purple and white superstructure of the *Star of Carmen* floating at anchor below. He donned a pair of binoculars resting on the patio table; he kept them around to watch ships out on the sea.

The *Star of Carmen*'s stern had swung towards the house with the incoming tide. Rashid was on the second deck near the pool.

"I see you," al-Seif said, "Is anyone on board?"

"Unconfirmed, sir," Rashid answered. "I am making my way to the bridge."

Al-Seif saw the dromedary draw a pistol from his robes and cautiously enter the second-deck lounge.

Several minutes passed before the mouflon heard a sudden eruption of sound and an exchange of gunfire. Moments later, the entire seventy-metre vessel exploded in a bright orange fireball.

The phone fell from Jirair al-Seif's numbed fingers. He staggered back as the shockwave hit him and the windows of the bedroom rattled, but they didn't shatter; the explosion was too far away, and the tempered glass was designed to withstand the violent storms that could sweep in from the Medean Basin.

Carmen came out and stood beside him, staring at the burning wreckage floating on the water.

"We cannot escape," she said, her voice almost a whisper.

Al-Seif turned to her and grabbed her shoulders. "No," he said, gazing steadily into her eyes. "We are still alive. And while we live, there is always a chance."

The ibex smiled weakly up at him. "You said it yourself, our demons have come to collect."

He took Carmen'sr face in his hands. "No! Stop it! We will be free! From now on we make new lives, we will start over."

Al-Seif kissed her fiercely.

Carmen kissed him back, then pulled away. "We cannot run forever," she said, the sad smile still on her face. "But I will follow you. To the ends of Amarthia."

Abar Kami appeared in the balcony doorway and al-Seif turned to him.

"Abar, my friend," al-Seif's voice cracked with uncharacteristic emotion. He had never referred to the panther in this fashion before, and the mouflon discovered it felt good. "Check the Regalia for booby traps. We're going into the city."

The panther nodded and left, but he gave his employer the faintest of smiles as he did so.

Al-Seif kissed Carmen again and led her back into the bedroom to finish packing. The small 9mm Bartelli pistol was in his shoulder holster as always, but he threw spare magazines and a small machine pistol into his luggage as insurance.

Carmen moved in a robotic state of shock, and her lover ended up assisting his mistress with her bags. The mouflon deliberately considered their next move while he worked. The airport of Pacé Acqua only supported small private aircraft, but Jirair al-Seif's plane was one of them. Even as he thought this, he knew it was useless, surely whoever had rigged the *Star of Carmen* would know about the plane.

But by air was not the only way out of the city.

Within minutes, they re-joined Kami on the sweeping driveway that led up to the house. The Regalia's engine was running, and the panther gave al-Seif a reassuring nod to signal he had thoroughly checked the vehicle for any explosive devices. The bodyguard had also attached the hard-cover shell over the flimsier armoured canvas roof. It ruined the lines of the elegant automobile, but al-Seif was glad of the added protection.

As he climbed into the driver's seat, Kami looked expectantly into the rear-view mirror. Al-Seif motioned for the car phone and had the panther dial the airport.

"Get my plane ready," the mouflon told his pilot when he answered, "Make a flight plan for Norsen. I don't care where, just do it quickly."

He handed the phone back to Kami, who hung it up.

"Yursa will expect us to make for the airport," al-Seif said, almost to himself. "It would be the fastest way out of

Medocci. So, we'll make for the train instead. We'll take the international rail into Maris, then board a boat to Libris. From there we can go anywhere, even the West United Kingdoms."

"I do not wish to challenge your judgement, Jirair," Abar Kami said, "But would it not be safer to simply drive out?"

Al-Seif shook his head. "This car is too well known. I am almost certain Yursa is not the only one who has betrayed us; we must find a way to vanish in a crowd. The airport and train stations in Scoliera Piatta are still closed after those explosions early yesterday morning, but we can still catch an international train here in Pacé Acqua."

He wrapped his arms around Carmen and held her close, but the ibex's smile was distant. She had resigned herself to a fate that her lover was still fighting.

Abar Kami threw the car into gear and started forward.

Jirair al-Seif watched the villa slip away behind them. He half expected to see it go up in flames just as his yacht had. But there was no explosion, no billow of smoke above the trees to warn him. He turned back to stare out the front window and hugged his mistress to his chest.

Carmen was muttering something under her breath, over and over. "There are no angels in this world. Only the demons we create for ourselves."

Al-Seif wanted her to stop, she was going into shock thanks to the loss of her—of *their*—only son. He tried to force himself to think logically, to go over what had happened and plan his next move, but the thoughts wouldn't come. For once in his life, Jirair al-Seif's mind was a blank, his rational processes refused to work, and all that drove him now was his primitive instinct to survive.

Before he knew it, they had reached the outskirts of Pacé Acqua and traffic began to increase as they approached the gates of the city. Al-Seif tensed and looked uneasily at the vehicles around them. During the day, traffic flowed in and out of the city freely, and the slow-moving line outside the narrow portal was a prime spot for an ambush.

But nothing happened. Soon, the Regalia merged with the tail end of the lunch-rush traffic, inching its way deeper into the city.

Abar Kami had few options when it came to choosing a route to the train station, the long Regalia was much larger than the typical compact cars found on Medoccian streets. Additionally, whichever direction Kami took would follow the same path that led to the airport for much of the way. If Yursa was going to plan an ambush inside the city, there was ample opportunity to do so.

There was a profusion of scooters and motorcycles on the road; such vehicles were the most efficient way for an individual to get around the narrow Medoccian streets. Kami adjusted his mirror again; one particular individual had caught his eye.

The rider was three cars behind them astride a red motorcycle. She dressed in acid washed jeans and a brown leather jacket. Black riding gloves covered her hands and a helmet designed to fit a feline head concealed much of her face. She was one of the so-called 'big cats', not a domestic breed; a white tail striped in black poked out from the seat of her pants, twitching now and again as if electrified.

She was good, but Kami caught on to her just before they entered the city gates and had watched her for several blocks now. This rider was exclusively interested in their car.

A scout, perhaps? Waiting for a signal or location to spring a trap? Abar Kami kept his eyes open for more unwanted attention, but for the moment the tigress appeared to be working alone.

"Sir," the panther said softly, "do not be alarmed, but we have a tail."

"Carry on," al-Seif ordered, "It's too late to change plans."

They were close to the station now, the white tigress still trailing behind. If Yursa had been planning an ambush, her window was closing fast. Al-Seif would not relax until they were safe aboard the train.

They started to cross the final intersection.

Carmen sat up suddenly and took al-Seif's head in her hands. "Jirair, I love you. Never forget that."

Al-Seif was staring at her in confusion when the right side of the car suddenly erupted in a shower of glass. He flew back against the left-hand door as the car rocked with the force of the impact. His vision blacked out for a few seconds but he could hear the screech of metal and the squeal of rubber as the traffic around them ground to a halt.

The mouflon wiped something warm and sticky from his eyes; his hand came away bloody. The engine was on fire, the flickering flames casting weird shadows through the spider web of the fractured front window. Abar Kami moaned in the driver's seat, stunned. A heavy garbage truck with its front-end forklift partly raised had slammed sidelong into the Regalia, skewering it like a bolvin roast over a firepit.

"Carmen!" al-Seif blurted out.

The ibex sat upright on the seat, facing him but without seeing him. One window, forced from its frame by the collision, had impacted with the back of Carmen's skull. She remained propped up because one of her ibex horns was wedged through the armoured glass and a tooth of the garbage truck's forklift now jammed into her spine. A spatter of crimson coated the cracked glass, framing Carmen in a halo of blood.

"No!" al-Seif's voice rasped, the tears already beginning to stream down his face to mingle with the blood matting his fur. "No, Carmen. Carmen!"

But Carmen Abbatelli was dead.

Jirair al-Seif wept openly now, the first time he had done so in many years. He reached up and gently closed the staring eyes.

The door opened behind him, and the mouflon felt strong arms wrap around him and yank him from the car. Al-Seif struggled fruitlessly against the iron grip until he found himself staring into the golden eyes of Abar Kami.

"Jirair," the panther shouted, "Jirair, she's gone! It's Nahas and Weis' men! I should have seen them coming. But you must live! For her, and for your son!"

The panther shoved al-Seif away in the direction of the train station. "Go! I will cover you!"

The mouflon was only partially aware of the figures that had begun to close in on them. He stumbled forward, not even conscious of the sound of his hooves against the cobblestone street. The flames were spreading, and he kept hearing the crash of glass. But it was not the echoes of the crash al-Seif heard, his assailants were trying to box him in with home-made firebombs.

A badger with spotted markings and large white patches around his eyes lunged at the retreating mouflon, but Abar Kami swatted the blow to the side and delivered three swift strikes to the broad face. A scrawny knife-wielding racoon tried to get in behind the panther, but Kami spun on his toe pads, grabbed the knife arm and with one powerful blow, snapped it in half at the wrist. The racoon's cry of pain cut off as the panther brought his knee into the racoon's chest, it caved inward with a sickening *crunch*.

The badger recovered and made a lunge at the panther. Kami ducked back and brought his elbow up under his attacker's chin, snapping the spotted head back before delivering a swift chop to the badger's throat that severed his windpipe.

Both the badger and the racoon had been wearing green coveralls like sanitation workers; Kami used this information to scan the crowd for more attackers. He spotted a group of them heading for the station, hard on the heels of his master. His friend.

Kami snarled and felt the rage of feral bloodlust rising inside him. He embraced it and leapt after the thugs.

The panther caught two henchmen at the edge of the crash site, now ringed with fire thanks to the attackers' firebombs. Kami cracked their feline and reptile skulls together and left their broken bodies where they were. Several metres on, he caught a stoat from behind with a vicious flying kick that broke the weasel's back. Further up, a wolf and a rat suffered broken arms and legs at the hands of Abar Kami.

Finally, a muscle-bound horse blocked the panther's path. Kami swept the equine's legs out from under him and brought his heel down on the long throat.

Abar Kami reached the doors of the train station and saw the coattails of his employer vanish inside. A crowd of bewildered civilians gathered around, but the panther hissed fiercely if they got too close.

Four more large assailants in green coveralls were forcing their way towards the station. Kami unhooked a pair of queue stanchions and wrapped the chains around his paws. Al-Seif had made it inside, the panther just needed to buy the mouflon time to disappear into the crowd.

He glared at the mammal and reptile faces that began to close on him and bared his teeth.

But in his rage, Abar Kami failed to note that none of his assailants was a white tigress.

36 – Cornered

Jirair al-Seif neared the platform for Scogliera Piatta and ducked into the men's room. He didn't check the restroom for other occupants, nor did he care. He leaned against an open sink and stared into the mirror, but all he could see was the face of his beloved Carmen, her head ringed in a bloody halo. Jirair al-Seif wept openly.

The mouflon had lost everything when he lost her. Even the loss of his son hadn't hit him as hard the death of his beloved. His businesses no longer mattered, his wealth and his power were all meaningless without Carmen Abbatelli.

If only that bitch Yursa could see him now.

Al-Seif pounded his fist against the counter. Yursa and that damned Freggs! The mouflon knew the mechanical voice must be behind this somehow. Al-Seif had outlived his usefulness as a pawn, and now it was time to remove him from the board.

The mouflon slammed his fist into the mirror and gritted his teeth as small shards of glass burrowed their way into his knuckles. He continued pounding his frustration out, alternating between the mirror and the counter. A parakeet and a fox entered, chatting politely about their separate travel plans. Their conversation halted abruptly on seeing the distraught mouflon, and the two exchanged bemused looks before promptly deciding to seek out a different restroom.

Al-Seif hadn't even noticed the interruption. Gaining control of his faculties once again, he straightened up and adjusted his suit jacket. The cauracua feather from his lapel was gone, as was one of his horn tassels; he plucked the remaining tassel off and threw it on the floor. Washing the blood from his face and hands, al-Seif made himself as presentable as he could under the circumstances.

Freggs hadn't beaten him yet, not while he was still alive. Al-Seif would track down the mechanical voice and feed him his own testicles. And if it turned out Freggs actually was an amphibian, then to hell with the medical complications involved in performing such a procedure.

Al-Seif left the men's room and started making his way toward the ticket counter. The mouflon's survival instincts were kicking in again; first, he must get out of this trap before he could start setting his own.

It was a Miriday afternoon, and the station was quite crowded with commuters. Since its invention over a hundred and fifty years ago, trains had become one of the most widely used methods of transportation on the continent of Aerenia. Many nations universally acknowledged the railway as the reason they had maintained a lasting peace for so long. With workers from so many different countries coming and going, the weaving of Aerenia's economies was irreversible.

It was for this reason that Jirair al-Seif felt confident he would have no trouble escaping Medocci. He had no luggage now, only the cash in his wallet and the reassuring bulk of the small pistol in his shoulder holster; and the former would assist him in getting the latter past security.

Once he was free, he could begin anew. Al-Seif had started from the bottom before, and he could do it again.

But without Carmen and Delshad, what's the point?

Al-Seif thrust the thought away with an angry shake of his horns and looked up at the departures board. It didn't really matter which international line he selected, as long as it was leaving Medocci soon. Once he was out of the country, he would have more time to carefully choose his next destination.

A flash of white caught al-Seif's eye. He turned and saw two pools of sapphire ice staring at him from across the long, crowded hall. Even at a distance, the mouflon's blood froze in the sheer hatred of that gaze. He had no idea who this white tigress was, but everything about her advertised her intent.

Al-Seif's eyes darted around like a cornered munski. She wouldn't do anything in this crowd, al-Seif knew because otherwise, he'd already be dead. But if she followed him onto the train.

Al-Seif didn't dare finish that line of thought. He needed an exit, some way he could lose the tigress. There was a door off to the mouflon's right, leading into the maintenance halls behind and beneath the station; if he could reach it. He discarded the idea immediately; they always locked such doors to keep out unauthorised personnel.

The tigress started pushing her way through the crowd. Al-Seif backed towards the door.

Maybe she wouldn't care if she murdered him in public? Where the hell was Abar?

Just as al-Seif's shoulder bumped into the door, he felt it open towards him. A platypus in the dark blue coveralls of a station utility worker came out, pulling a cart of cleaning supplies behind him.

Without thinking, al-Seif grabbed the edge of the door and shoved both worker and cart out of the way before darting inside. The platypus barked angrily, but the mouflon ignored him. Al-Seif heard the reassuring click of the door locking behind him, so that would slow his pursuer somewhat; the platypus would contact his supervisor before attempting to open the door again.

But that might not be the case should the tigress shove a gun in his face. The mouflon hurried on down the tunnel.

One of the wonders of Medocci's civil engineering was its underground. In addition to the intercity rails above ground, Pacé Acqua possessed a winding subway system. It also dealt with large amounts of water runoff when the spring melt came to the mountains in the northwest. The pipes and reservoirs of the drainage system, combined with the tunnels and tubes of the subway, created a maze-like substructure deep beneath the streets of the city above.

Vigo De Palma had once shown al-Seif a map of the tunnels and explained how they could be quite useful for smuggling. Naturally, the mouflon hadn't memorised the map, but he did remember that almost every section of subway had a maintenance door that connected it to the tunnel network. If he could make a loop, duck through the tunnel system and come back into the train station on the other side, maybe he could throw the tigress off and gain enough time to board the next train to out of Medocci before she caught on.

Al-Seif's current section of tunnel marched on with tiles of utilitarian white, occasionally smudged with dirt, but otherwise clean. Colour coded piping ran above the mouflon's head, and caged incandescent lights paced him along the wall. His cloven feet clacked on the smooth cement as he ran, but he didn't care about the noise right now; once he came to the first junction, the mouflon would try to move quieter and hide which direction he'd gone.

Al-Seif passed the maintenance closet that the platypus must have come from and hit the first break in the path not long after. Ahead, the tunnel started to curve downward in a gentle spiral with a low slope, to the left the tiled tunnel ran straight and true along what must be the back end of the station. The mouflon could see multiple doors on either side that must lead to offices or back into the station proper, but something kept him from turning that way.

I'm still too close, al-Seif thought, *Those doors will be locked, and she'll be checking them to see if I double back on her!*

The mouflon made for the spiralling tunnel, trying hard to be as light on his feet as possible. If only he hadn't left the velvet slippers he had stored in his luggage, the soft padding of the soles would do wonders to hide his footfalls.

The sound of rushing water rose to meet him as the tunnel descended.

Instead of another intersection of tunnels, the passage ended at a large square chamber with several levels of catwalks. Daylight filtered in from a grate in the street several metres above him. To al-Seif's left was a heavy metal door and a metal ladder down to the next level, to his right, a large open pipe dumped brackish water into the centre of the chamber, where it gathered into a dark pool at the bottom and flowed out an arched tunnel of grimy cobblestone. On the levels below, more open pipes spewed forth their contents, contributing to the dampness in the air. The catwalks and ladders on the lowest levels looked like they hadn't seen use in many years.

One glance at the dizzying collection of water-slicked platforms was enough to make the mouflon wonder how long it had been since the Medoccian Workplace Safety Commission had inspected this area. The thought brought a brief sardonic smile to his face. To think that Assad Alabwaq's own employees mostly had to worry about infection from bullets and knife wounds, not cuts from rusted gangplanks.

Al-Seif tried the door on his level. Locked. He could shoot the lock out, but that would let his pursuer know which way he had gone.

Precisely, he thought suddenly.

Wasting no time, al-Seif drew his pistol, shot out the lock and kicked the door in. Then he climbed down the ladder to the level below. If he could find an open door down here, or even just an alcove to duck into, his assailant might get off on the wrong track.

And if she didn't? Well, he had seven more rounds in the Bartelli, although this wasn't exactly al-Seif's choice of environment to make a stand. The mouflon was a decent swimmer, and if it came down to it, he could risk the water below.

The level two platform had two doors on his side, both also locked. Across the chamber, al-Sief could see another pair of doors, but no way to reach them. He continued downward.

The mist was heavier here, and heavier still below. Al-Seif's suit was thoroughly soaked and clung to his narrow frame. There were four doors on the third level as well; two on his platform and two more across the chamber, just like above. Along the left-hand wall, a rusted catwalk with no railing joined the two. A large pipe on the top level sent torrents of water crashing down across the catwalk, effectively blocking his path.

Again, al-Seif found both doors on his side locked. He could try descending to the fourth level, but the platforms there were in terrible condition and beneath that was nothing but the pool of dark water. He peered through the mist to the doors on the opposite side of level three. He couldn't be certain, but he thought one of them looked slightly ajar.

The mouflon examined the water pouring out from the pipe above him. It wasn't getting wet that made al-Seif pause, he was already soaked through. What troubled him was that he couldn't be certain of the strength of the catwalk or the water pressure. It wouldn't take much to push him off and send him hurtling into the water below, most likely to his doom.

But one thing was sure, the longer al-Seif waited, the less chance he would find a way out of the chamber, and his diversion would be for nothing.

The mouflon took one tentative step and heard the metal groan beneath his foot. Slowly shifting his weight forward brought more groans of protest, but the platform seemed to hold. In this manner al-Seif carefully made his way forward, keeping one hand on the slick wall for support.

He reached the torrent of water in the middle and crouched low in preparation to dash through it.

"Al-Seif!" a voice roared above him.

And roar was precisely the right word. It rang off the sides of the chamber, rising even above the thunder of the splashing water. There was a lot of repressed anger in that shout.

The mouflon looked up, and his eyes widened. There was the tigress on the top platform glaring down at him, a large white-gold pistol in her left hand.

Al-Seif ran forward as the thunder of the pistol added to the clash of noise in the chamber. The bullet was aimed at his temple, but the mouflon's hoof slipped on the metal grating, and the slug whizzed passed the bridge of his snout. He slid into the torrent of water, and the sudden force slammed him down on his back. The catwalk creaked in protest, and al-Seif heard a sickening *pop* as the supports gave way.

The ramp tilted down, and the mouflon found himself sliding with it. As he slipped off the end, al-Seif felt the jagged rusting edges tear through his clothes and into his back. He flailed desperately and caught the end of the catwalk on the fourth level below him.

The tigress' pistol thundered again, and the round ricocheted off the wall to his left. Al-Seif tried to lift himself onto the catwalk, but as he moved, his extra weight began to pull the platform down off its mountings. He made a final desperate reach and cried out in pain as a bullet took off the last two fingers of his left hand.

Fumbling through the pain and blood, Jirair al-Seif lost his grip and fell into the churning water below.

37 – Pursuit

Mohan found the blue and white police cruiser to be surprisingly spacious. Then again it was primarily used by a hippopotamus. The huge tiger had plenty of leg room in the passenger's seat, and his ears barely brushed the interior roof. However, the vehicle was not particularly wide, and both tiger and hippo struggled not to constantly bump elbows whenever they shifted.

Sergeant Delano leaned against the window of the driver's seat, drumming her chubby fingers on the steering wheel with obvious agitation.

The hippo was in uniform, and technically, so was Mohan. The tiger's hunting outfit consisted of dark denim pants and a woven shirt with leather patches over the chest and arms. The flimsy material might look like cotton, but a microscope would reveal a hybrid mesh developed by Tiger's Stripe; it was as strong as chain-linked steel and served much the same purpose against claws and blades. Had Jirair al-Seif followed up immediately on the case of Kevlar he stole so many years ago, he would have tracked it right to the scientists who pulled the ballistic weave apart to run their own experiments.

Mohan moved a hand towards the radio.

"Don't!" Delano said sternly.

The tiger dropped his hand and grinned sheepishly. "Sorry."

"You might outrank me, general," the hippo said, "But the radio is fine as it is. If we hear something, we'll hear something."

Mohan nodded. As a major general the tiger could have pulled rank on Delano, ranks were enforced in crisis situations, and Mohan couldn't think of a truer crisis than trying to stop his bloodthirsty daughter from making a huge mistake. But this was Delano's cruiser, and for the moment Mohan forced himself to exercise some patience.

"You realise that even if we hear something, I can't assist you in an official capacity?" the hippo said, "Pacé Acqua is out of my jurisdiction."

Mohan stretched his arms forward to work the kinks out of sore muscles. "Yeah, I know. But you can run interference while I nab Kitty. Most pedestrians are only going to see a uniform."

"And once the local police focus on me I'm going to have a lot of red tape to deal with," Delano said.

"You'll make do." Mohan grinned. "You're the PR department."

Delano smacked his arm with the back of her thick hand. "Oh, that makes me feel so much better," she said but smiled good-naturedly.

"I'll make sure Elder Tyrsus protects your career. We need you, Roberta."

The hippo's smile widened. "And don't you forget it. But what makes you think Lieutenant Katral will be here? Couldn't al-Seif drive out to Scogliera Piatta or Illia?"

"I admit, that's a risk," Mohan answered. "But I have a hunch. Al-Seif knows his car is easily identifiable. He'll try to find a less conspicuous route out of town. And I know Kitty's here because she'll stick to al-Seif like glue. Plus, I found the sidecar sans motorcycle when I got back to the airport in Scogliera Piatta."

The tiger leaned forward to check the position of the sun against his watch. "I think she's been watching al-Seif's villa like the proverbial hawk ever since she drove up here," Mohan said, "And remember that dispatch a half hour ago about an explosion in the bay? I think it's safe to assume we know what happened to al-Seif's yacht."

"Was that her doing?" Delano asked.

Mohan shook his head. "Not her style, or ours. Kitty lets Rizzo handle the explosives work, and she's..." The tiger paused and grimaced. "She's laid up at the rendezvous in Kirque with everyone else. Assuming al-Seif wasn't onboard when his boat went up, he'll make for the next closest escape route, and won't trust the open road. That means either the train or the airport."

"If someone bombed his yacht, they'd likely have the plane rigged as well," Delano said.

Mohan nodded. "That's fair dinkum, his options are very few now."

They sat in silence again for a few minutes.

"General Katral?" Delano began, tilting her large head towards the tiger. "Why is she doing this?"

Mohan stared out the window at the creeping traffic. He chuffed and fiddled with his ear as if debating how to answer.

"I should really bring my wife here on vacation," he said, "She teaches music, you know. And is something of a prodigy herself. There's a lot of classical music history in Medocci."

Delano opened her mouth to say something, but the tiger went on, "Her family stretches back a long way. Did you know the Ruo-Shang are the blood descendants of Singh Fang-Ruo?"

"*Dai!*" the hippo gasped in Mecci.

Mohan nodded. "Swear to Aaba. I learned that through Singh's brother, my first partner. It's funny, but it was his death that brought us together."

The tiger fell silent again, but Delano waited patiently, aware that he was probably going to connect the dots eventually.

"Singh's mother and father are very modern people," the tiger said at last, "but they respect their heritage. Their family has a lot of old legends. Doing this job, you come to learn which legends might be true and which ones are rubbish. In the Ruo-Shang family, white tigers are viewed as omens."

Mohan trailed off, looking at the city beyond the cruiser's windows without really seeing it. "In the Ruo-Shang legends, they believed that once every several generations a white tiger is...reborn in a way." He turned to Delano. "Do you know what an Onryō is?"

The hippo shook her head negatively.

"Literally translated it means 'vengeful spirit'," Mohan said, "A kind of avenging angel sent to deal out justice on the wicked. And they're killers."

Delano cocked her head to the side. "And you think?" she left the question hang.

Mohan was about to answer when the radio crackled to life. "We have a vehicle collision outside the train station on Via Santino and Via Gabrielle," the dispatcher intoned, "Someone drove a garbage truck into a white and burgundy nineteen fifty-four Baronville Regalia. There are believed to be casualties on the scene."

The agents looked at each other.

"That's Jirair al-Seif's car!" Delano said.

"Bloody right, it is!" Mohan said. "How close are we?"

"I'll get you there in five," the hippo answered, and the cruiser's engine roared to life.

Unfortunately, Delano must have meant five hours because even with lights and siren going the traffic was horrendous. If ever there was a time to lament the rising popularity of the automobile, it was now. After five minutes they had barely travelled three blocks.

"*Madre Dio*," the hippo cursed, pounding her beefy hands on the steering wheel. "I'm sorry, General. It must have been a very bad accident."

"We both know it was no accident," the tiger said with a growl. "And it wasn't Kitty either, but she'll be there if she's listening. How far to the station?"

"Another five blocks straight ahead then left onto Via Gabrielle."

Mohan opened the door and climbed out. "Keep going, meet us there. I can move faster on foot."

Delano nodded and continued inching her way through the traffic, leaning on the horn and cursing all the while.

The five blocks Mohan traversed were mostly every-day pedestrian traffic, but the mass of bodies thickened almost as soon as he turned onto Via Gabrielle. Whatever was happening was definitely drawing a crowd.

The huge tiger rose head and shoulders above most of the pedestrians, but all he could see was a column of black oily smoke rising from the end of the street. As Mohan pushed his way through the crowd, he eventually reached a point where he was the only one trying to get *to* the wreckage instead of away from it.

Mohan paused when he reached the Regalia. The garbage truck had not been able to flip the heavy luxury car, but it had made a massive dent in the right side. From the shards of green glass lying on the fender boards, the tiger deduced that a firebomb, probably what they called a Molotov cocktail, was what set the engine afire. More firebombs had been set off around the perimeter to clear the area, but the job was sloppy, leaving a considerable gap in the direction of the train station.

Sloppy, or intentional? Mohan wondered.

The tiger leaned down and glanced in the open rear door on the left side. Carmen Abbatelli hung propped up in the back seat, her eyes closed and a spatter of blood painting the shattered window behind her in a crimson halo.

Mohan chuffed once. Abbatelli had been no angel, but she didn't deserve what had happened to her. Not like the mouflon she had inexplicably fallen in love with.

Mohan turned from the grisly scene and studied the two bodies lying in the intersection—a badger with spotted markings and a racoon. Both wore green coveralls like garbage collectors. The racoon's wrist—now bent backwards at an ugly angle— had a tattoo of a banana piercing the skin and dripping blood, like someone had used the fruit as a knife.

Mohan chuffed again. It was a sick joke, but he recognised the emblem of Mody Nahas. Unzipping their coveralls, the tiger found more proof: two-toned blue and red sashes tied around their waists.

Mohan moved towards the station. Along the way, he passed six more bodies, each as mangled as the two in the intersection; only two would survive their injuries.

Two of the thugs had born the marks of Mody Nahas, but the other four bore tattoos Mohan was only vaguely familiar with. It was the stylized green and silver image of a griffon; a beast composed of a lion-like bahnger with the head and shoulders of a sevviks—a predatory avian not too dissimilar from an eagle except for the serpent eyes and tongue. Ironically, this was one mythical creature that actually didn't have a connection to the fiends that Tiger's Stripe hunted.

It took Mohan a moment to recognise the griffon as the mark of Kristoph Weis.

Outside the station entrance, the tiger found four more henchmen, all dead. He didn't take the time to identify them; instead, he turned to the mass of people giving a wide berth to the entryway. Their faces all bore looks of stunned terror.

"What happened?" Mohan snapped, "*Quello che successo?*" His Mecci was terrible, but the crowd seemed to understand.

"*P-pazzo pantera!*" a wide-eyed tamarind muttered, pointing a shaky finger toward the door.

Crazy panther.

Mohan nodded. Abar Kami had laid waste to the goons and gone inside the station.

"The police will be here soon. Stay back," Mohan told the crowd. He vanished through the doors.

The tiger's warning was unnecessary, the frightened masses huddled on the street had no interest in going anywhere near the station.

Mohan passed into the main entrance hall just in time to see the panther use a stanchion chain to choke the life from a ferret. The mustelid crumpled to the floor to join the small collection of other green-coveralled bodies surrounding Abar Kami. Bloody bananas and green griffons adorned their shattered wrists.

The panther turned to face him.

"Come," Abar Kami said in his deceptively soft voice, "Come meet your death!"

"Kami, I'm not here to fight you," Mohan said, but he raised his fist protectively in front of him.

The tiger could tell that the panther was on the threshold of feral bloodlust. If Kami was pushed any furth into that abyss, he could hurt a lot more people than just a few hired goons.

Mohan had neither the time nor the desire to test his own skills against Abar Kami. Thanks to the tiger's size and strength, Mohan had always preferred wrestling, but he had studied several forms of martial arts and was reasonably confident he could defend himself against a chut-ri master.

Kami lashed out with one of the chains. Mohan caught it and pulled. He knew the panther was expecting this, especially when Kami leapt forward and brought his legs up, trying to use the momentum of the pull to drive both knees into the tiger's chest. Mohan dropped the chain and spun to his right, swinging his leg out and catching Kami across the back as he flew past.

The panther tumbled and rolled back to his feet, leaping in for a slash at Mohan's arm. Had the tiger not been wearing his armoured shirt, Kami would no doubt have torn a good-sized chuck out of him. Mohan still grunted and turned with the ferocious impact, and Kami kicked him square in the chest. Again, the armour helped, but the tiger felt at least one of his ribs snap.

"Kami," Mohan roared, leaping back out of the range of another kick, "dammit, man, I'm trying to help!"

"Do not waste your breath!" Kami said.

The panther was actually panting now, and he contemplated that this massive tiger had been the first in many years to make him put up this much effort.

"You are not one of the mafia," Kami said, "But my master has many enemies."

The panther feinted with a kick, then jabbed out with a fist. Not only did the tiger block the blow, but he also used his blocking arm to deliver a quick and equally vicious backhand across the panther's snout, then lept back out of range again.

Kami spit out a gob of blood and grinned. "You are good."

"I'm just staying alive," Mohan said, wincing slightly at the pain in his ribs, "Yes, I'd love to see your boss locked in a cell for the rest of his life, but right now I'm trying to stop one of my agents from blowing his brains out."

Kami paused, suddenly remembering the white tigress that had tailed them from the city gate.

"She doesn't know what she's doing," the tiger went on, taking advantage of the panther's hesitation. "She's not a cold-blooded murderer, but if I don't stop her..."

Mohan dropped his arms and gave Kami a pleading look. "If I don't stop her she's going to head down a path she may never return from."

Abar Kami glared at the tiger, then past his shoulder into the station beyond. A strange feeling began to creep over him. He had nearly let the bloodlust consume him, and in the process had forgotten his obligation. Now his master, his friend, was in danger.

For the first time in his life, Abar Kami was afraid.

38 – Angel of Death

Kitty knelt on the wet rusting catwalk. She had seen Jirair al-Seif fall, saw the spurt of blood just before, but she wasn't stupid enough to believe that was his end. The tigress had to be sure, she couldn't leave things like some cut-rate action film, she needed to see the body.

Climbing down to the lowest level, Kitty examined the outflow pipe where the water drained from the hub chamber. It was nearly ten metres in diameter, and the water flowed out swiftly, suggesting a steady downward grade into the blackness beyond. The water didn't appear as deep as she first assumed. But it was deep enough.

The tigress stripped down to just her underwear and her holster, scratching absently at the burning sensation coming from the birthmark stretched between her left breast and arm. The irritating itch had started as soon as she saw the mouflon's Regalia leave the villa, and the closer she got to her target the more intense the sensation became.

Kitty threw the rest of her clothes in a pile at the foot of the ladder; though she hadn't seen him since leaping from the plane, some hidden instinct told the tigress that her father would be along shortly to collect them.

Kitty knew it would be Mohan that came after her, trying to capture his wayward daughter and prevent what he perceived as a heinous crime. But hadn't Assad Alabwaq committed worse atrocities than murder a hundred times over? The mouflon deserved the bullet Kitty was intent on putting through his head.

The tigress shook her head to clear it, focusing on the pain in her birthmark. While tracking al-Seif, Kitty had managed to stay one step ahead of her father, but now that the mouflon was out in the open, Mohan would close in swiftly. But would he do what she was about to?

Kitty didn't think so.

Securing her pistol in its holster, the tigress bent and dove into the churning water below.

It was dangerous, the pipe might narrow suddenly somewhere in the dark, and she would become stuck and drown alongside al-Seif. Again, some unknown instinct told her that wouldn't be the case.

This was one of the old drainage tunnels, an engineering monster designed to dump excess water into the sea during the spring melt and the rainy season. It would stay wide and true all the way to the coast, but Kitty would need one hell of a bath afterwards.

The tigress surfaced and tread water, allowing the swift current to carry her along the pipe. When she had drifted roughly thirty metres from the chamber, the current slowed noticeably, its rapid pace broken by the intersection of another tube half the size of the main channel.

Kitty was going to let herself drift past it when she felt a sudden pull. It wasn't physical, but the tigress was hesitant to call it anything else. None the less, there was something here, something calling her to swim into this new section.

Not far beyond the mouth of the connecting tube, Kitty discovered that her feline eyes could pick up a faint light. It came from a single grimy bulb set above a metal door barred with chains. At first, the door seemed to float roughly a metre above the water, but as her eyes adjusted, Kitty could see a short flight of cement stairs. The stairs ended at a platform that converted the tube into a semi-circular shape, with a narrow channel running down the centre.

The dirt and grime along the wall had been disturbed recently, most likely by someone trying to climb out of the water. As Kitty swam closer, the scent of blood mingled with the musty stink of the drainage water. The streaks continued along the wall until the tigress came to the platform at the foot of the stairs, where it was apparent that someone had climbed out. Someone who was bleeding from the left hand.

Kitty exited the water as silently as a ghost, which wasn't really necessary because the rushing water still echoed through the tunnels. A pistol lay on the ground not far from her landing point; it was a 9mm Bartelli, the same type of Medocci-made firearm al-Seif carried.

Kitty picked it up and ejected the magazine; fully loaded. She proceeded to clear the round in the chamber and pop out each of the magazine rounds with her thumb claw, letting them plop into the water. Her task completed, the tigress tossed the empty weapon back on the ground.

There was blood spattered along the platform, and Kitty felt the pull calling her down the tunnel. She resisted it long enough to inspect the chained door, and reassure herself that no one had come through it in a very long time; the tigress was surprised the light above it was even still working.

Her curiosity satisfied, Kitty turned and followed the trail of blood left by al-Seif's mangled hand.

The passage began to slope upwards and widened until it was at least eight meters in diameter. It retained the old cobblestone construction, meaning it was still most likely one of the older pipes in the system. Kitty's light was gone now, and she proceeded cautiously in total blackness, using the centre channel as a guide by brushing the bare pads of her feet against it. Al-Seif had used the wall to guide him, but Kitty could tell there were no breaks in the tunnel by the flow of the foul air against her damp fur.

Eventually, the light began to return and the tunnel levelled off. Grates appeared in the ceiling, spaced roughly ten metres apart. Soft afternoon sunlight filtered in from the world above along with the distant sound of traffic. Thin alcoves began to appear in the walls of the tube, ingress for smaller pipes that fed the main channel; but too small for someone al-Seif's size to crawl through. The rumble of a subway train passed close by.

He must think he can escape by looping back to the station, Kitty thought, the very idea of al-Seif eluding her caused her anger to flare up, and as it did, so did the fire in her birthmark.

The tigress moved to the wall on her left and examined the ground, noting that the droplets of blood had thinned out. The mouflon must have bandaged his hand.

Blood on your nice linen suit, you bastard? A wicked grin spread across the tigress' face.

A wider alcove with a door appeared on her left, and Kitty could see cloven hoof prints in the grime heading towards it. They didn't lead away.

It's unlocked, Kitty thought even before she began reaching for the knob, *It's supposed to be unlocked. He's supposed to go this way. How do I know that?*

Once again, the tigress felt that strange pull drawing her through the door, calling to her, nudging her in the direction she was supposed to go.

Kitty paused, struggling against the burning sensation creeping through her chest and arm.

What if it was leading her the way *it* wanted her to go? Had al-Seif felt the same pull, and without even realising it chosen this tunnel instead of trying the next?

Kitty reached for the knob again and found it unlocked just as she had thought. Carefully, she opened the door and peered beyond. A narrow utility tunnel stretched out roughly ten metres before ending in another door. This one was open.

The tigress approached, checked her corners, and stepped out into a second tunnel mirroring the first. This tube was the same size, but drier and made of concrete; Kitty guessed it was a new overflow pipe built to ease pressure on the original pipe.

The alcoves were broader and deeper in this tunnel, and the dim light from the surface world didn't reach into them.

The sound of running hooves echoed towards her from the right. Kitty swung her gun around but didn't have a target.

The tigress broke into a run, her anger rekindled. The tunnel flowed straight and true, but still, she couldn't see the mouflon ahead of her.

The tunnel came to a four-way split, and Kitty skidded to a halt. Her mind raced as she looked into each new tunnel.

He can't be allowed to escape! Not now, not when I'm so close!

As she paused in the intersection, flashes of pain crossed her arm and chest, her birthmark flaring with such intensity it made her wince. Only one thing would soothe the burn, seeing al-Seif's brains spattered across the floor. Deep inside, Kitty felt the rising bloodlust that had consumed her in Jar-Geshim.

A scrape to her left brought the tigress' gun up. There was a flash of movement, and she fired. A high-pitched squeak echoed briefly through the tunnel and was silent.

Dammit! Only a munski.

Kitty crept forward, gun at the ready, her right hand locked under and around her left. Bits of random detritus, food wrappers, broken bottles, and pieces of splintered wood clogged the floor of the tunnel. Every few steps, she had to manoeuvre around a wooden pallet that had somehow been swept down from the world above. The tigress began to wish she still had the hard rubber sandals that would protect her soft padded feet.

Kitty followed the munski's branch of the tunnel for another thirty metres, not even bothering to avoid the shafts of afternoon sunlight that shot through grates in the curved ceiling. Let the mouflon see his doom approaching.

Soft silt coated the floor, but much of it gathered at the centre of the tube. Kitty didn't possess her father's tracking skill, and al-Seif had wisely stuck to the hard cement along the sides, but the tigress was able to spy a few broken tracks left by the mouflon's passage.

There was a large pool of black in the distance signalling another break in the tunnel. Somehow, Kitty didn't think al-Seif had reached it yet. He was hiding in one of the alcoves, waiting for—

The scrape of metal on metal echoed behind her, and she turned sharply. A new shaft of sunlight appeared as someone in the world above opened a manhole cover roughly ten metres behind her. A large orange foot striped with black came down on the top rung, a foot Kitty recognised.

Shit! He finally tracked me down. It can't end like this. Not when I'm so close!

Heedless of the clutter on the floor, Kitty turned and began to run away from the manhole, following al-Seif's broken tracks. She heard a muffled voice behind her but ignored it.

Kitty hadn't gone more than ten metres when she entered the next junction. She skidded to a stop and felt a brief stab of panic; this junction had *five* tunnels branching off of hers. She searched the ground frantically, but couldn't find any hoofprints.

No, this couldn't be the end, she couldn't have lost the mouflon's trail!

A rustle of movement caught Kitty's attention, and she snapped her aim to her left, then straight ahead again as a flash of white linen fluttered through a shaft of sunlight.

Kitty's finger tightened on the trigger.

But she didn't fire. There was something wrong here, the coat was too high up and too billowy.

A distraction!

The tigress spun back to her left just in time to see a slender object come darting out of a dark alcove. The makeshift spear was a piece of broken PVC piping, the jagged end serving as well as a sharpened stake. Kitty was barely able to dodge the projectile and it glanced off her left shoulder, cutting a shallow gash in her arm.

The tigress gasped at the sudden pain. *That bastard actually managed to wing me!*

The dark form of al-Seif dashed towards the intersection and hopeful escape. Kitty raised her arm, fire lancing through her injured shoulder, and pulled the trigger. The tunnels filled briefly with the thunder of the Desert Hawk, and the figure gave a strangled yelp of pain as he fell.

Kitty moved forward, heedless of the blood that now streamed down her shoulder and matted her fur. She had him now, soon Jirair al-Seif and his criminal alter ego Assad Alabwaq would receive the justice they truly deserved. The tigress winced slightly, and not all the pain came from her injured shoulder, the heat of her birthmark was intensifying as her feral bloodlust continued to rise.

Jirair al-Seif continued to crawl feebly towards the centre of the intersection of tunnels. It wasn't until Kitty was standing over him that the mouflon finally gave up and lay crumpled in the filth of the tunnel floor. Blood streamed from his right leg; her bullet had shattered the bone just beneath the kneecap. Against his chest, al-Seif cradled the bloody stump of his left hand, now wrapped in a piece of his expensive linen coat.

The dreaded Assad Alabwaq's breath came in ragged pants as he slowly pushed himself to a sitting position with his good hand. His vest and shirt were little more than filthy tatters now, and his woolly body-fur was matted with dirt and blood. Dark-grey long-fur hung in damp strands across his brow.

Still, Al-Seif's eyes seemed to glitter in the twilight of the tunnel, but their gleam was no longer defiant, or even fearful. Instead, the mouflon looked tired, worn thin by the life he had chosen to live. The life that had finally taken everything from him.

Al-Seif spread his arms out to his sides, the first genuinely submissive gesture he had ever made in his life.

"If you're going to kill me, then do it!" he said in a harsh croak, "I make only one request: that you do the same to that bitch Yursa for what she did to my Carmen."

Kitty levelled her pistol between al-Seif's eyes; the white gold plating on the barrel was almost a perfect match to those pale-yellow orbs.

"A request?" the tigress hissed, "You dare ask for vengeance after everything you've done? After all the lives you've destroyed?"

Kitty's Mark was on fire now, burning with what she told herself was the righteous fury of everyone the mouflon had wronged. In her mind's eye, the tigress saw the faces of the slaves Assad Alabwaq had sold at auction, their eyes dull from forced heroin injections. She saw the greedy faces of the wealthy patrons, who used the slaves up like any other disposable commodity, then threw them into the arena to be fodder for the beasts and gladiators. She saw the dead eyes of the gazelle, Rijay din-Aden, sacrificed to bring war between the nations of Pytan and Barju.

A red fire began to creep into the edges of Kitty's vision, and her finger tightened on the trigger.

"Kitty!" a voice roared behind her.

Consumed by her hatred, the tigress had forgotten all about the opened manhole cover. But she recognised that voice and knew exactly who stood behind her now.

"We need him alive," Mohan said sternly, "He's a pawn, and you know it. Without him, we lose whatever he may know."

The gun stayed level, the righteous fire in Kitty's arm and chest now become an inferno.

Mohan remained where he was, barely three metres from his daughter, and arms at his side. "This isn't you, Kitty," he said calmly, "If you murder him like this, you'll be no better than him."

Kitty chuffed angrily at this. "That cliché is bolvinshit, and you know it. Some people need. To. Die!" The last three words were emphasised through clenched teeth.

But the gun began to waver. The pain from her birthmark was excruciating, and Kitty grit her teeth against it.

 This was right.

Wasn't it?

Kitty could hear the feral bloodlust in her own voice now, and could almost taste the merciless power it would give her. New faces began to flash across her vision, every bandit she had slaughtered in her bloody rampage through the streets of Jar-Geshim.

Their vengeance has been paid, a voice said.

Kitty thought it was her own, but there was something different about it. The voice was cold and cruel, filled with the fury of a thousand grieving souls.

The tigress shook her head to clear it. They were bandits, scum, they would have done worse to her and her fellow agents had she let them live.

Al-Seif mumbled under his breath.

"What was that?" Kitty roared.

"There are no angels in this world," al-Seif said looking up at her, "Only the demons we make for ourselves. But you are the angel of death, come to claim me."

Kitty's grip tightened around the pistol.

And then another face appeared before her, her own personal demon.

It was not the green-eyed lynx journalist, who even now waited anxiously to hear what had become of the tigress and her father. This was a face from Kitty's past, one that haunted her every time she looked into the face of a daisy blossom or smelt their sweet fragrance on the air.

It was the face of a cougar. A mop of shaggy brown long-fur framed his broad head. His jaw was strong, and his deep, golden-brown eyes had a slight dip on the outer corners that gave him a perpetually melancholy expression. But Kitty remembered his personality. She remembered his constant smile and deep-throated laughter.

"Tony?" the tigress whispered, her voice barely audible.

The mouth moved, but Kitty couldn't hear anything at first. Then a single word echoed through her head in a voice that she had almost forgotten.

"No."

A choked sob escaped the tigress' lips, and slowly the gun came down.

No, Kitty thought, *this wasn't right. As much as this piece of shit mouflon deserves to die, it cannot be me that pulls the trigger.*

The maleficent voice of her bloodlust cried out in defeat, but the fire in her arm and chest was already fading. Along with it went the face of the cougar.

"Don't go," Kitty whispered desperately, "Don't leave me again."

Mohan moved forward slowly until he was at his daughter's shoulder, but he made no move to take the gun from her hand.

"Are you OK?" the big tiger asked gently.

Kitty turned to Moahn. But as she started to answer, the deafening *CRACKOW* of a rifle shot filled the drainage tunnel.

39 – End of the Line

Jirair al-Seif stared dumbly as a dark stain spread across his chest. The mouflon slumped forward as if in acceptance that his quest for power had finally come to its end, then he toppled sideways to the floor of the tunnel, pale-yellow eyes now wide and blank, and his tongue hanging slack from a partially open mouth. Blood oozed from the chest wound to mingle with the rivulets of water snaking down the drainage channel.

Kitty and Mohan staggered briefly in the wake of the blast, ears ringing wildly. From out of the darkness they heard a distorted voice.

"Ah, how disappointing," it said, "For a moment I thought you might actually have the strength to follow through. But alas, I must do the dirty work. *C'est la vie.*"

Kitty recognised the voice instantly. Gregory Delany.

The tigress turned a slow circle, trying to identify which tunnel the voice came from; any one of them could have hidden the sniper. She wasn't worried about a second shot, if Delany wanted them dead, he wouldn't hesitate.

Al-Seif's body lay at the centre of the junction, and based on how the mouflon fell, Kitty narrowed the angle of the shot down to two of the five tunnels; both opposite the one she and Mohan approached from.

"I wish I could stay and play, *mon chéri*," Delany's voice echoed, "but I have more important matters to attend to."

Kitty heard a splash and the echo of footsteps. She turned to her father hesitantly.

"Well?" Mohan said, "Let's get after the bastard!"

Kitty nodded briefly and led the way down the leftmost passage, the one she judged most likely to have hidden the sniper. The tigress didn't know what kind of supernatural ability allowed Delany to camp out at just the right spot, but Kitty no longer believed al-Seif had come to this drainage intersection entirely at random.

Maybe it was the same mysterious force that had pulled the tigress through the tunnels. Perhaps it had even guided Mohan to the correct surface access so he could stop her from...

Kitty shook her head to clear it. No time to think about that now.

Somewhere ahead of them, the white tigress heard the squeak of a metal door opening, her father heard it as well. It was lost in the approaching rumble of a subway train.

Rounding a bend in the drainage tunnel, Kitty spotted flickering lights through a partially open door set in an alcove. Once the train had passed, the flickering was replaced by a steady red glow.

Kitty levelled her pistol at the opening. Her shoulder ached from the wound caused by al-Seif's makeshift spear, but at least the fire of her birthmark had subsided to a dull throb. The tigress didn't know it, but after hearing Delany's taunts, the mark on her father's back had also begun to tingle.

Despite the urgency she felt, Kitty waited patiently for Mohan to take up a position on the opposite side of the door, his massive Babylon revolver drawn and at the ready.

"Will another train come along?" the tigress asked.

Mohan shook his head negatively. "It shouldn't. After what happened at the station, Delano and the local police had all departures delayed. I'd imagine the subway would be included. That was probably the last one we'll see for a while."

Kitty nodded. The door was designed to open towards them, and she slowly nudged it wider with her foot.

The red glow grew brighter. It came from a signal lamp mounted high on the wall of a narrow subway tunnel. Long years of greasy dirt coated the stonework walls, but the steel rails gleamed with the shine of constant use. A narrow curb lined a metre-deep trough through the centre of the tube. Kitty hoped Mohan was right about the train, there would be very little if any room for them to get out of the way.

Kitty waved her father forward. "You're the tracker," she said, "Which way did he go?"

Mohan took a small electric torch out of a vest pocket and studied the ground. Medoccian subways ran the electricity along the ceiling, so there wasn't any danger of stepping on electrified rails. There were a surprising number of prints in the dirt, both animal and sentient; apparently, subway trains weren't the only thing that travelled this line.

But that in itself was a hopeful sign. If the vagrants who lived in the underground of Pacé Acqua frequented this tunnel, it meant it probably wasn't a long trek either to the next door or the nearest platform.

Mohan couldn't be sure of the species, but the most recent sentient prints led off to the right. The tiger rose and pointed, then gave a sudden wince of pain and put a hand to his side.

"Are you ok?" Kitty asked.

Mohan nodded. "Just a dust-up with Abar Kami. Which I hope not to repeat any time soon."

Kitty nodded and positioned herself next to the door. "If we're doing this, let's go, before Delany gets away."

The tiger nodded and adjusted the satchel over slung his shoulder; it was the first time Kitty had noticed it.

Mohan eased his way down into the trough, his huge frame blotting out the light of the signal lamp as he squeezed through the door. Kitty followed a moment later.

The big tiger set the pace, he couldn't run with his ribs injured, but Mohan didn't want to spend any more time than was necessary on the tracks, regardless of the police having halted the trains.

Ten metres into the tunnel they passed another red signal light, but there was still no hint of any approaching trains. The darkness ahead of them began to brighten as the path curved, but it was a white light this time. Brightly coloured squiggles of graffiti appeared on the walls, signs that subway cars definitely weren't the only travellers along the rail.

The light wasn't enough to illuminate the dark void that open ahead of them as the subway walls gave way on either side. It appeared they had reached the next platform.

Kitty threw her hand up over her eyes as a sudden blinding light appeared in front of them. There was a crackle of electricity and the screech of steel on steel as a sleeping subway car came to life at the far end of the platform. It began to pick up speed quickly.

The marks on both tigers flared to life, signalling them of approaching danger. Kitty instinctively raised her pistol, but she couldn't find a target beyond the light.

"Up!" Mohan roared, "Get out of the way!"

They leapt onto the darkened platform just as the train went speeding past. The interior lights of the railcars were brilliant against the darkness and cast dancing shadows that blinked across their vision like strobe lights. Kitty watched the windows, but as near as she could tell, the car was empty.

Then, just before the train vanished around the bend, Gregory Delany rose up into view. Just as he had from the back of a retreating speedboat, and again from the seat of a dirtbike, the greyhound placed a hand to his chest and gave the tigress a pretentious bow.

Kitty roared in fury and fired three futile shots into the now dark tunnel. She sank to her knees on the dirty cement, ignoring the fact that she was still in her underwear, and pounded her frustration out on the platform.

"The bloody bastard did it again!" the tigress shouted.

Mohan stood somewhere nearby, leaning on a pillar and shaking off the adrenaline rush. His broken rib screamed in protest, and his breath came in shallow gasps. The tiger was finding it increasingly difficult to shrug off the pain. Bloody hell, he hated getting old. Turning his back to the pillar, he slowly sank to the floor.

Mohan let his eyes adjust to the light. There was barely any illumination, and he soon discovered why. The platform on both sides of the rail was littered with plastic sheeting, scaffolding, scattered tools, and a myriad of other loose construction equipment. Apparently, the platform was under renovation.

The light came from two industrial lamps on the opposite platform, which had been left on.

"Think they're out to lunch?" Mohan said.

Kitty rose lept her feet. "Come on!" she said, "I'll bet Delany only took that car the to next station. We can't let him get away again!"

"Kitty," Mohan wheezed.

The tigress paused mid-stride. She looked towards her father and immediately knew their chase was done.

"I'm a bloody fool," Mohand said, "Delany wanted us down here, wanted us cut-off from the scene of the crime." The tiger drew in a ragged breath and winced at the pain. "We never had a chance at catching him."

Slowly, Mohan removed the satchel from around his neck and tossed it towards Kitty. "Your clothes. I managed to track you down to the drainage hub. That was a bloody fool thing you did, jumping in."

The tigress hesitated. The fire she had felt while hunting al-Seif was flaring again, but she knew her father was right. With an angry chuff, Kitty turned away from the tunnel and retrieved the bag.

"Thanks," Kitty said pulling the damp clothes from the satchel.

Mohan eyed the tigress cautiously as she wrung as much water as she could from the garments. He heard the manic strains of bloodlust in her voice; it was fading, but Mohan was concerned about how close she had come to losing control. Mohan hadn't wanted to believe his wife's family legends about the Onryō, but he couldn't deny the evidence before him.

"How did you find me anyway?" Kitty asked as she pulled on her jeans.

Mohan gave her a reproachful glance. "That platypus maintenance worker you scared half to death," he said, "Delano and I managed to convince him to show us a map of the tunnels leading off the reservoir. Underground, it feels complicated, but above it, you only went over about three blocks from the station." The tiger frowned. "But I'll admit it was sheer dumb luck I dropped down in the same tunnel you were in."

"Maybe it wasn't," Kitty said quietly.

Mohan looked at her sideways but said nothing. He didn't tell her that his birthmark had reacted in a manner he had never experience in all his thirty-plus years as an agent. The closer he got to his daughter, the stronger the fire from the mark became. It was like a beacon, guiding him in the right direction. As soon as Mohan laid eyes on Kitty in the tunnel, the sensation faded away.

"What happened to Abar Kami?" Kitty asked.

Mohan frowned. "I'm not sure. He almost tore my head off at the station entrance; got a broken rib as a souvenir. But I managed to convince him to stand down when I explained I was trying to stop you."

Kitty paused a moment. "I don't think he'll be happy to find al-Seif dead," she said, "Even if we proved we didn't do it."

Mohan nodded. "Too right," he said.

There was an uncomfortable silence as the tigress finished dressing.

Finally, Mohan asked, "What happened, Kitty?"

The tigress looked at the big tiger quizzically.

"Why didn't you pull the trigger on al-Seif?" he elaborated.

Kitty looked away into the darkness of the subway station. "I don't know," she lied.

Mohan said nothing. He had heard his daughter whisper something before lowering her gun, but he hadn't been able to make out what it was. There was no doubt in the tiger's mind that the spirit of the Onryō had very nearly manifested itself in his daughter. And yet something had beaten it back.

There was only one ghost from Kitty's past that Mohan believed strong enough to do that. And what frightened him the most was that he had been directly responsible for creating it.

Kitty got up and walked over to one of the abandoned workbenches, rummaging through its contents.

"Oi," she said holding up a set of blueprints, "I think I found out why this place isn't up and running on a Miriday afternoon. This project is under contract to Tortoise Construction."

"Tortoise?" Mohan said, "That's one of Yursa's companies, inherited through her brother."

Kitty nodded. "She probably gave them the day off, so Delany had a nice quiet getaway route."

The tigress rummaged through more construction equipment. Mohan heard a crash and the clatter of metal pipes, followed by Kitty cursing.

"What happened?" Mohan asked.

"Nothing," came Kitty's reply.

A few moments later, the tigress returned holding a length of lead pipe with one end wrapped in rags.

"Not a proper crutch," Kitty said, "But it'll work for the moment."

Mohan smiled. "Thanks for that, Kitty, but I'm not going anywhere fast. I'm afraid I overdid it on this rib."

Kitty tossed the make-shift crutch aside in exasperation. "Oh, bloody hell, Mohan. What? I'm just supposed to leave you here while I get help?"

Mohand frowned and nodded. "Exactly. I'll be fine. This station is probably closer than you think to the main terminal."

"And if Delany comes back to finish you off?" the tigress argued.

The tiger shook his big head. "He won't. They're done with us for now. Chalk another one up for the bad guys."

Kitty crossed her arms and glanced angrily at the tunnel that had facilitated Greg Delany's escapes. Then, without another word, she made her way for the platform exit and the streets above.

40 – The Road Ahead

Ric Barnes lay on a cot staring at the canvas ceiling of the tent. The lynx had woken sometime in the middle of the night and was hoping exhaustion would eventually knock him out again. It wasn't working.

Rising to one elbow, the journalist glanced at Vince on the other side of the tent. The hare sat between Rizzo and Vicki's beds, his large feet propped on a second chair. The basilisk and the bullfrog were still asleep, but Vince was busy perusing a trashy romance novel.

"The Trials of Rosella?" Ric read the book title aloud and raised an eyebrow.

"It was in Rizzo's bag," Vince replied without setting it down.

"Of course, it was," Ric said sagely.

Vince glanced up at the lynx over the edge of the paperback. "My dear sir," the hare said, "I'll have you know I proudly own three of Julie Moses' fine novels. I just haven't read this one yet."

Ric could only smirk in reply. Vince hadn't been shy about recalling scandalous adventure's that would probably make the likes of Ms Moses blush, but Ric began to see that wasn't all there was to the hare. Vince hadn't left the side of either teammate since the Soketh of the Emerald Dune clan had brought them in and treated their injuries. For all his bawdy stories, the hare proved himself nothing but a gentleman around his female comrades and showed genuine concern for their well being as they healed.

Unfortunately, the companions Ric kept thinking had yet to arrive at the camp.

The lynx checked his watch. "I can't sleep," he said, swinging his paws to the grassy floor, "I'm going to go catch the sunrise."

Vince simply nodded and went back to his book.

No one challenged the journalist as he made his way through the collection of tents arranged in a copse of hazel and cypress trees. Most of the dwellings were large square structures of canvas and ghuska wool stretched over sturdy poles, but the most interesting tents were those that seemed to spring from the bodies of off-road vehicles of varying size. The trucks had no discernable make or model as the Soketh had purpose-built them from the chassis up; Ric had to remind himself that, despite their nomadic existence, the Soketh were quite technologically savvy. They were also efficient and creative with their use of space and camouflage, concealing their dwellings with bits of netting and broken branches from the underbrush. Unless you knew it was there, the entire camp was practically invisible until you literally stumbled into it.

There were at least six separate families that made up the Soketh tribe of the Emerald Dune, and all of them were birds from the raptor families Falconidae and Accipitridae.

For the briefest of moments, Ric wondered if Vince ever felt uncomfortable under their keen gazes. After all, in the non-sentient world, the sevviks was disturbingly eagle-like, and they had a taste for the rabbit-like alhnem'rey.

Ric walked through the long, tree-lined clearing they had used as a runway three days ago; their plane rested nearby, the blue and white fuselage concealed by netting. On reaching the ridge at the far end, the journalist hunkered down and turned his emerald eyes to the shadow that split the horizon from the night sky.

This far from civilisation, the heavens were filled with countless numbers of stars; a cosmic blanket for Midori, the pale-green night moon. Ric had seen such sights before and was always marvelled by them. But not this night.

Several minutes past with only the rustle of leaves to break the silence. Slowly the sun rose, gently illuminating the vibrant green plains that lay south of the city of Beklenme.In Nitrik, the official language of Kirque, the name translated roughly to "the expected". The remaining agents of Mohan's Scrappers couldn't have planned things that way had they tried. For three days they camped in these foothills, guests of the Emerald Dune—a courtesy made possible through Zed's connections.

And there they had waited, expecting the missing members of their party to return soon.

Normally Ric would've used the time to make notes or examine the Soketh camp up close; after all, that was the excuse the journalist had given his editor to cover for his extended absence. In fact, once Elder Tysus had explained the situation, the tribe leaders supplied Ric with numerous war reports from Kirque, Pytan, and Barju.

He had yet to even glance at them.

With Mohan and Kitty gone, the lynx found it difficult to concentrate on anything but the horizon.

And it was a glorious horizon.

Western Kirque was the last piece of green on the contiguous continent of Estan before the arid deserts and rocky hills took over. Here the last gentle hills rolled out of Mata, the eastern province of Medocci before they were suddenly stopped by the northern edge of the Gen-Yeshif Desert.

However, this was also the edge of the "civilised" lands.

In Medocci, and throughout the continent of Aerenia, bandits were little more than small bands of youthful hoodlums, and the wildlife was carefully managed. Beyond these plains, the raiders became large organised tribes, willing to do anything to ensure their survival. And there was no taming the wildlife; the hides of the bahngers and ceravaags grew thick to compensate for the harsh environment, and they showed no fear in the face of firearms.

Ric picked up a stone, bounced it idly in his hand a few times, then dropped it. The Soketh had already chastised Vince for chucking a rock down into the plain below. The last thing they needed right now was unwanted attention, and even a single stone could alert a passing horde that fresh victims lingered outside the walls of Beklenme.

The faintest crunch of the underbrush made the journalist's ear twitch, and he turned to see a large falcon approaching. Ric had learned a lot about minding his surroundings in the past two weeks, but he had learned even more from the Soketh in the past three days. If the falcon hadn't wished the lynx to hear his approach, he wouldn't have.

Imram of the Emerald Dune was the *aloachm arashon*, or 'first warrior' in Netrik, and one of the lesser tribe leaders. He was an imposing figure in the morning shadows, not as tall as Mohan, but still several centimetres above Ric. Imram's feathers were jet black save for a crest of white on his chest and the grey feathers on his head. His clothing consisted of a drab thigh-length cotton thawb over loose cotton trousers and tied around the waist with a striped grey and red sash. Ric recalled that Zed preferred a similar style of dress, but the Soketh of the Emerald Dune wore leather hoods shaded a vibrant green instead of sky blue keffiyehs like Zed's Tribe of the Brown Paw.

Imram was also fully armoured; a reminder to Ric of the territory he now travelled in. Leather pauldrons with brass fittings covered the Soketh's arms, and he wore supple leather gloves with the tips open to accommodate his finger talons. His wings were similarly protected by an ingeniously designed sheath that could stretch out without hampering what limited mobility the appendages offered; even the healthiest sentient birds couldn't fly more than a couple kilometres without rest. Ric guessed this was nature's way of compensating for giving them sentience.

The falcon addressed the lynx in a voice that was surprisingly deep for a bird, "Your comrades have arrived."

Ric practically jumped to his feet. "Are they OK?" he asked, "Did they tell you what happened?"

Imram motioned for him to follow. "Would it not be better to ask them yourself?" he said.

Ric nodded and followed the Soketh warrior back to the camp. In the dawn light, the lynx thought he could pick out the sentries perched high in the branches of the cypress trees; they had been completely invisible in the dark.

The camp itself was waking with the sun. Eagles and falcons went about their morning rituals; but the business of cooking, cleaning, and general preparation for the coming day occurred with a practised air of caution. Those tribe members who were not in their tents remained in the shelter of broad canopies or under the boughs of trees. The children—who were surprisingly numerous—were silent and disciplined as they carried out errands for their parents or gathered for the lessons that comprised their education.

From the day they arrived, Ric was given the impression that these were a people who valued their privacy; and what better way of achieving that than to make sure nobody even knew you were there.

Imram led the way to the largest tent in the camp; three meters at its peak, eight on the long side, and six on the short. A single tall radio antenna mounted on the back of a truck rose behind the tent, but the clever masking on the tower made it almost indistinguishable from the cypress trees in the copse. The falcon pulled a flap aside and ushered the lynx in.

The interior was divided into five sections including the central meeting area, which was occupied by a folding table surrounded by simple folding stools. The attached radio station was set up at the far end of the tent.

A female golden eagle—whom Ric had been introduced to as Rahna, the Emerald Dune's eldest chieftain—sat at one end of the table flanked by Mohan and Kitty; the huge tiger opted to sit cross-leg on a pillow because the stool wouldn't support him. Basira Tyrsus and Zed were also in attendance; Vince remained in the medical tent with Rizzo and Vicki. A large laminated map of the region lay on the table with several coloured push-pins marking key locations.

Mohan was just finishing his report to Elder Tyrsus, "...after that, it was fairly easy for PR to smuggle us on a boat to Mata, and we hitchhiked all the way to the border."

"And you've had no further contacts?" Tyrsus asked.

The huge tiger chuffed and made a sour face. "Not since we left Pianure Rosso," Mohan said, "It seems we were half right, the bastards just wanted us out of the country."

Elder Tyrsus winced slightly as she attempted to shuffle her wings, as was her habit when agitated. Unfortunately, both appendages had been bound to heal.

"Very good, agent Katral," Tyrsus said at last, "We must move carefully from this point forward. Similar reports are beginning to filter in from teams across the globe, but this region seems to be the focal point."

Ric took a seat next to Kitty but the tigress didn't even notice, she just sat there staring at the table as if she might bore a hole in it with her eyes.

Mohan gave the journalist a nod. "How are we looking?" he asked.

"Not good," Ric replied, "Vicki's leg was broken in two places, and she lost a lot of blood. Rizzo suffered the worst of us; it's a miracle she wasn't killed in the crash. She has two broken ribs, a broken arm and an ankle, cuts, contusions, blood loss, and to top it all off a severe concussion. I think we all thanked God when she woke up yesterday."

"How are you holding up?" the tiger asked.

Ric folded his hands together and leaned against the table. "Well as can be expected, I guess. It seems Vince, Zed, and I are the only three to come out of this with barely a few cuts and bruises."

Rahna, the Soketh eagle, spoke up, "Your comrades will need to be moved to a hospital. Our medical facilities can treat many serious wounds, but they are ill prepared for patients who cannot heal on the road, and I'm afraid the tribe must move on shortly."

Elder tyrsus nodded.

"What about you?" Ric asked Mohan, "Al-Seif is he—"

"He's dead," Kitty spoke for the first time since Ric had entered, "Delany was waiting for us in the sewers beneath Pacé Acqua. He shot al-Seif right through the heart."

Ric didn't press the issue, but something in the tigress' voice told him there was much more to the story. He looked toward Mohan. "I take it you had PR cover up the incident?" he asked.

The tiger glanced from his daughter to Elder Tyrsus and back to Ric. "Only what happened at the station. We ran after Delany, but he doubled back on us and collected the corpse. At the moment we suspect he was working with Yursa De Palma and wanted proof the deed was done."

Ric nodded slowly. "What happens now?"

"That is the question," Rahna answered. The golden eagle was much older than Tyrsus, and her feathers had gone grey. It also showed in her wizened voice, which rose and fell like the hills her tribe roamed.

"This enemy has chased you from the deserts and the cities," Rahna continued, "Herding you like ghuskas. Perhaps it is time you slipped your harness."

Kitty gave an annoyed chuff. "Like we bloody know how," she said.

"Kitty," Mohan warned.

Elder Tyrsus raised a hand for silence. "All we know about this enemy is that they know us," she said, "With all our history, that provides a fairly long list of potential threats. We've outlasted most of them, but unfortunately, our advanced age also means we've grown arrogant. We believe we created the rules for this game, but the truth is we have only learned and adapted as the centuries go by."

The younger golden eagle folded her hands together and glanced at them each in turn. "This is a matter for the Elder Council to discuss now," she said quietly, "As far as you're concerned, the mission of Hunter Task Force Three is complete."

Ric glanced at Kitty, but the tigress remained uncharacteristically silent.

"And we failed," Mohan said with a chuff.

Elder Tyrsus' eyes soften, and she put a scaly hand on the huge tiger's arm. "I don't think you should count this against you, General," she said, "This was a test, and we've learned more from it than we initially suspected. The connections to

Jirair al-Seif may have been thin, but through him, we know that someone is using the *roulin yeshou* to create even more deadly creatures. Once you're given time to heal, I fear Mohan's Scrappers will be given another chance to prove that hunter teams with urban experience are necessary."

"If we get time to heal," Kitty said, breaking her silence.

The younger golden eagle nodded soberly. "That is true," she said, "But as I said before, your mission is over for now."

Tyrsus rose, and the other agents followed suit. "Now, you and major general Katral must prepare for your next assignment," she said and turned to Ric, "getting you to the Sanctuary."

The journalist nodded. "I understand, but it feels like there is more to do here."

"There always is, mate," Mohan replied, "Trust me you'll get used to not having all the pieces in place. Even if it never feels comfortable." Ric noticed the sideways glance the tiger shot at Elder Tyrsus as he said this.

The eagle seemed not to hear. "Well, you have your tasks," she said, "The day is young, so I suggest you use the time to prepare. Agents Vega and Littlepond will be moved into Beklenme tonight, and I expect us all to separate then. Dismissed."

Kitty was out of the tent before Ric could even manage a 'hello', but he caught the melancholy look that passed between her and Mohan. Something had happened between the two tigers while they were separated from the group, and every inquisitive nerve in the journalist's brain was screaming to find out what it was. The lynx turned to Mohan.

The huge tiger shook his head firmly in the negative. "For once, mate, you're going to have to let this go. It's between Kitty and me."

Ric scratched at an ear. "Sorry, just instincts, you know?"

Mohan nodded and winced as he stretched.

"Are you all right?" Ric asked.

'I broke a few ribs fighting with al-Seif's bodyguard," the tiger said, "Nothing to worry about. Go pack your bags, mate. We're finally taking you to Sanctuary, but it's a long road between here and the Strait of Adrakar."

Epilogue – Test

The shepherd-dog woke at four-thirty AM on the dot without the aid of an alarm clock. He immediately went into his morning routine: thirty push-ups, as many crunches, and a series of knee-bends. When he had finished, the shepherd made his way to the portable showers, where he cleaned and groomed himself in less than ten minutes. By five AM, with the sun only just beginning to lighten the eastern sky, the large canine was fastening the last button on his grey uniform shirt.

The shepherd ran a finger over the insignia on the collar: four silver diamonds arranged in a diamond. The rank held no meaning since he left the Zeichmacht, but he had his own reasons to continue wearing the studs. His hand moved up to the long scar on his cheek and traced it through the eyepatch over his left eye, then above it until his fingers caressed the remaining half of his left ear.

Donning a long grey trenchcoat and a tall-peaked cap, the shepherd made his way across the mercenary camp to a large tent set up well away from the others. The hum of electricity filled the air, and signs erected before the entrance warned of high voltage. Two guards—a rhinoceros and a giraffe—snapped to attention.

"Major," they greeted in unison, saluting with a hand to their brow, palms facing out.

The shepherd returned the salute and went inside.

Six more guards greeted the Major, each of them heavily armed with machine guns. Their charge was an amorphous bulk lying in a cage at the centre of the tent; the bars were as thick as the shepherd's arms and coursing with several thousand volts. The diamond-shaped scales of the creature's hide rose and fell in rhythmic slumber.

The Major had lost five men in the attempt to move the beast into its new holding cell. It had been conditioned to follow a series of whistles and commands, but clearly, it hadn't been perfected, and the tranquilliser dosage didn't act as swiftly as it should have.

The Major's employer had given him the complex origins of the creature and its official experiment name: Hazard 17. But after witnessing its destructive power, the mercenaries gave it their own name: Nachtpirscher. The Night Stalker.

It was a name out of Ziechlind folklore, but it was disturbingly appropriate. Even in broad daylight, the creature seemed to shroud itself in darkness, broken only by the bone-yellow horns that covered its sides and head. Its jaw could open wide enough to swallow a man the major's size whole—indeed, three of the five men he had lost had been bitten in half.

Yes, this beast was a terrible testament to the ingenuity of mad science.

There was a cough behind him, and the shepherd turned to see a small ocelot holding the tent flap aside.

"Major," the feline said, "We have a visitor. I think you know who sent them."

The major frowned. Yes, he knew, and if the money hadn't been so good, he'd be tempted to leave their guest to wait a while longer. And yet a voice in the back of his mind warned him that his anonymous employer was more dangerous than the creature left in his care, and whoever he had sent as a messenger was most likely the same.

The shepherd nodded and followed the ocelot out. Thick morning mist clung between the trees, a staple of the evergreen forests that marched up the slopes of the Khaskeya Mountains in southeastern Kolovania. Even when the sun rose to its height only half of the mist would burn away. But the gloomy atmosphere didn't bother the mercenaries; in fact, they preferred the isolation and used it to their advantage.

The Major and his attaché made their way across the camp to the radio tent. The major threw the flaw aside to find his visitor lounging against the radio table.

She was a red wolf, quite tall, and generously proportioned. She wore baggy military pants with a woodland camouflage pattern and a dark grey halter top, a red elastic band covered her right shoulder. The Major's first impression was that the wolf was about to go for a jog, but the gear she carried put that thought to rest instantly. There was a brace of throwing knives strapped to each hip and a pistol on her right hip; closer inspection revealed that the sidearm was actually a pistol crossbow, and she had a pouch of small bolts attached to her belt.

But the oddest addition to her outfit was the dark red riding cloak draped around her shoulders. It reminded the Major of an old Dollan fairy tale about a young pup who got lost in the woods and encountered a wolf who had gone feral; this she-wolf appeared to be mixing the roles of the cautionary tale, turning the pup into the 'Big Bad Wolf'.

The hood of the cloak was pulled back, allowing the she-wolf's feathered brown long-fur to cascade down to her shoulders, the bangs were cut straight across her forehead. She studied the Major through eyes of burnt gold, and her appraisal seemed more than purely professional.

The major stepped into the tent, letting the flap close behind him, and said, "Ja?"

"Good morning, Major," the she-wolf said in Locken. Her voice was low and sultry, with a distinct accent from somewhere in the northwest of the West United Kingdoms.

When she didn't offer anything more after a pause, the Major said, "This is no place for little girls. State the purpose of your visit quickly."

The she-wolf frowned in mock disappointment. "Oh, you're no fun," she said, "From the looks of things, I take you've had a little trouble with your new toy?"

The shepherd dog's eyes narrowed sharply. "I've lost five men," he growled, "Good men, and unless your employer wishes to renegotiate our agreement, I suggest you tell me what I'm supposed to do with this beast quickly. Or I will send it back to him in pieces."

"Temper, temper," the she-wolf said, clucking her tongue, "You have my condolences on your men, really. We had hoped to perfect the conditioning before moving the specimens, but our hand was forced. Perhaps that's why the larger one went berserk on the Resthoven? Seventeen always was the more docile of the pair."

"You call that docile?" the Major barked taking a step forward.

The she-wolf was on him in seconds, one of her knives pressed against his throat. "Oh, don't be cross," she growled into his ear, "And be more careful about making any sudden moves."

The shepherd returned her glare. "I would advise the same."

The she-wolf looked down. A large combat knife had appeared in the Major's hand and was poised just above her gut.

The wolf stepped back, twirling the knife around her fingers before returning it to its sheath. "Oh, I like you," she said.

The major didn't put his knife away. "Charmed, I'm sure," he growled, "I trust your employer advised you that I do not like games when there is work to be done?"

The she-wolf casually swept away several pieces of radio equipment and perched herself on the table, crossing her ankles. She sat there for several long moments before the radio began to buzz. The wolf picked up the receiver and answered the call, then held the microphone out to the Major. "It's for you," she said.

The shepherd grabbed the device and gruffly stated, "Ja?"

"I do apologise for Ms Reed's behaviour," a familiar unaccented mechanical voice replied, "However, I assure you she is quite talented."

"And I take it you've assigned her as a watchdog for your pet project," the Major growled.

"By now I am sure you have assumed that we wish to test our new...asset," the mechanical voice continued unperturbed, "Our efforts in Medocci have proven fruitful, and our...adversaries have pulled some of their most vital assets into Kirque. We did not anticipate this move, but it comes as an opportunity to remove some annoying pieces from the board."

"You're a fool to believe you can control this creature," the Major said, "Once unleashed, I doubt even your 'conditioning' will get it back into its cage."

"That may be so," came the reply, "But this is only a test, after all. We expect some margin of error, but the loss of another asset would prove unfortunate."

"And I cannot afford to lose any more men," the shepherd said, "I will not be so foolish as to ask for additional compensation now, our deal has already been made. But should I suffer additional casualties, I will demand a higher fee on future endeavours."

"That is fair," said the caller, "Your next assignment is to transport the creature to the field test site, on the Kirque-Kolovania border. Ms Reed will provide the coordinates."

"And after?" the Major asked.

The pause on the other end grew uncomfortably long. "We require a full test of Seventeen's abilities. A variety of scenarios must be presented to achieve accurate results. Once the basic command tests are complete, the scope of the experiment must be expanded. Release Seventeen on the city of Al Qureg."

The line went dead.

The Major stared at the microphone for a moment before handing it back to the wolf. "Well," he said, "It appears you will be joining us, Ms Reed."

"Priscilla," the she-wolf said with a toothy grin, "But you can call me Pris."

Find out more about the World of Amarthia at:

worldofamarthia.squarespace.com

Follow on Facebook:

@Amarthia Books